W9-CEO-452

SECRET HISTORY

AND

LAURA

broadview editions
series editor: L.W. Conolly

Life is better when I think
about the kind of Person I want to be.
Our values instilled determine this vision
and are therefore of great importance.

"It's obvious there is work to do,
deliberately"   strong and

Read, write, sing, play, cook, clean, work, rest, love,
sleep.

Haruki Murakami doesn't get writer's block.

SECRET HISTORY;

OR, THE HORRORS OF ST. DOMINGO

AND

LAURA

Leonora Sansay

edited by Michael J. Drexler

broadview editions

© 2007 Michael J. Drexler
Reprinted with corrections 2008

All rights reserved. The use of any part of this publication reproduced, transmitted in any form or by any means, electronic, mechanical, photocopying, recording, or otherwise, or stored in a retrieval system, without prior written consent of the publisher—or in the case of photocopying, a licence from Access Copyright (Canadian Copyright Licensing Agency), One Yonge Street, Suite 1900, Toronto, ON M5E 1E5—is an infringement of the copyright law.

Library and Archives Canada Cataloguing in Publication

Sansay, Leonora, b. 1773
     Secret history, or, The horrors of St. Domingo and Laura / Leonora Sansay ; edited by Michael J. Drexler.

(Broadview editions)
Includes bibliographical references.

ISBN 978-1-55111-346-3

     1. Haiti—History—Revolution, 1791–1804—Fiction. I. Drexler, Michael J. II. Sansay, Leonora, b. 1781. Laura. III. Title. IV. Title: Horrors of St. Domingo. V. Series.

PS2769.S35S42 2007   813'.3   C2007-902848-9

Broadview Editions

The Broadview Editions series represents the ever-changing canon of literature by bringing together texts long regarded as classics with valuable lesser-known works.

Advisory editor for this volume: Jennie Rubio

Broadview Press is an independent, international publishing house, incorporated in 1985. Broadview believes in shared ownership, both with its employees and with the general public; since the year 2000 Broadview shares have traded publicly on the Toronto Venture Exchange under the symbol BDP.

We welcome comments and suggestions regarding any aspect of our publications–please feel free to contact us at the addresses below or at broadview@broadviewpress.com / www.broadviewpress.com

North America
PO Box 1243, Peterborough, Ontario, Canada K9J 7H5
2215 Kenmore Ave., Buffalo, NY, USA 14207
Tel: (705) 743-8990; Fax: (705) 743-8353
email: customerservice@broadviewpress.com

UK, Ireland, and continental Europe
NBN International
Estover Road
Plymouth PL6 7PY UK
Tel: 44 (0) 1752 202 300
Fax: 44 (0) 1752 202 330
email: enquiries@nbninternational.com

Australia and New Zealand
UNIREPS, University of New South Wales
Sydney, NSW, 2052
Australia
Tel: 61 2 9664 0999; Fax: 61 2 9664 5420
email: info.press@unsw.edu.au

PRINTED IN CANADA

MIX
Paper from
responsible sources
FSC
www.fsc.org
FSC® C013916

Contents

Acknowledgements

As I put the final touches on this edition I am reminded that today, 28 July is the anniversary of the United States' invasion of Haiti. The US Marines occupied Haiti for 19 years. Though they constructed roads and distributed food and medicine, US military administrators censored the press, tried political prisoners in military tribunals, and trained the Haitian military, which after the invasion, brutally repressed the population. Fifteen thousand Haitians died during the occupation. As native Haitian novelist Edwidge Danticat wrote movingly in the *Miami Herald* earlier this week, "While it takes American leaders and their armed enforcers just a few hours, days, weeks, months to rewrite another sovereign nation's history, it takes more than 90 years to overcome devastations caused by such an operation, to replace the irreplaceable, the dead lost, the spirits quelled, to steer an entire generation out of the shadows of dependency, to meet fellow citizens across carefully constructed divides and become halfway whole again." Danticat's voice has often been raised to remind Americans of the intertwined histories of Haiti and the United States, a history that goes back to the founding of the hemisphere's first independent republics. I hope this edition lends support to the important task of recording, remembering, and reconnecting. In the years of the Haitian Revolution, from both sides of the political spectrum came the call to heed the lessons of St. Domingo. We can learn from the past only once we are prepared to review it with eyes wide open.

First, I would like to thank Joanne Pope Melish for introducing me to *Secret History*. Thanks, too, to Philip Gould and William Keach, who supported my dissertation work on Sansay. I am grateful as well for the help of Philip Lapsansky of the Library Company of Philadelphia, who shared with me his extensive research on Sansay's biography. Harry Anderson and Phyllis Morales provided interesting biographical leads as well. Thanks to Kay Freeman for her sleuthing. Thanks to my colleagues in the Society of Early Americanists. Conversations with Michelle Burnham, Jeffrey Richards, Timothy Sweet, Stephen Shapiro, Jared Gardner, Elizabeth M. Dillon, Bryan Waterman, Ed Cahill, Monique Allewaert, Laura Stevens, Andy Doolen, Phil Round, Eric Wertheimer, Chris Iannini, Duncan Faherty, and Robert Levine have enriched this project. Special thanks to Malini Schueller and Ned Watts for including an essay of mine on Sansay in their collection, *Messy Beginnings: Postcoloniality and Early American Studies*. And special thanks are due to Colin (Joan) Dayan, who gave me permission to reprint and adapt her chronology of the Haitian Revolution. Notes to Pope's "Eloisa to Abelard" (Appendix B1) © Broadview Press are used by kind permission of Laura Cardiff and Broadview Press. And it has been a pleasure to work with the editors at Broadview Press. Thanks to the staff of the John Hay Library at Brown University, to Special Collections at the Margaret Clapp Library at Wellesley College, the New York Historical Society, the New York Public Library, the Elmer Holmes Bobst Library at New York University, and the Yale Center for British Art. The support of Information Services and Resources at Bucknell University has been indispensable. I also benefited from a summer research fellowship at The John Nicholas Brown Center for the Study of the American Civilization. Thanks to the organizers of Bicentenary Conference on Haitian Independence at the University of the West Indies in St. Augustine, Trinidad for allowing me to share my research with and gain crucial insights from pan-American Caribbeanist scholars, and to the Deans at Bucknell University, who funded my travel to Trinidad. The St. Augustine conference was illuminating in many ways, but fundamentally what I valued most was my exposure to the rich diversity of reactions to Haiti both from around the Caribbean and from Europe. I am grateful for conversations with Wendy Sutherland, whose work on German literary responses to Haiti is especially exciting.

Thanks to my colleagues in the English Department at Bucknell University, who have invited me to share my work publicly and given me inestimable support, and especially to Saundra Morris and Harold Schweizer for their encouragement. My students in English 301 tried out this edition before it was ready for prime time. For their enthusiasm, insight, and patience I am grateful. Thanks especially to Sean Kirnan for helping with transcriptions and for inviting me to present my work informally with the Bucknell graduate students, and to Caleb Sheaffer as well for his help at the end. Linden Lewis has been incredibly generous with his time and good humor. Conversations with Linden brought the secondary literature on Caribbean history to life for me. There's so much more to read! Christopher Mayo helped me wade into subtle complexities of textual editing. His friendship and his insight have meant much to me. My frequent co-author, Ed White, read multiple drafts of papers and dissertation chapters on Sansay. His patience has surely been tested, but I'm blithely unaware of it. To Kimberley, my best editor and best friend, and our daughters, Hannah and Mariah, this work is dedicated with love.

Introduction

Over the past fifteen years, a parade of commemorative events has sparked the historical imagination in the United States. 1989 marked the bicentenary of the Constitution and the election of the first US president, George Washington. In 1992, celebrations vied with rituals of mourning as the world recalled Columbus' "discovery" of America five hundred years earlier. The 50th anniversary of D-Day in 1994 inspired President Clinton to declare over the tombs of the fallen on Omaha Beach that "these men saved the world." Then on 6 August of the following year, we remembered Hiroshima—the dawn of the nuclear age—and we continue to set our Doomsday clocks just minutes before the midnight of the world's destruction. And more recently, in April 2003, organizers hailed the bicentenary of the Louisiana Purchase, a treaty that doubled the size of the United States, as the "most significant real estate transaction in the history of civilization."[1] From beginnings to endings, from political consolidation to vast territorial expansion, creation to destruction, and from peace to war, the events of remembrance at this turn to the twenty-first century testify to both the exuberance and trauma of modernity.

2004 marked another anniversary, relatively unnoted in North America and of unacknowledged importance to its own history. On 1 January 1804, the black general Jean-Jacques Dessalines proclaimed the independence of Haiti, formerly the French colony of Saint Domingue. Dessalines' declaration brought twelve brutal years of warfare to an end; and, ending the only successful slave rebellion, the declaration also launched the second independent nation in the western hemisphere. To C.L.R. James, the foundational historian of the Haitian Revolution, "the transformation of slaves, trembling in hundreds before a single white man, into a people able to organise themselves and defeat the most powerful European nations of their day, is one of the greatest epics of revolutionary struggle and achievement" (ix). The struggle for Haitian independence profoundly reshaped the geopolitics of the hemisphere. Saint Domingue was to

---

[1] *Louisiana Purchase Bicentennial, 1803–2003.* 2 August 2004. [http://www.louisianapurchase2003.com/home.cfm].

have been the foothold for Napoleon to resume an imperial project in North America. In losing the jewel of its colonial holdings at tremendous cost in lives and resources, France was forced to abandon its aspirations in the West, conceding the port of New Orleans and the Louisiana Territory to the Jefferson administration for $15 million. Doubling its territory overnight, the United States leveraged the Haitian rebellion in its march toward continental supremacy. Slave resistance in Saint Domingue spread anticolonial energy across the Caribbean sparking independence movements in Spanish-held territories. Why, some have asked, has the Haitian Revolution been so often left out of the narrative of the revolutionary period whose keywords are liberty and equality when it was the only revolutionary event predicated on racial equality?[1]

Commemorations, though they may foster historical inquiry, rarely in themselves highlight historical complexity. How might one celebrate declarations of independence and proclamations of human equality if those declarations and proclamations must be held to the light of practice and forced to account for the ongoing traffic in human beings? The Haitian Revolution put the test to the philosophy, rhetoric, and practices of the revolutionary period. Neither France nor the United States could easily accommodate Haiti into universalizing visions of freedom and equality. In 1801, Napoleon endeavored to reenslave the black population while the US resisted recognizing Haitian Independence until 1865.[2] To Michel-Rolph Trouillot, the history of the Haitian Revolution was "unthinkable" to contemporaries, who could sustain both the rhetoric of revolutionary egalitarianism and the practice of slavery only by denying to enslaved Africans and their descendents the capacity to understand freedom or the ability to design strategies to achieve it.[3] This ideology of African infrahumanity—the view that Africans were not wholly human, and were thus inferior to whites—could comprehend slave resistance only as the barbaric, impulsive response of caged animals. Thomas Jefferson, readily aware of the contradiction between his own language of innate human equality in the *Declaration of Independence* and the entrenched institution of race-slavery, was

---

[1] See Fischer, ix; James; Buck-Morss; Trouillot; Genovese, xxvi, 173.
[2] See the chronology for a survey of these events.
[3] Trouillot, 73.

unwilling to consider ending slavery by enveloping enslaved peoples of African descent into the community of national citizenship. Instead, he dolefully predicted the inevitability of race-warfare. In 1782, years before the first sparks of the revolution in Saint Domingue, he wrote,

> Deep rooted prejudices entertained by the whites; ten thousand recollections, by the blacks, of the injuries they have sustained; new provocations; the real distinction which nature has made; and many other circumstances, will divide us into parties, and produce convulsions which will probably never end but in the extermination of the one or the other race.[1]

Well before Haiti, the opposition to slavery had already been scripted as a Manichean struggle through which only one race could prevail. Few considered extending the Rights of Man to slaves, an idea placed beyond the pale of sense or sensibility. The certainty that only violence and eternal race-enmity lay in the future justified increasing the harshness of servile incarceration and turning slave-owning centers into garrisons against insurrection. If at the end of the eighteenth century, drawing a comparison between Haiti and the revolutions in North America and in France was "unthinkable," today that comparison may be willingly suppressed. As Lester Langley has eloquently put it, "Haiti was at once an affirmation of the *universality* of such revolutionary credos of liberty and equality and a denial of that contemporary ideology, which subsumed slavery in the revolutionary cause" (5).

No event captures the contradictions of new world history more than the Haitian Revolution.[2] When the former slaves of Saint

---

[1] Jefferson, 186. Jefferson's position on slavery and the slave-trade is notoriously complex. As a young state legislator, Jefferson advocated granting slave-owners the right to emancipate their slaves and, as president, he signed into law a ban on the African slave trade. Yet both his public and private views on abolition and the rights of black people were more equivocal. Jefferson's most vigorous critics view him as "blinded by negrophobia and notions of black inferiority" (Finkelman 195). See also Zuckerman, esp. 175–218. Others see this as an overstatement. Tim Matthewson, for example, explains that Jefferson's decision-making on Haiti during his presidency is best explained by his unwavering commitment to the southern planter class with whom he continued to identify.

[2] In an important and forcefully argued book, Sibylle Fischer claims that any discussion of modernity that excludes colonial experience "is just a reinstantiation of a Eurocentric particularism parading as universalism [...] what happened in the Caribbean in the Age of Revolution was also," she contends, "a struggle over what it means to be modern, who

Domingue, having separated themselves from colonial domination, reclaimed the indigenous Arawak Taino name for their portion of the island of Hispaniola, their act of renaming exemplified the ambiguities of the modern world.[1] "I have avenged America," Dessalines would write later the same year, identifying Haiti's birth with a broader resistance to the European colonization of the hemisphere.[2] The creation of Haiti did not, of course, restore the period before Columbian contact, but grew out of three centuries of conflict, including the evisceration of the indigenous population and the forced immigration of Africans to the Caribbean. At the beginning of the Haitian Revolution, the population of the island comprised 28,000 whites of French descent, 30,000 free people of color, and over 500,000 black slaves. Independent Haiti would become a black republic, a result sealed by both symbol and action. The first official flag of the new Haitian Republic appropriated the tri-color model of France. The blue band to represent the blacks[3] and the red to commemorate their blood were retained if re-appropriated. The white band, however, was discarded. France would never again control Haiti. The symbolic act of stripping whiteness from the flag was doubled by the strategic, if tragic, massacre of the remaining white French inhabitants in 1804. And yet, while the defeat of French rule signaled the end of slavery in Haiti, the decision by France to retreat from its new world colonial holdings after the loss of Saint Domingue enabled the most significant expansion of slavery in North America. Owing much to the outcome of the Haitian Revolution, the United States completed the Louisiana Purchase. As Haiti entered the new century having cast off the shackles of race-slavery, the United States used its new territories to begin a vast expansion of its slaveholding economy. By 1810, the slave population of the United States had more than doubled since 1770.[4] Moreover, as the

---

can claim it, and on what grounds; that the suppression and disavowal of revolutionary antislavery and attendant cultures in the Caribbean was also a struggle over what would count as progress, what was meant by liberty, and how the two should relate" (24).

[1] For an extensive commentary on why "Haiti" was chosen as the name of the new Black Republic, see David Patrick Geggus, *Haitian Revolutionary Studies*, 207–20.

[2] Proclamation of 28 April 1804 (quoted in Geggus, *Haitian Revolutionary Studies*, 207).

[3] No racial distinctions were to be recognized in the new Haitian Republic. In the first Haitian Constitution, all citizens of the island were called "black" regardless of their racial status prior to the revolution.

[4] Peter Kolchin, 63.

Purchase opened the west to white settlers, American Indians were aggressively displaced from fertile, tribal lands further westward.

I. "What kind of free is this?"[1]

Out of the three great revolutions of the late eighteenth century come three different ideas of freedom. Only in the case of Haiti are all three present. From the American Revolution comes the idea of freedom as self-governance. The American colonists rejected a colonial administrative system that did not award local assemblies control over issues of taxation and trade. With the rallying cry of "no taxation without representation," the American rebels at first sought to reform the colonial bureaucracy and then, in response to imperial intransigence, won independence from its centralized, authoritarian control. Grounded in the abstract concept of freedom as freedom from restraint, the American idea of freedom celebrated autonomy. The individual, free of institutional and therefore arbitrary constraints, was liberated to pursue private goals.

The French Revolution differed from the American precedent fundamentally in that its anti-authoritarian charge emerged from within the traditional geographical bounds of the nation-state. With the convening of the National Constituent Assembly and then the storming of the infamous prison, the Bastille, in 1789, the *ancien régime* fell and the path toward the French Republic was cut. Freedom for the French combined the procedural apparatus of constitutional republicanism with a more radical social dimension. As in the American cause, the French Revolutionaries authored their own manifesto of liberty and equality, *The Declaration of the Rights of Man*, which, as in the *Declaration of Independence*, identified freedom as a natural right. Both revolutionary movements renounced the existing basis of political authority and assumed a new legitimacy to govern by proclaiming themselves representatives of the general will of the people of the nation. Nevertheless, unlike France, the American Revolution did not topple a monarch or transform an economic social order (feudalism). For the French, liberty and equality were conjoined. Freedom could be realized only through social leveling.

---

[1] Quoted in Sheller, 81.

Social distinctions based on class rank were abolished. The communal identity of *citoyen* was needed to replace entrenched class and clerical prerogatives.[1]

What became known as the Haitian Revolution included elements of both American and French models. Some historians prefer to name the early stages of the Haitian Revolution the "Revolution on Saint Domingue," to highlight the French colonial crisis that preceded the massive slave uprising and, later, the War of Independence (1802–1804). Much like the American revolutionaries, who resented metropolitan regulation of trade, the white planters on Saint Domingue wanted to gain political representation in the French Assembly to win more local control over the production and export of sugar and molasses. They objected most to the *exclusif*, the trade provision that forced all colonial exports to go through France. The revolutionary re-organization taking place in the home country gave the planters an opening to press their economic agenda. What the planters underestimated was the radically universalist impulse of French revolutionary ideology. Seeking relief from royalist trade restrictions, the planters failed to imagine that the entire structure of the colonial economy would prove controversial in the midst of discussions about how to secure and extend inherent human rights. When the planters, in an attempt to make the most of their political power, requested seats in the Assembly on the basis of the entire population of the island—including the free men of color and the black slaves—members of the recently founded *Société des Amis des Noirs* seized the opportunity to press the issue.[2] With influential members including Brissot, Mirabeau, l'abbé Grégoire, and Lafayette, the *Amis des Noirs* insisted revolutionary change extend to the

---

[1] Though symbolic social leveling did occur in the United States with the confiscation of loyalist estates and the abolition of primogeniture and entail (rules governing inheritance that ensured property was retained, intact, within a family) the distribution of income and wealth remained static from 1776 to 1800. See Langley, 64. For two different presentations of the case that the American Revolution did radically transform social realities, see Jameson and Wood.

[2] Gordon Brown draws the connection between this debate in revolutionary France and the 3/5 compromise agreed to by delegates to the Constitutional Convention in Philadelphia in 1787. The third clause of Article 1, Section 2 of the US Constitution apportions representatives and taxes "according to their respective Numbers, which shall be determined by adding to the whole Number of free Persons, including those bound to Service for a Term of Years, and excluding Indians not taxed, three fifths of all other Persons." See Brown, 36–44.

colonies. Along with their campaign both for the immediate abolition of the slave trade and the gradual emancipation of colonial slaves,
the *Amis des Noirs* vigorously opposed the seating of the colonial
delegates. For the Saint Dominguan delegates to ask for political
representation on the basis of the entire population of the island, they
argued, was the height of hypocrisy. Mirabeau hit the nail squarely:
"The free blacks are proprietors and taxpayers, and yet they have not
been allowed to vote. And as for the slaves, either they are men or
they are not; if the colonists consider them men, let them free them
and make them eligible for seats; if the contrary is the case, have we,
in apportioning deputies according to population of France, taken
into consideration the number of our horses and mules?"[1]

The planters, of course, had no design on radically redistributing
political or economic power in the colonies. Relaxed trade policies
would be moot in the absence of the massive slave-labor force that
guaranteed the profitability of sugar. And sugar production on Saint
Domingue was incredibly profitable. Known during the eighteenth
century as the "Pearl of the Antilles," Saint Domingue out-produced
the sugar economies of the British West Indies almost two to one.
It had also become twice as profitable. In 1713, there were only 18
sugar works on the island. By 1790, that number had grown to 793.[2]
A slave population reaching to as many as 500,000 worked the 8,000
plantations devoted to sugar, coffee, indigo, and other crops destined
for export to Europe and North America. The expropriation of
labor for profit from a captive and potentially rebellious workforce
required a regimented, coercive, and brutal exercise of supervisory
power. Greatly outnumbered by their slaves, some 28,000 whites[3]
refined the plantation system to maintain order and productivity.
They treated their slaves like beasts of burden, subjecting them to
workdays that, during the sugar harvest, lasted from eighteen to
twenty hours. As Carolyn Fick explains, the plantation system could
be maintained only through a "regime of calculated brutality."

[1] Quoted in Laurent Dubois, *Avengers of the New World*, 75.
[2] For a comparison of sugar production in the British and French West Indies, see
Blackburn, 403–56.
[3] It is important to note that the white population, though racially unified, was wracked by
an internal schism along the axis of class. The *petit blancs*, small landholders, poor whites,
and white laborers, were adversaries to the *grand blancs*, the wealthy plantation owners,
who controlled most of the wealth on the island.

"Punishment, often surpassing the human imagination in its grotesque refinements of barbarism and torture," she writes, "was often the order of the day" (Fick, *Making of Haiti* 34). As the white planter regime subjected black slaves to physical and psychological terror, other forms of social management were needed to deal with the substantial population of free men and women of color.[1] The *gens de couleur libres* were a socially and economically diverse population that included recently emancipated slaves,[2] artisans, petty traders, white men's mistresses,[3] and a number of wealthy, French-educated landowners. Free coloreds also served in the colonial militia.[4] While the socio-economic breadth of the free colored population may suggest social integration in Saint Dominguan society, an elaborate system of regulations severely restricted anything resembling civic equality. Though the term *mulatto*, or mixed-race, was often the generic designation for all free coloreds, Saint Dominguan society recognized a staggering 128 racial categories to discriminate all conceivable gradations from white to black.[5] Nevertheless, the hyper-rational frenzy to distinguish fractional quantities of black blood had the effect of solidifying the difference between white and nonwhite. As Joan Dayan explains, such pseudo-scientific excess functioned "to demonstrate how these people, even if freed, were still slaves with a damning defect: black blood" (229). Especially at the top of the socio-economic scale, where visible distinctions between white and nonwhite were minute, and where property and acculturation through education in France even raised some nonwhites above many *petit blancs*, racial

---

[1]   The population of *gens de couleur libres* was larger on Saint Domingue than on other colonial islands.

[2]   Who was emancipated and why? Stewart King, noting that freed females outnumbered males 2 to 1, identifies familial relationship between master and slave as the primary reason for manumission.

[3]   According to Moreau de Saint-Méry, "most of the [free colored] women live with white men. There, under the little-deserved title of 'housekeepers,' they have all the functions of wives ..." (quoted in Socolow, 294n8).

[4]   According to Stewart King, free coloreds made up more than half of the island's militia by the end of the eighteenth century. They were integral to the defense of the colony. More surprising, perhaps, was the use of free colored soldiers for military expeditions overseas. In 1779, a force of Saint Dominguan soldiers including free coloreds attacked Savannah, Georgia in support of the American War of Independence. See King, 52–77.

[5]   Moreau de St. Méry catalogued the island's racial taxonomy in his *Description Topographique, Physique, Civile, Politique Et Historique De La Partie Française De L'ile Saint-Domingue*. The most extensive discussion of these categories of racial distinction can be found in Dayan, 219–37.

distinctions remained crucial to colonial order. Free coloreds, regardless of the remoteness of black ancestry, could not hold public office, could not carry weapons in towns, and were subject to sumptuary laws restricting the wearing of silk and other finery. Theaters, churches, and eateries were segregated. Despite their wealth and cultural refinement, and perhaps even because of these accomplishments, free coloreds were denied political authority. The revolution in France did nothing to incline the white planters to alter their political monopoly.

Events in Versailles and Paris did, however, inspire the *gens de couleur* to seek redress for civic inequality. The controversy over the seating of the Saint Dominguan delegates provided a fresh opportunity to sue for civil rights. While the Constituent Assembly would not abolish slavery in the colonies until 1794, delegates were receptive to the demands to extend rights and equality to the *gens de couleur*. Pleading that color alone had deprived them of political rights, the *gens de couleur* advocated both home and abroad for reform, occasionally opting for armed resistance when rebuffed. The execution of the free-colored leader Vincent Ogé in 1790 and the resultant outrage in Paris proved determinative. Though the result would fall far short of full citizenship regardless of color, the Revolution in Saint Domingue had compelled French revolutionaries to test the limits of their commitment to universal rights and equality. A compromise left white planters and *gens de couleur* to face off in a simmering, if not openly hostile, engagement. Convinced that the complete elimination of the legal recognition of racial difference would undermine the slave economy, the National Assembly empowered the colonial assemblies to control their own destiny. In exchange, however, the white planters were forced to concede rights to certain free coloreds, provided that both their parents were free. In principle, if not practice, Saint Domingue was transforming the relationship of freedom to equality.

Efforts to win civil equality for free coloreds on Saint Domingue pointedly excluded changing the status of the black slaves. Free coloreds, in fact, shared with the white planters a feeling of superiority over enslaved plantation workers. The campaign for free colored rights was based on the entitlements that accrued to their free status. Free, propertied, and now marginally granted civil rights, the free coloreds recognized some common interests with the white planters in sustaining race-slavery and the society that depended upon it. These paradoxical allegiances and antinomies of race were dramatically intensified in August 1791. Beginning in the north of the island, the 500,000 black slaves opened a new challenge to colonial stability, launching a massive, coordinated, and sustained rebellion against the plantation regime.

The Haitian Revolution thus began with the convergence of three forces: 1) opposition to centralized, imperial mercantilism on the American revolutionary model; 2) the circulation of universalist and equalitarian rhetoric from France; and 3) a slave uprising that violently but categorically redefined freedom in the Americas. Out of the material conditions of existence and oppression, the slave rebels crafted a freedom from below.[1] To freedom as self-government and freedom as social and civic equality, the slave uprising in Haiti contributed a novel definition. Though the American and French precedents may have set the conditions for the slave revolt, the slaves of Saint Domingue transformed resistance to oppression into the liberation of the "person as property." Haitian freedom would be a freedom from domination.[2]

Resistance to colonial slavery prior to 1791 had taken many forms. Slaves refused to work. They forged communal solidarity through religious ritual, blending what was retained from Africa with local adaptations. On Saint Domingue, this syncretic religious experience became vodou. Slaves also fled from plantations to form small, independent, and sustainable communities.[3] Periodically, slaves did attempt organized rebellion. The most famous of these on Saint Domingue was the Makandal plot, in which a long-time fugitive slave distributed poisons on several plantations. Makandal was caught and executed in 1758. The slave revolt of 1791 was, however, of an

---

[1] See Sheller, 18–40. The idea of the Haitian Revolution as a revolution from below is argued most forcefully in Carolyn E. Fick's, *The Making of Haiti: The Saint Domingue Revolution from Below*. See also her article, "The French Revolution in Saint Domingue: A Triumph or a Failure?" 54, 70.

[2] "Haitian liberty by challenging this domination was a different kind of freedom than the practices of natural liberty of the period. It was a freedom which allowed for the creation of a free state and created the conditions for human equality of laws, which were unconditional" (Bogues).

[3] Escaped slaves were known as "maroons." David Geggus argues that marronage on Saint Domingue may help explain the absence of slave insurrection throughout the eighteenth century on the island. It may have served as "an alternvative to rebellion, a safety valve" (*Haitian Revolutionary Studies* 74).

unprecedented scale. Under the leadership of Toussaint Louverture, a previously emancipated slave, the rebel army cut a swath across the island. In time, the slave rebels "defeated in turn the local whites and the soldiers of the French monarchy, a Spanish invasion, a British expedition of some 60,000 men, and a French expedition of similar size" (James ix).

The military success of the slave rebels provides perhaps the surest proof of the non-Eurocentric, African contribution to the Haitian Revolution. As many as 70 percent of the slaves on Saint Domingue in the 1780s and 1790s were born in Africa. What this staggering statistic tells us is of two-fold importance. It underscores foremost the devastatingly high mortality and low fertility rate of recently imported slaves. Robin Blackburn cites planters' estimation that "the young African brought to their estates had an average life expectancy of little more than seven years," and five to six percent of any given slave crew died annually (339). Second, the high percentage of recent arrivals from Africa may explain the slave rebels' military skill. According to John Thornton, who has compared patterns of slave trafficking to wars in Africa, "a great many of the slaves had served in African armies prior to their enslavement and arrival in Haiti. Indeed, African military service had been the route by which many, if not most, of the recently arrived Africans became slaves in the first place, since so many people had been enslaved as a result of war" (Thornton, "African Soldiers in the Haitian Revolution" 59). In this light, the Haitian victory over Spanish, British, and French regulars seems less improbable. While disease and climate may offer some clues to the difficulties faced by European troops in Saint Domingue, surely it is relevant that so many of the rebel slaves had military combat experience prior to becoming enslaved agricultural laborers in the West Indies.

Together, Thornton's evidence of African military skill and the articulation of a distinctive, Caribbean form of freedom answer longstanding suppression of the history of the Haitian Revolution. As documented by Bénot, Trouillot, and Fischer, revolutionary anti-slavery has consistently been written out of histories of modernity and the so-called Age of Revolutions.[1] Despite voluminous scholarly attention to slavery since the 1970s, slave resistance rarely plays

---

[1]   See Bénot, 205–17.

a significant role in discussions about revolutionary ideology or political economy. Recent encyclopedic surveys of the American and French Revolutions make at most marginal, if any, references to slavery, colonialism, or slave rebellion.[1]

Few white contemporaries of the revolution on Saint Domingue were prepared to acknowledge its significance either. In the United States, reaction to the ongoing conflict in the French colonies diverged predictably by region. Southerners responded anxiously to the news of race-war in the Caribbean. Saint Domingue represented an example of what could happen to an unstable slaveholding regime. While southerners initially expressed compassion for the white refugees from Saint Domingue then arriving in Richmond, Charleston, and Norfolk, they also grew concerned that the "horrors of St. Domingo" might happen locally.[2] In response, all of the southern states placed restrictions on the Atlantic slave trade during the 1790s. Many laws were specifically designed to prevent the importation of slaves from the West Indies.[3] Concurrent with the implementation of these laws, attitudes began to shift toward the white refugees from Saint Domingue, who frequently arrived at US ports of asylum with their black servants. And other types of French imports became suspect as well. As southerners feared that blacks schooled in rebellion might bring violence to their doorstep, they also began to blame "French ideas" for spreading abolitionist propaganda "fatal" to social stability.[4] Nativism and paranoia led some to call for suppressing all news of slave rebellion from the West Indies. "Slave-holding societies were," Ed White writes, "at once cultures of (white) fear and censorship of the action feared. Newspapers, journals, and government bodies fairly consistently restricted information about slave resistance, for the obvious reason that the more you talk about it, the more likely it is to occur" (96). Telling the truth about slave insurrection was considered risky if not grossly negligent. Editors of the *Norfolk Herald*, for example, reported on 10 June 1802 that they were "authorised to state, that an insurrection of a very serious nature has broken out amongst the Negroes in Perquimens and Hartford Counties, N. Carolina," but then demurred

---

[1] See Fischer, 6–11 and Trouillot, 98.
[2] Hunt, 42.
[3] Du Bois; Scott, 73, 84.
[4] Rusticus, Columbia *Herald*, 14 July 1794 (quoted in Hunt, 111).

further comment with the observation that "the particulars, we are constrained to observe, must be withheld for the present, from motives of precaution."[1] Slaveholders worried that news of rebellion or the circulation of radical Jacobin ideology to slaves could inspire local unrest, and they may have been correct. It is possible that Gabriel Prosser, who led a failed rebellion in Virginia in 1800, found inspiration in both radical republicanism and the example of Haiti.[2]

In the North, public opinion about Saint Domingue tended to shift in keeping with attitudes toward revolutionary France. After the French Republic abolished religion and entered the bloody months of the Reign of Terror, news of massacres and civil war from Saint Domingue reinforced popular disillusion with Jacobinism. Relations with France continued to sour in the middle of the decade. Following the "XYZ Affair" (1797–98), in which an American delegation seeking to reaffirm the 1778 treaty with France was rebuffed, the US moved to a war footing. Ironically, the so-called Quasi-War with France (1798–1800) had the effect of severing associations of the rebellion in Saint Domingue and the French Revolution. Led by mercantilists in the North, Americans sought to open trade access to the lucrative commodities of the island formerly controlled by France. Breaking the imperial *exclusif* would work doubly to enrich commercial interests in the US and economically wound the aggressive French government, then the Directory. Quickly, Federalists in Congress passed a law to suspend all trade with France, "or elsewhere under the acknowledged authority of France." This clause, named Toussaint's Clause, opened Saint Domingue to American merchants and was a "virtual invitation" to Toussaint Louverture to declare independence from France.[3] But when the Quasi-War with France came to a peaceful conclusion in 1801, the Toussaint Clause expired. Trade with war-ravaged Saint Domingue no longer seemed as desirable. The new president from Virginia, Thomas Jefferson, yielded to the influence of Southern planters, who were intent to maximize profitable cotton production

---

1 "Last mail. Insurrection in North-Carolina," *Balance and Columbian Repository* 1.25 (1802): 198.
2 For the history of slave revolts after the Haitian Revolution see Aptheker. On the revolutionary consciousness of the black diaspora, see Scott and Bolster.
3 Brown, *Toussaint's Clause*, 129. For an exploration of Federalist support for independent Saint Domingue, see Zuckerman, 215.

reliant on an obedient, enslaved workforce. Jefferson worked to re-establish ties with France and signaled to Napoleon's delegate in Washington that the US would not interfere with French efforts to regain control of Saint Domingue.

On one point, there was widespread agreement: both north and south, many were horrified by the widely circulated tales of butchery related by eyewitnesses in graphic detail. In newspapers and periodicals, Americans read about "crimes unknown to past ages" committed by "black dæmons of slaughter:"

> Thousands of French have been massacred there lately, for being *white*—for being patriots—for being rich proprietors—and the metropolis of that colony is now a heap of ashes. [...] Thousands of women, old men and children who could not find the necessary means to embark and to fly from a land of desolation, await, with consternation and terror, their turn to be massacred.[1]

Descriptions of atrocity focused on the savage inhumanity of the black rebels and the corresponding vulnerability of the white victims:

> With one hand the black dæmons of slaughter were seen holding up the writhing infant, and hacking off its limbs with the sword in the other. Those that escaped the sword were preserved to witness more horrid sensations, being dragged by the negroes, (who evacuated the town during the fire, and after the demolishing of the forts) to their strong places in the mountains, to serve as hostages or to glut their fury.[2]

It was not uncommon for descriptions of black on white violence to highlight sexual atrocities as well.[3] The slave rebellion was drained of political and historical context in the American periodical press and became instead a theater of horror and gore perpetrated by animalistic brigands loosed from their chains.

Few writers took the cause of the black slaves of Saint Domingue as their own. Abraham Bishop, a graduate of Yale and a radical Republican,

---

[1]   "From the New-York Journal. To All Sympathizing Souls," *New Jersey Journal* September 28, 1793: 1.
[2]   "Conflagration of the Cape," *The Republican, or Anti-Democrat* 4 March 1802: 2.
[3]   See Letter XXII, 124–25, below.

was exceptional. In three pamphlets published under the pseudonym J.P. Martin in 1791, Bishop urged Americans to support the rebel slaves, comparing their struggle to the American Revolution of 1776. "Believing our cause to have been just," Bishop wrote, "I believe firmly, that the cause of the Blacks is just." Bishop even defended Black armed struggle and contextualized violence against whites as a response to the brutality of slavery: "They are asserting those rights by the sword which it was impossible to secure by mild measures.—Stripes, imprisonment, hunger, nakedness, cruel tortures and death, were the portion of those Blacks who even talked of liberty, or who, for a moment, conducted like Freemen." The choice was clear: Americans ought to support the rebel slaves because freedom has no color. "I wish success to their arms, with all my heart, and lament, that it is not in my power to afford them effectual assistance," he wrote. "The sword is drawn, blood must be shed, and freedom must be obtained."

In England and France, favorable presentation of the slave rebels was spare and more moderate. But a common element of these early accounts was the conclusion that slavery had created the conditions for the Caribbean insurrection. If writers stopped short of endorsing black armed resistance, as Bishop had, they did situate violence against whites as a foreseeable response to injustice. This muting of "the horrors of St. Domingo" might accompany fulsome praise for the emergent leaders of the black army and admiration for the social order that they and the black masses were creating in the wake of the conflict. "It is on ancient record," wrote Englishman Marcus Rainsford (1805),

> that negroes were capable of repelling their enemies with vigour, in their own country [...] but it remained for the close of the eighteenth century to realize the scene, from the state of abject degeneracy:— to exhibit, a horde of negroes emancipating themselves from the vilest slavery, and at once filling the relations of society, enacting laws, and commanding armies, in the colonies of Europe.[1]

American writer Charles Brockden Brown chided Europeans generally for failing to recognize "the faculties which the negroes of the

---

[1] Rainsford, 6–7. Jeremy Popkin has identified a similar attitude in early French language accounts of the revolution. See Popkin, 511–33.

West Indies possess." To Brown, the Haitian Revolution had demonstrated an important lesson about the irrelevance of race:

> The war of St. Domingo reads us a memorable lesson; negroes organizing immense armies; laying plans of campaigns and sieges, which, if not scientific, have at least been successful against the finest European troops; arranging forms of government, and even proceeding some length in executing the most difficult of human enterprises; entering into commercial relations with foreigners, and conceiving the idea of alliances; acquiring something like a maritime force, and, at any rate, navigating vessels in the tropical seas, with as much skill and foresight as that complicated operation requires.
>
> This spectacle ought to teach us the effects of circumstances upon the human faculties, and prescribe bounds to that arrogance, which would confine to one race, the characteristics of the species.[1]

Of course, it would be a mistake to overestimate the influence of these, in the least, equitable views of the Haitian Revolution. Following the Louisiana Purchase, the Jefferson administration embargoed the Haitian Republic and refused to recognize its independence. France did not officially recognize the loss of its signature western colony until 1825. If the distinctive features of Haitian freedom failed to receive popular or diplomatic recognition in the years following independence, there are, nevertheless, unexplored avenues to follow its influence on Anglo-American culture. Women's writing about Haiti and news from abroad more generally is especially promising.[2]

II. Novel History: Leonora Sansay's Secret for America

In 1808, Leonora Sansay published *Secret History; or The Horrors of St. Domingo, in a Series of Letters, Written by a Lady at Cape Francois, to Col.*

---

[1]   The complete text of Brown's article is reprinted in Appendix C.
[2]   Interest in American women's travel and historical writings has generally focused on domestic travel and US history. See for example anthologies compiled by Martin and Harris. Study of the transatlantic participation of women in the abolitionist movement has yielded some correction. See Ferguson and Yellin. See also Kadish, "The Black Terror: Women's Responses to Slave Revolts in Haiti." Kaplan and Smith-Rosenberg contest the view that women's writing stands outside dominant racial and imperial ideology.

Aaron Burr, Late Vice-President of the United States, Principally During the Command of General Rochambeau, a novel that offers the observation near its beginning that the "negroes, notwithstanding the state of brutal subjection in which they were kept, have at length acquired a knowledge of their own strength." This critical description of a fundamental reversal of the relations of power is the basis on which Sansay will describe not only the disintegration of French rule in Saint-Domingue, but from which she will speculate that other discursive categories describing relations of power might also crumble.[1]

Unlike the racial taxonomer, Moreau de Saint-Méry,[2] Sansay used fiction not to stabilize ideologically rigid distinctions of caste, but to draw relations between multiple fluid categories. Among the oppositions that Sansay describes as being on shaky ground in both Saint Domingue and the United States are geographic hierarchies (such as the distinction between creole and native French), and political hierarchies (such as the distinctions between French subjects under Napoleon and the "citoyens" of the collapsed French Republic); similarly unstable is the partisan divide in the United States between Federalism and Antifederalism. These are categories already unsettled by Sansay's patron Aaron Burr. Add to these oppositions racial hierarchies. Sansay describes the status competition over white Frenchmen among white creoles and mulatresse mistresses, which leads to the distinction between the politics of race and the politics of the domestic sphere. If, as Sansay suggests, the struggles for political- and caste-status in Saint Domingue are best exemplified through the observation of women and the domestic and sexual economy, then meaningful distinctions between public and private spheres also disappear. Marriage, like the political world, is marked by a duplicitous and combative struggle between individuals who "talk of sentiments they never feel," nuns are prostitutes, and wives are potential murderers.

Of all the socio-political hierarchies under strain, Sansay is most overtly interested in what happens to marital and sexual relations in moments of intense socio-political change. The black slaves of Saint

---

[1] The first scholar to treat Sansay seriously as a writer was Joan Dayan, who broke new ground and set the agenda for future efforts in *Haiti, History, and the Gods*. For Dayan, the novel is both a social history of French decadence and a glimpse of trans-cultural, or trans-racial, mimicry, fantasy, and desire.

[2] See note 1, p. 301 and note 1, p. 308.

Domingue "acquired a knowledge of their own strength," a moment of self and communal empowerment necessary for freedom, but also unleashing—at least in the eyes of many white observers—violent and libidinous excess: "the horrible catastrophe which accompanied the first wild transports of freedom" (*SH*, 77). Might social instability grant a comparable recognition of previously obscured power to women as well? Would the passions be similarly provoked, and what form would their eruption take? In *Secret History*, we encounter, among other extreme examples, a woman who cuts off the head of her husband's black mistress and serves it to him on a platter. The aftershocks of the Haitian Revolution could be surprising and unpredictable. For Sansay, most formative if apparently distant from the drama of slave revolt, emancipation, and political independence, was her own entrance into the privileges of publicly recognized subjective agency—becoming an author.

Almost everything we know about the life of Leonora Sansay comes from her sporadic appearance in the memoirs and private journals of Aaron Burr, where letters from her and about her surface over the course of twenty years.[1] Philadelphia city directories establish that she was the daughter of William Hassell,[2] the inn-keeper of the Sign of the Half Moon, centrally located across from the statehouse at 185 Chestnut Street. Hassell died in 1793, perhaps a victim of the Yellow Fever epidemic that swept the city in that year. It is tempting to imagine Leonora maintaining the business, which may explain her access to the eminent men of society with whom she associated. To the third Vice President of the United States, she was a sometime mistress, a confidante, and, perhaps, a political operative as well. Among Burr's circle of associates she was "too well known under the name of 'Leonora.'"[3] The suggestion is clear; Leonora Sansay was a public woman, a coquette. She was capricious, witty, and inconstant in her attachments.[4] For Burr, the Boston physician William Eustis, scientist and economist Erich Bollman, Navy Lieutenant Robert Spence, wealthy New Orleans merchant Daniel Clark, architect Benjamin

---

[1]   I am indebted to Philip Lapsansky for sharing his biographical research on Leonara Sansay.
[2]   Sometimes spelled Hassall.
[3]   Burr, *Memoirs*, II:326.
[4]   In a letter to Aaron Burr, Sansay's husband wrote of Leonora, "You know, Monsieur, the lightness and inconstancy of Madame Sansay" (from the *Papers of Aaron Burr* dated 2 April 1802).

Latrobe, and for her husband, the refugee Saint Dominguan planter Louis Sansay, Leonora was an object of desire. To Burr, Louis Sansay wrote, "my love for her is invincible and I would sacrifice everything to have her in my possession" (Ibid). But though inspiring great passion, she was no celebrity. Only glimpses of her life are available on the margins of history. Sansay perhaps recognized herself in her protagonist Mary's description of "that unfortunate class of beings, so numerous in my own [country]—victims of seduction, devoted to public contempt and universal scorn" (*SH*, 95). That she envisioned more for herself, however, is also clear. To what extent did Sansay's experiences in Saint Domingue shape her own desires and her means of pursuing them? Certainly her time in Saint Domingue inclined her to become a writer. The story of her emergence from the sphere of private letter-writing to the public stage of professional authorship runs through both her experiences on Saint Domingue and her relationship with Aaron Burr.

Sansay's friendship with Aaron Burr dates from as early as 1796. The Federal Government located to Philadelphia from New York in 1790 and remained there for ten years. Hassell's tavern, the Sign of the Half Moon, was a likely gathering place where the young Leonora could have become acquainted with Burr, the senator from New York and a recent widower. Little, however, is known about these early years. In 1800, apparently at Burr's suggestion, Leonora married Louis Sansay, a refugee from Saint Domingue, who had sold his plantation to the black revolutionary Toussaint Louverture and fled to New York to escape the retribution meted out against the former slave holders of the revolted French colony. Burr's notes indicate the Sansays kept house in New York at 115 Fly Market,[1] but Leonora maintained her romance with him as well. In March 1802, she was in Washington, presumably with Burr. Now, however, Louis Sansay's prospects seemed on the verge of change. The French had re-invaded Saint Domingue. Napoleon Bonaparte had directed a French expeditionary force of 20,000 veteran soldiers to recapture Saint Domingue, depose Toussaint Louverture (the black general who was governing the island as if it were a semi-autonomous

---

[1] Fly Market was located in lower Manhattan, near Fulton Street where the fish market remained until recently. "Fly" is likely an adaptation of the Dutch *vlie*, meaning valley. Mispronunciation may explain the origin of the term "flea market."

territory), and re-establish slavery on the island. Louis Sansay decided to go back and reclaim his plantation, but he was unwilling to go without Leonora. In an impassioned letter to Burr, Sansay pleaded with him to send Leonora home to New York:

> I tremble that it is her intention to abandon me and I myself have decided to abandon everything, and even to sacrifice my life, rather than to leave her in the possession of another; pardon me, Monsieur, that I write to you of these things, but I am not in the position to master and vanquish the love, friendship, and attachment I have for her. I beg of you to urge her to return as soon as possible.[1]

Whatever reservations Leonora may have had were overcome, and she was persuaded to accompany her husband on his return to Saint Domingue. If dates in *Secret History* are faithful, the Sansays arrived at Cap Français on 7 June 1802, the day Toussaint Louverture was captured and embarked for France. It seemed that soon Leonora would become mistress of Sansay's property and slaves. Burr had assured her that the island would be subdued in less than three weeks. A year later, however, the situation on the island had yet to stabilize. On 6 May 1803, Leonora wrote to Burr of her frustration: "I have been coop'd up in the hollow bason in which the town is built, for there is no means of going a mile in any direction beyond it without I chose [sic] to make a sortie on the brigands which I have not yet determined on."[2] The remainder of this letter comprises the first half of what will become *Secret History* in compressed form. Adopting her alter-ego, Leonora "commences the adventures of Clara." "Do you recollect her?" she writes, "that Clara you once loved?" At first a flirtatious device to provoke Burr to recall the woman he had passed off on another, the invention of Clara is the first breakthrough in Leonora Sansay's entrance into the public sphere of letters. Writing of herself as another, Sansay reverses her own objectification by the male gaze. If Clara is the object of desire, it is Sansay as author who renders her so compelling:

---

[1] Louis Sansay to Aaron Burr, 2 April 1802.
[2] The text of this substantial letter, appended to Charles Burdett's novel *Margaret Moncreiffe; the First Love of Aaron Burr*, appears in Appendix A.

Dressed with a licence which can be authoriz'd only by the heat (for she was almost naked) she was led round the room by an officer, where as a belle-femme and a stranger her vanity was fully gratified by the buzzes of admiration, her husband delighted by the splendor of what he deem'd his property follow'd her at a small distance [...]

The pleasure of authorial control leads Sansay to aspirations for a larger audience, and at the end of this remarkable letter, she asks Burr to become her publishing agent:

Should the story of Clara, with many incidents which I have omitted, and some observations on all that is passing here, be written in a pretty light style, could it be printed in America in a tolerable pamphlet in french and english, & a few numbers sent here. [...] There's certainly matter enough in it to form a romance; but whose life has afforded so many subjects for romance as that of its writer?

Events in Saint Domingue, for Sansay, and at home, for Burr, would put a temporary hold on Sansay's aspirations. The last half of 1803 saw the triumph of the black army against the French forces at Le Cap. By 1804, the Sansays had fled to Cuba. Burr's strange odyssey from Vice President to his indictment for treason was about to begin. Settling his affairs on 10 July, the eve of the fateful duel with Alexander Hamilton, Burr wrote to his son-in-law: "If you can pardon and indulge a folly, I would suggest that Madame Sansay, too well known under the name of Leonora, has claims on my recollection. She is now with her husband at St. Jago of Cuba."[1] Burr also directed his daughter, Theodosia, to secure from his private correspondence the "letters of *Clara* [...] sometimes 'L.'" The next day, Hamilton would die from Burr's pistol shot on the shores of the Hudson.[2] By the time Sansay returned to Philadelphia, Burr was busy with a new venture to repair his bruised reputation.

To his many critics, numbering among them the current president (Thomas Jefferson), Aaron Burr remained dangerous, his

---

[1] Burr, *Memoirs*, II:326.
[2] This is not the place to retell what led Aaron Burr and Alexander Hamilton to the duel at Weehawken on the morning of 11 July 1804. That story can be found in the numerous biographies of the two principals as well as in Fleming.

designs suspect. Little is conclusive about Burr's plans. He did travel west along the Ohio and down the Mississippi along the border of the newly acquired Louisiana territories. Rumor had it that he was assembling an army with the intent of capturing New Orleans, forming a new empire in Mexico, or, most wild of all and equally implausible, marching on Washington. Whatever his intent, Burr numbered Leonora Sansay among his associates. She couriered messages for him in anticipation of his arrival at the Mississippi Delta in 1806.[1] The specific details of her involvement or utility to Burr remain unclear and Burr's plans never reached fruition. Nevertheless, historians are in error when they relegate the Burr Conspiracy to the margins of early American culture.

The Burr Conspiracy belongs as much to the history of the Haitian Revolution as it does to the intrigues of political partisanship in the Early Republic. The departure of European imperial rivals from the Louisiana territory following the Haitian Revolution far from settled the question of the disposition of the inhabitants of that region. Among others, Aaron Burr and his associates were inclined to wade into the vaccuum to try to consolidate power. Had Leonora Sansay gleaned valuable lessons in her Caribbean travels that might prove useful organizing previously colonized territories? Consider Clara's response to the Cuban farmers she encounters once free from Saint Domingue and her husband in Letter XXVIII. Like the land crabs that frightened Clara in her sleep and "appeared like a brown stream rolling over the surface of the earth," might these rural inhabitants achieve consciousness of their collective strength and, under proper leadership, transform their existence as had the slaves on Saint Domingue? Were the inhabitants of the North American western frontier similarly situated?[2]

---

1   Records of Sansay's role are documented in Latrobe, 2:598, 3:105n27. In my article, "Brigands and Nuns," I speculate that Sansay, perhaps herself of Irish descent, was a go-between for Burr and the Irish laborers he hoped to recruit with Latrobe's assistance. The laborers were requested under the guise of constructing a canal on the Ohio River in Kentucky. Latrobe feared he had unwittingly helped Burr secure an able bodied force of 500 men for his paramilitary operations.

2   Charles Brockden Brown makes the connection of Saint Domingue and Louisiana explicit in his anonymously published pamphlet, *An Address to the Government of the United States, on the Cession of Louisiana to the French: And on the Late Breach of Treaty by the Spaniards; Including the Translation of a Memorial, on the War of St. Domingo, and Cession of the Mississippi to France, Drawn Up by a French Counsellor of State.* Philadelphia: John Conrad & Co, 1803.

While tempting, these suppositions must remain at the level of speculation. Burr's expedition was cut off before fully forming. Jefferson had Burr arrested and he was put on trial for treason against the United States in 1807. Though ultimately acquitted—found by the jury "not proved to be guilty"—Burr sought voluntary exile in Europe for four years following the trial.

Leonora Sansay returned north with new ambitions. Though she would still correspond periodically with Burr—her last known letter was addressed to him in 1817—Sansay envisioned a different kind of publicity for herself. No longer satisfied to be a satellite to influential men, she aimed to attract the admiration of the public at large. In 1808, she offered through her publishers Bradford & Inskeep, *Secret History; or The Horrors of St. Domingo, in a Series of Letters, Written by a Lady at Cape Francois, to Col. Aaron Burr, Late Vice-President of the United States, Principally During the Command of General Rochambeau*. The following year, her novel *Laura* appeared from the same press.[1] Feminist theorist Leigh Gilmore coined the term *autobiographics* to analyze how women use self-representational strategies including, but not limited to, autobiography "to become no longer primarily subject to exchange but subjects who exchange the position of object for the subjectivity of self-representational agency" (12). Sansay's writing, clearly adapted from her own experience, exemplifies this practice. In fact, the very practice of publishing *Secret History* is an act of transgression, eviscerating the separation of the private from the public sphere. Having killed Alexander Hamilton and following his acquittal for treason, Burr chose voluntary exile in Europe; he was no longer in a position to offer protection or guidance to Sansay. In *Secret History*, Sansay leveraged her relationship with Aaron Burr. While she certainly traded on the public's appetite for descriptions of racialized violence,[2] she also capitalized on its hunger for news

---

[1] Bradford and Inskeep took over the partisan Federalist periodical *Port-Folio* in 1809 from Joseph Dennie. The new printers transformed it from a divisive political journal into a review of science and the arts "with all the extensive and variegated department of polite literature, merriment and wit." Bradford and Inskeep used the *Port-Folio* to promote their own books, publishing anonymous and favorable reviews of *Laura* in its pages.

[2] While Sansay does narrate black on white violence akin to the periodical writings to stoked racist anxiety during the 1790s, it is interesting that these stories are all related second-hand in *Secret History*. Neither Mary nor Clara reports any eyewitness accounts of black violence in the text.

about the scandalous Aaron Burr, converting what for her had become a potentless patronage into something of value.

The public exposure of her ties with Burr also provides a link between *Secret History* and Sansay's subsequent novel *Laura*. Her second novel features as its protagonist a beautiful impoverished orphan, who throws herself headlong into a secret marriage with a young medical student, afraid to acknowledge her to his family. When Belfield dies in a duel in an effort to protect his wife's reputation, Laura finds herself once more alone in the world, only now pregnant, having only her intuitive wit and wisdom to guide her. Though Sansay appended a heavy-handed moral signature to the end of *Laura*, declaring "that perpetual uneasiness, disquietude, and irreversible misery, are the certain consequences of fatal misconduct in a woman" (*Laura*, 222), her indictment falls as squarely on Belfield and his reckless participation in the violent code of gentlemanly honor (dueling). Belfield has to duel to reclaim Laura's reputation because he had previously been unwilling to claim her publicly as his wife. His reticence leaves Laura subject to accusations that she is a prostitute. Thus the stupid violence of the duel is critiqued alongside Belfield's failure to publish his attachment. This latter flaw casts Sansay's decision to publish as itself a form of feminist practice. And it may be that this nascent feminism is the glue that binds Sansay's portrait of Saint Domingue to her views of the United States. For Sansay, the revolution in Saint Domingue did not offer a stark contrast to the United States or even a salutary lesson in the dangers of mixed societies. Rather, both Sansay's narrative technique and her pursuit of a public voice illustrate affinities between the society of post-revolutionary United States and that of revolutionary Saint Domingue, where men in positions of authority are consistently portrayed as bungling, venal, malicious, or sadistic. Whether at home or abroad, in the environs of placid Schuylkill River or on the shores of the turbulent Caribbean, Sansay envisions a world in which women's happiness seems all but circumscribed by violent masculinity.

In this regard, it is of signal importance that the final push of the black revolution on Saint Domingue triggers Clara's escape from her jealous and increasingly abusive husband. Clara's emancipation from St. Louis is, moreover, doubled by her authorial liberation as well. The narrative trajectory of *Secret History* required Sansay to shift away from the univocal epistolary style of the first twenty-six letters. The sisters, Mary and Clara, are separated after Clara runs away from her husband while in St. Jago de Cuba after he rapes her and threatens to disfigure her face. Thus, in the last third of *Secret History*, readers encounter letters Clara writes herself in addition to more descriptions of her from the frequently judgmental pen of her sister, Mary. Sansay's split persona does not resolve completely to a unified voice; however, it seems significant that free from both her husband and the violent throes of the revolution, Clara is granted the ability to speak for herself. The shift has at least three consequences that could prove fruitful for more critical attention. First, as the letters pass between the sisters, Burr is displaced as the sole receiver and, as a consequence, readers no longer view Clara as if from the position of his sole oversight. Second, the homosocial exchange invites readers to consider whether bonds between women offer a satisfying alternative to heterosocial and heterosexual relations. And finally, Clara's empowerment as the scribe of her own experience frees readers to turn a more critical eye on Mary, previously uncontested as the voice of narrative authority.

How does the sororal relationship compare to other heterosexual and homosocial attachments as Clara makes her way from Saint Domingue to Cuba and then to Jamaica? What are the attractions of the Cuban Donna Jacinta in contrast to the community of creole evacuees, whose social cohesion is formed on the endlessly repeated tales of horror, suffering, displacement, and loss? Similar questions can be raised about *Laura*, where the cloistered, world-renouncing security of the convent is numbered among the few options for protection from the structural inequality and injustice of heterosexual competition.[1] In the United States "victims of seduction [are] devoted to public and universal scorn" while in Saint Domingue, where non-marital sex has become the norm, "she who has only one [extra-marital] lover, and retains him long in her chains, is considered a model of constancy and discretion" (*SH*, 95). In which circumstances are women most likely to find happiness? If in the United

---

[1] In my essay, "Brigands and Nuns: The Vernacular Sociology of Collectivity after the Haitian Revolution," I argue that Sansay uses the convent and the whorehouse to define the spectrum of options from isolated, privatized homosociality to fully commodified heterosexuality within which women might pursue happiness.

States, marriage removes women from the dangers of seduction, on Saint Domingue "every girl sighs to be married to [...] enjoy the unbounded liberty she so often sees abused by her mother." Little does she realize the sadness that awaits her. "She joins with unblushing front, the crowd who talk of sentiments they never feel, and who indulge in the most licentious excesses without having the flow of passion to gild their errors" (*SH*, 96). Under Sansay's scathing comparative survey, it is easy to understand the occasional despondency of her heroines. But Sansay's characters do, at times, find solace in the communality of other women. Analysis of Sansay's views about homosociality might productively compare these works to other early American novels that diverge on the constraints and freedoms offered through friendship between women.[1] Because Sansay evidently admired the French salonnière Germaine de Staël, it would be fruitful to query the status of the American salon circa 1800.[2] We might provisionally speculate that publication substituted for the absence of an established salon culture or for Sansay's class estrangement from the forms of the salon that did exist in the United States.

From the little we know of Sansay's career as a professional writer, the boldness of her venture into print was not rewarded with money, fame, or the social tranquility she sought. She reported to Burr earning only $100 for *Laura*, which sold, as did *Secret History*, for the modest fee of one dollar.[3] By 1812, she had moved on, seeking other avenues to pursue happiness. She tells Burr that she has opened a factory to manufacture artificial flowers, itself another example of Sansay's willingness to try out alternative social arrangements.[4] Surrounded by her employees, girls ranging in age from eight to eighteen, Sansay tells Burr that she is now too busy to hurry to meet him upon his return from Europe. "Had I been the wife of a prince or a king," she writes, "I should have flown to you as soon as your arrival was announced,

---

[1] Of note here are Susanna Rowson's *Charlotte* (1794), Hannah Foster's *The Coquette* (1797), Charles Brockden Brown's *Ormond* (1799), and Tabitha Tenney's *Female Quixotism* (1801).

[2] See *Secret History* (*SH*, 67–68). A selection from de Staël is reprinted in Appendix B. Regarding the salon in the United States see Branson, 125–42 and Stabile. Branson and Stabile are concerned with political and economic elites. It is hard to imagine Sansay having access to either of the social circles surveyed in these nonetheless important works.

[3] Titles advertised alongside Sansay's from her publisher, Bradford & Inskeep, were more than twice as expensive.

[4] This letter is reproduced in Appendix A.

bongré malgré[1] the royal permission. But you will readily conceive how much I am the soul of this establishment. So much so am I, that though the city lays before me as if it was painted on a map, I am often several months without going to it" (Appendix A, 235).

III. A Note on Later Texts Attributed to Leonora Sansay

Two later novels have been discovered that some attribute to Leonora Sansay. Both appeared from the publisher A.K. Newman in London: *Zelica, the Creole* in 1821 and *The Scarlet Handkerchief* in 1823. A third novel, referenced by the publisher as in the press and entitled *The Stranger in Mexico*, has not been found. *Zelica, the Creole* is a much expanded version of *Secret History* from which much of the earlier text is reproduced with slight but important alterations. Most apparent is the absence of the epistolary form. Another major difference between the two works is the addition of the character Zelica, the mixed-race daughter of radical egalitarian and supporter of the black revolt on Saint Domingue, De la Riviere. Riviere's commitment to the black elite leaders of the revolution leads him paradoxically to deny his daughter freedom to fix her romantic attachments.[2] He commits her against her will to marry Christophe, portrayed in the novel as an enlightened black leader, the heir to Toussaint and rival of the despot Dessalines. What gives me pause about attributing this novel to Sansay is the disposition of Clara. In *Zelica*, Clara no longer laments her marriage to St. Louis, who in *Secret History* is jealous, abusive, and dull. Instead, St. Louis is the gallant. Clara pines for his attention, her attachment to him verging on idolatry. Moreover, in place of the fascinating Caribbean travels featured in the final third of *Secret History*, Clara is killed![3] In her place, Zelica and Lastour, the French officer she prefers over the black general Christophe, escape Saint Domingue for the United States. *The Scarlet Handkerchief* is set during the War of 1812. We are introduced to Sophia Seaton in the company of first lady Dolley Madison. After the death of her guardian, she follows the hints of a mysterious British admirer and the call to celebrity and leaves for England to pursue romance and literary fame. At the conclusion of the novel, she gets

---

[1]   A neologism or pun, implying "should he [the king or prince] deign to grant his permission."
[2]   For a provocative reading of *Zelica*, see Smith-Rosenberg.
[3]   A short selection from *Zelica* is reprinted in Appendix B.

both, becoming a famous novelist and marrying into elite society, as the wife of Lord Edgeville. Whether these later works are authored by Leonora Sansay, they surely are interesting in their own right and deserve the attention of scholars of American literature.

Leonora Sansay's writings challenge the notion of an early American fiction solely obsessed with the problems and promises of early national republican citizenship. In their comparative scope and generic experimentation, Sansay's novels invite scholars, teachers, and students of American literature to draw connections between the institutions of Euro-American colonialism, race-slavery, the discourses of enlightenment and emancipation, gender roles and the transgression of domesticity, and the production of narrative prose genres around the turn of the century. Both *Secret History* and *Laura* need to be situated not only alongside other early American novels, but among the cosmopolitan, circum-Atlantic fiction about Haiti and New World colonization including François-René Chateaubriand's *Atala et René* (1801), Heinrich von Kleist's "Die Verbolung in Santo Domingo" (1811), and Victor Hugo's *The Bug-Jargal* (1826).

Chronology: Haiti/USA/France/Leonora Sansay

Adapted from Joan Dayan, *Haiti, History, and the Gods* (Berkeley: U of California P, 1995).

Year	Haiti/*USA*/**Sansay**	France
1492	6 December Columbus lands at Môle St. Nicholas, names island Hispaniola.	
1685		March Louis XIV issues Colbert's *Code Noir.*
1697	20 September Treaty of Ryswick. Spain officially recognizes French presence and cedes western third of island to France, henceforth referred to as Saint-Domingue.	
1758	March Execution of François Makandal, an African-born maroon who, after escaping slavery, organized a revolt to begin with the mass poisoning of plantations across the island.	
1763	*10 February* *Treaty of Peace ends the Seven Years' War between England and France.* *British Empire in North America extends to the Mississippi River.* 24 November Jesuits expelled from Saint-Domingue.	

Year	Haiti/*USA*/**Sansay**	France
1771		May Louis XV decrees *Instructions to Administrators*, a new code of restrictions and prejudices designed specifically to oppose *gens de couleur*.
1773	*December* *Sons of Liberty,* *revolutionary political group* *based in Massachusetts, dump* *British Tea in Boston Harbor.*	
1776	*4 July* *Thomas Jefferson's Declaration* *of Independence ratified by the* *Continental Congress.*	
1777		17 December France recognizes the independence of the United States of America.
1783	3 September Treaty of Paris brings the American Revolution to a close.	
1789	*March* *US Constitution takes effect* *after having been ratified by* *11 states. Constitution tables* *any law to prohibit the* *importation of slaves* *until 1808.*	4 July The National Assembly votes to seat six delegates from Saint-Domingue.
	George Washington becomes *first president of the* *United States.*	9 July The National Assembly becomes the National Constituent Assembly.

Year	Haiti/*USA*/**Sansay**	France
1789		14 July French Revolution officially begins with the fall of the Bastille. 20 August Colonists in Paris found Club Massiac to oppose colonial participation in the French Revolution. 26 August Declaration of the Rights of Man and Citizens adopted by National Assembly.
	October Formation of Colonial Assembly in order to combat actions of National Assembly on behalf of *gens de couleur*. Mulatto leaders, including Vincent Ogé, Jean-Baptiste Chavannes, and Julien Raymond, ally themselves with the Amis des Noirs, while white deputies from Saint-Domingue seek colonial representation.	5 October Louis XVI assents to the Declaration of Rights of Man and Citizens: "granted to all men by natural justice." 22 October National Assembly accepts petition of rights of "free citizens of color" from Saint-Domingue.
1790		8 March Decree grants full legislative powers to the Colonial Assembly in Saint Marc. The ambiguous article 4 gives political rights to persons aged twenty-five years or older who own property or pay taxes and have resided for two years in the colony.
	May News of 8 March decree reaches Saint-Domingue. Constitutional Assembly in Saint Marc issues radical decrees	

Year	Haiti/*USA*/**Sansay**	France
1790	and reforms, pushing colony toward independence from the dictates of the metropole and resulting in the colonial conflict between the *pompons blancs* (the royalists) and the *pompons rouges* (the patriots). The Colonial Assembly at Saint Marc declares the royal governor Comte de Peynier a traitor, while the Provincial Assembly at Le Cap sides with the governor. Both sides exclude mulattoes from the provisions of article 4.	
		12 October National Assembly dissolves Assembly at Saint Marc, reaffirming the colonists' right to legislate the future of free persons of color.
	23–28 October Ogé lands in Saint-Domingue, fails in petition to Peyneir demanding mulatto rights and begins rebellion.	
1791	9 March Chavannes and Ogé executed at Le Cap.	
		15 May National Assembly declares a limited number of free-born persons of color eligible to be seated in future assemblies, with "the rights of voting citizens."
	14 August Ceremony of Bois Caïman, Voudou ritual that some credit with initiating the Haitian Revolution.	

Year	Haiti/*USA*/**Sansay**	France
1791	22–23 August Slave insurrection in the North.	
		24 September National Assembly revokes 15 May decree.
	26 September Cap Français, the oldest, richest, and most densely populated city of the colony, burned to the ground by rebelling slaves.	
1792		4 April Louis XVI affirms Jacobin decree granting equal political rights to all persons of color and free blacks in Saint-Domingue. 9 July Rochambeau appointed lieutenant general in command of the French Windward Islands (the southern islands of the French Lesser Antilles including Martinique and Saint Lucia). Fights against British in West Indies until besieged at Martinique in 1794. Surrenders and is allowed to reside in United States as
	18 September Jacobin commissioners Poverel, Sonthonax, Ailhaud, and General Laveaux arrive in Le Cap with troops.	British prisoner until exchanged.
		21 September Monarchy abolished. National Convention elected. The Republic declared. 21 January Louis XVI beheaded.
1793	February While Spain, Britain, and France fight for Saint-Domingue, Toussaint,	1 February France declares war on Great Britain and Holland.

Year	Haiti/*USA*/**Sansay**	France
1793	Jean François, and Bissou join Spanish forces. 20–21 June Cap Français again consumed by flames and deserted by the white inhabitants. 10,000 refugees arrive in the United States. *Summer* *Yellow Fever epidemic strikes Philadelphia. 4,000 die and 20,000 flee to the countryside, including members of the Federal government.* 29 August Sonthonax issues a General Emancipation decree abolishing slavery in the North. 20 September The British invasion of Saint-Domingue begins.	10–13 March Royalist uprisings in La Vendée and military reverses lead to a Reign of Terror in which tens of thousands of opponents of the Revolution and criminals are executed. September 1793–October 1795. National reforms include the abolition of colonial slavery, economic measures to aid the poor, support for public education, and a short-lived de-Christianization. 16 October Marie Antoinette beheaded.
1794	24 March Rochambeau, having returned to the Windward Islands on 30 January, surrenders to the	4 February The Convention officially abolishes slavery in France and French territories, including Saint-Domingue. 5 February Mixed delegation from Saint-Domingue seated at National Convention.

Year	Haiti/*USA*/**Sansay**	France
1794	British at Fort Royal in Martinique.	
	6 May Toussaint turns on the Spanish and joins Republicans under Laveaux.	
	4 June The British take Port-au-Prince. British troops occupy most of major seaports in western and southern provinces; Spanish troops and a number of former slaves occupy western provinces.	25 June The French legislature recalls commissioners Poverel and Sonthonax.
		28 July Robespierre, Saint-Just, and 19 adherents executed.
1795	**Louis Sansay evacuates Saint-Domingue.**	22 July France signs peace treaty with Spain that cedes Santo Domingo to France.
		26 October National Convention dissolved. Directory established.
1796	**Leonora Sansay (née Hassell) begins affair with Aaron Burr.**	
	11 May Rochambeau arrives in Le Cap as governor with new civil commissioners, including Sonthonax, and republican reinforcements.	
	June Final withdrawal of Spanish forces.	

Year	Haiti/*USA*/**Sansay**	France
1796	18 July Rochambeau clashes with Sonthonax; is dismissed as governor and returns to France.	September Laveaux and Sonthonax elected delegates from Saint-Domingue to Legislative Assembly under Directory.
1797	2 May Sonthonax appoints Toussaint governor general. 25 August Toussaint forces Sonthonax to return to France.	
1798	March British general Maitland arrives to negotiate peace. April Commissioner Hédouville arrives in Le Cap. *13 June Congress suspends commercial trade with France and her possessions.* October British forces evacuated from Saint-Domingue. 23 October Toussaint forces Hédouville to return to France.	
1799	June Civil war between mulatto André Rigaud and Toussaint breaks out. *26 June President Adams issues proclamation lifting embargo imposed on Saint-Domingue and promises cooperation with Toussaint.*	

Year	Haiti/*USA*/**Sansay**	France
1799		9 November As part of a planned coup d'état, General Bonaparte is illegally named commander of the troops in Paris. The Directory is officially ended.
1800	**Leonora marries Louis Sansay, but continues affair with Burr.** 25 July Dessalines defeats Rigaud with help of American vessels at port of Jacmel.	
1800	*30 August* *In Richmond, Virginia, General Gabriel's plan for slave insurrection revealed.*	
1801	**4 March** **Jefferson and Burr inaugurated as third president and vice president of the United States.** 8 July New Constitution proclaimed. Toussaint declared governor general for life. *19 July* *Jefferson assures French minister Pichon that he opposes independence of Saint-Domingue and supports Napoleon's agenda.*	
		24 October Victor-Emmanuel Leclerc named commander in chief of the largest expeditionary army ever to sail from France. Rochambeau named second in command and returns for the third time to the Caribbean.
	24 November *Thomas Jefferson writes to Virginia Governor James Monroe regarding the relocation of emancipated slaves*	

Year	Haiti/*USA*/**Sansay**	France
1801	*and free negroes to Saint-Domingue.*	
1802	4 February General Christophe, following Toussaint's orders, sets fire to Le Cap.	
	6 February Leclerc enters Le Cap. **Louis and Leonora Sansay return to Saint-Domingue to reclaim the Sansay plantation forfeited when Louis Sansay evacuated the island in 1795.**	24 March Loss of Battle of Crête-à-Pierrot.
		25 March Treaty of Amiens between England and France.
	26 April Christophe meets with and joins Leclerc's forces.	27 April Bonaparte approves decree reestablishing slavery and the slave trade.
	6 May Toussaint agrees to surrender to Leclerc.	
	23 May At Saint Marc, Dessalines assumes command of the Artibonite under Leclerc.	
	7 June Toussaint tricked, taken prisoner, and deported to Fort de Joux in the Jura mountains.	
	13–14 October Dessalines, Pétion, and Clerveaux defect from the French. Christophe then joins them.	

Year	Haiti/*USA*/**Sansay**	France
1802	2 November Leclerc dies of yellow fever. Rochambeau takes command as capitaine général de la colonie.	
1803		7 April Toussaint dies at Fort de Joux.

18 May
Dessalines rips white from
French tricolor at Arcahaie,
and Haitian flag is born. Black
and mulatto generals swear
allegiance to Dessalines.

18 November
Battle of Vertières. French
evacuate Le Cap.

19 November
Rochambeau sails from Le Cap
and surrenders to the British
admiral who had offered
Dessalines naval support.

28 November
Môle Saint Nicholas evacuated
by French troops.

29 November
8,000 survivors of 43,000 men
sent by Napoleon surrender to
the British.

30 November
Dessalines, at the head of 8,000
men, takes possession of Cap
Français and renames it
Cap Haïtien.

18 May
War declared between
England and France.

1804   1 January
In Gonaives, Dessalines
proclaims independence for the
first black republic.

Year	Haiti/*USA*/**Sansay**	France
1804	February–April Dessalines orders the slaughter of the remaining French after promising them protection.	
	11 July Aaron Burr kills Alexander Hamilton in a duel at Weehawken, New Jersey.	
	8 October Dessalines crowned Emporer Jacques I of Haiti.	
	Leonora Sansay returns to Philadelphia from Saint-Domingue via Cuba.	2 December Napoleon Bonaparte crowns himself emperor.
1805	20 May Dessalines ratifies Haiti's first constitution as independent nation and the first Black Republic in the New World.	
	1805–1806 Burr develops and begins to execute a western expedition for which he will be suspected and tried for treason against the United States.	
1806	**Leonora Sansay participates in aborted Burr Conspiracy.**	
	17 October Dessalines betrayed and murdered in an ambush at Port-Rouge.	
1807	17 February Christophe proclaimed president of newly created state of Haiti in the North.	

Year	Haiti/*USA*/**Sansay**	France
1807	11 March Alexandre Sabès Pétion elected president of republic of Haiti in Port-au-Prince. The struggle between the *noirs* of the North and the *jaunes* of the South and West results in a divided Haiti. **1 September** **Federal jury finds Burr "not** **proved to be guilty under this** **indictment by any evidence** **submitted to us."**	
1808	**Publication of *Secret History;*** ***or the Horrors of St. Domingo.*** **Burr leaves for Europe,** **not to return until 1812.**	
1809	**Publication of *Laura*.**	
1811	2 June Christophe crowned King Henry I.	
1816	2 June Pétion declared president for life.	
1817	**Last known letter from** **Sansay to Burr.**	
1818	29 March Pétion's death. 30 March Jean-Pierre Boyer elected president for life.	
1820	30 April President Boyer offers blacks emigrating from the United States land for homesteads in Haiti. 8 October Christophe commits suicide.	

Year	Haiti/*USA*/**Sansay**	France
1820	26 October Boyer enters Le Cap. Haiti reunited.	
1821	**Publication of *Zelica, the Creole*.**	
1822	9 February Boyer enters the city of Santo Domingo. *30 May* *In Charleston, South Carolina,* *Denmark Vesey's plot for a* *massive slave uprising exposed.*	
1823	**Publication of** ***The Scarlet Handkerchief.***	
1824	*4 February* *Thomas Jefferson writes to Jared* *Sparks with an emancipation plan* *that calls for "colonization" of US* *blacks to Haiti.*	
1825		17 March Charles X recognizes independence of Haiti, and conveys his royal recognition to Port-au-Prince with two admirals and the 494 guns of 14 warships.
	April Haitian government abandons program of US black emigration.	
1826	6 May Boyer signs into effect the *Code* *Rural*, consigning most Haitians, especially rural cultivators, to severe laws, amounting to nothing less than compulsory labor and curtailed freedom of movement.	
1831	*28 August* *Nat Turner revolt in Southampton,* *Virginia.*	

Year	Haiti/*USA*/**Sansay**	France
1832	July Thirty-two black slaves arrive in Port-au-Prince from New Orleans under the auspices of Miss Frances Wright, a Scottish inhabitant of the United States.	
1836	**14 September** **Aaron Burr dies.**	
1843	13 March Boyer abdicates and leaves for Jamaica.	
1844	3 April During provisional government of Charles Rivière-Hérard, Piquet uprising begins in the South, led by Louis Jean-Jacques Acaau. 3 May Rivière-Hérard deposed. Philippe Guerrier becomes president.	
1845	16 April Council of State elects Jean-Louis Pierrot president.	
1846	1 March Pierrot deposed. Jean-Baptiste Riché declared president.	
1847	1 March General Faustin Soulouque becomes president.	
1848		24 February The Second Republic proclaimed after popular insurrection, leading to massacre of the June days and defeat of working-class struggle. 4 March The provisional government of the Second Republic decrees the

Year	Haiti/*USA*/**Sansay**	France
1848		emancipation of the slaves in Guadeloupe and Martinique.
	16 April President Faustin Soulouque begins massacre of mulattoes suspected as conspirators in Port-au-Prince.	
1849	25 August President Soulouque declares himself Emperor Faustin I.	
1851		2 December Louis Napoleon announces coup d'état and becomes president in token election.
1852		20 November Louis Napoleon proclaims himself Emperor Napoleon III.
1859	15 January Soulouque abdicates and leaves for Jamaica.	
	18 January Fabre Nicholas Geffrard becomes president.	
1860	Concordat between Haiti and the Vatican.	
1861	*May Reverend James Theodore Holly, black Episcopalian priest, and nearly 2,000 blacks emigrate to Haiti from New Haven, Connecticut.*	
1862	*5 June US government recognizes Haiti.*	
	22–24 September "Preliminary Emancipation Proclamation" contains a plan "to colonize persons of African descent," which would not appear in the final Proclamation.	

Year	Haiti/USA/Sansay	France
1862	*31 December* *Lincoln signs a contract to pay the* *adventurer Bernard Kock $250,000* *for the colonization of 5,000 freed* *men at Ille-â-Vache.*	
1915	28 July Admiral Caperton and US marines land in Haiti, occupying Haiti until 1934.	

Maps of Haiti (1853) and the Caribbean (2005)

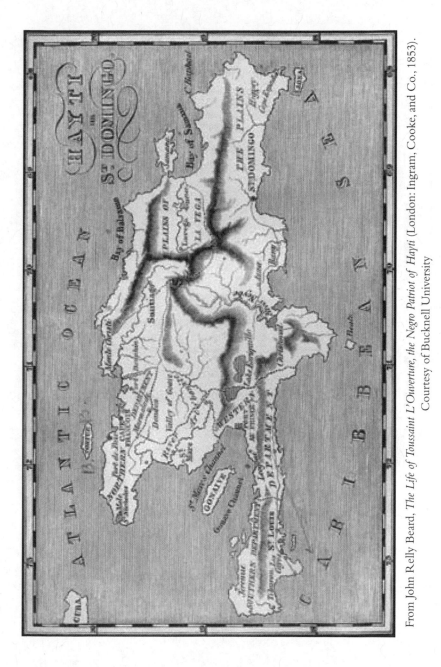

From John Relly Beard, *The Life of Toussaint L'Ouverture, the Negro Patriot of Hayti* (London: Ingram, Cooke, and Co., 1853). Courtesy of Bucknell University

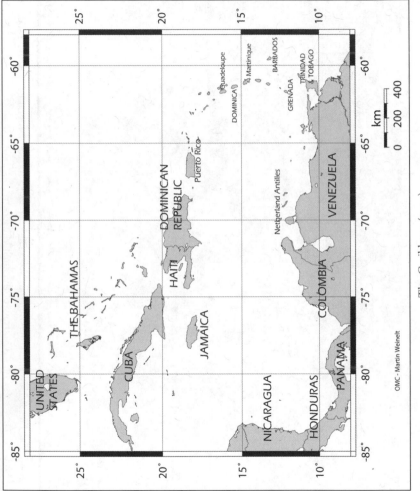

The Caribbean (2005)

OMC – Martin Weinelt

A Note on the Text

The text of this Broadview edition has been transcribed from the first editions of *Secret History* (1808) and *Laura* (1809). The text has not been modernized or regularized, but for a few typographical errors and other features I consider nontextual. Variant spellings have been preserved. Obvious printer's errors have been corrected.

Original author notes have been retained in the appendices and are identified by asterisks.

SECRET HISTORY;
OR,
THE HORRORS OF ST. DOMINGO,

IN

A SERIES OF LETTERS,
WRITTEN BY A LADY AT CAPE FRANCOIS.

TO

COLONEL BURR,
LATE VICE-PRESIDENT OF THE UNITED STATES,
PRINCIPALLY DURING THE COMMAND OF
GENERAL ROCHAMBEAU.

PHILADELPHIA:

PUBLISHED BY BRADFORD & INSKEEP.

R. CARR, PRINTER

****

1808.

the obvious Preface

I am fearful of having been led into an error by my friends, when taught by them to believe that I could write something which would interest and please; and it was chiefly with a view to ascertain what confidence I might place in their kind assurances on this subject, that I collected and consented, though reluctantly, to the publication of these letters.

Should a less partial public give them a favourable reception, and allow them to possess some merit, it would encourage me to endeavour to obtain their further approbation by a little work already planned and in some forwardness.

THE AUTHOR.

Philadelphia, Nov. 30th*, 1807.*

LETTER I.

Cape Francois.

We arrived safely here, my dear friend, after a passage of forty days, during which I suffered horribly from sea-sickness, heat and confinement; but the society of my fellow-passengers was so agreeable that I often forgot the inconvenience to which I was exposed. It consisted of five or six French families who, having left St. Domingo at the beginning of the revolution, were now returning full of joy at the idea of again possessing the estates from which they had been driven by their revolted slaves. Buoyed by their newly awakened hopes they were all delightful anticipation. There is an elasticity in the French character which repels misfortune. They have an inexhaustible flow of spirits that bears them lightly through the ills of life.

Towards the end of the voyage, when I was well enough to go on deck, I was delighted with the profound tranquillity of the ocean, the uninterrupted view, the beautiful horizon, and wished, since fate has separated me from those I love, that I could build a dwelling on the bosom of the waters, where, sheltered from the storms that agitate mankind, I should be exposed to those of heaven only. But a truce to melancholy reflections, for here I am in St. Domingo, with a new world opening to my view.

My sister, whose fortunes, you know, I was obliged to follow, repents every day having so precipitately chosen a husband: it is impossible for two creatures to be more different, and I foresee that she will be wretched.

On landing, we found the town a heap of ruins. A more terrible picture of desolation cannot be imagined. Passing through streets choaked with rubbish, we reached with difficulty a house which had escaped the general fate. The people live in tents, or make a kind of shelter, by laying a few boards across the half-consumed beams; for the buildings being here of hewn stone, with walls three feet thick, only the roofs and floors have been destroyed. But to hear of the distress which these unfortunate people have suffered, would fill with horror the stoutest heart, and make the most obdurate melt with pity.

When the French fleet appeared before the mouth of the harbour, Christophe,[1] the Black general, who commanded at the Cape, rode through the town, ordering all the women to leave their houses—the men had been taken to the plain the day before, for he was going to set fire to the place, which he did with his own hand.

The ladies, bearing their children in their arms, or supporting the trembling steps of their aged mothers, ascended in crowds the mountain which rises behind the town. Climbing over rocks covered with brambles, where no path had been ever beat, their feet were torn to pieces and their steps marked with blood. Here they suffered all the pains of hunger and thirst; the most terrible apprehensions for their fathers, husbands, brothers and sons; to which was added the sight of the town in flames: and even these horrors were increased by the explosion of the powder magazine. Large masses of rock were detached by the shock, which, rolling down the sides of the mountain, many of these hapless fugitives were killed. Others still more unfortunate, had their limbs broken or sadly bruised, whilst their wretched companions could offer them nothing but unavailing sympathy and impotent regret.

On the third day the negroes evacuated the place, and the fleet entered the harbour. Two gentlemen, who had been concealed by a faithful slave, went in a canoe to meet the admiral's vessel, and arrived in time to prevent a dreadful catastrophe. The general, seeing numbers of people descending the mountain, thought they were the negroes coming to oppose his landing and was preparing to fire on them, when these gentlemen informed him that they were the white inhabitants, and thus prevented a mistake too shocking to be thought of.

The men now entered from the plain and sought among the smoking ruins the objects of their affectionate solicitude. To paint

---

[1] Together with Toussaint Louverture and Jean-Jacques Dessalines, Henri Christophe was a principal leader of revolutionary Haiti. Depicted here as a Haitian Nero, Christophe indeed led the defense of Cap François and, forced to retreat from the city, burned and reduced it to rubble. Though he joined Dessalines in a brief period of compliance with the French after Toussaint's capture and deportation, Christophe eventually joined the black rebels, who had refused to disarm in the wake of the successful French assault on Le Cap. The Saint Dominguan letters in *Secret History* are framed by Christophe's retreat and then by his triumphant return to Le Cap on 19 November 1803, the date Rochambeau conceded defeat and began the negotiated evacuation of French troops and citizens from Haiti. Christophe became independent Haiti's second President and, in 1811, its first and only King. He committed suicide in 1820.

these heart-rending scenes of tenderness and woe, description has no powers. The imagination itself shrinks from the task.

Three months after this period we arrived and have now been a month here, the town is rapidly rebuilding, but it is extremely difficult to find a lodging. The heat is intolerable and the season so unhealthy that the people die in incredible numbers. On the night of our arrival, Toussaint[1] the general in chief of the negroes, was seized at the Gonaives and embarked for France. This event caused great rejoicing. A short time before he was taken, he had his treasure buried in the woods, and at the return of the negroes he employed on the expedition, they were shot without being suffered to utter a word.

Clara has had the yellow fever. Her husband, who certainly loves her very much, watched her with unceasing care, and I believe, preserved her life, to which however she attaches no value since it must be passed with him.

Nothing amuses her. She sighs continually for the friend of her youth and seems to exist only in the recollection of past happiness. Her aversion to her husband is unqualified and unconquerable. He is vain, illiterate, talkative. A silent fool may be borne, but from a loquacious one there is no relief. How painful must her intercourse with him be; and how infinitely must that pain be augmented by the

---

[1] Toussaint Louverture (1745?–1803) had been a coachman on a plantation near Cap Français. Born on All Saint's Day (thus the name Toussaint), he adopted the name Louverture during the revolution to signify the opening of freedom. Emancipated when he was 30, Toussaint would become a complex, heroic figure. A brilliant military strategist and a cunning and deceptive politician, Toussaint gained fame and admiration even among white observers of events on Saint Domingue, who promoted him as the black Napoleon. He was Christian, but retained his ties to his African roots. Though free, he quickly became a leader of the black army after the slave uprising in the north in 1791. He led them to startling victories over French regulars in 1793 before accepting a truce with newly Republican France in 1794. When slavery was abolished, Toussaint rallied the army of former slaves in support of the French Republic and helped defeat both Spanish and English invasions of the island. By 1800, Toussaint had become the dominant military and civil leader of Saint Domingue. He named himself governor for life and began to rebuild the Saint Dominguan plantation economy. By 1800, Napoleon had gained control of the French army and the Directory ended. Toussaint's power threatened Napoleon, who had plans to reinstitute slavery in the French colonies and to reinvigorate French settlements in North America. Napoleon sent General Leclerc to reclaim power in Saint Domingue, and on 7 June 1802, Toussaint was taken prisoner and sent to France, where he died in a prison cell in the Jura Mountains in 1803.

idea of being his forever? Her elegant mind, stored with literary acquirements, is lost to him. Her proud soul is afflicted at depending on one she abhors, and at beholding her form, and you must know that form so vilely bartered. Whilst on the continent she was less sensible of the horrors of her fate. The society of her friend gave a charm to her life, and having married in compliance with his advice, she thought that she would eventually be happy. But their separation has rent the veil which concealed her heart; she finds no sympathy in the bosom of her husband. She is alone and she is wretched.

General Le Clerc[1] is small, his face is interesting, but he has an appearance of ill health. His wife, the sister of Buonaparte,[2] lives in a house on the mountain till there can be one in town prepared for her reception. She is offended, and I think justly, with the ladies of the Cape, who, from a mistaken pride, did not wait on her when she arrived, because having lost their cloaths they could not dazzle her with their finery.

Having heard that there were some American ladies here she expressed a desire to see them; Mr. V— proposed to present us; Clara, who would not walk a mile to see a queen, declined. But I, who walk at all times, merely for the pleasure it affords me, went; and, considering the labour it costs to ascend the mountain, I have a claim on the gratitude of Madame for having undertaken it to shew her an object which she probably expected to find in a savage state.

She was in a room darkened by Venetian blinds, lying on her sofa, from which she half rose to receive me. When I was seated she reclined again on the sofa and amused general Boyer, who sat at her feet, by letting her slipper fall continually, which he respectfully put on as often as it fell. She is small, fair, with blue eyes and flaxen hair. Her face is expressive of sweetness but without spirit. She has a voluptuous mouth, and is rendered interesting by an air of languor which spreads itself over her whole frame. She was dressed in a

---

[1] Charles Victor Emmanuel Leclerc (1772–1802) led the French invasion force with which Napoleon hoped to reestablish French control of Saint Domingue and, following the model of Guadeloupe, to reinstitute slavery on the island. Leclerc was married to Napoleon's sister, Pauline.

[2] Pauline Bonaparte; Napoleon Bonaparte; Buonaparte is the Italian form of the name used by Napoleon himself until 1796 when he adopted the French form, dropping the "u."

muslin morning gown, with a Madras handkerchief[1] on her head. I gave her one of the beautiful silver medals of Washington, engraved by Reich,[2] with which she seemed much pleased. The conversation languished, and I soon withdrew.

General Le Clerc had gone in the morning to fort Dauphin.

I am always in good spirits, for every thing here charms me by its novelty. There are a thousand pretty things to be had, new fashions and elegant trinkets from Paris; but we have no balls, no plays, and of what use is finery if it cannot by shewn?

The natives of this country murmur already against the general in chief; they say he places too much confidence in the negroes. When Toussaint was seized he had all the black chiefs in his power, and, by embarking them for France, he would have spread terror throughout the Island, and the negroes would have been easily reduced, instead of which he relies on their good faith, has them continually in his house, at this table, and wastes the time in conference which should be differently employed. The Creoles[3] shake their heads and predict much ill. Accustomed to the climate, and acquainted with the manner of fighting the Negroes, they offer advice, which is not listened to; nor are any of them employed, but all places of honour or emolument are held by Europeans, who

---

[1]   Fabric from Madras, India was widely available and popular among women of color in colonial Saint Domingue and throughout the West Indies. It came into use as a headdress in response to sumptuary laws designed to punish women of color, who were often the sexual rivals of white creole women (see Letter X, p. 95, below). Women of color were prohibited from wearing silk or keeping their heads uncovered. The madras handkerchief met the principle if not the spirit of the restrictive codes. Artfully worn, the madras handkerchief attracted attention and, when folded to display one to four points, was used to indicate whether the wearer was engaged or free to be approached. That elite French women like Pauline Bonaparte would adopt the madras headdress illustrates how successfully women of color subverted any stigma attached to its use.

[2]   John Reich came from Bavaria to the United States in 1800 as an indentured servant; though a highly skilled craftsman, he evidently could not afford passage to the United States. Thomas Jefferson attempted to secure a position for him at the US mint in 1801, but Reich would not receive work as an assistant engraver until 1807. Reich did engrave the first, if unofficial, Presidential inaugural medal for Jefferson in 1802. In Sansay's letter to Burr (1803; see Appendix A, p. 225), she writes of giving Pauline Leclerc the Medal of Jefferson, not of Washington. Perhaps the change was made by Sansay's publishers, Bradford and Inskeep. Having recently purchased the partisan Federalist journal *The Port-Folio*, Bradford and Inskeep, or certainly their readers, would have had slight interest in commemorating Jefferson as a great leader.

[3]   Creole refers to white inhabitants of European descent but born in the colonies.

appear to regard the Island as a place to be conquered and divided among the victors, and are consequently viewed by the natives with a jealous eye. Indeed the professed intention of those who have come with the army, is to make a fortune, and return to France with all possible speed, to enjoy it. It cannot be imagined that they will be very delicate about the means of accomplishing their purpose.

The Cape is surrounded; at least the plain is held by the Negroes; but the town is tranquil, and Dessalines[1] and the other black chiefs are on the best terms with general Le Clerc.

We are to have a grand review next week. The militia is to be organized, and the general is to address the troops on the field. He has the reputation of being very eloquent, but he has shocked every body by having ordered a superb service of plate, made of the money intended to pay the army, while the poor soldiers, badly cloathed, and still more badly fed, are asking alms in the street, and absolutely dying of want.

A beggar had never been known in this country, and to see them in such numbers, fills the inhabitants with horror; but why should such trifling considerations as the preservation of soldiers, prevent a general in chief from eating out of silver dishes?

We have neither public nor private balls, nor any amusement except now and then a little scandal. The most current at this moment is, that Madame Le Clerc is very kind to general Boyer, and that her husband is not content, which in a French husband is a little extraordinary. Perhaps the last part of the anecdote is calumny.

Madame Le Clerc, as I learned from a gentleman who has long known her, betrayed from her earliest youth a disposition to gallantry, and had, when very young, some adventures of éclat[2] in Marseilles. Her brother, whose favourite she is, married her to general Le Clerc, to whom he gave the command of the army intended to sail for St.

---

[1] Jean-Jacques Dessalines (1758–1806) defeated the French army under Leclerc and proclaimed Haitian independence on 1 January 1804. Under the constitution written under his stewardship, Haiti became a black republic. No distinctions of race were recognized among citizens. Whites, however, were banned forever from owning land. Dessalines is infamous for ordering and supervising the massacre of the remaining white inhabitants on the island, an event that tragically allowed both France and the US to refuse to recognize independent Haiti for decades. Dessalines named himself first emperor of Haiti. He was assassinated in 1806 by rebels loyal to Henri Christophe, who succeeded Dessalines.

[2] Great brilliance, success, or scandal.

Domingo, after having given that island, as a marriage portion, to his sister. But her reluctance to come to this country was so great, that it was almost necessary to use force to oblige her to embark.

She has one child, a lovely boy, three years old, of which she appears very fond. But for a young and beautiful woman, accustomed to the sweets of adulation, and the intoxicating delights of Paris, certainly the transition to this country, in its present state, has been too violent. She has no society, no amusement, and never having imagined that she would be forced to seek an equivalent for either in the resources of her own mind, she has made no provision for such an unforeseen emergency.

She hates reading, and though passionately fond of music plays on no instrument; never having stolen time from her pleasurable pursuits to devote to the acquisition of that divine art. She can do nothing but dance, and to dance alone is a triste[1] resource; therefore it cannot be surprising if her early propensities predominate, and she listens to the tale of love breathed by General Boyer, for never did a more fascinating votary offer his vows at the Idalian shrine.[2] His form and face are models of masculine perfection; his eyes sparkle with enthusiasm, and his voice is modulated by a sweetness of expression which cannot be heard without emotion. Thus situated, and thus surrounded, her youth and beauty plead for her, and those most disposed to condemn would exclaim on beholding her:

Prettyness trumps all

"If to her share some female errors fall,
Look in her face, and you'll forget them all."[3]

I suppose you'll laugh at this gossip, but 'tis the news of the day, nothing is talked of but Madame Le Clerc, and envy and ill-nature pursue her because she is charming and surrounded by splendor.

I have just now been reading Madame de Stael[4] on the passions, which she describes very well, but I believe not precisely as she felt

---

1   Sad.
2   Idalium is a mountain city in Cyprus, sacred to Venus, or Aphrodite.
3   Adapted from Alexander Pope (1688–1744), *The Rape of the Lock* (1714), Canto 2, line 17.
4   Anne Louise Germaine Necker, Madame de Staël-Holstein (1766–1817) was the daughter of Jacques Necker, the Swiss-born finance minister of French King Louis XVI, and salonnière Suzanne Necker. Necker's dismissal was one of the triggering events of the French Revolution. Madame de Staël, as she was known, fled France for England during

their influence. I have heard an anecdote of her which I admire; a friend, to whom she had communicated her intention of publishing her memoirs, asked what she intended doing with the gallant part, —Oh, she replied, je ne me peindrai qu'en buste.[1]

LETTER II.

Cape Francois.

What a change has taken place here since my last letter was written! I mentioned that there was to be a grand review, and I also mentioned that the confidence General Le Clerc placed in the negroes was highly blamed, and justly, as he has found to his cost.

On the day of the review, when the troops of the line and the guarde nationale were assembled on the field, a plot was discovered, which had been formed by the negroes in the town, to seize the arsenal and to point the cannon of a fort, which overlooked the place of review, on the troops; whilst Clairvaux,[2] the mulatto[3] general, who commanded the advanced posts, was to join the negroes of the plain, overpower the guards, and entering the town, complete the destruction of the white inhabitants. The first part of the plot was discovered and defeated. But Clairvaux made good his escape, and in the evening attacked the post General Le Clerc had so imprudently confided to him. The consternation was terrible. The guarde nationale, composed chiefly of Creoles, did wonders. The American captains and sailors volunteered their services; they fought bravely, and many of them perished. The negroes were repulsed; but if they gained no ground they lost none, and they occupy at present the same posts as before. The pusillanimous General Le Clerc, shrinking from

the Reign of Terror, but returned in 1794. She opened her own salon, a private gathering place for intellectuals, writers, artists, and arbiters of taste and fashion. After Napoleon's rise to power in 1795, she was forcibly exiled until 1814. Abroad, she became a prolific writer of novels, political essays, and literary criticism. See Appendix B for a selection from *On the Influence of Passions* (1796).

[1] "I will paint myself only from the shoulders up."
[2] Augustin Clerveaux, a general who led the black rebels against Leclerc during the war of independence.
[3] A person of colour, of mixed race.

danger of which his own (imprudence) had been the cause, thought only of saving himself. He sent his plate and valuable effects on board the admiral's vessel, and was preparing to embark secretly with his suite, but the brave admiral La Touche de Treville sent him word that he would fire with more pleasure on those who abandoned the town, than on those who attacked it.

The ensuing morning presented a dreadful spectacle. Nothing was heard but the groans of the wounded, who were carried through the streets to their homes, and the cries of the women for their friends who were slain.

The general, shut up in his house, would see nobody; ashamed of the weakness which had led to this disastrous event, and of the want of courage he had betrayed: a fever seized him and he died in three days.

Madame Le Clerc, who had not loved him whilst living, mourned his death like the Ephesian matron,[1] cut off her hair, which was very beautiful, to put it in his coffin; refused all sustenance and all public consolation.

General Rochambeau,[2] who is at Port au Prince, has been sent for by the inhabitants of the Cape to take the command. Much good is expected from the change, he is said to be a brave officer and an excellent man.

Monsieur D'Or is in the interim Captain General, and unites in himself the three principal places in the government: Prefect Colonial, Ordonnateur, and General in Chief.[3]

All this bustle would be delightful if it was not attended with such melancholy consequences. It keeps us from petrifying, of which I was in danger.

---

[1] The tale of the Ephesian Matron appears in Petronius' *Satyricon* (64 AD), and was popularized by the French writer Jean de La Fontaine (1621–95). The tale tells of a woman who sobbed continuously for five days by her dead husband's corpse, refusing to eat, and tearing out her hair in grief. She is eventually comforted and then seduced by a soldier sent to guard the tomb.

[2] Donatien Marie Joseph Rochambeau (1755–1813) served with his father at Yorktown during the American Revolution. In 1792, he was appointed to defend the French Windward Islands against the British. He surrendered at Martinique in 1794. Returning to France after a prisoner exchange, he was recommissioned to take over the Leclerc expedition after his predecessor died of yellow fever in 1802.

[3] Chief administrative officer of the Northern Department of Saint Domingue, Financial Director, and highest ranking military officer.

I have become acquainted with some Creole ladies who, having staid in the Island during the revolution, relate their sufferings in a manner which harrows up the soul; and dwell on the recollection of their long lost happiness with melancholy delight. St. Domingo was formerly a garden. Every inhabitant lived on his estate like a Sovereign ruling his slaves with despotic sway, enjoying all that luxury could invent, or fortune procure.

The pleasures of the table were carried to the last degree of refinement. Gaming knew no bounds, and libertinism, called love, was without restraint. The Creole is generous, hospitable, magnificent, but vain, inconstant, and incapable of serious application; and in this abode of pleasure and luxurious ease vices have reigned at which humanity must shudder. The jealousy of the women was often terrible in its consequences. One lady, who had a beautiful negro girl continually about her person, thought she saw some symptoms of *tendresse*[1] in the eyes of her husband, and all the furies of jealousy seized her soul.

She ordered one of her slaves to cut off the head of the unfortunate victim, which was instantly done. At dinner her husband said he felt no disposition to eat, to which his wife, with the air of a demon, replied, perhaps I can give you something that will excite your appetite; it has at least had that effect before. She rose and drew from a closet the head of Coomba. The husband, shocked beyond expression, left the house and sailed immediately for France, in order never again to behold such a monster.

Many similar anecdotes have been related by my Creole friends; but one of them, after having excited my warmest sympathy, made me laugh heartily in the midst of my tears. She told me that her husband was stabbed in her arms by a slave whom he had always treated as his brother; that she had seen her children killed, and her house burned, but had been herself preserved by a faithful slave, and conducted, after incredible sufferings, and through innumerable dangers to the Cape. The same slave, she added, and the idea seemed to console her for every other loss, saved all my madrass handkerchiefs.

The Creole ladies have an air of voluptuous languor which renders them extremely interesting. Their eyes, their teeth, and their hair are

---

[1] Tenderness.

remarkably beautiful, and they have acquired from the habit of commanding their slaves, an air of dignity which adds to their charms. Almost too indolent to pronounce their words they speak with a drawling accent that is very agreeable: but since they have been roused by the pressure of misfortune many of them have displayed talents and found resources in the energy of their own minds which it would have been supposed impossible for them to possess.

They have naturally a taste for music, dance with a lightness, a grace, an elegance peculiar to themselves, and those who, having been educated in France, unite the French vivacity to the Creole sweetness, are the most irresistible creatures that the imagination can conceive. In the ordinary intercourse of life they are delightful; but if I wanted a friend on any extraordinary occasion I would not venture to rely on their stability.

LETTER III. .

Cape Francois.

The so much desired general Rochambeau is at length here. His arrival was announced, not by the ringing of bells, for they have none, but by the firing of cannon. Every body, except myself went to see him land, and I was prevented, not by want of curiosity, but by indisposition. Nothing is heard of but the public joy. He is considered as the guardian, as the saviour of the people. Every proprietor feels himself already on his habitation and I have even heard some of them disputing about the quality of the coffee they expect soon to gather; perhaps these sanguine Creoles may find that they have reckoned without their host.

However, *en attendant,*[1] the General, who it seems bears pleasure as well as conquest in his train, gives a grand ball on Thursday next. We are invited, and we go.

Clara is delighted! for the first time since our arrival her eyes brightened at receiving the invitation, and the important subject of what colours are to be worn, what fashions adopted, is continually

---

[1]   Meanwhile.

discussed. Her husband, whose chief pleasure is to see her brilliant, indulges all the extravagance of her capricious taste. She sighs for conquest because she is a stranger to content, and will enter into every scheme of dissipation with eagerness to forget for a moment her internal wretchedness. She is unhappy, though surrounded by splendor, because from the constitution of her mind she cannot derive happiness from an object that does not interest her heart.

My letter shall not be closed till after the ball of which I suppose you will be glad to have a description.

But why do you not write to me?

I am ignorant of your pursuits and even of the place of your abode, and though convinced that you cannot forget me, I am afflicted if I do not receive assurances of your friendship by every vessel that arrives!

Clara has not written, for nothing has hitherto had power to rouse her from the lethargy into which she had sunk. Perhaps the scenes of gaiety in which she is now going to engage may dispel the gloom which threatened to destroy all the energy of her charming mind. Perhaps too these scenes may be more fatal to her peace than the gloom of which I complain, for in this miserable world we know not what to desire. The accomplishment of our wishes is often a real misfortune. We pass our lives in searching after happiness, and how many die without having found it!

In Continuation

Well my dear friend the ball is over—that ball of which I promised you a description. But who can describe the heat or suffocating sensations felt in a crowd?

The General has an agreeable face, a sweet mouth, and most enchanting smile; but

"Like the sun, he shone on all alike,"[1]

and paid no particular attention to any object. His uniform was *a la hussar*,[2] and very brilliant; he wore red boots:—but his person is bad.

---

[1] Adapted from Pope, *Rape of the Lock*, Canto 2, line 14.
[2] As a member of a light cavalry unit, elegantly uniformed in many European armies.

he is too short; a Bacchus-like figure,[1] which accords neither with my idea of a great General nor a great man.

But you know one of my faults is to create objects in my imagination on the model of my incomparable friend,[2] and then to dislike everything I meet because it falls short of my expectations.

I was disappointed at the ball, because I was confounded in the crowd, but my disappointment was trifling compared with that felt by Clara. Accustomed to admiration she expected to receive it on this occasion in no moderate portion, and to find herself undistinguished was not flattering. She did not dance, staid only an hour, and has declared against all balls in future. But there is one announced by the Admiral which may perhaps induce her to change her resolution.

Madame Le Clerc has sailed for France with the body of her husband, which was embalmed here.

The place is tranquil. The arrival of General Rochambeau seems to have spread terror among the negroes. I wish they were reduced to order that I might see the so much vaunted habitations where I should repose beneath the shade of orange groves; walk on carpets of rose leaves and frenchipone;[3] be fanned to sleep by silent slaves, or have my feet tickled into extacy by the soft hand of a female attendant.

Such were the pleasures of the Creole ladies whose time was divided between the bath, the table, the toilette and the lover.

What a delightful existence! thus to pass away life in the arms of voluptuous indolence; to wander over flowery fields of unfading verdure, or through forests of majestic palm-trees, sit by a fountain bursting from a savage rock frequented only by the cooing dove, and indulge in these enchanting solitudes all the reveries of an exalted imagination.

But the moment of enjoying these pleasures is, I fear, far distant. The negroes have felt during ten years the blessing of liberty, for a blessing it certainly is, however acquired, and they will not be easily deprived of it. They have fought and vanquished the French troops, and their strength has increased from a knowledge of the weakness of their opposers, and the climate itself combats for them. Inured to a savage life they lay in the woods without being injured by the sun, the dew

---

1 Roman god of wine and intoxication.
2 Aaron Burr.
3 Possibly frangipani, or plumeria, a fragrant ornamental shrub or tree native to the tropics. Its flowers are famously used in Hawaii to make leis.

or the rain. A negro eats a plantain, a sour orange, the herbs and roots of the field, and requires no cloathing, whilst this mode of living is fatal to the European soldiers. The sun and the dew are equally fatal to them, and they have perished in such numbers that, if reinforcements do not arrive, it will soon be impossible to defend the town.

The country is entirely in the hands of the negroes, and whilst their camp abounds in provisions, every thing in town is extremely scarce and enormously dear.

Every evening several old Creoles, who live near us, assemble at our house, and talk of their affairs. One of them, whose annual income before the revolution was fifty thousand dollars, which he always exceeded in his expenses, now lives in a miserable hut and prolongs with the greatest difficulty his wretched existence. Yet he still hopes for better days, in which hope they all join him. The distress they feel has not deprived them of their gaiety. They laugh, they sing, they join in the dance with the young girls of the neighbourhood, and seem to forget their cares in the prospect of having them speedily removed.

LETTER IV.

Cape Francois.

The ball announced by the admiral exceeded all expectations and we are still all extacy. Boats, covered with carpets, conveyed the company from the shore to the vessel, which was anchored about half a mile from the land, and on entering the ball room a fairy palace presented itself to the view. The decks were floored in; a roof of canvas was suspended over the whole length of the vessel, which reached the floor on each side, and formed a beautiful apartment. Innumerable lustres of chrystal and wreaths of natural flowers ornamented the ceiling; and rose and orange trees, in full blossom, ranged round the room, filled the air with fragrance. The seats were elevated, and separated from the part appropriated to dancing, by a light balustrade. A gallery for the musicians was placed round the main-mast, and the whole presented to the eye an elegant saloon, raised by magic in a wilderness of sweets. Clara and myself, accompanied by her husband and Major B——, were among the first who arrived. Never had I beheld her so interesting. A robe of white crape shewed to advantage the contours of her elegant person. Her arms and bosom were bare; her black hair, fastened on the top with a brilliant comb, was ornamented by a rose which seemed to have been thrown there by accident.

We were presented to the admiral, who appeared struck by the figure of Clara, and was saying some very flattering things, when a flourish of martial music announced the arrival of the General in chief. The admiral hastened to meet him, and they walked round the room together.

When the dances began the general leaned against the orchestra opposite Clara. Her eyes met his. She bent them to the ground, raised them timidly and found those of the general fixed on her: a glow of crimson suffused itself over her face and bosom. I observed her attentively and knew it was the flush of triumph! She declined dancing, but when the walses began she was led out. Those who have not seen Clara walse know not half her charms. There is a physiognomy in her form! every motion is full of soul. The gracefulness of her arms is unequalled, and she is lighter than gossamer.

The eyes of the general dwelt on her alone, and I heard him inquire of several who she was.

The walse finished, she walked round the room leaning on the arm of Major B——. The general followed, and meeting her husband, asked (pointing to Clara) if he knew the name of that lady. Madame St. Louis, was the reply. I thought she was an American said the general. So she is, replied St Louis, but her husband is a Frenchman. That's true, added the general, but they say he is a d——d jealous fool, is he here? He has the honour of answering you, said St Louis. The general was embarrassed for a moment, but recovering himself said, I am not surprised at your being jealous, for she is a charming creature. And he continued uttering so many flattering things that St. Louis was in the best humour imaginable. When Clara heard the story, she laughed, and, I saw, was delighted with a conquest she now considered assured.

When she sat down, Major B—— presented the General to her, and his pointed attention rendered her the object of universal admiration. He retired at midnight: the ball continued. An elegant collation was served up, and at sunrise we returned home!

The admiral is a very agreeable man, and I would prefer him, as a lover, to any of his officers, though he is sixty years old. His manners are affable and perfectly elegant; his figure graceful and dignified, and his conversation sprightly. He joined the dance at the request of a lady, with all the spirit of youth, and appeared to enjoy the pleasure which his charming fête diffused.

He told Clara that he would twine a wreath of myrtle to crown her, for she had vanquished the General. She replied, that she would mingle it with laurel, and lay it at his feet for having, by preserving the Cape, given her an opportunity of making the conquest.

Nothing is heard of but balls and parties. Monsieur D'Or gives a concert every Thursday; the General in chief every Sunday: so that from having had no amusement we are in danger of falling into the other extreme, and of being satiated with pleasure.

The Negroes remain pretty tranquil in this quarter; but at Port-au-Prince, and in its neighbourhood, they have been very troublesome.

Jeremie, Les Cayes, and all that part of the island which had been preserved, during the revolution, by the exertions of the inhabitants, have been lost since the appearance of the French troops!

The Creoles complain, and they have cause; for they find in the army sent to defend them, oppressors who appear to seek their destruction. Their houses and their negroes are put under requisition, and they are daily exposed to new vexations.

Some of the ancient inhabitants of the island, who had emigrated, begin to think that their hopes were too sanguine, and that they have returned too soon from the peaceful retreats they found on the continent.[1] They had supposed that the appearance of an army of thirty thousand men would have reduced the negroes to order; but these conquerors of Italy, unnerved by the climate, or from some other cause, lose all their energy, and fly before the undisciplined slaves.

Many of the Creoles, who had remained on the island during the reign of Toussaint, regret the change, and say that they were less vexed by the negroes than by those who have come to protect them.

And these negroes, notwithstanding the state of brutal subjection in which they were kept, have at length acquired a knowledge of

---

[1]   North America. Many French families fled to New Orleans, Virginia, New York, and Philadelphia during the early stages of the Haitian Revolution.

their own strength. More than five hundred thousand broke the yoke imposed on them by a few thousand men of a different colour, and claimed the rights of which they had been so cruelly deprived. Unfortunate were those who witnessed the horrible catastrophe which accompanied the first wild transports of freedom! Dearly have they paid for the luxurious ease in which they revelled at the expense of these oppressed creatures. Yet even among these slaves, self-emancipated, and rendered furious by a desire of vengeance, examples of fidelity and attachment to their masters have been found, which do honour to human nature. (2)

For my part, I am all anxiety to return to the continent. Accustomed from my earliest infancy to wander on the delightful banks of the Schuylkill, to meet the keen air on Kensington bridge, and to ramble over the fields which surround Philadelphia, I feel like a prisoner in this little place, built on a narrow strip of land between the sea and a mountain that rises perpendicularly behind the town. There is to be sure an opening on one side to the plain, but the negroes are there encamped; they keep the ground of which general Le Clerc suffered them to take possession, and threaten daily to attack the town!

There is no scarcity of beaux here, but the gallantry of the French officers is fatiguing from its sameness. They think their appearance alone sufficient to secure a conquest, and do not conceive it necessary to give their yielding mistresses a decent excuse by paying them a little attention. In three days a love-affair is begun and finished and forgotten; the first is for the declaration, the second is the day of triumph if it is deferred so long, and the third is for the adieu.

The Creoles do not relish the attacks made on their wives by the officers. The husband of Clara in particular is as jealous as a Turk, and has more than once shewn his displeasure at the pointed attentions of the General-in-chief to his wife, which she encourages, out of contradiction to her husband rather than from any pleasure they afford her. The boisterous gaiety and soldier-like manners of general Rochambeau, can have made no impression on a heart tender and delicate as is that of Clara. But there is a vein of coquetry in her composition which, if indulged, will eventually destroy her peace.

A tragical event happened lately at Port-au-Prince. At a public breakfast, given by the commandant, an officer just arrived from

France, addressing himself to a lady, called her *citoyenne*.[1]—The lady observed that she would never answer to that title. The stranger replied that she ought to be proud of being so called. On which her husband, interfering, said that his wife should never answer to any mode of address that she found displeasing. No more passed at that time, but before noon Monsieur C— received a challenge: the choice of weapons being left to him, he said that it was absolutely indifferent: the stranger insisted on fighting with a rifle; Monsieur C— replied that he should have no objection to fight with a cannon: it was however, finally settled, that the affair should be decided with pistols; and at sun-rise next morning they met: the officer fired without effect. Monsieur C—, with surer aim laid his antagonist lifeless on the ground.

On what trifles depends the destiny of man! but the Europeans are so insolent that a few such lessons are absolutely necessary to correct them.

Monsieur C— is a Creole, and belonged to the Staff of the general who commands at Port-au-Prince, from which he has been dismissed in consequence of this affair, which is another proof of the hatred the French officers bear the inhabitants of this country.

We have here a General of division, who is enriching himself by all possible means, and with such unblushing rapacity, that he is universally detested. He was a blacksmith before the revolution, and his present pursuits bear some affinity to his original employment, having taken possession of a plantation on which he makes charcoal, and which he sells to the amount of a hundred dollars a day. A carricature has appeared in which he is represented tying up sacks of coal. Madame A—, his mistress, standing near him, holds up his embroidered coat and says, "Don't soil yourself, General."

---

1   Citizen, a common title of greeting during the First French Republic (1792–1804). Many of the elite white planters, or *grand blancs*, opposed the Revolution in France and the fall of the French monarchy. To these royalists, used to the titles of rank and privilege, being called *citoyenne* was an insult.

LETTER V.

Three of your letters arriving at the same time, my dear friend, have made me blush for my impatience, and force me to acknowledge that I have wronged you. But your friendship is so necessary to my happiness that the idea of losing it is insupportable. You know what clouds of misfortune have obscured my life. An orphan without friends, without support, separated from my sister from my infancy, and, at an age when the heart is most alive to tenderness and affection, deprived by the unrelenting hand of death, of him who had taught me to feel all the transports of passion, and for whose loss I felt all its despair—Cast on the world without an asylum, without resource, I met you:—you raised me—soothed me—whispered peace to my lacerated breast! Ah! can I ever forget that delightful moment when your care saved me? It was so long since I had known sympathy or consolation that my astonished soul knew not how to receive the enchanting visitants; fleeting as fervent was my joy: but let me not repine! Your friendship has shed a ray of light on my solitary way, and though removed from the influence of your immediate presence, I exist only in the hope of seeing you again.

In restoring me to my sister, at the moment of her marriage, you procured for me a home not only respectable, but in which all the charms of fashionable elegance, all the attractions of pleasure are united. Unfortunately, Clara, amidst these intoxicating scenes of ever-varying amusement, and attended by crowds, who offer her the incense of adulation, is wretched, and I cannot be happy!

You know her early habits have been different from mine; affluence might have been thought necessary to her, yet the sensibility of her heart rejects the futile splendour that surrounds her, and the tears that often stain her brilliant robes, shew that they cover a bosom to which peace is a stranger!

The fortune of her husband was his only advantage. The friend who had been charged with Clara from her infancy had accustomed her to enjoy the sweets of opulence, and thought nothing more desirable than to place her in a situation where she could still command them. Alas her happiness has been the sacrifice of his mistaken, though well meant, intentions. St. Louis is too sensible of the real superiority of his wife not to set some value on that which he derives from his money, and tears of bitterest regret often fill her eyes when contemplating the splendor which has been so dearly purchased. Though to me he has been invariably kind yet my heart is torn with regret at the torments which his (irascible) temper inflict on his wife. They force her to seek relief in the paths of pleasure, whilst destined by nature to embellish the sphere of domestic felicity.

LETTER VI.

Cape Francois.

General Rochambeau has given Clara a proof of his attention to her wishes at once delicate and flattering. She dined with a large party at the Government house, where, as usual, he was entirely devoted to her. After dinner, he led her, followed by the company, to a saloon, that was fitting up for a dining-room. It was ornamented with military trophies, and on every panel was written the name of some distinguished chief.

On one Buonaparte, on another Frederic, on another Massena, &c.[1]

Clara said it was very pretty, but that Washington should also have found a place there!

A few days after, a grand ball was given, and, on entering the ballroom, we saw, on a pannel facing the door,

Washington, Liberty, and Independence!

This merited a smile, and the general received a most gracious one. It was new-year's eve. When the clock struck twelve, Clara, approaching the general, took a rose from her bosom, saying, let me be the first to wish you a happy new-year, and to offer you les entrennes.[2] Saucy He took the rose, passed it across his lips, and put it in his bosom.

---

[1] Napoleon Bonaparte (1769–1821); Frederick the Great (1712–86), King of Prussia; and André Masséna (1758–1817), an officer who rose to the rank of general during the French Revolution.

[2] Presents that are given on New Year's Day in France.

The next morning, an officer called on her, and presented her a pacquet in the name of the general in chief. On opening it she found a brilliant cross, with a superb chain, accompanied by an elegant billet, praying her acceptance of these trifles.

Take it back, she exclaimed, I gave the general a flower, and will accept nothing of greater value.—The officer refused, and, as the eyes of her husband expressed no disapprobation, she kept it.

We have since learned that it is customary to make at this season, magnificent presents, and this accounts for the passiveness of St. Louis on this occasion.

Shortly after, at a breakfast given by Madame A—, Clara appeared with her brilliant cross: the General was there.

When they sat down to table, he offered her an apple, which she declined accepting. Take it, said he, for on Mount Ida I would have given it to you, and in Eden I would have taken it from you.[1]

She replied laughing, no, no; since you attach so much value to your apple I certainly will not accept it, for I wish equally to avoid discord and temptation.

Her husband looked displeased, and withdrew as soon as possible.

On their return home, he told her that her flirting with the General, if carried much farther, would probably cost her too dear. She became serious, and I foresee the approaching destruction of all domestic tranquillity.

Clara, proud and high spirited, will submit to no control. If her husband reposed confidence in her she would not abuse it. But his soul cannot raise itself to a level with that of his wife, and he will strive in vain to reduce her to that of his own.

He has declared that she shall go to no more balls; and she has declared as peremptorily, that she will go where she pleases. So on the first public occasion there will be a contest for supremacy, which will decide forever the empire of the party that conquers.

---

[1]   Rochambeau refers to two stories with apples at their core: the Judgment of Paris, or The Apple of Discord, from Greek mythology and the Garden of Eden from the Judeo-Christian Bible. In the Greek myth, which takes place at the wedding of Peleus and Thetis on Mount Ida, Zeus orders Paris to judge who among the three most beautiful goddesses (Hera, Athena, and Aphrodite) is fairest; the winner is to receive a golden apple tossed in disgust at the wedding guests by Eris (goddess of discord), who was not invited to the ceremony. Paris chooses Aphrodite. In the Garden of Eden, Eve offers Adam a bite from an apple taken from the Tree of Knowledge, an act forbidden by God but too tempting to resist.

Their jarrings distress me beyond measure. I had hoped to find tranquillity with my sister, but alas! she is herself a stranger to it.

I have no pleasure but that which the recollection of your friendship affords, which will be dear to my heart whilst that heart is conscious of feeling or affection.

LETTER VII.

Cape Francois.

The brigands have at length made the attack they so long threatened, and we have been terribly alarmed.

On Thursday last, one party approached the fort before day break, whilst another, passing behind the barrier, which is at the entrance of the plain, unobserved by the guard, surprised fort Belleair, which stands on an elevation adjoining the town, and killed the officer and twelve soldiers. The wife of the officer, who commanded that post, had gone, the day before to stay with her husband. Herself and her child were pierced by the same bayonet. The body of the officer lay across the bed, as if he had died in the act of defending them.

The negroes were advancing silently into the town, when they were discovered by a centinel who gave the alarm.

The troops rushed to arms. The Brigands were repulsed: but those who had taken possession of fort Belleair made a vigorous resistance.

St. Louis, who commands a company in the guarde nationale,[1] was the first on the field. It was discovered that the negroes in the town intended to join those who attacked it from without and to kill the women and children, who were shut up in their houses, without any one to defend them; but the patroles of the guarde d'honneur[2] prevented, by their vigilance, the execution of this design.

At nine o'clock the general sent to tell Clara that the part of the town she lived in being very much exposed, she had better come to his house and he would send her on board the admiral's vessel.

---

[1] National guard, troops drawn from the inhabitants of the colony.
[2] Honor guard, generally composed of younger men from elite families, who bore the costs of outfitting them.

She replied that it was impossible for her to go, her husband having desired her on no account to leave the house; therefore she added, "Here I must stay if I am sure to perish."

The action continued at the barrier and advanced posts during the day. The negroes, depending on their numbers, seemed determined to decide at once the fate of the town, and we passed the day in a situation which I cannot describe.

In the evening the general sent an officer to tell Clara that he had some news from her husband which he could communicate to none but herself.

The first idea that presented itself was, that St. Louis had been killed. She seized my arm and without waiting to take even a veil hurried out of the house.

A gloomy silence reigned throughout the streets. She arrived breathless at the government house. The general met her in the hall, took her gravely by the hand and led her into a parlor.

What have you to tell me? she cried, where is St. Louis?

Calm your spirits said the general. Your agitation renders you unfit to hear any thing! But seeing that his hesitation encreased her distress, he said, laughing, your husband is well, has behaved gallantly, and seems invulnerable; for though numbers have been killed and wounded at his post, he has remained unhurt!

Then why, she asked, have you alarmed me so unnecessarily, and made me come here, when you knew he had desired me not to leave the house? He will never believe my motive for coming, and I shall be killed!

The general strove to soothe her, said that it would be highly improper to pass the night in her house, that several ladies had embarked, and that she must go on board, which she positively declined.

At that moment the officer who had accompanied us, entered, and presenting some papers to the general, they both went into another room.

Directly after the general called Clara. She went, and I followed her. He was alone, and looked as if he thought me an intruder, but I continued at her side.

The papers he held in his hand were dispatches from the camp. He told her that St. Louis would remain out all night, and again requested her to think of her own safety. But she would not listen to his proposal of sending her on board; and, attended by the officer who had accompanied us, we returned home.

Whilst the general was talking with Clara, I examined the apartment, which had been Madame Le Clerc's dressing-room.

The sofas and curtains were of blue sattin with silver fringe. A door, which stood open, led into the bedchamber. The canopy of the bed was in the form of a shell, from which little cupids descending held back with one hand, curtains of white sattin trimmed with gold, and pointed with the other to a large mirror which formed the tester.[1] On a table, in the form of an altar, which stood near the bed, was an alabaster figure representing silence, with a finger on its lips, and bearing in its hand a waxen taper.

The first thing we heard on our return was that a soldier, sent by St. Louis, had enquired for Clara, and not finding her, had returned immediately to the camp.

She was distressed beyond measure, and exclaimed, "I had better go forever, for St. Louis will kill me!"

I endeavoured to console her, though I felt that her apprehensions were not groundless. She passed the night in agony, and awaited the return of her husband in the most painful agitation.

At ten the next morning he arrived, having left his post without orders, and thus exposed himself to all the rigours of a court-martial.

He was trembling with rage, transported with fury, and had more the air of a demon than a man.

I know of your conduct madam, he cried, on entering, you left the house contrary to my desire; but I shall find means of punishing you, and of covering with shame the monster who has sought to destroy me!

He seized her by the arm, and dragging her into a little dressing-room at the end of the gallery, locked her in, and, taking the key in his pocket, went to the government house, and without waiting till the officers in the antichamber announced him, entered the room where the general was alone, reclining on a sofa, who arose, and approaching him familiarly said, "St. Louis, I am glad to see you, and was just thinking of you; but did not know that you had been relieved."

I have not been relieved, replied St. Louis, but have left a post where

---

[1] The vertical part at the head of the bed which ascends to and sometimes supports the canopy.

I was most unjustly placed and kept all night, to give you an opportunity of accomplishing your infernal designs. You expected, no doubt, that I would have shared the fate of my brave companions, which I have escaped, and am here to tell you what every body believes but which no body dares utter, that you are a villain!—I know to what I am exposed in consequence of leaving my post. You are my superior, it is true; but if you are not a coward you will wave all distinction, and give me the satisfaction due to a gentleman you have injured.

He then walked hastily away, before the general could recover from his surprise.

The officer, who had accompanied us the night before, followed and attempted to soothe him.

He said that he had been sent by the general to take Clara to his house because the part of the town in which she lived was absolutely unsafe, and that he had used a little stratagem to induce her to come, but that she had absolutely refused staying;—that Mademoiselle, (meaning my ladyship) had gone with her, and that he had not left her till he had conducted her home.

This a little softened the rage of St. Louis! He has a good opinion of this young man, who by the bye, is a charming creature. They entered the house together. I was alone, and joined my assurances to those of the officer, that we had not quitted Clara an instant.

He was now sorry for having treated her so harshly; but did not regret the scene that had passed at the general's.

At this moment a soldier entered, who told him that they had been relieved directly after he had left them, and that no notice had been taken of his departure.

I now learned that St. Louis, with sixty men, had been placed in the most advanced post, on the very summit of the mountain, where they were crowded together on the point of a rock. In this disadvantageous position, they had been attacked by the negroes; forty men were killed; and the troops of the line, who were a little lower down, had offered them no assistance. It being the first time that the guarde nationale had been placed before the troops of the line the common opinion is, that it was the general's intention to have St. Louis destroyed, as it was by his order that he was so stationed, and kept there all night, though the other posts had been relieved at midnight.

St. Louis forgot his rage and his sufferings in the assurance that

Clara had not been faithless. He went to the room in which he had confined her, threw himself at her feet, and burst into tears.

Clara, affected by his pain, or ashamed of having so tormented him,—or fatigued with their eternal broils, leaned over him, and mingled her tears with his.

When the violence of her emotion subsided, she entreated him to forgive the inconsiderateness of her conduct, and vowed that she would never again offend him.—But you have destroyed yourself, she continued, the general will never pardon you: let us leave this hated country, where tranquillity is unknown.

After much debate, it was agreed that he should send us to Philadelphia, and that he would follow himself as soon as he had arranged his affairs.

Clara keeps her room and sees nobody, her husband is in despair at parting with her, but proposes following her immediately.

We embark in ten days. What power shall I invoke to grant us favourable winds? Whose protection solicit to conduct me speedily to my native shores, and to the society of my friends?

LETTER VIII.

Cape Francois.

We are still here, my dear friend, and my disappointment and vexation have been so great, that ten days have passed since I have written a single line.

The general, thinking Clara was sent away against her will, and determined to thwart the intentions of her husband, laid an embargo on all the vessels in the port.

St. Louis raved, and swore she should not leave her room till he conducted her on board.

To prevent all intercourse from without, he keeps her locked up in a small room, adjoining her chamber.—Nobody, not even myself, can see her, except in his presence; and thus all confidence is at an end between them.

She weeps continually, and I am afraid the torments she suffers will destroy her health.

St. Louis is unworthy of her: he thinks it possible to force her to love him:—How much more would a generous confidence influence a heart like hers!

Many of his friends have represented to him the impropriety of his conduct. The challenge he gave general Rochambeau filled every body with terror, for it exposed him to certain death. To have left his post without orders was a crime equally serious; and, if the general has passed them both over in silence, it is supposed that his vengeance only slumbers for a time to be more sure in its effect.

He thinks Clara attached to the general. I know she is not! her vanity alone has been interested. To be admired was her aim, and she knew that, by attracting the notice of the general in chief, her end would be accomplished. She succeeded even beyond her wishes, but it has been a dangerous experiment; and will cost her, I fear, the small portion of domestic *peace* she enjoyed.—Domestic *felicity* she never knew! I am convinced that she has never been less happy than since her marriage!

Nothing can be more brutal than St. Louis in his rage! The day of his affair with the general, he threw her on the ground, and then dragged her by the hair:—I flew to her, but his aspect so terrified me that I was obliged to withdraw: and when his fits of tenderness return he is as bad in the other extreme. He kneels before her, entreats her pardon, and overwhelms her with caresses more painful to her than the most terrible effects of his ill-humour. And then his temper is so capricious that he cannot be counted upon a moment. I have seen him oblige her to stay at home and pass the evening alone with him after she had dressed for a ball.

This does not accord with the liberty French ladies are supposed to enjoy. But I believe Clara is not the first wife that has been locked up at St. Domingo, yet she excites little sympathy because she has not the good fortune to be one of the privileged.

In Continuation

Certain events, which shall be related, prevented me from finishing my letter. The same events have produced an entire change in our affairs, and we are now fixed at St. Domingo for some time.

The embargo is raised:—the general in chief is gone to Port-au-Prince; all the belles of the Cape have followed him. Clara is at liberty, and her husband content!

As soon as we had an opportunity of conversing together, Clara related to me occurrences which seem like scenes of romance, but I am convinced of their reality. Under the window of the little apartment in which she was confined, there is an old building standing in a court surrounded by high walls. The general informed himself of the position of Clara's chamber, and his intelligent valet, who makes love to one of her servants, found that it would not be difficult to give her a letter, which his dulcinea[1] refused charging herself with. He watched the moment of St. Louis's absence, entered the deserted court, mounted the tottering roof, and, calling Clara to the window, gave her the letter, glowing with the warmest professions of love, and suggesting several schemes for her escape, one of which was, that she should embark on board a vessel that he would indicate, and that he would agree with the captain to put into Port-au-Prince, whither he would speedily follow her.—Another was, to escape in the night by the same window, and go to his house, where he would receive and protect her. But the heart of Clara acknowledged not the empire of general Rochambeau, nor had she even the slightest intention of listening to him.

If her husband knew all this it would cure him, I suppose, of his passion for locking up. But, incapable of generosity himself, he cannot admire it in another, and would attribute her refusal of the general's offers to any motive but the real one.

How often has she assured me that she would prefer the most extreme poverty to her present existence, but to abandon her husband was not to be thought of. Yet to have abandoned him, and to have been presented as the declared mistress of General Rochambeau, would not have been thought a crime nor have excluded her from the best society!

Madame G——, who has nothing but her beauty to recommend her, (and no excess of that) lives with the admiral on board his vessel. She is visited by every body; and no party is thought fashionable if not

---

[1] In Miguel de Cervantes Saavedra's *Don Quixote* (1606), Dulcinea is the imaginary princess in whose name Don Quixote carries out his quests of knight-errantry.

graced by her presence, yet her manners are those of a poissarde[1] and she was very lately in the lowest and most degraded situation. But she gives splendid entertainments: and when good cheer and gaiety invite, nobody enquires too minutely by whom they are offered.

Clara laughs at the security St. Louis felt when he had her locked up. Yet in spite of bolts and bars love's messenger reached her. The general's letters were most impassioned, for, unaccustomed to find resistance, the difficulty his approach to Clara met added fuel to his flame.

You say, that in relating public affairs, or those of Clara, I forget my own, or conceal them under this appearance of neglect. My fate is so intimately connected with that of my sister, that every thing concerning her must interest you, from the influence it has on myself: and, in truth, I have no adventures. I described in a former letter, the gallantry of the French officers, but I have not repeated the compliments they sometimes make me, and which have been offered, perhaps, to every woman in town before they reach my ear. But a civil thing I heard yesterday, had so much of originality in it that it deserves to be remembered. I was copying a beautiful drawing of the graces,[2] when a Frenchman I detest, entered the room. Approaching the table he said, What mademoiselle do you paint? I did not know that you possessed that talent. Vexed at his intrusion, I asked if he knew I possessed any talents. Certainly, he replied, every body acknowledges that you possess that of pleasing. Then looking at the picture that lay before me, he continued: The modesty of the graces would prevent their attempting to draw you. Why? I asked. Because in painting you, they would be obliged to copy themselves.

With all this *bavardage*[3] receive my affectionate adieu!

---

[1] Plebian.

[2] The goddesses Aglaia (of beauty), Euphrosyne (of joy), and Thalia (of blooming), who together often accompanied Aphrodite.

[3] Chattering.

LETTER IX.

Cape Francois.

We have had some novelty here my dear friend, for general Closelle, who commands during the absence of the general in chief, has taken a new method to amuse the people, and courts popularity under the veil of religion. He gives no balls, no concerts; but he has had the church fitted up, and the fete dieu[1] has been celebrated with great order, magnificence and solemnity.

At break of day the fete was announced by the firing of cannon: at eight o'clock the procession left the church, and passed through the principal streets, which were strewn with roses; the fronts of the houses were decorated with green branches, formed into arches, intermingled with wreaths of flowers. The troops under arms were placed in double ranks on each side of the street. The procession was opened by a number of young boys dressed in white surplices,[2] singing a hymn in honour of the day. They were followed by young girls, crowned with myrtle, bearing in their hands baskets of flowers, which they strewed on the ground as they passed along. The band of music followed, and then the priests, bearing golden censors, in which were burning the most exquisite perfumes, preceded by four negroes, carrying on their shoulders a golden temple, ornamented with precious stones, and golden angels supporting a canopy of crimson velvet, beneath which the sacred host was exposed in a brilliant sagraria.[3] After them marched general Closelle, and all the officers of the civil and military departments. The procession was closed by a number of ladies, covered with white veils. As the temple passed along, the soldiers bent one knee to the ground; and when it returned to the church, high mass was sung, accompanied by military music.

Clara and myself, attended by her everlasting beau, major B—, went all over the town, and so fatigued our poor cavalier, that he actually fell down; but he is fifty years old, and at least five hundred

---

[1] The Feast of Corpus Christi, or the body of Christ, commemorates the sacrament of communion in the Roman Catholic Church. It was traditionally celebrated on Maundy Thursday, the Thursday after Trinity Sunday, with great pageantry.

[2] Loose-fitting, white ecclesiastical gowns with wide sleeves, worn over a cassock.

[3] Cathedral.

in constitution; he has been very handsome, has still the finest eyes in the world, is full of anecdote, and infinitely amusing.

General Closelle is very handsome, tall, and elegantly formed, but not at all gallant, consequently not a favourite with the ladies; and for the same reason, a great one with the gentlemen, particularly those who are married. Since the departure of the general in chief he has put every thing on a new footing: the fortifications are repairing, and block-houses are erecting all round the town.

A few days since the negroes attacked a block-house which was nearly finished. A detachment commanded by general Mayart, was instantly sent out to support the guard. As he passed under my window, I told him to hasten and gather fresh laurels. He replied, that at his return he would lay them at my feet; but, alas! he returned no more. The negroes were retreating when he arrived: a random shot struck him, and he fell dead from his horse. This young man came from France about a year ago, a simple lieutenant; he was very poor, but being powerfully protected, advanced rapidly in the army; and, what is infinitely surprising, thirty thousand dollars, and a great quantity of plate, were found in his house at his death.

Madame G——, a pretty little Parisian, who was his favourite, is inconsolable. She faints when any body enters the room, and repeats his name in gentle murmurs. In the evening she languishingly reposes on a sopha placed opposite the door, and seems to invite by the gracefulness of her attitudes, and the negligence of her dress, the whole world to console her.

The most distressing accounts arrive here daily from all parts of the island.

The general in chief is at Port-au-Prince, but he possesses no longer the confidence of the people. He is entirely governed by his officers, who are boys, and who think only of amusement. He gives splendid balls, and elegant parties; but he neglects the army, and oppresses the inhabitants.

A black chief and his wife were made prisoners last week, and sentenced to be shot. As they walked to the place of execution the chief seemed deeply impressed with the horror of his approaching fate: but his wife went cheerfully along, endeavoured to console him, and reproached his want of courage. When they arrived on the field, in which their grave was already dug, she refused to have her eyes bound; and turning to the soldiers who were to execute their sentence, said "Be expeditious, and don't make me linger." She received their fire without shrinking, and expired without uttering a groan. Since the commencement of the revolution she had been a very devil! Her husband commanded at St. Marks, and being very amorously inclined, every white lady who was unfortunate enough to attract his notice, received an order to meet him. If she refused, she was sure of being destroyed, and if she complied she was as sure of being killed by his wife's orders, which were indisputable. Jealous as a tygress, she watched all the actions of her husband; and never failed to punish the objects of his amorous approaches, often when they were entirely innocent.

How terrible was the situation of these unfortunate women, insulted by the brutal passion of a negro, and certain of perishing if they resisted or if they complied.

This same fury in female form killed with her own hand a white man who had been her husband's secretary. He offended her; she had him bound, and stabbed him with a penknife till he expired!

How often, my dear friend, do my sighs bear my wishes to your happy country; how ardently do I desire to revisit scenes hallowed by recollection, and rendered doubly dear by the peaceful security I there enjoyed, contrasted with the dangers to which we are here exposed. Yet the Creoles still hope; for

"Hope travels through, nor quits us when we die."[1]

They think it impossible that this island can ever be abandoned to the negroes. They build houses, rebuild those that were burned, and seem secure in their possession. The measures of general Closelle inspire them with confidence; and they think that if he was commander in chief, all would go well. But when general Rochambeau was second in command, he was a favorite with every body; and it is only since he has attained the summit of power that he has appeared regardless of public opinion! He is said to have the talents of a soldier, but not those of a general. Whatever may be the fate of this country, here I must wait with patience, of which mulish virtue I have no great share, till some change

---

[1]   Alexander Pope, *Essay on Man*, Epistle II (1732), line 274.

in its affairs restores me to my own. Yet when there, I can hope for nothing more than tranquillity. The romantic visions of happiness I once delighted to indulge in, are fading fast away before the exterminating touch of cold reality.—

The glowing hand of hope grows cold,
And fancy lives not to be old.[1]

But whilst your friendship is left me life will still have a charm.

LETTER X.

Cape Francois.

It is not often in the tranquillity of domestic life that the poet or the historian seek their subjects! Of this I am certain, that in the calm that now surrounds us it will be difficult for me to find one for my unpoetical pen.

Clara is dull, St. Louis contented, and I pass my time heavily, complaining of the fate which brought me here, and wishing to be away. We go sometimes to the concerts given by monsieur d'Or, where madame P——, a pretty little Parisian sings; and where madame A——, acccompanied by her daughter, presides with solemn dignity. This lady, who is at present a most rigid censor of female conduct, and not amiable either in person or manners, lived many years with monsieur A——, who raised her from the rank of his house-keeper, to that of his mistress. But he fell in love with another lady, whom he was going to marry. The deserted fair one threw herself in despair at the feet of Toussaint, with whom she had some influence, and so forcibly represented the injustice of the proceeding, that Toussaint ordered A—— to be confined, saying he should not be released till he consented to marry the lady he had so long lived with. A—— resisted some time, but at length yielded, and exchanged his prison for the softer one of her arms.

Before the revolution there was a convent at the Cape. The nuns in general were very rich, and devoted themselves chiefly to the

---

[1] Adapted from John Langhorne (1735–79), *The Fables of Flora* (1771), 26.

education of young ladies: some of their pupils, I have heard, would have done honour to a Parisian seminary.

When religion was abolished in France,[1] the rage for abolition, as well as that of revolutionizing reached this place, and the nuns were driven from the convent by Santhonax,[2] a name which will always fill every Frenchman's breast with horror: he caused the first destruction of the Cape. On the arrival of Galbo, who was sent to supercede him, he said, "if Galbo reigns here, he shall reign over ashes," and actually set fire to the town.[3] The convent was not then burned; but the society was dissolved, the habit of the order laid aside; and some of the nuns, profiting by the license of the times, married. One of these became the wife of a man who, during the reign of the negroes committed crimes of the deepest die. He has not yet received the punishment due to them; but he awaits in trembling the hour of retribution. I often see her. She has been very handsome, but her charms are now in the wane; she has a great deal of vivacity, and that fluency of expression in conversing on the topics of the day, which gives to a French woman the reputation of having *beacoup d'esprit*.

I know also the lady abbess, who is an excellent woman of most engaging manners. She lives in a miserable chamber, and supports herself by her industry. The greatest part of the community have perished; and general Le Clerc found it more convenient to have the convent fitted up for his own residence, than to restore it to its owners, the government house having been entirely destroyed.

There are also here two hospitals, neither of which have been injured, though the town has been twice burned. The *Hopitale de la Providence* is an asylum for the poor, the sick and the stranger; the building is decent: but the *Hopitale des Peres de la Charite* is superb,

---

[1] In 1793, Sans-culottes functionaries (representatives of the radical and working-class faction) designed a campaign to dechristianize France. The plan was scrapped with the fall of Robespierre in July 1794.

[2] Léger Félicité Sonthonax was the Republican commissioner of Saint Domingue from 1792–97. Sonthonax brought the most radical elements of the French Revolution to his administration of the colony, abolishing slavery in the Northern Province on 29 August 1793.

[3] In June 1793, the colonial governor, François-Thomas Galbaud du Fort, planned a violent campaign against Le Cap François to depose the radical commissioners, Poverel and Sonthonax, who were viewed as hostile to the interests of the white inhabitants. During the failed insurrection, parts of Le Cap were burned. Rumors circulated that Sonthonax deliberately sought to destroy the town rather than turn it over to the counterrevolutionary governor.

surrounded by gardens, ornamented with statues and fountains, and finished with all the magnificence which their vast revenues enabled its owners to command.

The streets of the town cross each other at right angles, like those of Philadelphia, and there are several public squares which add greatly to the beauty of the place. In the centre of each is a fountain, from which the water, clear as crystal, flows into marble basons. The houses are commodious, particularly those of two stories, which have all balconies; but the streets are narrow, and the heat would be intolerable if it was not for the relief afforded by bathing, which is here an universal custom, and for the sea-breezes which, rising every afternoon, waft on their wings delicious coolness.

The mulatto women are the hated but successful rivals of the Creole ladies. Many of them are extremely beautiful; and, being destined from their birth to a life of pleasure, they are taught to heighten the power of their charms by all the aids of art, and to express in every look and gesture all the refinements of voluptuousness. It may be said of them, that their very feet speak. In this country that unfortunate class of beings, so numerous in my own,—victims of seduction, devoted to public contempt and universal scorn, is unknown. Here a false step is rarely made by an unmarried lady, and a married lady, who does not make one, is as rare; yet of both there have been instances: but the *faux pas* of a married lady is so much a matter of course, that she who has only one lover, and retains him long in her chains, is considered as a model of constancy and discretion.

To the destiny of the women of colour no infamy is attached; they have inspired passions which have lasted through life, and are faithful to their lovers through every vicissitude of fortune and chance. But before the revolution their splendor, their elegance, their influence over the men, and the fortunes lavished on them by their infatuated lovers, so powerfully excited the jealousy of the white ladies, that they complained to the council of the ruin their extravagance occasioned to many families, and a decree was issued imposing restrictions on their dress. No woman of colour was to wear silk, which was then universally worn, nor to appear in public without a handkerchief on her head. They determined to oppose this tyranny, and took for that purpose a singular but effectual resolution. They shut themselves up in their houses, and appeared no more in public. The merchants soon felt the bad effects of this determination, and represented so forcibly the injury the decree did to commerce, that it was reversed, and the olive beauties triumphed.

But the rage of the white ladies still pursued them with redoubled fury, for what is so violent as female jealousy? The contest however was unequal, and the influence of their detested rivals could not be counteracted. Some of them were very rich. There is a friendliness and simplicity in their manners which is very interesting. They are the most caressing creatures in the world, and breathe nothing but affection and love. One of their most enviable privileges, and which they inherit from nature, is that their beauty is immortal—they never fade.

The French appear to understand less than any other people the delights arising from an union of hearts. They seek only the gratification of their sensual appetites. They gather the flowers, but taste not the fruits of love. They call women the "*beau sexe*," and know them only under the enchanting form of ministers of pleasure. They may appear thus to those who have only eyes; by those who have hearts they will always be considered as sacred objects of reverence and love. A man who thinks and feels views in woman the beneficent creature who nourished him with her milk, and watched over his helpless infancy; a consoling being who soothes his pains and softens his sorrows by her tenderness and even by her levity and her sports. But here female virtue is blasted in the bud by the contagious influence of example. Every girl sighs to be married to escape from the restraint in which she is held whilst single, and to enjoy the unbounded liberty she so often sees abused by her mother. A husband is necessary to give her a place in society; but is considered of so little importance to her happiness, that in the choice of one her inclination is very seldom consulted. And when her heart, in spite of custom, feels the pain of being alone, and seeks an asylum in the bosom of her husband, she too often finds it shut against her; she is assailed by those whose only desire is to add another trophy to their conquests, and is borne away by the torrent of fashion and dissipation till all traces of her native simplicity are destroyed. She joins with unblushing front, the crowd who talk of sentiments they never feel, and who indulge in the most licentious excesses without having the glow of passion to gild their errors. These reflections were suggested by a most preposterous marriage, at which I was present. A girl of fifteen was sacrificed by her grandmother to a man of sixty, of the most disagreeable appearance and forbidding manners. The soul of this unfortunate victim is all melting softness; she is of the most extraordinary beauty; she is now given to the world, and in those who surround her she will find the destroyers of her delicacy, her simplicity, and her peace.

LETTER XI.

Cape Francois.

To give you some idea of the despotism that reigns in this country, I must relate an event which, though it originated with Clara, was certainly carried farther than she either expected or desired.

On our arrival here she engaged a young Frenchman to give her lessons in his language, which she spoke tolerably before, but in which she wished to acquire perfection. After he had attended her some time she perceived that his lessons were considerably lengthened and that he chose for his themes the most amorous and affectionate pieces. Some observations made on the subject, drew from him a confession of the extraordinary passion she had inspired. After laughing at his folly, she dismissed him, and thought of him no more; but shortly after was informed that he had circulated reports highly injurious to her. General Rochambeau, whose ears they had reached, asked her from whence they arose? and she related to him with great simplicity the whole affair. The general said he should be embarked, and the next morning he was actually sent on board an armed vessel which was to sail in a few days. Whilst there he wrote a pathetic and elegant little poem in which he represented himself as the victim of the general's jealousy, who thus sought to destroy him for having interfered, and not unsuccessfully, with his pursuits. This paper was sent to the man with whom he had lived, and who handed it to every body. Clara was in despair. She informed the general in chief that he had rendered the affair, which was at first only ridiculous, seriously provoking: in consequence of which the house of this man was surrounded by guards, who, without giving him time to take even a change of clothes, conducted him on board the vessel where his friend was confined; it sailed immediately for France, and his house and store, which were worth at least thirty thousand dollars became the prey of the officers of the administration: but the poem was heard of no more.

LETTER XII.

Cape Francois.

The general in chief has returned from Port-au-Prince. Three days after his arrival the Cape was blockaded by five British ships, and news was received of war having been declared between England and France.[1]

Every body is in the greatest consternation, for inevitable ruin threatens the place. The English will no doubt prevent all vessels from entering the port, and take all that go out; at the same time the negroes are said to be preparing another attack.

The general brought in his train all the belles of Port-au-Prince, and has given a ball, at which, incredible as it may appear to you, Clara and myself appeared. When the cards of invitation were brought, St. Louis declared that they should not be left; but major B—, who was present, represented so forcibly the danger of irritating the general, who has shewn some symptoms of a disposition to tyrannize, since his return which were never remarked in him before, that he consented to our going. When we entered the room attended by B, every eye was fixed on Clara, who never was so lovely. Dressed in a robe ornamented with wreaths of flowers, she joined the sweetness of Flora[2] to the lightness of the youngest of the graces, and the recollection of certain late events gave an air of timidity to her looks which rendered her enchanting. General Rochambeau, by the warmth of his manner increased her confusion, and fixed on her more pointedly the attention of every beholder. He was surprized at seeing her without her husband, and enquired what had

---

[1] Britain declared war against France on 18 May 1803.
[2] Roman goddess of flowers.

wrought so wonderful a change? She replied that he had found a very good representative in major B—, and that he had acquired a little confidence in herself. She waltzed with more than her usual grace, and the general seemed flattered by the notice she attracted. Most of the ladies from Port-au-Prince are widows

"Who bear about the mockery of woe
To midnight dances and the public shew."[1]

None of them are remarkable for their beauty or elegance. The only new face worth looking at was a madame V—, lately arrived from France; her hair was dressed *a la Ninon de l'Enclos*,[2] part of it fastened on the top of the head, the rest hanging about her neck in loose curls. The ball room had been newly furnished with regal splendor; all the chairs were removed, and long sophas with large cushions offered delightful seats. A recess at one end of the room had been fitted up *a la Turc*;[3] the walls were entirely concealed with large looking glasses, which reached the ceiling; the floor was covered with carpets and the only seats were piles of crimson sattin cushions thrown on the ground. The lustres, veiled with green silk, gave a soft light, imitating that of *Colors* the moon, and the *ensemble* breathed an air of tranquillity that invited to repose after the fatigue of dancing, and offered a retreat from the heat which it was almost impossible to resist. To this retreat general Rochambeau led Clara. A lady was lolling in one corner, and I entered at the same moment. He looked as if he wished us both away, but I never attend to looks that I am resolved not to understand.

lots of cultural references

---

[1] Alexander Pope, "Elegy To the Memory of an Unfortunate Lady" (1717) line 57.
[2] Like Germaine de Staël (1766–1817), Anne "Ninon" de L'Enclos (1616?–1705) may have been a model for Sansay's self-fashioning. Reputedly the most beautiful woman of the seventeenth century, fiercely independent, and intellectually vibrant, L'Enclos was an influential figure of the French salon, a patron of the arts, and a wit. She befriended and encouraged the young Molière (1622–73) and Jean-Baptiste Racine (1639–99), two of the most important playwrights of seventeenth-century France, and late in life counseled Voltaire (1694–1778). A devotee of Epicureanism, the uncompromising pursuit of physical and mental pleasure, she was renowned for espousing the equality of the sexes and for discounting the necessity of religion.
[3] In the Turkish style.

Cape Francois.

A few days after the ball mentioned in my last, St. Louis determined to send Clara and myself to St. Jago de Cuba, and to follow us as soon as possible. This measure was opposed by major B——; but Clara insisted, and the day of our departure was fixed. The next day B—— breakfasted with us; and as soon as we were alone, told Clara that she was wrong in being so entirely governed by her husband. She replied that she had suffered much in consequence of coquetting with general Rochambeau, in which her only intention had been to find amusement; but she was now convinced of its being highly dangerous and improper; and that it had been productive of much ill. She added, that she lived in continual inquietude, and that nothing would induce her to stay in the Cape if she could get away.

B—— spoke of the passion of the general,—said he had seen him that morning, and as a proof of her having been the subject of their conversation, gave her a letter from him. Is it possible, (she exclaimed) you in whom my husband has so much confidence? You are a fool, replied B——, and your husband is not better: and if his insolence to the general has not been punished it is owing to my interference.

Clara read the letter. It was filled with professions of admiration and unalterable love. He begged her not to think of leaving the Cape, which was in no danger; and further said he had taken measures to prevent her being sent away. He requested her to write to him, but this she positively refused.

Towards noon a proclamation was issued ordering all the passports which had been granted during the last three months to be returned. St. Louis was in despair: he had intended sending Clara off without eclat, having procured passports before, but B—— betrayed him. Yet in B—— he has the most unbounded confidence; and suffers Clara to receive nobody else. She walks with him when she pleases, and he never fails on such occasions to give the general an opportunity of speaking to her.

A few days ago we went to Picolet, to see the fort. The road to it winds along the seashore at the foot of the mountain. The rocks are covered with the Arabian jessamin,[1] which grows here in the greatest profusion. Its flexible branches form among the cliffs moving festoons and fantastic ornaments, and its flowers whiter than snow, fill the air with intoxicating fragrance. After having visited the fort we were preparing to return, when we saw a troop of horsemen descending the mountain. They came full speed. We soon discovered they were the general and his suite; and as they followed the windings of the road, with their uniform *a la mameluc*,[2] and their long sabres, they appeared like a horde of Arabs.

The general arrived first, and jumping from his horse, told Clara that he had left the table an hour sooner than usual to have the pleasure of seeing her. Then, said she, looking reproachfully at B—, you have a familiar spirit who informs you of my movements! Why not, he replied, are you not an enchantress, and have you not employed all the powers of magic to enslave me? You are in an error said Clara; I was flattered by your admiration, and gratified by the attentions with which you honoured me; but I used no art to attract the one, and am too sensible of my own defects not to feel that I am indebted for the other entirely to your goodness. That is too modest to be natural, cried the general. Nobody who possesses your charms can be ignorant of their power; nor could any one mistake the passion I have evinced for you, for the common attention every lady receives as her due. Then you do not believe a woman can be modest? asked Clara. Modest if you please, but not insensible, he replied. And suffer me to observe,—Oh no observations, I entreat, interrupted Clara; for this interview will, I fear, occasion too many.—But tell me, how did you learn I was to be here; and why have you left the table where you so often sacrifice till a late hour to the rosy god, to wander among these rugged rocks where despairing lovers alone would seek a retreat? And are you of that number? he enquired. No, she replied: but I have not your motives for staying at home: I was led here by curiosity; It is my first visit to this spot. Then believe, said the general, that I came here to offer at your feet that homage which envious fate has hitherto deprived me of an opportunity of paying. During this conversation, he had drawn her to a point of the rock; and the officers of his suite,

---

[1] Jasmine, a flowering shrub.
[2] Turbans became popular accoutrements of fashion for both military officers and for women after Napoleon's campaign in Egypt (1798).

surrounding me, sought to divert my attention by all the common place compliments of which they are so profuse. I had forgotten Clara for a moment, when, turning, I beheld the general, who bending one knee to the ground, seized her hand passionately, and at the same time I saw St. Louis ascending the mountain.

Pressing through the crowd I flew to her, saying, are you mad? Rise general, for heaven's sake! her husband approaches! what means this exhibition of folly? Yes I am mad, he replied, I adore your sister, and she refuses to listen to me. My sister is married, I answered. But, said he, she loves not her husband. At least I love no one more than him, said Clara, trembling at the idea of having been seen by St. Louis. Fortunately I had discovered him at the foot of the mountain, and the road winds round its base with so many turnings that it is of considerable length and before he arrived she was tolerably composed.

You have deceived me, said the general. I never listened to you, she replied. But you have read my letters.—I could not avoid receiving, but I never answered them. Still, he observed, interrupting her, I will hope; for your eyes cannot utter falsehood, and from them I have received encouragement.

At that instant St. Louis arrived; he appeared astonished at seeing Clara so surrounded, and advancing involuntarily, as if to defend her, took her arm.

The general, with his usual levity, told St. Louis, that he came in time to prevent him from running away with his wife. Then twining round her arm a wreath of jessamin he had taken from my hand, said, with such fetters only you should be bound! Does she find those that bind her too heavy? asked her husband. No, replied the general, she seems content. Then casting a look of disappointment at Clara, he mounted his horse and rode off.

Major B— engaged St. Louis in a conversation on the situation of the colony, which made him forget the dangerous one in which he had found his wife.

Clara, leaning on my arm, seemed oppressed by a variety of sensations, among which indignation predominated. The security and presumption of the general shocked her, and the recollection of having, at least negatively encouraged him, gave an additional pang to her heart. We returned slowly home. Our meeting with general Rochambeau was thought accidental by St. Louis, and was taken no notice of.

LETTER XIV.

Cape Francois.

Ah, my dear friend, where shall I find expressions to convey to you an idea of the horror that fills my soul; how describe scenes at which I tremble even now with terror?

Three negroes were caught setting fire to a plantation near the town. They were sentenced to be burnt alive; and the sentence was actually executed. When they were tied to the stake and the fire kindled, one of them, I understand, held his head over the smoke and was suffocated immediately. The second made horrible contortions, and howled dreadfully. The third, looking at him contemptuously said, Peace! do you not know how to die? and preserved an unalterable firmness till the devouring flames consumed him. This cruel act has been blamed by every body, as giving a bad example to the negroes, who will not fail to retaliate on the first prisoners they take. But it has been succeeded by a deed which has absolutely chilled the hearts of the people. Every one trembles for his own safety, and silent horror reigns throughout the place.

A young Creole, who united to the greatest elegance of person the most polished manners and the most undaunted courage, had incurred, I know not how, the displeasure of general Rochambeau, and had received a hint of approaching danger, but neither knew what he had to fear, nor how to avoid it, when he received an order to pay into the treasury, before three o'clock, twenty thousand dollars on pain of death. This was at ten in the morning. He thought at first it was a jest; but when assured that the order was serious, said he would rather die than submit to such injustice, and was conducted by a guard to prison. Some of his friends went to the government-house to intercede for him. Nobody was admitted. His brother exerted himself to raise the sum required; but though their house has a great deal of property, and government is indebted to them more than a hundred thousand dollars, it was difficult, from the scarcity of cash, to raise so large a sum in so short a time, and nobody thought there was any danger to be apprehended. At half after two o'clock he was taken to the fosset,[1]

---

[1] La Fossette: an area on the outskirts of Cap Français where the cemetery was located.

where his grave was already dug. The captain of the guard sent to know if there was no reprieve: and was told that there was none. He sent again, the same answer was returned, with an order to perform his duty, or his life would be the forfeit of his disobedience. He was a Creole, the friend, the companion of the unfortunate Feydon. Ah! how could he submit to be the vile instrument of tyranny? How could he sacrifice his friend? Why did he not resign his commission on the spot, and abide by the consequence? Approaching Feydon, he offered to bind his eyes; but he refused, saying, No, let me witness your horrors to the last moment. He was placed on the brink of his grave. They fired: he fell! but from the bottom of his grave cried, I am not dead—finish me! My heart bleeds: I knew him; and while I live, the impression this dreadful event has made on me will never be effaced. At the moment he was killed his brother, having collected the required sum, carried it to the general, who took the money, and sent the young man, who was frantic when he heard of his brother's fate, to prison. It is said a reprieve had been granted, but had been suppressed by Nero the commandant de la place, who is as cruel, and as much detested as was the tyrant whose name he bears.[1]

A few days after, nine of the principal merchants were selected. One hundred thousand dollars was the sum demanded from them; and they were imprisoned till it should be found. It was then the virtuous Leaumont approached, fearless of consequences, the retreat of the tyrant, and obliged him to listen to the voice of truth. He represented the impossibility of finding the sum demanded from these unfortunate men, and entreated to have a tax laid on every individual of the place in proportion to his property, which, after much debate was consented to. The money was soon furnished, and the prisoners released.

Since the death of Feydon the general appears no more in public. A settled gloom pervades the place, and every one trembles lest he should be the next victim of a monster from whose power there is no retreat. St. Louis, above all, is in the greatest danger, for he has the reputation of being rich, and, having excited the aversion of general

---

[1]   Nero Claudius Caesar Drusus (37–68 AD) was a scandal-ridden and tyrannical Roman Emperor. He was rumored to have been personally responsible for the Great Fire of Rome in 64. An infamous and widely-circulated account depicts Nero blithely playing his lyre as Rome burned.

Rochambeau, it is not probable that he will escape without some proof of his animosity.

Clara is in the greatest dejection. She repents bitterly the levity of her conduct, and is torn with anxiety for the fate of her husband. She loves him not, it is true, but would be in despair if through her fault the least evil befel him, and feels for the first time the danger of awakening the passions of those who are capable of sacrificing all considerations to gratify their wishes or revenge their disappointment. She requested the general to give her a passport for St. Jago de Cuba. He replied that he could only grant them to the old and ugly, and she, not being of this description, he was obliged to refuse her; however, after much solicitation, she obtained one for herself for me and her servants, and we shall sail in a few days. All the women are suffered to depart, but no man can procure a passport. Some it is true, find means of escape in disguise, and they are fortunate, for it is much feared that those who remain will be sacrificed. Every vessel that sails from hence is seized and plundered by the English; but, as we are Americans, perhaps we may pass.

Our intention is to stay at St. Jago till St. Louis joins us. God knows whether we shall ever see him again. With what joy I shall leave this land of oppression! how much that joy would be increased if I was going to the continent; but in all places, and in all countries I shall be affectionately yours.

LETTER XV.

Barracoa.[1]

You will no doubt be surprised at receiving a letter from hence, but here we are my dear friend, deprived of every thing we possessed, in a strange country, of whose language we are ignorant, and where, even with money, it would be impossible to procure what we have been accustomed to consider as the necessaries of life. Yet here we have found an asylum, and met with sympathy; not that of words, but active

---

[1] The oldest Spanish settlement on Cuba (1512), Baracoa is located near Cuba's easternmost point.

and effectual sympathy, from strangers, which, perhaps, we should have sought in vain in our own country, and among our own people.

We embarked at the Cape, Clara, myself and six servants, in a small schooner, which was full of women, and bound to St. Jago. As soon as we were out of the harbour a boat from a British frigate boarded us, condemned the vessel as French property, and, without further ceremony, sent the passengers on board another vessel which was lying near us, and was going to Barracoa, where we arrived in three days, after having suffered much from want of provisions and water. Every thing belonging to us had been left in the schooner the English made a prize of. St. Louis, having forseen the probability of this event, had made Clara conceal fifty doubloons in her corset.

On our arrival at Barracoa, a Frenchman we had known at the Cape came on board. He conducted us ashore, and procured us a room in a miserable hut, where we passed the night on a board laid on the ground, it being impossible to procure a mattrass. The next morning the first consideration was clothes. There was not a pair of shoes to be found in the place, nor any thing which we would have thought of employing for our use if we had not been obliged by the pressure of necessity. Clara had given a corner of our hut to a lady who, with two children, was without a shilling.

While we were at breakfast, which we made of chocolate, served in little calabashes, lent us by the people of the house, a priest of most benign aspect entered, and addressing Clara in French, which he speaks fluently, told her that having heard of our arrival and misfortunes, he had come to offer his services, and enquired how we had passed the night? Clara shewed him the boards on which we had slept. He rose instantly, and calling the mistress of the house, spoke to her angrily. I afterwards learned that he reproached her for not having informed him of our distress as soon as we arrived. He took his leave and returned in half an hour with three or four negroes who brought mattrasses, and baskets filled with fowls, and every kind of fruit the island produces. Then, telling Clara that his sister would call on her in the evening, and begging her to consider him as her servant, and every thing he possessed at her disposal, he went away. In the afternoon he returned with his sister. She is a widow. Her manners are interesting, but she speaks no language except her own, of which not one of us understood a word.

Father Philip sent for the only shopkeeper in the place, who furnished us with black silk for dresses, and some miserable linen. By the next day we were decently equipped. We were then presented to the governor, whose wife is divinely beautiful. Nothing can equal the lustre of her eyes, or surpass the fascinating power of her graceful and enchanting manners. The changes of her charming countenance express every emotion of her soul, and she seems not to require the aid of words to be understood. She conceived at once a fervent friendship for Clara, and having learned our misfortunes from father Philip, insisted on our living in her house whilst we remained at Barracoa. This point was disputed by Donna Angelica, who said she had provided a chamber for us in her own. But madame la Governadora was not to be thwarted; she seized Clara by the arm, and drawing her playfully into another room, insisted on dressing her *a la Espagnole*,[1] which is nothing more than a cambric *chemise*, cut very low in the bosom, an under petticoat of linen, made very stiff with starch, and a muslin one over it, both very short. To this is added, when they go out, a large black silk veil, which covers the head and falls below the waist. By this dress the beauty of the bosom, which is so carefully preserved by the French is lost.

Clara looked very well in this costume, but felt uncomfortable. As Donna Jacinta would not hear of our leaving her we consented to stay; and a chamber was prepared for us. In the evening we walked through the town, and were surprised to see such extreme want in this abode of hospitality. The houses are built of twigs, interwoven like basket work, and slightly thatched with the leaves of the palm tree, with no other floor than the earth. The inhabitants sit on the ground, and eat altogether out of the pot in which their food is prepared. Their bed is formed of a dried hide, and they have no clothes but what they wear, nor ever think of procuring any till these are in rags.

There are only three decent houses in the place, which belong to the governor, to father Philip, and his sister; yet these good people are happy, for they are contented. Their poverty is not rendered hideous by the contrast of insolent pride or unfeeling luxury. They dose away their lives in a peaceful obscurity, which if I do not envy, I cannot despise. There are many French families here from St. Domingo; some

---

[1]   In the Spanish style.

almost without resource; and this place offers none for talents of any kind. It is not uncommon to hear the sound of a harp or piano from beneath a straw built shed, or to be arrested by a celestial voice issuing from a hut which would be supposed uninhabitable.

Clara studies with so much application the Spanish language that she can already hold with tolerable ease a conversation, especially with seignora Jacinta, whose eyes are so eloquent that it would be impossible not to understand her. She is a native of the Havanna, was married very young, and her husband having been appointed governor of Barracoa, was obliged to leave the gaiety and splendour of her native place for this deserted spot, where fashion, taste or elegance had never been known. It has been a little enlivened since the misfortunes of the French have forced them to seek in it a retreat.

Jacinta has too much sensibility not to regret the change of situation; but she never repines, and seeks to diffuse around her the cheerfulness by which she is animated. From early prejudice she loves not the French character. Fortunately Clara is an American; and the influence of her enchanting qualities on the heart of her fair friend is strengthened by the charm of novelty.

We are waiting for a vessel to carry us to St. Jago, and its arrival, I assure you will fill us with regret.

LETTER XVI.

St. Jago de Cuba.[1]

We have left Barracoa, the good Father Philip, his generous sister, and the beautiful Jacinta. Removed from them for ever, the recollection of their goodness will accompany me through life, and a sigh for the peaceful solitude of their retreat will often heave my breast amid the mingled scenes of pleasure and vexation in which I shall be again engaged. Fortunate people! who, instead of rambling about the world, end their lives beneath the roofs where they first drew breath. Fortunate in knowing nothing beyond their horizon; for

---

[1] Santiago de Cuba is located on the south-eastern side of the island. Many refugees from the Haitian Revolution settled there.

whom even the next town is a strange country, and who find happiness in contributing to that of those who surround them! The wife of the governor could not separate herself from us. Taking from her neck a rosary of pearls, she put it round that of Clara, pressed her in her arms, wept on her bosom, and said she never passed a moment so painful. She is young, her soul is all tenderness and ardour, and Clara has filled her breast with feelings to which till now she has been a stranger. Her husband is a good man, but without energy or vivacity, the direct reverse of his charming wife. She can never have awakened an attachment more lively than the calmest friendship. She has no children, nor any being around her, whose soul is in unison with her own. With what devotion she would love! but if a stranger to the exquisite pleasures of that sentiment she is also ignorant of its pains! may no destructive passion ever trouble her repose.

She walked with us to the shore and waited on the beach till we embarked. She shrieked with agony when she clasped Clara for the last time to her breast, and leaning against a tree, gave unrestrained course to her tears.

The good father Philip accompanied us to the vessel, and staid till the moment of our departure. He had previously sent aboard every thing that he thought would be agreeable to us during the voyage. His friendly soul poured itself forth in wishes for our happiness. May all the blessings of heaven be showered on his head!

It is Clara's fate to inspire great passions. Nobody loves her moderately. As soon as she is known she seizes on the soul, and centres every desire in that of pleasing her. The friendship she felt for Jacinta, and the impression father Philip's goodness made on her, rendered her insensible to all around her.

The vessel was full of passengers, most of them ladies, who were astonished at beholding such grief. One of them, a native of Jeremie, was the first who attracted the attention of Clara. This lady, who is very handsome, and very young, has three children of the greatest beauty, for whom she has the most impassioned fondness, and seems to view in them her own protracted existence. She has all the bloom of youth, and when surrounded by her children, no picture of Venus with the loves and graces was ever half so interesting. She is going to join her husband at St. Jago, who I hear, is a great libertine, and not sensible of her worth. An air of sadness dwells on her lovely countenance, occasioned, no doubt, by his neglect and the pain of finding a rival in every woman he meets.

There is also on board a beautiful widow whose husband was killed by the negroes, and who, without fortune or protection, is going to seek at St. Jago a subsistence, by employing her talents. There is something inconceivably interesting in these ladies. Young, beautiful, and destitute of all resource, supporting with cheerfulness their wayward fortune.

But the most captivating trait in their character is their fondness for their children! The Creole ladies, marrying very young, appear more like the sisters than the mothers of their daughters. Unfortunately they grow up too soon, and not unfrequently become the rivals of their mothers.

We are still on board, at the entrance of the harbour of St. Jago, which is guarded by a fort, the most picturesque object I ever saw. It is built on a rock that hangs over the sea, and the palm trees which wave their lofty heads over its ramparts, add to its beauty.

We are obliged to wait here till to-morrow; for this day being the festival of a saint, all the offices are shut. No business is transacted, and no vessel can approach the town without permission.

This delay is painful; I am on the wing to leave the vessel, though it is only four days since we left Barracoa.—I wish to know whether we shall meet as much hospitality here as in that solitary place. Yet why should I expect it? Hearts like those of father Philip and the lovely Jacinta do not abound.—How many are there who, never having witnessed such goodness, doubt its existence?

We have letters to several families here, from the governor of Barracoa and father Philip, and St. Louis has friends who have been long established at this place. Therefore, on arriving, we shall feel at home; perhaps too, we may find letters from the Cape;—God grant they may contain satisfactory intelligence.

LETTER XVII.

St. Jago de Cuba.

A month has passed, since our arrival in this place, in such a round of visits and such a variety of amusements, that I am afraid, my dear friend, you will think I have forgotten you. We were received by the gentleman, to whom Clara was directed, with the most cordial friendship. He is an ancient Chevalier de St. Louis,[1] and retains, with much of the formality of the court of France, at which he was raised, all its elegance and urbanity; and having lived a number of years in this island, he is loved and respected by all its inhabitants.

The letters which father Philip and the governor of Barracoa gave us to their friends, have procured us great attention.

The people here are much the same as at Barracoa; perhaps they are a little more civilized. There is some wealth, with much poverty. The women have made great progress towards improvement since such numbers of French have arrived from St. Domingo.—They are at least a century before the men in refinement, but women are every where more susceptible of polish than the lords of creation. Those of this town are not generally remarkable for their beauty. There are some, however, who would be admired even in Philadelphia, particularly the wife of the governor; but they are all remarkable for the smallness of their feet, and they dress their hair with a degree of taste in which they could not be excelled by the ladies of Paris.

We arrived in the season of gaiety, and have been at several balls; but their balls please me not!—Every body in the room dances a minuet,[2] which you may suppose is tedious enough; then follow the country dances, which resemble the English, except that they are more complicated and more fatiguing.

There are in this town eleven churches, all of them splendid, and the number of priests is incredible! Many of them may be ranked among the most worthless members of the community. It is not at all uncommon to see them drunk in the street, or to hear of their

---

[1] Knight of the military order.
[2] Stately dance for two in triple time. Fashionable throughout Europe during the eighteenth century, it became increasingly complex and stylized.

having committed the most shocking excesses. Some, however, are excellent men, who do honour to their order and to human nature. But the thickest veil of superstition covers the land, and it is rendered more impervious by the clouds of ignorance in which the people are enveloped!

Clara, who speaks the language with the facility of a native, asked some of her Spanish friends for books, but there was not one to be found in the place. She complained some days ago of a head-ache, and a Spanish lady gave her a ribbon, which had been bound round the head of an image of the Virgin, telling her it was a sovereign remedy for all pains of the head.

The bishop is a very young man and very handsome. We see him often at church, where we go, attracted by the music. But one abominable custom observed there, destroys our pleasure. The women kneel on carpets, spread on the ground, and when they are fatigued, cross their legs, and sit Turkish fashion; whilst the men loll at their ease on sofas. From whence this subversion of the general order? Why are the women placed in the churches at the feet of their slaves?

The lower classes of the people are the greatest thieves in the world, and they steal with so much dexterity, that it is quite a science. The windows are not glazed, but secured by wooden bars, placed very close together. The Spaniards introduce between these bars long poles, which have at one end a hook of iron, and thus steal every thing in the room, even the sheets off the beds. The friars excel in this practice, and conceal their booty in their large sleeves!

In the best houses and most wealthy families there is a contrast of splendour and poverty which is shocking. Their beds and furniture are covered with a profusion of gilding and clumsy ornaments, while the slaves, who serve in the family, and even those who are about the persons of the ladies, are in rags and filthy to the most disgusting degree!

How different were the customs of St. Domingo! The slaves, who served in the houses, were dressed with the most scrupulous neatness, and nothing ever met the eye that could occasion an unpleasant idea.

The Spanish women are sprightly, and devoted to intrigue. Their assignations are usually made at church. The processions at night, and the masses celebrated before daylight, are very favourable to the completion of their wishes, to which also their dress is well adapted. They wear a black silk petticoat; their head is covered with a veil of the same colour, that falls below the waist; and, this costume being universal, and never changed, it is difficult to distinguish one woman from another. A man may pass his own wife in the street without knowing her. Their attachments are merely sensual. They are equally strangers to the delicacy of affection or that refinement of passion which can make any sacrifice the happiness of its object may require.

To the licentiousness of the people, more than to their extreme poverty, may be attributed the number of children which are continually exposed to perish in the street. Almost every morning, at the door of one of the churches, and often at more than one, a newborn infant is found. There is an hospital, where they are received, but those who find them, are (if so disposed) at liberty to keep them. The unfortunate little beings who happen to fall into the hands of the lower classes of the people, increase, during their childhood, the throng of beggars, and augment, as they grow up, the number of thieves.

The heart recoils at the barbarity of a mother who can thus abandon her child; but the custom, here, as in China, is sanctioned by habit, and excites no horror!

LETTER XVIII.

St. Jago de Cuba.

We have received no news from the Cape, my dear friend, but it is generally expected that it will be evacuated, as several parts of the island have been already.

This place is full of the inhabitants of that unfortunate country, and the story of every family would offer an interesting and pathetic subject to the pen of the novelist.

All have been enveloped in the same terrible fate, but with different circumstances; all have suffered, but the sufferings of each individual derive their hue from the disposition of his mind.

One catastrophe, which I witnessed, is dreadfully impressive! I saw youth, beauty and affection sink to an untimely grave, without having the power of softening the bitterness of their fate.

Madame C——, a native of Jeremie, had been sent by her husband to Philadelphia, at the beginning of the revolution, where she continued several years, devoting all her time to improving the mind and cultivating the talents of her only child, the beautiful Clarissa.

Sometime after the arrival of the French fleet, Madame C——, and her daughter returned to Jeremie. She had still all the charms of beauty, all the bloom of youth. She was received by her husband with a want of tenderness which chilled her heart, and she soon learned that he was attached to a woman of colour on whom he lavished all his property. This, you may suppose, was a source of mortification to Madame C——, but she suffered in silence, and sought consolation in the bosom of her daughter.

When the troubles of Jeremie encreased, and it was expected every day that it would be evacuated, Monsieur C—— resolved to remove to St. Jago de Cuba. He sent his wife and child in one vessel, and embarked with his mistress in another. Arriving nearly at the same time, he took a house in the country, to which he retired with his superannuated favourite, leaving his family in town, and in such distress that they were often in want of bread.

Madame C——, too delicate to expose the conduct of her husband, or to complain, concealed from her friends her wants and her grief.

A young Frenchman was deeply in love with her daughter, but his fortune had been lost in the general wreck, and he had nothing to offer to the object of his adoration except a heart glowing with tenderness. He made Madame C—— the confidant of his affection. She was sensible of his worth, and would willingly have made him the protector of her daughter, had she not been struggling herself with all the horrors of poverty and therefore thought it wrong to encourage his passion.

He addressed himself to her father, and this father was rich! He lavished on his mistress all the comforts and elegances of life, yet refused to his family the scantiest pittance! He replied to the proposal that his daughter might marry, but that it was impossible for him to give her a shilling.

Clarissa heard the unfeeling sentence with calm despair. She had just reached the age in which the affections of the heart develope themselves. The beauty of her form was unequalled, and innocence, candour, modesty, generosity, and heroism, were expressed with ineffable grace in every attitude and every feature. Clarissa was adored. Her lover was idolatrous. The woods, the dawning day, the starry heavens, witnessed their mutual vows. The grass pressed by her feet, the air she respired, the shade in which she reposed, were consecrated by her presence.

Her mother marked, with pity, the progress of their mutual passion, which she could not forbid, for her own heart was formed for tenderness, nor could she sanction it, seeing no probability of its being crowned with success. But the happiness of her daughter was her only wish, and moved by her tears, her sighs, and the ardent prayers of her lover, she at length consented to their union. They were married and they were happy. But alas! a few days after their marriage a fever seized Clarissa. The distracted husband flew to her father who refused to send her the least assistance. She languished, and her mother and her husband hung over her in all the bitterness of anguish. The impossibility of paying a physician prevented their calling one, till it was too late, and, ten days after she had become a wife, she expired. I have held this disconsolate mother to my breast, my tears have mingled with hers: all the ties that bound her to the world are severed, and she wishes only for the moment that will put a period to her existence, when she fondly hopes she may be again united to her daughter. To the husband I have never uttered a word. His sorrow is deep and gloomy. He avoids all conversation, and an attempt to console him would be an insult on the sacredness of his grief. He has tasted celestial joys. He has lost the object of his love, and henceforth the earth is for him a desert.

For the brutal father there is no punishment. His conscience itself inflicts none, for he expressed not the least regret when informed of the fate of his daughter.

But when the story became known, the detestation his conduct excited was so violent, that the friends of Madame C— have caused her to be separated from him, and obliged him to allow her a separate maintenance. Unfortunately their interest has been exerted too late. A few weeks sooner it might have saved her daughter.

How terrible is the fate of a woman thus dependent on a man who has lost all sense of justice, reason, or humanity; who, regardless of his duties, or the respect he owes society, leaves his wife to contend with all the pains of want, and sees his child sink to an untimely grave, without stretching forth a hand to assist the one or save the other!

LETTER XIX.

I write continually, my dear friend, though the fate of my letters is very uncertain. If they arrive safe they will prove that I have not forgotten you, and that I suffer no opportunity to pass without informing you that I exist.

I understand that, after our departure from the Cape, the tyranny of the general in chief encreased, and that the inhabitants were daily exposed to new vexations. St. Louis, in particular, was the distinguished object of his hatred. Eternally on guard at the most dangerous posts, it was finally whispered that something, more decidedly bad, was intended him, and he thought it was time to try to escape from the threatening danger. Being informed of a vessel, that was on the point of sailing, he prevailed on a fisherman to put him outside of the fort in his boat, and wait till it came out, the captain not daring to take him on board in the harbour. On the day appointed, St. Louis, disguised as a fisherman, went into the boat, and, working at the oar, they were soon beyond the fort. The vessel approached shortly after, and St. Louis, embarking, thought himself out of danger. As soon as they were in reach of the English ships they were boarded, plundered and sent to Barracoa.

St. Louis had no trunk, nor any clothes but what were on him, in which however was concealed gold to a great amount.

A gentleman, who left the Cape the day after him, informed us of his escape, and of his having been sent to Barracoa, and also that, as soon as the general had heard of his departure, he had sent three barges after the vessel with orders to seize him, take him back, and, as soon as he was landed, shoot him without further ceremony.

The whole town was in the greatest consternation. The barges were well manned and gained on the vessel, but a light wind springing up put it soon beyond their reach, and it was even believed that the officer, who commanded the barges, did not use all possible diligence to overtake them.

We were rejoiced to hear of the fortunate escape of St. Louis but felt some anxiety at his not arriving, when lo! he appeared and gave us himself an account of his adventures.

He is in raptures with the governor of Barracoa, his charming wife and the good father Philip, who, hearing that he was the husband of Clara, shewed him the most friendly attention. He brought us from them letters glowing with affectionate recollection. He talks of buying a plantation and of settling here. If he does I shall endeavor to return to the continent, but poor Clara! she weeps when I speak of leaving her, and when I consider the loneliness to which she will be condemned without me, I have almost heroism enough to sacrifice my happiness to her comfort.

Before the arrival of St. Louis we lived in the house of the gentlemen to whose care he had recommended us. He is a widower, the most cheerful creature in the world, but he lives in the times that are past; all his stories are at least forty years old. He talks continually of the mystification of Beaumarchais,[1] and the magic of Cagliostro.[2] He told me, with all the solemnity of truth, that a lady at the court of France, who was past fifty, bought from Cagliostro, at a great price, a liquid, a single drop of which would take off, in appearance, ten years of age. The lady swallowed two drops, and went to the opera with her charms renewed, and her bloom restored to the freshness of thirty.—At her return she called her waiting woman, who had been her nurse and was at least seventy. She was nowhere to be found, but a little girl came skipping in. The lady, enquiring who she was, learned that old Ursula, intending to try the effect of the drops, had taken too large a dose, and was skipping about with all the sprightliness of fifteen.

Nothing enrages the old gentleman so much as to doubt the truth of what he relates, or even to question its probability. He assured me that he knew the lady, and that he witnessed the effect of the drops

---

1 Pierre-Augustin Caron de Beaumarchais (1732–99) was the author of *Le Barbier de Séville* (1773) and *Le Mariage de Figaro* (1778) comedic plays known today primarily through operatic adaptations by Mozart and Rossini (1786 and 1816 respectively). Previously, Beaumarchais had worked for Louis XVI's secret service, and, following the publication of his memoirs, became a figure of international intrigue. Though patronized by the French court, Beaumarchais considered himself a republican. Napoleon regarded Beaumarchais' plays as "the revolution already in action."

2 Allesandro, Count di Cagliostro (1743–95) was a celebrated occult figure in French high society, holding séances and selling elixirs and aphrodisiacs in the years before the French Revolution. Banished from France in 1789, Cagliostro was arrested by the Inquisition in Rome for practicing Freemasonry. He spent the rest of his life in prison.

on herself and the chambermaid. As I can discover no purpose the invention of such a tale would answer, I listen without reply, and almost suffer myself to be persuaded of its reality.

Nothing can equal the unpleasantness of this town: it is built on the declivity of a hill; the streets are not paved; and the soil, being of white clay, the reflection is intolerable, and the heat insupportable. The water is brought on mules, from a river three miles off, and is a very expensive article. The women never walk, except to church, but every evening they take the air in an open cabriolet,[1] drawn by mules, in which they exhibit their finery, and, not unfrequently, regale themselves with a segar.[2]

Every body smokes, at all times, and in all places; and from this villanous custom arises perhaps, the badness of their teeth, which is universal.

The American consul, who has lived here many years, says that the people are much improved since he resided among them. At his arrival there was not a gown in the place. They are now generally worn.

This old consul is the greatest beau in the place. He gives agreeable parties, and makes love to every body, but I believe with little success. His very appearance would put all the loves to flight.

LETTER XX.

St. Jago de Cuba.

The French emigrants begin to seek in their talents some resource from the frightful poverty to which they are reduced, but meet with very little encouragement. The people here are generally poor, and unaccustomed to expensive pleasures. A company of comedians are building a theatre; and some subscription balls have been given, at which the Spanish ladies were quite eclipsed by the French belles, notwithstanding their losses.

Madame D—, of Jeremie, who plays and sings divinely, gave a concert, which was very brilliant.

---

[1] Two-wheeled, one-horse carriage that has two seats and a folding top.
[2] Cigar.

The French women are certainly charming creatures in society. The cheerfulness with which they bear misfortune, and the industry they employ to procure themselves a subsistence, cannot be sufficiently admired. I know ladies who from their infancy were surrounded by slaves, anticipating their slightest wishes, now working from the dawn of day till midnight to support themselves and their families. Nor do they even complain, nor vaunt their industry, nor think it surprising that they possess it. Their neatness is worthy of admiration, and their taste gives to their attire an air of fashion which the expensive, but ill-chosen, ornaments of Spanish ladies cannot attain. With one young lady I am particularly acquainted whose goodness cannot be sufficiently admired. Ah! Eliza, how shall I describe thy sweetness, thy fidelity, thy devotion to a suffering friend? Why am I not rich that I could place thee in a situation where thy virtues might be known, thy talents honoured? Alas! I never so deeply regret my own want of power as when reflecting that I am unable to be useful to you.

This amiable girl was left by her parents, who went to Charleston at the beginning of the revolution, to the care of an aunt, who was very rich, and without children. At the evacuation of Port-au-Prince, that lady embarked for this place. Her husband died on the passage; and they were robbed of every thing they possessed by an English privateer. The father of Eliza wrote for them to join him in Carolina; but the ill health of madame L— would not suffer her to undertake the voyage, and Eliza will not hear of leaving her, but works day and night to procure for her aunt the comforts her situation requires. She is young, beautiful and accomplished. She wastes her bloom over the midnight lamp, and sacrifices her health and her rest to soothe the sufferings of her infirm relation. Her patience and mildness are angelic. Where will such virtues meet their reward? Certainly not in this country; and she is held here by the ties of gratitude and affection which, to a heart like hers, are indissoluble.

In the misfortunes of my French friends, I see clearly exemplified the advantages of a good education. Every talent, even if possessed in a slight degree of perfection, may be a resource in a reverse of fortune; and, though I liked not entirely their manner, whilst surrounded by the festivity and splendour of the Cape, I now confess that they excite my warmest admiration. They bear adversity with cheerfulness, and resist it with fortitude. In the same circumstances I fear I should be inferior to them in both. But in this country, slowly emerging from a state of barbarism, what encouragment can be found for industry or talents? The right of commerce was purchased by the Catalonians,[1] who alone exercise it, and agriculture is destroyed in consequence of the restraints imposed on it by the government. The people are poor, and therefore cannot possess talents whose acquisition is beyond their reach; but they are temperate, even to a proverb, and so hospitable that the poorest among them always find something to offer a stranger. At the same time they are said to be false, treacherous, and revengeful, to the highest degree. Certainly there are here no traces of that magnanimous spirit, which once animated the Spanish cavalier, who was considered by the whole world as a model of constancy, tenderness, and heroism.

They feel for the distressed, because they are poor; and are hospitable because they know want. In every other respect this is a degenerate race, possessing none of the qualities of the Spaniards of old except jealousy, which is often the cause of tragic events.

A young gentleman of this place fell in love with a beautiful girl who rejected him because she was secretly attached to another. Her lover was absent; and she feared to avow her passion lest his rival might use some means to destroy him, for she knew he was cruel and vindictive; but her lover returning, she declared her attachment, and declined receiving the visits of him who had pretended to her hand. A few evenings previous to that fixed on for her marriage, she was returning from church with her mother, when at the door of her house a man, wrapped in a large cloak, seized her arm, and plunging a dagger in her breast, fled, leaving her lifeless on the ground. The cries of her affrighted mother brought people to her assistance, but the blow was directed by a secure hand; she breathed no more. Every body was convinced that the perpetrator of this abominable act was her rejected lover; but, as no proofs existed, the law could not interfere. Shortly after he was found dead in the street; and probably it was the hand of him he had driven to despair, that inflicted the punishment due to his crime.

---

[1] Catalonia is the region of northeastern Spain comprising the provinces of Barcelona, Gerona, Lérida, and Tarragona.

Nothing is more common than such events. They excite little attention, and are seldom enquired into. How different is this from the peaceful security of the country in which I first drew breath, and to which I so ardently, but I fear hopelessly, desire to return.

LETTER XXI.

St. Jago de Cuba.

General Rochambeau, after having made a shameful capitulation with the negroes, has evacuated the Cape. He presented his superb horses to Dessalines, and then embarked with his suite, and all the inhabitants who chose to follow him, intending to fight his way through the British ships. They were, however, soon overpowered and taken. The English admiral would not admit the general in chief into his presence. He has been sent to Jamaica, from whence he will be transported to England.

Many of the inhabitants of the Cape have arrived here, after having lost every thing they possessed. Numbers have remained. After the articles of capitulation were signed three days were allowed for the evacuation, during which the negroes entered the town, and were so civil and treated the inhabitants with so much kindness and respect, that many who had embarked their effects, allured by the prospect of making a fortune rapidly, paid great sums to have them relanded, supposing they would be protected as they had been in the time of Toussaint. But in less than a week they found that they had flattered themselves with false hopes. A proclamation was issued by Dessalines, in which every white man was declared an enemy of the *indigenes*, as they call themselves, and their colour alone deemed sufficient to make them hated and to devote them to destruction.[1] The author of this eloquent production, a white man, became himself the first sacrifice.

The destined victims were assembled in a public square, where

---

[1] Following independence, Jean-Jacques Dessalines ordered the massacre of the white inhabitants of the island. Proof to critics of the barbarity of the Haitians, the killing of the whites was defended by Dessalines as necessary to secure the liberation of the country: "Yes, we have rendered to these true cannibals, war for war, crime for crime, outrage for outrage; Yes, I have saved my country; I have avenged America."

they were slaughtered by the negroes with the most unexampled cruelty. One brave man, who had often distinguished himself in the defence of the Cape, and who had been weak enough to stay in it, seized with desperate fury the sword of one of the negroes, and killing several, at length fell, overpowered by numbers. A few were preserved from this day's massacre by their slaves. Some were concealed by the American merchants,[1] though it was very dangerous to venture on such benevolent actions. One vessel was searched, and several inhabitants being found on board, they were taken and hanged. The mate of the vessel, though an American, shared their fate. The captain saved himself by declaring that he was ignorant of their being on board. Major B——, whom I have so often mentioned, had also the folly to stay. One of his slaves concealed him on the day of the massacre, and, shut up in a hogshead, he was put on board an American vessel. After many perilous adventures he has arrived here, and relates scenes which cannot be thought of without horror.

The women have not yet been killed; but they are exposed to every kind of insult, are driven from their houses, imprisoned, sent to work on the public roads; in fine, nothing can be imagined more dreadful than their situation.

Two amiable girls, whom I knew, hung to the neck of their father when the negroes seized him. They wept and entreated these monsters to spare him; but he was torn rudely from their arms. The youngest, attempting to follow him, received a blow on the head with a musquet which laid her lifeless on the ground. The eldest, frantic with terror, clung to her father, when a ruthless negro pierced her with his bayonet, and she fell dead at his feet. The hapless father gave thanks to God that his unfortunate children had perished before him, and had not been exposed to lingering sufferings and a more dreadful fate.

Some ladies have found protectors in the American merchants, who conceal them in their stores. Some have been saved by the British officers; but the greatest number have been driven into the streets, and many are forced to carry on their heads baskets of cannon balls from the arsenal to the fosset, a distance of at least three miles.

---

[1] Americans continued to trade with Haiti during the revolution and after independence, despite the fact that Jefferson refused to recognize the new Haitian nation.

I enquired after a most accomplished and exemplary woman, who with three beautiful daughters remained at the Cape after the evacuation, and I have wept at the story of their sufferings till I am unable to relate them.

What could have induced these infatuated people to confide in the promises of the negroes? Yet to what will not people submit to avoid the horrors of poverty, or allured by the hope of making a rapid fortune.

During the reign of Toussaint the white inhabitants had been generally respected, and many of them, engaging in commerce, had accumulated money which they sent to the United States, where they are now living at their ease. Even at the arrival of the French fleet, the lives of the people, except in a few solitary instances, had been spared. These considerations had without doubt great weight, but alas! how soon were their hopes blasted, and how dearly have they paid for their credulity. Yet even these monsters, thirsting after blood, and unsated with carnage, preserved from among the devoted victims those whose talents could be useful to themselves. A printer and several artists have been suffered to live, but are closely guarded, and warned that their lives will be the forfeit of the first attempt to escape. With the sword suspended over their heads they still cherish perhaps a secret hope of eluding the vigilance of their savage masters.

LETTER XXII.

St. Jago de Cuba.

Madame G—, a native of Gonaives, having lost her husband at the beginning of the revolution, left St. Domingo, and sought a retreat from the horrors that ravaged that devoted island in the peaceful obscurity of Barracoa. Three infant daughters cheered her solitude; and she found in cultivating their minds a never failing source of delight. Some faithful slaves who had followed her, supplied by their industry her wants. The beauty of her person, the elegance of her manners, and the propriety of her conduct, rendered her the admiration of all who beheld her, whilst her benevolence, which shared with the poor the scanty pittance she possessed, made her the idol of those whose wants she relieved. Thus she lived, contented, if not happy, till the arrival of the French army at St. Domingo recalled its inhabitants to their deserted homes.

Madame G——, lured by the hope of reinstating her children in their paternal inheritance, left Barracoa, followed by the blessings and regret of all to whom she was known. On arriving at the Cape she found a heap of ashes, and shuddered with horror at the dreary aspect of her native country. But she viewed her children, recollected that on her exertions they depended, and determined to sacrifice every thought of comfort to their advancement. Some houses she owned in the Cape, upon being rebuilt, promised to yield her a handsome revenue; and she passed in anxious expectation the time during which the army kept possession of the Cape. At length the moment of the evacuation arrived, and the wretched Creoles were again reduced to the dreadful alternative of perishing with want in foreign countries, or of becoming victims to the rage of the exasperated negroes in their own. Whilst Madame G—— hesitated, she received a letter from one of the black chiefs, who had been a slave to her mother. He advised her not to think of leaving the country; assured her that it was the intention of Dessalines to protect all the white inhabitants who put confidence in him, and that herself and her children would be particularly respected. The dread of poverty in a strange country with three girls, the eldest of whom was only fifteen, induced her to stay. Many others, with less reason to expect protection, followed her example.

When the time allowed for the evacuation had expired, the negroes entered as masters. During the first days reigned a deceitful calm which was followed by a dreadful storm.

The proclamation of Dessalines, mentioned in my last letter was published. Armed negroes entered the houses and drove the inhabitants into the streets. The men were led to prison, the women were loaded with chains. The unfortunate madame G——, chained to her eldest daughter, and the two youngest chained together, thus toiled, exposed to the sun, from earliest dawn to setting day, followed by negroes who, on the least appearance of faintness, drove them forward with whips. A fortnight later the general massacre took place, but the four hopeless beings of whom I particularly write, were not led to the field of slaughter. They were kept closely guarded, without knowing for what fate they were reserved, expecting every moment to hear their final sentence. They were sitting one day in mournful silence, when the door of their prison opened, and the chief, whose letter had induced them to stay, appeared. He saluted madame G— with great familiarity, told her it was to his orders she owed her life, and said he would continue his friendship and protection if she would give him her eldest daughter in marriage. The wretched mother caught the terrified Adelaide, who sunk fainting into her arms. The menacing looks of the negro became more horrible. He advanced to seize the trembling girl. Touch her not, cried the frantic mother; death will be preferable to such protection. Turning coldly from her he said, You shall have your choice. A few minutes after a guard seized the mother and the two youngest daughters and carried them out, leaving the eldest insensible on the floor. They were borne to a gallows which had been erected before their prison, and immediately hanged. Adelaide was then carried to the house of the treacherous chief, who informed her of the fate of her mother, and asked her if she would consent to become his wife? Ah! no, she replied, let me follow my mother. A fate more dreadful awaited her. The monster gave her to his guard, who hung her by the throat on an iron hook in the market place, where the lovely, innocent, unfortunate victim slowly expired.

LETTER XXIII.

St. Jago de Cuba.

I finished my last letter abruptly, my dear friend, but a good opportunity offered of sending it, and the story of madame G— had so affected me that I could think of nothing else.

St. Louis is determined to buy a plantation here, and establish himself on it till he can return to St. Domingo. His old disease has seized him with fresh violence, and he intends to carry his wife beyond the reach of men. He is jealous of an interesting Spaniard who has lately been very assiduous towards my sister; and who is, I believe, much more dangerous than the redoubted general Rochambeau. His person is perfectly elegant; his face beautiful; his large black eyes seem to speak every emotion of his soul, but I believe they express only what he pleases. Clara listens to him, and looks at him as if she was fully sensible of his advantages, and frequently holds long conversations with him in his own language, which, if gestures deceive not, are on no uninteresting subject. But I hope, and would venture to assert, that she will never, to escape from the domestic ills she suffers, put her happiness in the power of a Spaniard. She is violent in her attachments, and precipitate in her movements, but she cannot, will not, be capable of committing such an unpardonable act of folly. All idea of her going to the continent is abandoned; and when I only breathe a hint of leaving her, she betrays such agony that I yield and promise to stay; yet I render her little service, and destroy myself, being wearied of this place, which has no charm after the gloss of novelty is gone, and that has been long since worn off.

A company of French comedians had built a theatre here, and obtained permission from the governor to perform. They played with eclat, and always to crowded houses. The Spaniards were delighted. The decorations, the scenery, above all the representation of the sea, appeared to them the effect of magic. But the charm was suddenly dissolved by an order from the bishop to close the theatre, saying, that it tended to corrupt the morals of the inhabitants.[1] Nothing can be more ridiculous, for the inhabitants of this island have long since reached the last degree of corruption; devoted to every species of vice, guilty of every crime, and polluted by the continued practice of every species of debauchery. But it is supposed the order was issued to vex the governor, with whom the bishop is at variance, and the orders of the latter are indisputable. It is impossible for him not to know that even the vices of the French lose much of their deformity by the refinement that accompanies them, whilst those of his countrymen are gross, disgusting, and monstrously flagrant. Gaming is their ruling passion; from morning till night, from night till morning, the men are at the gaming table. They all wear daggers, and a night very seldom

---

[1] Similar views were held in much of British North America during the eighteenth century. During the American Revolution, the theater was banned by an act of the Continental Congress, associated with gambling, prostitution, and other social vices. The Congress also viewed the theater as a British import, much like English tea, unwelcome in American cities. Theaters reopened and gained popularity in Philadelphia, New York, and Boston toward the end of the century.

passes without being marked by an assassination, of which no notice is taken. The women have recourse to intrigue, sipping chocolate, or reciting prayers on their rosaries. The custom is to dine at twelve, then to sleep till three, and this is the hour favourable to amorous adventures. Whilst the mother, the husband or the guardian sleeps, the lover silently approaches the window of his mistress, and in smothered accents breathes his passion. It is not at all uncommon to see priests so employed; nor are there more dangerous enemies to female virtue, or domestic tranquillity, than these pretended servants of the Lord.

I was at first shocked beyond measure, at their licentiousness, for I had been taught to consider priests as immaculate beings; but when I reflect that they are men, and doomed to an unnatural condition,[1] I pardon their aberrations, and abhor only their filth, which is abominable. Consider how agreeable a monk must be in this hot country, clothed in woolen, without a shirt, without stockings, and his legs so dirty that their colour cannot be distinguished, to which is added a long beard; and yet these creatures are favourites with women of all ranks and all descriptions.

There are many religious orders here, among which the Franciscan friars are the richest, and they are also the most irregular in their conduct.[2] They had begun, a number of years since, to build a church, which they were obliged to discontinue for want of funds. Shortly after our arrival here the wife of a very rich merchant fell dangerously ill. When her life was despaired of by the physicians, she made a vow to St. Francis, that if she recovered, she would finish his church. The saint, it seems, was propitious, for she was restored to health, and her husband instantly performed the promise of his wife, which has cost him a hundred and fifty thousand dollars. The church was consecrated last week, with great pomp and due solemnity. The lady, who is certainly very beautiful, assisted at the ceremony, covered with diamonds, and displaying in her dress almost regal splendour. She kneeled on the steps of the great altar, and more than shared the adoration offered to the saint by the admiring multitude.

Half the money expended in this pious work would have raised

---

[1] Mary refers to clerical celibacy.

[2] The Franciscan Order was founded by St. Francis of Assisi. Friars, itinerant monks, followed a strict rule of poverty, disavowing private property, an ideal at odds with their depiction here.

thousands of the inhabitants of this place, who are in the greatest want, to comparative ease. But it would not if thus employed, have had such an effect on the minds of the people; nor would the lady have had any hope of becoming herself a saint, an honour tó which she aspires, and which she may perhaps attain.

LETTER XXIV.

St. Jago de Cuba.

Clara and her husband are separated for ever! St. Louis is frantic, and I am distressed beyond measure. My heart is torn with anxiety for her fate, and I shall know no tranquillity till I hear that she is at least content. Being acquainted with many of the circumstances which led to this event, I pity and pardon her. As for the world, its sentence is already pronounced, and she will be condemned by those who possess not a thousandth part of her virtues. Her husband spares neither pains nor expense in searching after her retreat; but, though I am absolutely ignorant of it, I believe she is beyond his reach. His house is so disagreeable to me, since she left it, and the wry faces made by all our friends, seeming to involve me in the scandal occasioned by her elopement, excite such unpleasant sensations that it will be impossible for me to remain here. Therefore I shall leave this place immediately with a lady who is going to establish herself in Jamaica. I have always desired to see that island, and there I intend to stay till I have some positive information of Clara. If she is gone to the continent I shall follow her immediately; if she is in Cuba my friendship, my presence will console her, and they shall not be wanting. One of my friends, a man of intelligence and discretion, has promised to find her, if possible, and has promised also not to betray her, for she must never be restored to the power of her husband. Far from being an advocate for the breach of vows so sacred as those which bound her to St. Louis, I have always expressed with unqualified warmth, my disapprobation of the levity of many women who had abandoned their husbands. But there are circumstances which palliate error. Many of those which led to Clara's elopement plead for her; but if she has sought protection with another, if she will not accompany me, my heart renounces her, and she will no longer have a sister.

We sail in three days. St. Louis makes no objection to my going, and I leave Cuba without regret, for in it I have never been happy. Write to me at Kingston. Never was the assurance of your friendship more necessary to my heart than at this moment.

LETTER XXV.

Kingston, Jamaica.

We arrived at Kingston after a passage of twenty-four hours. On entering the harbour our little vessel, as it passed near the admiral's ship, appeared like an ant at the foot of a mountain. Nothing is more delightful than the bustle and continual movement that strikes the eye on entering this port. Innumerable boats are continually plying round the vessels, offering for sale all the fruits of the season. I like the town. There is an air of neatness in the houses which I have no where seen since I left my own country; but the streets are detestable; none of them are paved, and at every step you sink ankle deep in sand.

I have found numbers of my French friends here, and among others madame M——, who was more than gallant at the Cape, and who at St. Jago appeared not insensible to the pleasure of being loved. She left her sister in a fit of jealousy and went to Jamaica, hoping to captivate some Englishman, or at least to rival him in his attachment to roast beef and Madeira. But it seems she has been disappointed, no lover having yet offered his homage to her robust attractions. She accuses them of wanting taste, and hates the place and all who inhabit it.

I have also met here my little friend Coralie, whose adventures since I parted with her at the Cape, have been distressing and romantic.

Her mother and herself had been persuaded to remain at the Cape, after the evacuation, by a brother on whom they entirely depended, and who, seduced by the hope of making a fortune, staid and shared the melancholy fate of the white inhabitants of that place.

Coralie and her sister were concealed by an American merchant in his store, among sacks of coffee and boxes of sugar. Their mother had been led, with the rest of the women, to the field of slaughter.

The benevolent man who concealed these unfortunate girls at the risk of his life, after some weeks had elapsed, and the vigilance of the negroes a little relaxed, entreated the captain of an English frigate to receive them on board his vessel, to which he readily agreed. Disguised in sailors' clothes, and carrying baskets of provisions on their heads, they followed the captain to the sea side. As they approached the guard placed on the wharf to examine all that embarked, they trembled, and involuntarily drew back. But their brave protector told them that it was too late to recede, and that he would defend them with his life. As the English were on the best terms with the negroes, the supposed boys were suffered to pass. On entering the ship the captain congratulated them on their escape, and Coralie, overpowered by a variety of sensations, fainted in the arms of her generous protector.

A few days after, they sailed for Jamaica. On entering Port Royal, the frigate was driven against a small vessel, and so damaged it, that it appeared to be sinking. The boat was instantly hoisted out, and the captain of the frigate went himself to the assistance of the sufferers. The passengers and crew jumped into the boat, and were making off, when the screams of a female were heard from below, and it was recollected that there was a sick lady in the cabin. The English captain descended, brought her up in his arms, and put her in the boat. Then, saying that the vessel was not so much injured as they imagined, ordered some of his people to assist him in saving many things that lay at hand. Four sailors jumped on board, and followed their commander to the cabin, where they had scarcely descended, when the vessel suddenly filled and sunk. They were irrecoverably lost.

Coralie, standing on the deck of the frigate, beheld this catastrophe, saw perish the man to whom she owed her life, and whose subsequent kindness had won her heart.

The lady found in the sinking vessel was her mother, who had escaped almost miraculously from the Cape, fully persuaded that her daughters existed no longer. The joy of their meeting was damped by the melancholy fate of their deliverer, which has been universally lamented.

The scenes of barbarity, which these girls have witnessed at the Cape, are almost incredible. The horror, however, which I felt on hearing an account of them, has been relieved by the relation of some more honourable to human nature. In the first days of the massacre, when the negroes ran through the town killing all the white men they encountered, a Frenchman was dragged from the place of his concealment by a ruthless mulatto, who, drawing his sabre, bade him prepare to die. The trembling victim raised a supplicating look, and the murderer, letting fall his uplifted arm, asked if he had any money. He replied, that he had none; but that if he would conduct him to the house of an American merchant, he might probably procure any sum he might require. The mulatto consented, and when they entered the house, the Frenchman with all the energy of one pleading for his life, entreated the American to lend him a considerable sum. The gentleman he addressed was too well acquainted with the villainy of the negroes to trust to their word. He told the mulatto, that he would give the two thousand dollars demanded, but not till the Frenchman was embarked in a vessel which was going to sail in a few days for Philadelphia, and entirely out of danger. The mulatto refused. The unfortunate Frenchman wept, and the American kept firm. While they were disputing, a girl of colour, who lived with the American, entered, and having learned the story, employed all her eloquence to make the mulatto relent. She sunk at his feet, and pressed his hands which were reeking with blood. Dear brother, she said, spare for my sake this unfortunate man. He never injured you; nor will you derive any advantage from his death, and by saving him, you will acquire the sum you demand, and a claim to his gratitude. She was beautiful; she wept, and beauty in tears has seldom been resisted. Yet this unrelenting savage did resist; and swore, with bitter oaths to pursue all white men with unremitting fury. The girl, however, hung to him, repeated her solicitations, and offered him, in addition to the sum proposed, all her trinkets, which were of considerable value.

The mulatto, enraged, asked if the Frenchman was any thing to her? Nothing, she replied; I never saw him before; but to save the life of an innocent person how trifling would appear the sacrifice I offer. She continued her entreaties in the most caressing tone, which for some time had no effect, when softening all at one, he said, I will not deprive you of your trinkets, nor is it for the sum proposed that I relent, but for you alone, for to you I feel that I can refuse nothing. He shall be concealed, and guarded by myself till the moment of embarking; but, when he is out of danger, you must listen to me in your turn.

She heard him with horror; but, dissembling, said there would be always time enough to think of those concerns. She was then too much occupied by the object before her.

The American, who stood by and heard this proposal, made to one to whom he was extremely attached, felt disposed to knock the fellow down, but the piteous aspect of the almost expiring Frenchman withheld his hand. He gave the mulatto a note for the money he had demanded, on the conditions before mentioned, and the Frenchman was faithfully concealed till the vessel was ready to sail, and then embarked.

When he was gone, the mulatto called on the girl, and offering her the note, told her that he had accepted it as a matter of form, but that he now gave it to her; and reminded her of the promise she had made to listen to his wishes. Her lover entering at that moment told him that the vessel was then out of the harbour, and that his money was ready. He took it, and thus being in the power of the American gentleman, who had great weight with Dessalines, he probably thought it best to relinquish his projects on the charming Zuline, for she heard of him no more.

The same girl was the means of saving many others, and the accounts I have heard of her kindness and generosity oblige me to think of her with unqualified admiration.[1]

LETTER XXVI.

Kingston, Jamaica.

I pass my time agreeably enough here, though I am obliged to stay in a boarding house till madame L— can be fixed in her own. A few

---

[1] Perhaps the model for Zelica, the title character of the later adaptation and expansion of *Secret History* published in 1821.

days ago a Spanish sloop of war was captured by a British frigate, and brought into Jamaica. The officers were suffered to land, and came to lodge in the house where I stay. When called to dinner I was surprized at finding myself among a group of strangers. As the mistress of the house never dines at table, and madame L— was abroad, I would have retreated, but curiosity prompted me to remain.

The Spanish captain is an elderly man of most respectable appearance. All the rest are young, full of spirits, and two of them remarkably beautiful. Taking it for granted that I was French, and not imagining I could understand their language, as soon as they were seated at table they indulged very freely in their remarks on myself. One said I was not pretty; another, that I was interesting; another, that I resembled somebody he had seen before; and one elegant young man, who sat next me, having brushed his arm against mine made in Spanish an apology, which I appeared not to understand. He then asked me if I spoke English? I shook my head; and he observed to his companions, that he had never so much regretted his ignorance of the French. They laughed; and he continued lamenting the impossibility of making himself understood. After dinner I withdrew, and having been engaged by Coralie to pass the evening at her house, I forgot the strangers, and thought of them no more till the next morning at breakfast, where they were all assembled, and where madame L— related to me an adventure she had met with the day before. She spoke English, and as I was answering her my eyes met those of the young officer, and his look covered me with confusion. Ah! he said, you speak English, and were cruel enough to refuse holding converse with a stranger and a prisoner. I speak so little, I replied. No, no, he cried, your accent is not foreign; I could almost swear that it is your native language. He looked at the others with an air of triumph; and the one who had said I was not pretty, observed, that he was glad I did not speak Spanish; but I understand it perfectly, I answered in the same language.

He looked petrified; and the old captain was delighted. He made many inquiries after his friends at Cuba, with all of whom I was acquainted. The young officer who speaks English, is by birth an Irishman.[1] He entered the Spanish service at the age of fifteen; had

---

[1] After the devastating loss at the Battle of Kinsale (1601), many Irish were exiled to the West Indies.

been several years at Lima; had returned to Europe, and was on his way to Vera Cruz[1] when they were taken by the English. With him my heart claimed kindred, for in every Irishman I fancy I behold a brother and a friend.[2] His manners are elegant and interesting beyond expression. There is an appearance of sadness in his face, which heightens the interest his fine form creates; and if I had an unoccupied heart, and he a heart to offer, I believe we should soon forget that he is a prisoner and I a stranger!

I have learned from him, that on his arrival at Lima, he was lodged in the house of a gentleman who had a beautiful daughter. She was a widow, though very young. The seclusion in which the ladies of this country live rendered such a companion as Don Carlos doubly dangerous, and the beauty and sweetness of Donna Angelina, made an indelible impression on his heart. Their mutual passion was soon acknowledged; but obstacles, which appeared insurmountable, seemed to deprive them even of hope.

Angelina had inherited the immense fortune left by her husband, on condition of remaining a widow. Her father was very rich, but avarice was his ruling passion. He had sacrificed his only child at the age of thirteen to an old man, merely because he was wealthy, and there was no reason to expect that he would suffer her to abandon the fortune she had so dearly acquired, and marry a man who had no inheritance but his sword. Though these considerations cast a cloud over their mutual prospects, they still cherished their mutual affection, and hoped that some fortunate event would at length render them happy. The father of Angelina never suspected the situation of his daughter's heart, and her intercourse with Don Carlos was without restraint. Delightful moments of visionary happiness how quickly ye passed; delivering in your flight two victims to the gripe[3] of despair!

A new viceroy[4] arrived from Spain and Angelina was obliged to appear at a ball given to celebrate his entry into Lima.

---

[1] Mexico.
[2] See introduction (note 1, p. 31) for the possible significance of Sansay's favor for the Irish.
[3] Grip.
[4] The Viceroy was the highest-ranking government official, the direct representative of the Spanish crown, for the Spanish colonial territories. There were two Viceroys, one to govern New Spain and stationed in Mexico City and the other in Lima, Peru.

She danced with Don Carlos, and her beauty, eclipsing all other beauty, attracted universal notice, but particularly that of the viceroy, who went the next day to offer at her feet the homage of his adoration. She received him coldly, but the father was transported with joy, and when, a few days after, the viceroy demanded her hand, without hesitation favoured his suit. Angelina declined, and acquainted him with the conditions on which she inherited her husband's wealth, and her resolution to remain a widow. He told her that his own fortune was more than sufficient to replace that he wished her to sacrifice, but her evident aversion raised a suspicion of other reasons than those she avowed, and his jealous watchfulness soon discovered her attachment to Don Carlos. He informed her father of his discovery, who, furious at seeing his hopes of aggrandizing his family thwarted by a boy, forbad all intercourse between them.

The means employed by the viceroy to separate them were still more effectual. A vessel was on the point of sailing for Spain, and Don Carlos received orders to embark instantly to bear dispatches of importance to the court. Resistance would have been vain. He sailed without being permitted to see the object he had so long adored.

When he arrived in Spain, he learned that his rival had taken every precaution to prevent his return to Lima. Fortunately he knew the heart of his Angelina, and felt assured that the hopes of the detested rival would never be crowned with success; nor was he disappointed.

She had been deprived by her father and the viceroy of the man she loved, but their power extended no farther. There was an asylum to which she could retreat from their tyranny; that asylum was a convent. She entered one, took the vows, and gave her immense fortune to the society of which she became a member.

On the eve of entering the convent she wrote to Don Carlos, informing him of her intention; of the impossibility of preserving herself for him, and her determination never to belong to another. He received this letter the day on which he sailed for Vera Cruz, and I believe, does not regret being a prisoner, since he has found in the place of his captivity a kind being who listens to his tale of sorrows and seeks to pour the balm of consolation into his wounded heart.

He amuses me continually with his stories of Lima; describing the splendour of its palaces, the magnificence of its churches, filled with golden saints and silver angels, and the beautiful women with which it abounds. He tells me there can be nothing more fascinating than their manners; nor more singular and picturesque than their dress, which consists of a petticoat, reaching no lower than the knee, and a veil that covers the head and waist, but through which a pretty face is often shewn in a most bewitching manner. At the same time I perceive that he talks on every subject with reluctance, except on that nearest his heart; and when speaking of this, he seems animated by all the energy of despair.

I have heard of Clara by a person just arrived from Cuba, and have written to her. My heart is torn with anxiety for her fate, and will remain a stranger to repose till I receive more satisfactory intelligence. I fear she was not born to be at ease. She lives continually in an ideal world. Her enthusiastic imagination filled with forms which it creates at pleasure, cherishes a romantic hope of visionary happiness which never can be realized.

Yet with all my fine sentiments of correctness and propriety, and the duty of content and resignation, my heart refuses to condemn her for having left her husband. Never was there any thing more directly opposite than the soul of Clara, and that of the man to whom she was united. Their tempers, their dispositions, were absolutely incompatible. And should I abandon this poor girl to misfortune? Should I leave her to perish among strangers? Ah! no, she is twined round my heart, and I love her with more than a sister's affection. As soon as I hear from her again, you shall be informed of my intentions. If I can induce her to return with me to Philadelphia, in rejoining you I shall think myself no longer unhappy.

LETTER XXVII.

To Clara.

Kingston, Jamaica.

I have received the message, sent me by Anselmo, my dear Clara, and my joy at hearing of your welfare, made me forget for a moment, the many causes you have given me of complaint. Yet what more have I learned than that you exist? Of all that concerns you I remain ignorant. Unkind Clara! thus you repay my friendship! thus console me for all the solicitude I have felt for you! To have staid with St. Louis, after you left him, was not possible, for he did not conceal his suspicions of my having been in your secret, nor could I find in Cuba an eligible retreat; for all my friends were his, and all disposed to condemn you. I accepted therefore, with pleasure, the offer made by Madame L—, to take me with her to Jamaica.

Write to me, my dear sister, immediately. Tell me every thing. Does not your heart require the affectionate sympathy it has been accustomed to receive from mine? Can you live without me?—without me who have followed you, and love you with an affection so tender? Dearest Clara, speak, and I will fly to you! Means shall be found to return to Philadelphia, where, in peaceful obscurity we may live, free from the cares which have tormented you, and filled myself with anxiety.

Anselmo will be careful of your letter. Write fully, and remember that you are writing to more than a sister; to a friend, who loves you, who adores your virtues, and who pardons, while she weeps, your faults!

LETTER XXVIII.

To Mary.

Bayam, 20 leagues from St. Jago.

I know your heart, my dear Mary! On the affection which glows for me in that heart, I have counted for the pardon of my errors, and your letter convinces me that I have not been deceived. You know, for you witnessed, my domestic infelicity; yet, how many of my pains did I not conceal, to spare you the anguish of lamenting sorrows which you could not alleviate!

St. Louis, after his arrival at St. Jago, had connected himself with a company of gamesters, and with them passed all his time.—Often returning at a late hour from the gaming table, he has treated me with the most brutal violence,—this you never knew; nor many things which passed in the loneliness of my chamber, where, wholly in his power, I could only oppose to his brutality my tears and my sighs. To his intolerable and groundless jealousy at Cape Francois you were no stranger: it embittered my days. Since our arrival in this island it increased. In every man that approached me he saw a rival! and the more amiable the object, the more terrible were his apprehensions.

He became acquainted, at some of the haunts of gaming, with Don Alonzo de P— and brought him to our house, but, when his visits had been repeated two or three times, all the tortures of jealousy were awakened in the breast of St. Louis.

If I received this young stranger with pleasure, it was because I found him interesting. If I avoided him it was an acknowledgement of his power!

He had insisted on my learning the Spanish language, yet if I spoke in that language it was to express sentiments I sought to conceal from him. How often, in the bitterness of anguish, have I thought that the direst poverty would be preferable to the ease I had purchased at the expence of my peace! but alas! the colour of my fate was fixed,—I was united to St. Louis by bonds which I had been taught to consider sacred, and, though my heart shuddered at the life-long tie, yet I always recoiled with horror from the idea of breaking it.—That tie however is broken; those bonds are dissolved! and there is no fate so dreadful to which I would not submit, rather than have them renewed.

Believe me when I assure you that my flight was not premeditated. It is true, the eloquent eyes of Don Alonzo often spoke volumes, but I never appeared to understand their language, nor did a look of encouragement ever escape me. For some days previous to my elopement the ill humour of St. Louis had been intolerable. My wearied soul sunk beneath the torments I endured and death would have been preferable to such a state of existence. The night before I left him he came home in a transport of fury, dragged me from my bed, said it was his intention to destroy me, and swore that he would render me horrible by rubbing aqua-fortis[1] in my face. This last menace deprived me of the power of utterance; to kill me would have been a trifling evil, but to live disfigured, perhaps blind, was an insufferable idea and roused me to madness. I passed the night in speechless agony. The only thought I dwelt on was, how to escape

---

[1]   Nitric acid, used in the production of dyes.

138   LEONORA SANSAY

from this monster, and, at break of day, I was still sitting, as if rendered motionless by his threats. From this stupor I was roused by his caresses, or rather by his brutal approaches, for he always finds my person provoking, and often, whilst pouring on my head abuse which would seem dictated by the most violent hatred, he has sought in my arms gratification which should be solicited with affection, and granted to love alone.

You must recollect my unusual sadness that day; for well do I remember the kind efforts you made to divert me.

I awaited the approach of night with gloomy impatience, determined that the dawn of day should not find me beneath that hated roof. When I left you in the evening it was with difficulty I restrained my tears. My heart was breaking at the idea of being separated from you, if not forever at least for a considerable time, and the thought of the pain my flight would occasion you almost determined me to relinquish it.

But St. Louis was in my chamber, and his presence dispelled every idea, except that of avoiding it forever. After seeing me undressed, he left me, as usual, to pass the greatest part of the night abroad. His vigilant guard, the faithful Madelaine, lay down near the door of my apartment, and I, taking a book, appeared to read. At eleven o'clock I knew by her breathing that she was asleep.

Taking off my shoes, I passed her softly—opened the door that leads into the garden, and was instantly in the street.

The moments were precious for I had the whole town to pass, in order to gain the road to *Cobre*,[1] where I intended to request an asylum of Madame V—.

I flew with the rapidity of lightning, nor stopped to breathe till I had passed the town. Beginning to ascend the mountain, I paused, and leaning against a tree, reflected for a moment on the singularity of my situation.—Alone, at midnight, on the road to an obscure village, whose inhabitants are regarded as little better than a horde

---

[1] El Cobre is located 12.5 miles to the north-west of Santiago de Cuba. Cobre is an interesting choice for Clara to seek refuge from St. Louis—and from the Haitian Revolution. In 1731, Cobre was the site for a large slave revolt at the state-run copper mines. The rebel slaves, who were called *cobreros*, fled into the mountains and maintained a significant if dispersed population through the end of the eighteenth century. The cobrero maroons welcomed runaway slaves from surrounding plantations and from throughout the Caribbean.

of banditti!—Flying from a husband, whose pursuit I dreaded more than death; leaving behind a sister, for whom my heart bled, but whom I could never think of involving in my precarious fate!

The night was calm. The town, which lies at the foot of the mountain, was buried in profound repose. The moon-beams glittered on the waves that were rolling in the bay, and shed their silvery lustre on the moving branches of the palm trees. The silence was broken by the melodious voice of a bird, who sings only at this hour, and whose notes are said to be sweeter than those of the European nightingale. As I ascended the mountain, the air became purer. Every tree in this delightful region is aromatic; every breeze wafts perfumes! I had six miles to walk, and wished to reach the village before day, yet I could not avoid frequently stopping to enjoy the delightful calm that reigned around me!

I knew that, as soon as I was missed, the town would be diligently searched for me, but of the retreat I had chosen St. Louis could have no idea, for he was totally unacquainted with the residence of Madame V—. To this lady I had rendered some essential services at the Cape, which gave me a claim on her friendship. She left that place before us, and on her arrival here, bought a little plantation in *Cobre*, where she lives in the greatest retirement. I had heard of her by acci-dent, and thought it the surest retreat I could find. As the day broke I perceived the straggling huts which compose this village, and, approaching the most comfortable one of the group, found to my great satisfaction, that it was inhabited by the lady I sought. She had just risen, and was opening the door as I drew near it. Her surprise at seeing me was so great, that she doubted for a moment the evidence of her senses; but, seizing my hand, she led me to her cham-ber, where, pressed in her arms, I felt that I had found a friend, and the tears that flowed on her bosom were proofs of my gratefulness.

I began to explain to her my situation. "I know it all!" she cried, "you have escaped from your husband. My predictions are verified, though a little later than I expected.—But where" continued she, "is your sister?" I replied that my flight had not been premeditated, and that you had not been apprised of it. There was no necessity for giving her a reason for having left my husband. She had always been at a loss to find one for my staying with him so long. The next consideration was my toilette. I was bare-headed, without stockings:—my shoes were torn to pieces by the ruggedness of the road, and I had no other covering than a thin muslin morning gown. The kind friend, who received me, supplied me with clothes, and checked her eagerness to learn the particulars of my story till I had taken the repose I so much required.

Towards evening she seated herself by my bedside, and I related to her all that I had suffered since she left me at the Cape.

But when I spoke of the threat which had determined me to the step I had taken, she made an exclamation of horror.

I told her that my intention was to remain concealed till the search after me was over, and then to embark for the continent.

She approved the project, and said, that I could be no where in greater security than with her; for, though the village is only six miles from town, it is as much secluded as if it was in the midst of a desert, except at the feast of the holy Virgin which is celebrated once a year.

The festival lasts nine days, and all the inhabitants of St. Jago come to assist at its celebration. Unfortunately the season of the feast was approashing, during which it would have been impossible for me to remain concealed in the village. However, as there was still time to consider, she bade me be tranquil, and promised to find me a retreat. Two days after she went to town and at her return I learned that nothing was talked of but my elopement.

St. Louis, in the first transports of his rage, has entered a complaint against Don Alonzo and, declaring that he had carried me off, had him imprisoned!

It was feared this step would be attended with ill consequences, for this young Spaniard, being related to the bishop and some of the most distinguished families, it was supposed the indignity of his imprisonment would be resented by them all!

Besides, he was entirely innocent of the charge exhibited against him, not having had the slightest idea of my flight.

This information filled me with alarm. I felt insecure so near the town and entreated madame V— to indicate a more remote and safe asylum.

She told me that she had a friend, twenty leagues from town, to whom she had often promised a visit; that the inconvenience of travelling in this barbarous country, had hitherto prevented her going, but that these considerations vanished before the idea of obliging me, and that the pleasure of making the journey in my company would be a sufficient inducement.

Two days were past in procuring horses and making preparations for our departure. In the evening we walked among the rocks, which surround the village, and, had my heart been at ease, I should have wandered with delight in these romantic regions.

The place was once famous for its valuable copper mines, from which it takes its name, but they have been long abandoned. The inhabitants, almost all mulattos, are in the last grade of poverty, and too indolent to make an exertion to procure themselves even the most necessary comforts. Yet, in this abode of wretchedness, there is a magnificent temple, dedicated to the blessed Virgin.[1] Its ornaments and decorations are superb. The image of the Virgin, preserved in the temple, is said to be miraculous and performs often wonderful things. The faith of these people in her power is implicit. The site of the temple is picturesque, and the scenery, that surrounds it, beautiful beyond description, standing near the summit of a mountain, at the foot of which lies the village. You ascend to it by a winding road, and see its white turrets, at a great distance, glittering beneath the palm trees that gracefully wave over it.

After passing through the miserable village and following the winding path through craggy cliffs, over barren rocks aud precipices which the eye dares not measure, the mind almost involuntarily yields to the belief of supernatural agency. On entering the church the image of the Virgin, fancifully adorned and reposing on a bed of roses, appears like the presiding genius of the place. The waxen tapers, continually burning, the obscurity that reigns within, occasioned by the impenetrable branches of the trees which overshadow it, and the slow solemn tone of the organ, re-echoed by the surrounding rocks, fill the mind with awe; and we pardon the superstitious faith of the ignorant votaries of this holy land, cherished as it is by every circumstance that can tend to make it indelible.

At the appointed time, before the dawn of day, our little cavalcade set out. Madame V— and myself on horseback, preceded by a

---

[1]   The Basilica de Nuestra Señora del Cobre began as a hermitage to display a wooden image of the Virgin Mary found by three fishermen in 1606. It remains Cuba's most sacred pilgrimage site.

guide, and followed by a boy, leading two mules charged with provisions, and every thing requisite for the journey. We wore large straw hats, to defend us from the sun, with thick veils, according to the custom of the country. Leaving Cobre behind us, we ascended the mountain. The road passed through groves of majestic trees, intermingled with the orange and the lime, which being in blossom, the senses were almost overpowered by the odours which filled the air. We proceeded slowly and silently.—I thought of you my dear sister!—My tears flowed at the idea of your pain, and I trembled to think that I was not out of danger of being discovered.

About eight o'clock our guide said it was time to breakfast, and, tying our horses, he struck a light, kindled a fire, and made chocolate.[1] The repast finished, we continued on our way through the same delightful country; still breathing the purest air, but without discovering any vestige of a human habitation.

About noon we saw a little hut. The guide, alighting, half opened the door, saying "May the holy virgin bless this house!" This salutation brought out a tall sallow man, who gravely taking his segar from his mouth, bowed ceremoniously, and bid us enter. We followed him, and saw, sitting on an ox hide, stretched on the ground, a woman, whose ragged garments scarcely answered the first purposes of decency. She was suckling a squalid naked child, and two or three dirty children were lolling about, without being disturbed by the appearance of strangers. A hammock, suspended from the roof, was the only article of furniture in the house. Whilst the guide was unloading the mules to prepare our dinner, I went out to seek a seat beneath some trees; for the filth of the house, and appearance of its inhabitants filled me with disgust.

To my infinite astonishment, the plains which extended behind the house, as far as the eye could reach, were covered with innumerable herds of cattle, and on enquiring of the guide to whom they belonged, I learned, with no less surprise, that our host was their master. Incredible as it may appear, this miserable looking being, whose abode resembled the den of poverty, is the owner of countless multitudes of cattle, and yet it was with the greatest difficulty that we could procure a little milk.

---

[1] Most likely a beverage.

A small piece of ground, where he raised tobacco enough for his own use, was the only vestige of cultivation we could discover. Nothing like vegetables or fruit could be seen. When they kill a beef, they skin it, and, cutting the flesh into long pieces about the thickness of a finger, they hang it on poles to dry in the sun; and on this they live till it is gone and then kill another.

Sometimes they collect a number of cattle and drive them to town, in order to procure some of the most absolute necessaries of life. But this seldom happens, and never till urged by the most pressing want. As for bread, it is a luxury with which they are entirely unacquainted. After dinner the guide, and the host, and all the family, lay down on the ground to sleep the siesta, which, you know no consideration would tempt a Spaniard to forget. Madame V— walked with me under the trees, near the house, and remarked the striking difference between this country and St. Domingo. There, every inch of ground was in the highest state of cultivation, and every body was rich, here, the owners of vast territories are in the most abject poverty.

This she ascribed to the different genius of the people, but I think unjustly, believing that it is entirely owing to their vicious government.

After our guide had taken his nap he led up the horses, and bidding adieu to our hosts, we continued our journey.

We passed during the afternoon several habitations similar to the one where we dined. The same wretchedness; the same poverty exhibited itself, surrounded by troops of cattle, who bathed in plains of the most luxuriant pasturage.

As the sun declined our guide began to sing a litany to the Virgin, in which he was joined by the boy who followed us. The strain was sweet.

"And round a holy calm diffusing
In melancholy murmurs died away."[1]

At the close of day we stopped at a hut, where the guide told us we must pass the night, and I learned that we had come ten leagues, though we had advanced at a snail's pace. The hut we entered was

---

[1] Adapted from William Collins (1721–59), "The Passions: An Ode for Music" (1747), lines 66–68.

inhabited by an old man who, retiring with the guide to an adjoining shed, left us the house to ourselves. The couch, which invited us to repose, was a hide laid on the ground. Madame V— had brought sheets, and, spreading them on the hide, I soon sunk to rest. But my slumbers were interrupted by a most unaccountable noise, which seemed to issue from all parts of the room, not unlike the clashing of swords; and, as I listened to discover what it was, a shriek from Madame V— increased my terror. In sounds scarcely articulate, she said a large cold animal had crept into her bosom, and in getting it out, it had seized her hand.

Frightened to death I opened the door and called the guide, who discovered by his laughing that he had foreseen our misfortune, and guarded against it by suspending his hammock from the branches of a tree. When I asked for a light to search for what had disturbed us, he said it was nothing but land crabs, which, at this season, descend in countless multitudes from the mountain, in order to lay their eggs on the sea shore.

The ground was covered with them, and paths were worn by them down the sides of the mountain. They strike their claws together as they move with a strange noise, and no obstacle turns them from their course. Had they not found a passage through the house they would have gone over it; and one finding Madame V— in his way, had crept into her bosom. The master of the house gave his hammock to madame V—. I mounted in that of the guide; but the curiosity excited by our visitors, rendered it impossible for us to sleep. I asked the guide if it was common to see them in such numbers. He said that it was; and told me that the English having some years ago made a descent on the island, had seized a Spaniard whom they found in a hut, and threatened to kill him if he would not shew them the way to St. Jago, which they had always wished to possess, but which they could not approach by sea. The terrified Spaniard promised to comply. In the night, as they were encamped on the mountain, waiting for daylight in order to proceed, they heard a noise stealing through the thickets, like that of an approaching host. They asked their prisoner what it meant? He replied, that it could be nothing but a body of Spaniards who, apprized of their descent, were preparing to attack them. The noise increasing on all sides, the English, fearful of being surrounded, embarked, and in their haste suffered the prisoner to escape, who by his address probably prevented them from becoming masters of the island, for the pretended host was nothing more than an army of these crabs.

The man, I understand, received no reward; but the anniversary of this event is still celebrated; and if the crabs have not been canonized,[1] they are at least spoken of with as much reverence as the sacred geese, to which Rome owed its preservation.[2]

During the night their noise prevented me effectually from sleeping. They appeared like a brown stream rolling over the surface of the earth. Towards morning they gradually disappeared, hiding themselves in holes during the day.

At the first peep of dawn we set out, and arrived in the evening in Bayam. The friend of madame V— received us with great cordiality. She lost her husband soon after her arrival in this country. She is very handsome, and has an air of sadness which renders her highly interesting. She was informed of my story, and requested me to think myself at home in her house.

It was determined that I should pass for a relation of her husband; and soothed by her kindness and attentions I began to hope that beneath her roof I should find repose.

Madame V—, after staying with us eight days, returned to Cobre, promising to inform herself of you, and to write me all that was passing. She wrote me immediately that you had sailed for Jamaica: that Don Alonzo was out of prison; that he had commenced a suit against St. Louis for false imprisonment, and that the latter was actually confined. Don Alonzo is powerfully supported by the bishop and all his family, who have long been at variance with the governor, and gladly seek this opportunity of revenging themselves. She finally told me, my dear Mary, that she had discovered a young man who owned a small vessel in which he goes constantly to Jamaica, and that she had entreated him to find you, to tell you that I am well, and to charge himself with your letter, not doubting but you would write. That kind letter I received yesterday, and it has given me the first agreeable sensation I have known since we parted. I am convinced

---

1   To declare (a deceased person) to be a saint and entitled to be fully honored as such.
2   When the Gauls sacked and burned Rome (390–338 BCE), the citizens of Rome evacuated to the heavily fortified garrison on Capitoline Hill. According to legend, sacred geese alerted the citizens of an impending night-time attack against the fortress.

of your affection for me, but do not let that affection hurry you into imprudencies which may perhaps betray me. Do not think of returning to St. Jago; and, may I add, do not think of leaving Jamaica till I can join you. We will return to the continent together, and I hope together we shall be happy. Two or three doubloons, which I brought with me, prevent my being dependant on the lady in whose house I am, for any thing but her friendship.

I was struck with the resemblance of a Spanish lady who lives near us to Don Alonzo, and found, on enquiring, that she is his sister. She spoke to me of her brother, but is as ignorant of his affairs as if he dwelt in the moon.

This place is the abode of poverty and dullness, yet the people are so hospitable that from the little they possess they can always spare something to offer to a stranger. And they are content with their lot—how many reasons have I not to be so with mine!

LETTER XXIX.

To Mary

Bayam.

I thank you a thousand times, my dear sister, for your affectionate letter, and for the parcel that accompanied it. I knew with what pleasure you would share with me all you possess, and to be indebted to you adds to my happiness.

What you have heard of St. Louis is true. The affair of Don Alonzo and himself was made up by the interposition of some of their mutual friends who represented him as half mad; and somebody having spread a report that I had sailed for the city of Santo Domingo, he embarked immediately for that place. What he could think I should seek at Santo Domingo,[1] I am at a loss to imagine.

---

[1] Santo Domingo was the name of the Spanish-controlled, eastern portion of the island of Hispaniola and also the name of its capital city, located in the south. It became The Dominican Republic on 27 February 1844. Saint Domingue, or St. Domingo, was the western portion of the island and is now known as Haiti.

My retreat has been discovered, and though by one who would not betray me, yet he is the last person on earth, except St. Louis, to whom I could have wished it to be known.

The husband of Donna Maria, the Spanish lady whom I mentioned to you before, had gone to St. Jago, some days previous to my arrival here. Having, as is the universal custom, visited a gaming house, he had a dispute with a gambler of bad reputation, and on leaving the house received a blow with a poinard,[1] which proved mortal.

Such occurrences are too frequent to create much public interest, and it is considered useless to seek the assassin.

When the senora Maria expected the return of her husband, she heard that he existed no longer. The news was brought by her brother. Her house joins the one I live in. Hearing the most lamentable cries from her chamber I ran in. Judge of my surprise at seeing Don Alonzo. His, I believe, was not less, for abandoning his sister, he approached me; but I was too much terrified at her situation, to attend to him. When informed of the cause, I felt that in that moment she could not be consoled, and I saw also that the violence of her sorrow would soon exhaust itself.

Don Alonzo sought an opportunity of speaking to me, which I avoided. Learning afterwards where I lived, he so ingratiated himself with madame St. Clair, that he received an invitation to her house, and in that house he now passes all his time. He has been the innocent cause of much of my suffering, yet I cannot find fault with his conduct; and madame St. Clair, devoting much of her time to his widowed sister, I have no means of escaping from him. He has informed me of many of the follies of St. Louis, of the obstinacy with which he affirmed that Don Alonzo had aided my flight, and of the means he had employed to discover me. And why, he sometimes asks, did you not suffer me to aid you? Why did you not repose confidence in me?

You know my dear Mary, how eloquent are his eyes! you know the insinuating softness of his voice! Sometimes, when listening to him, I forget for a moment all I have suffered, and almost persuade myself that a man can be sincere.

---

[1]   Long dagger.

The governor of Bayam is an Irish Spaniard, at least he is of an Irish family, and was born in Spain. I have become acquainted with him since the arrival of Don Alonzo, and felt, the instant I beheld him, as if I was in the society of an old acquaintance. His Irish vivacity is a little tempered by Spanish gravity. He speaks English as if he had been raised in his own country, and his mind is stored with literary treasures. He has a handsome collection of books, which he offered me. Judge of my delight at meeting with Shakspeare in the wilds of Cuba.

What could have induced him to accept this sorry government I have not yet learned, but he certainly possesses talents which merit a more important employment, and his elegant manners would add lustre to the most distinguished situation. He laughs heartily at his ragged subjects, by whom however he is regarded as a father and a friend. He says with better laws they would be the best fellows in the world; but situated as they are, their indolence is their best security.

We often make excursions in the beautiful environs of this place and dine beneath the shade of the palm tree, or the tall and graceful cocoa, which offers us in its fruit a delicious dessert, whilst the gaiety of the governor diffuses around us an indescribable charm.

But my dear sister, think not that I forget you in these delightful scenes. On the contrary I long to see you, and am hastening the moment of my departure.

Madame St. Clair, seduced by the description I have made of our peaceful country, and wearied of a place where she has known nothing but misfortune, where the talents she possesses are absolutely lost, intends going with me to Philadelphia, as soon as she can arrange her affairs, and has consented to accompany me to Kingston, from whence we can all sail together. You will love her, I am sure, for her kindness to me; but, independently of that consideration, her beauty, the graceful sweetness of her manners, and her divine voice, render it impossible to behold or listen to her with indifference.

The governor says, if he loses his two most amiable subjects, his little empire will not be worth keeping. Don Alonzo

"Looks and sighs unutterable things,"[1]

---

[1] Adapted from James Thomson (1700–48), "The Seasons: Summer" (1727), line 1188.

and sometimes hints, in broken accents, the passion he has felt for me since the first moment he saw me, at all which I laugh. For me, henceforth all men are statues. I was so ill-fated as to meet that phenomenon a jealous Frenchman, and with my wounds still bleeding, would I put my happiness in the power of a Spaniard? Ah! no, let me avoid the dangerous intercourse, let me fly to my sister! Why are you so far removed from me? Why did you so hastily leave the island, where you knew I must be, and in a situation too in which your counsel, your support is doubly necessary?

It will be impossible for me to leave Bayam in less than a month. We shall sail for Kingston with Anselmo. Much precaution must be used, for I must embark from St. Jago, and if I was discovered, should certainly be arrested by the governor, who is exasperated against me. Write to me, my dear girl, by the return of the vessel; and believe me that I wait with the utmost impatience for the moment that will reunite us.

LETTER XXX.

To Clara

Kingston.

Let me entreat you, my dear sister, to leave Bayam as soon as possible. I cannot describe the pain with which I learned of Don Alonzo being near you. You pass hours, days with him; you talk of his eloquent eyes, his sweet voice. Ah! fly, dearest creature, fly from the danger that surrounds you. Listen not to that insinuating Spaniard. If you do you are irrecoverably lost.

Why indeed am I not near you? Yet after your flight, to stay in Cuba was impossible, and my leaving it was, I believe, one of the principal reasons which determined St. Louis to leave it also: so far it was fortunate. My heart always acquitted you for having taken the resolution to abandon your home; for though, as you say, I knew not all, I knew enough to awaken in my breast every sensation of pity. Yet it is not sufficient that you are acquitted by a sister, who will always be thought partial; and if you cannot conciliate general approbation, at least endeavor to avoid meriting general censure. Who that hears of your being at Bayam, in the house of the sister of Don Alonzo, knowing that he had been publicly accused of having taken you off, and learns, that as soon as the affair was hushed up in St. Jago, that he went to Bayam, that he passes all his time in your society, that at home and abroad he is ever at your side, who can hear all this, and not believe that it was preconcerted? Ah! Clara, Clara, I believe that it was not, because I love you, and cannot think you would deceive me. But why stay a month, a week, a day, where you are? Why not come to me when Anselmo returns? when with me, my friendship, my affection, will soothe and console you? I will remove from your lacerated breast the thorns which have been planted there by the hand of misfortune. You shall forget your sorrows, and I will aid you against your own heart, for I believe at present *that* is your most dangerous enemy.

LETTER XXXI.

To Mary

Bayam.

You frighten me to death, my dear sister, with your apprehensions. You paint my situation in terrifying colours; yet could I forsee that I should be led into it, when alone and friendless I fled at midnight from a house where I suffered continual torture? Did I imagine that in Bayam I should become acquainted with Don Alonzo's sister, and that I should meet him in her house? Sentence, I know, has been passed against me, and that sentence will be confirmed by what has happened subsequent to my elopement. The testimony of my own heart will be of little avail. But will you also join against me? I cannot believe it. Condemn me not, at least suspend all opinion till we meet, which will be in a fortnight. To avoid the danger of passing through St. Jago, we go by land to a place called Portici, from whence we shall embark. The journey will be delightful. We intend making it on horseback. The governor and Don Alonzo will accompany us. Start not at this, for it cannot be otherwise; nor could I, by refusing his services, discover that I thought it dangerous to accept them.

In my anxiety to see you, every moment seems an age, yet I feel something like regret at leaving this country. The friendliness of the people can never be forgotten. Here, as in Barracoa, they are poor but contented. They sip their chocolate, smoke a segar, and thrum the guitar undisturbed by care. Often, when reviewing the events of my past life, I wish that their calm destiny had been mine; but alas! how different has been my fate.

I write this letter to prepare you for my arrival. When Anselmo goes next, I go with him; and, when I embrace my sister, I shall be happy.

LETTER XXXII.

Kingston, Jamaica.

Clara, my dear friend, is at length arrived. I have held that truant girl to my heart, and have forgotten whilst embracing her all the reproaches I intended to make, and which I thought she deserved. I cannot help loving her, though I approve not of all she does; but I will blame her fate rather than herself, for who can behold her and not believe that she is all goodness? Who can witness the powers of her mind and withhold their admiration? Whatever subject may engage her attention, she seizes intuitively on what is true, and by a sort of mental magic, arrives instantaneously at the point where, even very good heads, only meet her after a tedious process of reasoning and reflection. Her memory, surer than records, perpetuates every occurrence. She accumulates knowledge while she laughs and plays: she steals from her friends the fruits of their application, and thus becoming possessed of their intellectual treasure, without the fatigue of study, she surprises them with ingenious combinations of their own materials, and with results of which they did not dream. Her heart keeps a faithful account, not only of every word but of every look, of every movement of her friends, prompted by kindness and affection, and never is her society more delightful than in those moments of calm and sublime meditation, when her genius surveys the past, or wanders through a fanciful and novel arrangement of the future. Who that thus knows Clara, and is sensible of her worth, can have known her husband and condemn her?

It is true, Clara is said to be a coquette, but have not ladies of superior talents and attractions, at all times and in all countries been subject to that censure? unless indeed theirs was the rare fortune of becoming early in life attached to a man equal or superior to themselves! Attachments between such people last through life, and are always new. Love continues because love has existed; interests create interests; parental are added to conjugal affections; with the multiplicity of domestic objects the number of domestic joys increase. In such a situation the heart is always occupied, and always full. For those who live in it their home is the world; their feelings, their powers, their talents are employed. They go into society as they take a ramble; it affords transient amusement, but becomes not a habit. Their thoughts, their wishes dwell at home, and they are good because they are happy. But if on the contrary a woman is disappointed in the first object of her affections, or if separated from him she loved, fate connects her with an inferior being, to what can it lead? You might as well expect to confine a sprightly boy, in all the vigour of health to sedate inaction, as to prevent talents and beauty, thus circumstanced, from courting admiration. A feeling heart seeks for corresponding emotions; and when a woman, like Clara, can fascinate, intoxicate, transport, and whilst unhappy is surrounded by seductive objects, she will become entangled, and be borne away by the rapidity of her own sensations, happy if she can stop short on the brink of destruction.

If Clara's husband had been in every respect worthy of her she would have been one of the best and happiest of human beings, but her good qualities were lost on him; and, though he might have made a very good husband to a woman of ordinary capacity, to Clara he became a tyrant.

Sensible of the impossibility of her leaving him, he took it for granted that she bestowed on another those sentiments he could not hope to awaken himself. Yet Clara never deceived him. There is in her character a proud frankness which renders her averse to, and unfit for intrigue. When at the Cape, she was not dazzled by splendour, though it courted her acceptance; nor could the ill-treatment of her husband force her to seek a refuge from it in the arms of a lover who had the means of protecting her. At St. Jago his conduct became more insupportable, and when at length she fled from his house, alone and friendless, she was unseduced by love, but impelled by a repugnance for her husband which had reached its height, and could no longer be resisted.

Delivered from the weight of this oppressive sentiment, she now enjoys a delightful tranquillity, which even the thought of many approaching struggles with difficulty and distress, cannot disturb.

In such a situation I am more than ever necessary to my sister; and, perhaps, it is the consciousness of this, that has given birth to many of the sentiments expressed in this letter.

We have learned that St. Louis sailed from the city of Santo Domingo to France, from which I hope he may never return.

Clara and myself will leave this for Philadelphia, in the course of the ensuing week. There I hope we shall meet you; and if I can only infuse into your bosom those sentiments for my sister which glow so warmly in my own, she will find in you a friend and a protector, and we may still be happy.

THE END.

LAURA

BY

A LADY OF PHILADELPHIA

Die Mutter Starb, fand mich init mir selbst
Ein schwaches rohr, und in dem sturm allein.

Goethe in Tancred

My Mother died, I found myself deserted
A feeble reed, and in the storm alone.

PHILADELPHIA:

PUBLISHED BY BRADFORD & INSKEEP.

PRINTED BY ROBERT CARR.

★★★★★★★★★★★★

1809.

PREFACE

With the exception of a few slight deviations, which were thought indispensible, the following narrative is a faithful account of real occurrences. I am aware that it can claim no merit unless it be that of correctness and simplicity; at no other at least have I aimed, and should my endeavours in this respect not have been entirely unsuccessful, should the little book interest, and have a tendency to promote virtue; my most sanguine wishes on the subject will be gratified.

THE AUTHOR.
Philadelphia, Feb. 14th, 1809.

CHAPTER I

Rosina, a destined victim to monastic gloom, leaned weeping against the grated window that terminates one of the vast corridors of the convent of Santa Clara.

The lady abbess had just finished a sermon on the advantages of a life devoted to religion within her sacred walls, beneath her holy auspices. She concluded it by dooming to eternal torments all those whose wishes strayed from these consecrated precincts; and as Rosina withdrew from the apartment and bent her way towards the garden, the repugnance she felt at spending her life in the convent filled her with sadness, and she forgot that the short interval of amusement, allowed by her rigid guardians, was passing.

Her thoughts were interrupted by the loud ringing of the convent bell, and soon after Rosina was summoned by one of the nuns.

Expecting to receive letters from a young lady who had lately left the convent, and who had promised to write to her all that was passing in the gay world, she flew to the parlour, and saw standing at the grate, a young gentleman of the most elegant appearance.

Surprised, she waited in silence to learn the purport of his visit, which he seemed in no haste to declare: at length presenting a letter, he told her it was from his sister, who had charged him to deliver it into her own hands.

The name of her friend, recalled to the heart of Rosina recollections that were inexpressibly dear. Her timidity and her sadness yielded to the desire of talking on a subject so interesting, and she learned that after a short passage, she had arrived safely in Dublin, and was now the delight of her friends, the idol of her family.

How kind of your sister, said Rosina sorrowfully, to think of me amid the happiness which surrounds her. The tearful look that accompanied this observation, sunk deep into the bosom of the stranger, but some ladies entering the parlour prevented his reply, and he retired after promising to call for an answer to his sister's letter.

Rosina hastened to her chamber. She opened the pacquet, and as she read its fascinating contents, her affectionate heart glowed with pleasure at the happiness of her friend, whilst the too striking contrast offered by her own situation gave new poignancy to her regret.

Every scene, every occurrence rendered brilliant by the charm of novelty, was related whilst the impressions they made were still warm. Her voyage, her arrival, her joy at meeting her family, the balls given to celebrate her return, her beautiful dresses, were all minutely described; but suddenly checking her transports, and recurring to the gloomy destiny of her friend, she continued:

"Dearest Rosina, we live not in the convent. There, from the perform-ance of a tiresome routine of constantly succeeding duties, we can claim no merit; they are prescribed, and we have no choice but to obey; we are good because all occasion of doing ill is kept from us.

"How different it is when the heart left to its own impulses expands spontaneously.

"Some days ago I was hastening to purchase a superb trimming and met in the way a poor emaciated woman, who begged for some-thing to save her children from starving. I instantly gave her the contents of my purse, and returned to relate the adventure to my mother, who pressed me to her bosom, but looked so grave that I at first feared I had done wrong: it was, however, merely for having given more money than the poor woman had probably ever seen before. And as they contrived to give me some idea of the impor-tance of this article, I insisted upon going to the ball dressed with the greatest simplicity; in which I was indulged, and believe me, though the least fine, I was far from being the least happy.

"I should have no wish ungratified if you my dear girl were here; but dearest Rosina I fear for you there is no hope! Your father and sisters, whom I have seen since my return talk of your taking the veil as of a thing long since decided on. And your inflexible aunt, the abbess, will never relinquish so fair a victim.

"My brother William, who is going to Lisbon, promises to deliver this letter to you and to send me yours:—How sincerely do I wish that the spirit of knight-errantry would seize him, and that he might bear you from your hated prison to your

CECILIA."

Rosina's father was a wealthy merchant in Dublin, who had sent her at a very early age to the convent of Santa Clara in Lisbon, the abbess of which was her aunt, and Rosina from the moment of her entrance, was considered as one of the order.

But the abbess knew not the art of dressing religion with smiles: rigid in the performance of her duty, and proud of that severity which gave to every human frailty the coloring of a crime, she regarded the reluctance of Rosina to enter her novitiate, as a sin of the greatest magnitude; and instead of seeking to draw her into the number of the elect by persuasion and caresses, unremittingly assailed her ear with terrifying images of the punishment awaiting refractory dispositions.

Whilst Cecilia was the companion of her solitude, Rosina had borne all this with patience; but by their separation she was deprived of her only comfort, and the last faint hope that lingered in her breast was totally destroyed by the letter of her friend.

Its concluding sentence raised a blush on her cheek, whilst a wish that it might be realized stole insensibly through her bosom.

Among the numerous boarders that were continually received in the convent some novels, though strictly prohibited, had found their way. Rosina had gathered from them enough to know that such occurrences were not unfrequent; and even the legends which the nuns repeated, were often founded on the story of some beautiful lady delivered from enchantment by a valiant knight.

The idea gradually took possession of Rosina's mind, till at last she dwelt with so much pleasure on the hope of being freed, and thought so little of the improbability of such an event, that she arose in the morning with a lighter heart than usual, and for the first time entered the refectory with a smiling countenance. But the iron bars, the gloomy windows, the impenetrable walls that surrounded her, dispelled the charming vision, and, as if she had been really disappointed, she fell again into her former despondency.

At noon she was called to the parlour where the brother of her friend was waiting. He enquired if she had written to his sister. Alas, no! replied Rosina, what time have I to relate but my regret for her loss? and why should I disturb the happiness of my dear Cecilia with a relation of sorrows which all her goodness cannot alleviate? But tell her that among the few happy hours of my life, those which were cheered by her friendship were the brightest,—tell her that I hope to live in her remembrance, as she will in mine, till I cease to exist!

In all ages, in all countries, youth and beauty in tears have been found irresistible. The heart of Cecilia's brother felt their influence, and he conceived the thought of freeing Rosina from a fate she seemed to abhor.

He informed her that he intended passing several months in Lisbon, and requested permission to see her often. He soon discovered the interest he had created in her bosom; his ardour increased with his admiration; and at length, the triple walls of Santa Clara were found insufficient to prevent the flight of Rosina.

A friend of William gave them an asylum in a solitary house on the shores of the Tagus,[1] where they were privately married by his chaplain.

But finding it impossible to remain long undiscovered in that country, where the crime of stealing from a convent a person intended for a nun, could only have been expiated on the rack, they embarked on board a vessel that was on the point of sailing for America; and after a long and dangerous passage arrived at Philadelphia.

CHAPTER II

Scarcely were they landed, when William received intelligence of the death of his father. This unexpected event obliged him to return to Europe, and he sailed for Dublin three weeks after Rosina had given birth to a daughter, with the intention of converting his property into money, and returning to form a permanent establishment.

After the departure of her husband, the care of her child formed the only amusement of Rosina, and she dwelt continually on the moment of his return; as if by seeking to forget, she could annihilate the interval of their separation. But alas! that separation was destined to be eternal. When she expected to receive letters from him, perhaps fixing the period of his return, she learned that the vessel in which he sailed, had foundered, and that not a soul had escaped.

The woman in whose house she lived, was humane, and by her kindness softened the misfortune of the afflicted Rosina. The sale of some trinkets of value which she possessed, and her own industry supported her during four years. She wrote to her family the

---

[1]   A river that runs from Spain into Portugal.

most supplicating letters, which were only answered by severe injunctions to write no more. She addressed herself to the family of her husband, but she learned from them that her marriage was doubted, and that they never would receive her. Cecilia was married; and giddy with happiness, or restrained by prudential considerations, seemed to have forgotten her friend.

The extreme beauty of Rosina, her industry, and domestic habits, attracted the attention of a gentleman who was an inmate of the same house. Possessed of property himself, he would have considered fortune with a wife as very desirable; but he saw that Rosina, though poor, was in herself a treasure, and he made her an offer of his hand. The heart of Rosina recoiled at the idea of forming second ties, as from an act of sacrilege. But at length the representations of the few friends she had acquired, and the fear of seeing her daughter grow up in poverty and neglect, vanquished her scruples, and she became the wife of another, whilst her heart renewed in bitter regret its vows of fidelity to the husband she had lost.

Neither the mind, the manners, nor the person of the man she had married, were calculated to efface the impressions of her first attachment: yet from a sense of duty, she concealed the real state of her feelings. To the children she bore him, she performed, with the strictest attention, all the duties of a mother, but the daughter of her love engrossed her affection.

In the opening features of Laura, Rosina traced a likeness of her father. In her temper, sometimes eccentrically gay, sometimes sad even to gloom, she saw his disposition renewed, and the sound of her voice awakened recollections which often became so painful, that they seemed to set at defiance even the soothing influence of time.

As Laura grew she became the friend, the companion of her mother. She shared every sentiment of her heart, and so closely became the existence of these two beings interwoven, that the disparity of years was forgotten.

The simplicity of Rosina's character had not been altered by her intercourse with the world; her piety had been increased by affliction. Shocked by the misfortunes that had attended her entrance into society, and disgusted by the mode in which she continued to exist, she cherished the secret wish of sending her daughter to the convent of Santa Clara, and of devoting her to that religious solitude from which she had herself so thoughtlessly fled. She therefore endeavoured to impress on her infant mind an idea of the futility of worldly pleasures, and the lively imagination of Laura entered readily into the holy visions of her mother.

She already fancied herself enrolled in the sacred number of women consecrated to the service of God. And whilst wandering in imagination through the marble halls, beneath the lofty domes of the magnificent convent, she sighed to witness the pomp,—to behold the splendor of its festivals.

But these delusive prospects were destroyed by a most unexpected misfortune.

The delicacy of Rosina's constitution had not been able to resist the sorrow which preyed on her mind, and her health, which had been long on the decline, yielded to a sudden attack, which, in its very first stage, was supposed to be dangerous.

Laura marked with distraction the progress of the disease; and Rosina from the intenseness of her sufferings, was herself convinced that she should not recover. She saw her daughter weeping by her bedside during the lonely nights and regarding her with eyes in which more than mortal attachment was expressed. She sought to comfort her, but the effort was beyond her strength; her faltering voice could give no utterance to the conflicting sensations that rent her breast.

Laura perceived the struggle with deep affliction. Her lips were pressed on the burning forehead of her mother, her tears streamed on her burning hands, but they streamed in all the bitterness of unavailing anguish, and were only the harbingers of lasting and impotent regret.

After a short interval of ease, during which she slumbered, Rosina seemed to rise by a sudden effort above the languor of mortality, and pressing with feverish energy her beloved child to her bosom, she exclaimed: "I have loved thee with more than a mother's love! I have cherished thee with more than a mother's care! oh thou dearest object of my affection! but alas, it will only aggravate the ills of thy orphan state; for soon wilt thou be indeed an orphan.

"Yet thy step-father is good, and will protect thee. Respect him; deserve his affection. Ah why can I not live to direct thee—to save thee from the dangers to which thou wilt be exposed! but my spirit shall hover round thee!—shall guard thee from evil!—No greater blessing can await the soul of a mother!—"

As the last faint accents expired on her lips, a sudden paleness overspread her face; her head sunk back on the pillow, and the hands that fell from the neck of her weeping daughter were cold as clay. A scream from Laura roused the drowsy attendant: she flew to the bed, where both lay apparently lifeless. Laura was restored, but the spirit of her mother had flown forever.

CHAPTER III

Laura had just entered her fifteenth year when she was deprived, by the death of her mother, of her only friend.

Sad and disconsolate she wept the irreparable loss, nor did the soothing voice of sympathy alleviate her sorrows; for she knew no heart with which her own could claim kindred. The world contained no being from whose voice she could expect consolation, on whose bosom she could seek repose.

The seclusion in which she had lived, gave a shade of melancholy to her disposition, which rendered her more exquisitely sensible of the folornness of her fate.

The delicacy of her feelings was shocked by the common-place condolence offered by those who surrounded her, and she concealed from them her sufferings: but sorrow, deep as that which preyed on the soul of Laura, acquires fresh force from concealment, and she retired to her sacred hoard of grief like a miser to his treasure. In her lonely walks she wept in bitterest agony the friend whose protecting care no longer accompanied her: and often leaning against a tree, beneath whose shade she had frequently reposed with her mother, she called in wildest anguish on her sainted spirit, and she prayed to be restored to her even in death.

In her lonely wanderings on the banks of the Schuylkill, Laura had been remarked by a young gentleman whose family lived on the borders of that delightful stream. Her nymph-like form, the beauties of which were not obscured by her sable habit, had attracted his notice, whilst unconscious of the curiosity she had excited, she returned repeatedly to the retired spot she had chosen, and there yielded without restraint, to the indulgence of her woe.

One evening, seated on a little hillock, she retraced the many happy moments she had passed in that neighborhood with her from whom she was now forever separated, still overcome by the painful variety of her sensations, she reclined on the grass and wept aloud.

Roused from her recumbent attitude by the sound of approaching footsteps, she raised her eyes, and fixed them on a face in every lineament of which was blended the sweetest expression of pity. A voice which seemed to tremble lest its softest accent should be found intrusive, sounded on her ear, and the hand that was stretched forth to raise her, appeared to entreat her acceptance of its support.

Laura, covered with unspeakable confusion, turned away in silence, but the stranger was too deeply interested to be easily avoided; he walked slowly by her side, and sought to apologize for his intrusion, or to excuse its continuance.

After a silence of some minutes, during which the confusion of Laura had painfully increased, he offered her his arm, and begged permission to attend her home. She refused both. Ah refuse me not, he said, suffer me to guard you from the danger that may lurk in this sequestered place, whilst I regret that, being unknown to you prevents my offering more;—Laura raised her eyes to his face:—prevents, he continued, my offering that sympathy which the tears I witnessed have so powerfully awakened. The tears of Laura glistened on her cheek: sighs which she vainly endeavoured to suppress, broke from her bosom. Fair suffering being, said the stranger, my heart bleeds for your pain: so young are you already the victim of misfortune?—has affliction chosen for her poisoned arrows a mark so fair? Who are you that thus even in silence so irresistibly seizes on my feelings? Speak to me. No impertinent curiosity seeks its own gratification, by prying into your sorrows,—but animated by the purest motives, I flew to soothe your pains—to arrest the sighs which you supposed were unheard by all except that heaven to whom they were addressed, and to dry those tears, which fell as you thought, unregarded, on the earth's cold bosom.

The heart of Laura had been wrung with pain even beyond the power of endurance, and the sweetly insinuating voice of pity had not soothed its sufferings: that heart revived beneath the consoling powers of the stranger, her tears flowed, but they were not tears of bitterness: she would have thanked him for his care, but her sensations defied the power of utterance. She reached her home without having spoken a word. When turning to take leave of her conductor, he entreated to be allowed to see her again; she continued silent: a moment only, he urged, tomorrow evening, at this hour, at this place,—my name is Belfield—

But Laura disappeared. She hastened to her chamber. There her busy fancy eagerly retraced the voice, the look, the accent of the amiable stranger, whose name declared him to belong to one of the most respectable families.

Wrapped in pleasing recollections, as she sunk to sleep, new images mingled with her thoughts, and she floated in the dreams that had before only been inspired by her mother.

CHAPTER IV

When Belfield presented himself for the first time to the tear-swoln eyes of Laura he had just completed his twentieth year.

Tall, and formed with the most perfect symmetry, the gracefulness of his movements added to the elegance of his person, which was more than equalled by the beauty of his face. In his hazle eyes sat youth and health sparkling with unspeakable lustre. His auburn hair played in glossy ringlets over his forehead, and on his lips

"Persuasion slept on roses."[1]

The sweetness of his smile tempered the vivacity of his eyes, and he could assume a look of tenderness that was irresistible.

Belfield had not beheld Laura without emotion. The air of superiority in which she seemed enveloped, the profound sorrow of which she was the prey, had awakened in his heart a warmer sentiment than mere curiosity, and on a nearer view of her face he discovered traces of a soul susceptible of the strongest affection.

Her image accompanied him to his pillow, where he sought in vain for sleep: and at earliest dawn he left his bed, and went to the spot where she had first met his eye; to that spot where he had beheld her sinking to the earth, and had obeyed the impulse of his heart in flying to her assistance.

---

[1] Unidentified.

The crystalline surface of the Schuylkill glowed with the first blush of the morn, and reflected back the craggy rocks glittering with dew. The refreshing coolness of the hour, the cloudless sky, the tranquillity that reigned around, soothed his agitation, expanded his feelings, and ushered in the soft emotions of new-born affection. Tears of tenderness filled his eyes as he regarded the hillock on which Laura had reclined. Sweet suffering creature! he exclaimed, perhaps thy heart is bleeding for some friend of thy youth—How delightful would be the task of soothing thy sorrows, of changing into smiles of hope thy tears of regret and anguish, and of whispering peace and love to thy wounded breast. His tears fell on the ground that had been moistened by her tears, he kneeled on the grass on which she had rested, and sensations of pity for a creature so young and afflicted blended themselves with the warmer sentiment which had been excited by her beauty.

Sweet sensations! Celestial sentiments! It is in the genial season of youth alone that the heart owns your enchanting influence, that the soul flies spontaneously to the relief of the sufferer, and is borne away without resisting the torrent of sympathy.

CHAPTER V

At the close of day Belfield directed his steps to the abode of Laura, and found her sitting beneath the trees that overshadowed her house.

She arose to meet him and sought by the cheerfulness of her manner to atone for her melancholy silence at their first interview. Belfield related to her, how often he had observed her on the banks of the Schuylkill, how he had been interested by her pensive manner so forcibly expressive of the state of her mind, and how much he wished for the power of relieving her pains.

Whilst listening to him Laura forgot that he was a stranger, and he soon ceased to be one to her affecting story.

She mentioned the death of her mother, dwelt with enthusiasm on her virtues, and her perfections, and wept again her loss with a warmth of regret which she sought not to conceal.

She was my only friend, said Laura, in almost inarticulate accents. Deprived of my father from my birth, my mother alone and friendless struggled through want and woe to shield my helpless infancy from harm. Her cares were unremitted, her affection knew no bounds. She was still young, but alas she has been torn from me, I am now truly an orphan, nor is there on earth a being on whom I can assert even an orphan's claim for sympathy or protection.

As Belfield listened to the artless recital, his bosom swelled with a variety of emotions. Every beam that emanated from the eyes of Laura, every sound that conveyed her grief fraught story to his ear, impressed themselves indelibly on his heart. He would have consoled her, but the words he sought to utter died on his lips; he pressed her hand in silence, and the trembling of his own betrayed an interest beyond the power of words to impart.

Laura felt the eloquence of his silence, and was pleased with a delicacy of mind so congenial to her own. She was at that perilous stage of female existence when the glowing heart expands to every new impression; when the lustre of the melting eye bespeaks the tender disposition of the soul; when the throbbing bosom beats with undefinable sensations, and the elastic, bounding step betrays an exuberance of life, and health and fire, which frequently bewilders its unguarded possessor. At the same time her heart was desolated by grief, a situation in which more than in any other it is susceptible of tender impressions, and under such circumstances Belfield presented himself, as a heaven-sent messenger of peace. Can it be wondered at that her soul hailed with joy the gentle visitant? Her tears no longer checked by coldness or restrained by fear, flowed, but flowed in all the sweetness of indulgence. To talk of her mother to one who could feel her worth, and who listened with interest to a description of her merit, was a pleasure she had never before known. The darling theme was inexhaustible, and it was late in the evening when Belfield retired full of love and admiration, and leaving Laura overwhelmed with feelings as delightful as they were new.

CHAPTER VI

Laura felt no longer alone and desolate, for she had found one gentle being who listened to her with sympathy and soothed her by tender attention. Those only can tell the effects of kindness on a heart like

Laura's, who like herself have been borne down by the hand of afflic-tion. Her memory fondly retraced each word, each look of the amiable stranger; the moon's silver light, resting on the snowy curtains of her bed, restored her to the mild lustre of his expressive eye, and the breezes that played along the branches which shaded her windows were soft as the sighs he had re-echoed to her own. She wept, but there was a luxury in her tears, and sleep was no longer solicited for its oblivious balm. Borne on the wings of imagination the night flew rapidly away, and when the sun's first rays illumined her chamber she hailed them with a smile, for she hoped, and a blush was the herald of the unac-knowledged hope, that with the setting sun she would see Belfield.

The day appeared insufferably long; the evening came and she flew to her accustomed seat. The shades of night fell deep around her, but the anxiously expected object met not her eye. She listened to every noise; the step so much desired approached her not. It grew late, she was obliged to retire, and disappointment strewed thorns on that pillow where a few hours before she had shed its freshest roses.

Whilst restless and inquiet she sought in vain for that repose which even her ardent desire of obtaining tended perhaps to remove, she was surprised by sounds of celestial sweetness. At first she thought it was a dream and feared to move lest the illusion should vanish, but as a louder and sweeter strain reached her ear she arose, went softly to the window and beheld several young men, among whom she distinguished her new acquaintance, standing under a tree opposite to her house. Some had flutes and clarinets, which others accompa-nied with their voices. The moon beams played among the branches that waved over their heads and illuminated the beautiful counte-nance of Belfield. He sung a pathetic little song in which his compan-ions joined. The serenity of the night, the novelty of the music which stole with magic influence on the enchanted sense of Laura filled her with extacy: leaning against the window, and fearing to breathe lest she should lose a single sound she stood motionless and concealed her face with her hands that she might not be discovered.

When Belfield ceased to sing, he remained sometime with his eyes fixed on her window, which was partially covered by the luxu-riant honeysuckles that surrounded it. The little group then slowly withdrew. Peace and joy on the wings of harmony, had regained possession of Laura's heart; she returned to bed and the thought of

Belfield still trembled in her mind when consciousness retired.

CHAPTER VII

The disappointment of the preceding evening was strongly impressed on the intelligent countenance of Laura, and veiled with reserve the native warmth of her manner, as Belfield, anxious to account for his absence, approached her.

He related the cause of his absence with an eagerness that almost defeated its purpose, and the features of Laura betrayed the satisfaction she felt whilst hearing his excuses. He had been taken into the country and detained notwithstanding all his efforts. Returning late at night, he continued, and wishing to make some atonement for my apparent negligence, I collected a few friends and led them towards your house, hoping that their melodious strains might plead for me, and obtain your pardon.

Laura acknowledged that she had expected him. She confessed, also, that she had heard the music, and sought not to conceal the pleasure it had given her. As she spoke, her cheeks glowed, her voice faltered, and she turned from the ardent gaze of Belfield who listened to her with rapture. "Oh turn not from me," he said, "that sweet face, let me still hear that enchanting voice!" With burning lip she pressed her hands; fixed on her blushing face his speaking supplicating eyes, and marked in the soft confusion there portrayed the effect of surprise, and the conflict between timidity and the new born feelings he had excited in her bosom.

How delightful were the hours passed by Laura and Belfield at this period! The declining health of her step-father confined him to his room and left her at liberty. The days flew by winged with her wishes, and she was only conscious of her existence as the evening approached, which seldom failed to bring her the society of Belfield. He was the companion of her walks. His refined and elegant manners were strongly contrasted by those of the few men she had sometimes conversed with. The beauty of his person had fascinated her at the first, and the delicacy, the constancy of his attentions, completed the enchantment.

The friendless state of Laura, rendered his approaches to her easy, and when the familiarity of continued intercourse had removed the veil which modesty threw over the native treasures of her mind, he considered with astonishment the extent of her intellectual powers. Her understanding was excellent, her memory uncommon, and she possessed a degree of refinement very unusual, and not at all congenial to the humble sphere in which she moved. Alas! why was a being so fair, so promising, so innocent, deprived at this dangerous period of a mother's care; of that sagacious solicitude which would have given the true direction to her talents, and prevented the romantic enthusiasm of her disposition, from becoming inimical to her peace!

Finding that a mind so capable of cultivation was unembellished by literary acquirements, Belfield furnished her with books, and most of the classic poets of the English language, with whom she had been hitherto unacquainted, passed gradually through her hands. She read them with avidity and infinite pleasure, but it would be in vain to attempt describing the effect produced on her ardent imagination by Pope's letter of Eloisa to Abelard.[1] In every passage she discovered sentiments of which she felt herself susceptible, and to experience, even during a short interval, the tenderness, the passion, the transports of Eloisa, she thought would be cheaply purchased by a life of torture.

Fatal illusion! which was still more fatally augmented when she heard the eloquent, the pathetic voice of Belfield, repeat the tenderest, the most impassioned lines of that dangerous poem. When she dwelt enraptured on his melodious accents and marked in his eye, now brilliant with enthusiasm, now melting in tears, the sudden transitions from love to despair, which the poet has painted in traits of fire.

As thus she wept the sorrows of Eloisa, when all her sensibility was awakened and her soul trembled on her lips, Belfield caught her emotions, and borne away by their violence he sunk at her feet, and addressed to his sweet auditress strains as passionate as those which had excited their transport. Surprised, confused, Laura felt that her tears flowed no longer for imaginary pains. Her heart gave him credence, and throbbed, as she hung over him, with sensations of the purest affection!

---

[1] Alexander Pope, "Eloisa to Abelard" (1717); see Appendix B.

CHAPTER VIII

Great and extraordinary were the changes produced in Laura by her new situation. Stepping from the chill circle in which her heart had been confined; rising from the grave of her mother, over which she had wept in hopeless sorrow; a new world of feeling opened before her; a new and dazzling creation burst on her astonished view.

The soul of Laura was formed for love. By the hand of love she had been cherished from her birth, and now love in its most seducing form, spread his rosy influence around her. She yielded without restraint to that influence, and followed her vagrant fancy through regions of unimagined bliss.

Cheerful as the dreams of infancy were the images that floated in her mind, and fair her hopes as those which gild life's dawn. Her heart beat high with transport. Her thoughts ranged freely in the boundless regions of intellectual existence, and her sentiments flowed warm and unrestrained into the bosom of her lover, whom the torrent of her ideas, as novel as they were original, astonished and delighted. Of the world she knew nothing but what she had learned from books. With those books Belfield had supplied her. From him she derived her improvement, and to him she returned her acquired ideas, newly modified and embellished by all the imagery with which a glowing fancy adorns an interesting subject.

Wrapped in enchanting illusions her life was a continued trance; love's soft visions danced before her; she saw, she heard, she thought of nought but Belfield. On him she rested, to him she listened, for him she studied; nothing had value but in its relation to him.

Often alone with her face resting on her hands, she passed whole hours repeating the lines she had heard him recite, and retracing on the tablets of her memory every look, every word, every movement of her friend. At church amid the organ's swelling tones, she heard his voice only; with the prayers she offered up for her mother, some sighs for Belfield were mingled; at the altar's foot, where she kneeled in humble adoration, her thoughts still strayed to him, and she could have said with Eloisa,

"Not on the cross my eyes were fixed, but you."[1]

The longer Belfield knew Laura the more he was forced to admire her; the flights of her genius not unfrequently surprized him, and he was often delighted with the charms of her imagination. He had himself enriched it, yet dazzled by its brilliant coruscations, he bowed involuntarily before the work of his own hands.

"I am your creature," Laura would say to him, "before I knew you all around me was darkness and desolation; the morning brought no gladness to my heart, the shades of evening cast only an additional gloom over my sufferings; by what magic have you wrought this change? how in your presence has

"Grief forgot to groan, and love to weep?"[2]

Still I weep, but not in sadness, still I regret, but my grief is without pangs!"

If Belfield heard not these questions with stoical equanimity; if his answers were impressed on the rosy lips of Laura, we must remember that Belfield was only twenty, and that he had never loved before.

CHAPTER IX

A celebrated German poet says, that the purest delights of love bring us too near the condition of immortals to admit duration; and unfortunately for poor Laura this observation proved true in the instance before us.

A young Englishman, whom business brought frequently to her step-father's house, saw her, was pleased with her, requested permission to visit her, which was readily granted, and after a few interviews asked her for his wife.

Her stepfather, whom a confirmed consumption, with slow but certain progress, brought daily nearer to his grave, rejoiced at the idea of seeing Laura established before his death, and told her of the

---

[1] Pope, "Eloisa," line 116.
[2] Adapted from Pope, "Eloisa," line 314.

proposal in a tone that conveyed his certainty of her approbation. She heard him with suppressed but inconceivable horror. Her acquaintance with Belfield was unknown; she did not dare to plead a prior attachment, yet; with her heart devoted to him, to become the wife of another was impossible. Overpowered by the shock she remained silent. This silence was ascribed to her youth and timidity, and no idea being entertained by her offering any objection, the marriage was concluded on and an early period mentioned for its celebration.

Wild with anguish, Laura sought in vain in her own mind for a refuge from the terror that awaited her. To resist the will of a dying father was beyond her power, and to doom herself to never-ending misery by complying with it, was an idea not to be endured. She loved Belfield to idolatry, and turned with disgust from the idea of belonging to another.

When in a voice almost unintelligible by weeping, she related to Belfield, the unfortunate occurrence; not less agitated than herself, he swore that he would not suffer her to be disposed of against her inclination. "You must quit this house," he exclaimed, "I will find you an asylum, and take upon myself the care of your happiness."

The drooping heart of Laura was comforted by these assurances of affection, which supported her as she attended her stepfather, who was on the brink of dissolution. Several weeks elapsed in the torture of suspense, and his increasing danger made it probable that the fatal moment would be deferred; at length, however, a day was fixed for her marriage, but on that very day, her stepfather died.

Laura was now free. No creature on earth had a right to control her; no being could force her to a marriage her soul abhorred; yet whilst indulging her grief, which the death of a friend never fails to awaken in a bosom of sensibility, she forgot the danger to which she had been exposed, and remembered only, the kindness of him who had so long supplied to her, the place of a parent. But the officiousness of her intended husband soon roused her to a sense of her real situation, the pains of which were not lessened when informed by her relatives that she had no other protection to expect than that of the gentleman who had been approved of by her father.

Belfield employed, during this painful interval, to console her, all the tenderness, all the persuasion, of Love. "Be comforted my poor girl," he said, whilst pressing to his bosom her pensive head, "consign your fate to me, and whilst I live, your happiness shall be dearer to me than my own."

Laura, without friends, without resource, had no alternative between marrying a man whom she loved not at all, and against whom, her reason found objections, not less weighty than those of her heart, or flying to the protection of him, whom she loved with all her soul. She hesitated, she doubted, she was lost in embarrassment and uncertainty, but at length her feelings and the entreaties of Belfield prevailed. She consented to meet him the following evening not far from her home; a home to which she was no longer held by any ties of sentiment or of duty, and which she now resolved to abandon forever.

The intervening hours were passed in the most tormenting conflicts. Agitated by fear, yet supported by hope, her mind was restless, though she flew from reflection, and sought courage in recollecting the many virtues of her friend, and the sincerity of his attachment.

With trembling steps she left her house at the appointed hour. Belfield was waiting for her in a chaise.[1] They drove to the habitation of a respectable farmer, where he had engaged lodgings, and there, lulled into delusive tranquillity, she forgot, in the presence of the man she adored, that a step however apparently harmless, if incorrect, leads invariably to ruin and destruction.

CHAPTER X

The flight of Laura occasioned some alarm; for though among her connexions few were interested for her happiness, yet, as her acquaintance with Belfield was wholly unknown, and the seclusion in which she had lived rendered any improper intercourse highly improbable, no satisfactory conjecture could be formed on the occasion.

Laura, safe in her retreat, with all her hopes built on a basis which she thought could not be shaken, felt happy. She loved, she was loved, and her romantic imagination was filled with visions of unfading felicity.

But the bosom of Belfield was often visited by less welcome

---

[1]   Any of various light open carriages, often with a collapsible hood, especially a two-wheeled carriage drawn by one horse.

guests. His family, once opulent, had become victims of misfortune. His parents were dead and he depended for his actual subsistence, and the expenses of his professional education, on a brother who was not rich. Thus situated he had felt uneasiness, even during the first days of his intercourse with Laura, on observing that the interest he had created in her bosom daily gained strength and ripened by degrees into the most sincere and ardent attachment: but now, when he saw that she depended on him solely, with all the bonds that joined her to society severed; when he reflected that he had prevented her marriage, and thus rendered himself responsible for her fate; the importance of the task, and the insufficiency of his means, for moments appalled him.

Soon, however, he found relief in the energies of his mind, and the consciousness of the rectitude of his intentions. Returning to his studies with increased application, he justly hoped ere long to be able to suffice to his own wants and those of the amiable being to whom he had devoted his existence.

Laura lived in a small farm-house on the heights near Germantown which border on the Wissahickon; and whilst climbing, attended by Belfield, the rocks through which this wild little stream forces its boisterous way, her fancy winged its flight through regions of anticipated happiness, not less romantic, though less real than the scenery that surrounded her.

Through the avenues of hope she beheld every coming hour gilded by the affection of Belfield. Love twined round her brow unfading roses, and strewed her path with undecaying sweets.

She passed the day in reading the books Belfield brought to increase her intellectual stores. In the evening she flew down the hills to meet him as he came from town; her heart beat quicker at his approach; her hands were stretched ere he could meet their touch to welcome his arrival.

Alas, poor girl! why were you placed in this strange world with nought but a heart, overflowing with sensibility, to oppose the dangers that beset your way; why did destruction approach you in a form so fair that even from suspecting it of ill you would have shrunk as from a crime!

CHAPTER XI

It was early in the spring when Laura had taken possession of her lodgings with the farmer. Belfield pursued his studies in town, but went every afternoon to see her.

Exquisitely happy was this interval of purity and peace the fleeting hours of which succeeded each other, ushered in by hope, and led on by joys which no regret embittered. My heart delights to dwell on them and bleeds when reflecting that they were harbingers of error and of pain; for Laura was a creature of sentiment; she extended not her views beyond the passing moment, nor ever cast one look on the world of reality, from that ideal, the enchanting world, which her fancy and the love of Belfield had created around her.[1] Deprived of parents and of friends, no one taught her to distinguish the visions of a luxuriant imagination from the soberer pleasures which life affords and reason sanctions! no one shewed her the tranquil path of virtue, nor warned her of the dangers of that into which love now lured her.

Belfield intended no wrong, but Laura was beautiful, and both were glowing with youth and health; both felt the power of the same irresistible impulse. Their walks were solitary; their meetings without intrusion; nature in the finest season shed over them her magic influence. Yet many weeks elapsed ere love's last tribute was demanded, and when at length the fatal moment arrived, the deepest shades of night veiled Laura's blushes!

The intoxicating excess of rapture steeped in delirium the senses of Belfield and shielded him, for a season, from the stings of regret. He was too much affected when approaching Laura to reflect, and nothing but endless transport seemed to hover round the retreat which she embellished. For such was her form that love himself would not have hesitated to choose it for a model of his most perfect votary; and in her face, the faithful image of her soul, the softest shades of her sentiments and all the energy of her feelings were equally legible.

Twining round the object of her idolatry, she felt the inadequacy of language to express her emotions, and thought it arose from some

---

[1] This is the most overt occasion of authorial intervention, when the narrator speaks directly to the reader and refers to herself in first-person, a common device in eighteenth-century fiction.

fault inherent to herself. "Teach me, she would sometimes say to him, teach me I pray you, to describe the happiness I feel, to paint the sensations of insupportable delight that overwhelm me, whilst thus I listen to you; 'tis you I know, who spread this charm around me, for when you are away, all is different, all is cold and cheerless. If I walk beneath these shades alone I only feel that you are absent; if I take a book I close it soon in sadness, for I can enjoy no pleasure which you do not share."

Yet amid this artless prattle, beneath these shades which Laura's love enlivened, Belfield felt that he had wronged her. All her extraordinary qualities, all that rendered her eminently lovely, added to his regret. But he resolved, in his inmost soul, to unite his destiny to hers by legal ties, and thus repair his fault ere she was aware of the ills to which she was exposed. In that intended reparation he sought refuge from his pangs, and excuse for the unhallowed pleasures in which he continued to indulge.

CHAPTER XII

The summer passed on in mutual transport. Autumn approached, and with it the yellow-fever made its appearance in Philadelphia.[1] Laura heard of the desolation it spread, and though the accounts of it were exaggerated by Belfield, who laughed at all idea of personal danger, they filled her with uneasiness.

The physician with whom Belfield studied was one of the very few who fled not from their post in the hour of danger. Many of his students fell victim to the dire disease, and Belfield also caught at length the infection. His friends, as was too generally the case, abandoned him to the care of a negro on the first appearance of the disorder, and left the city.[2] The violence of the attack rendered him incapable of giving coherent orders; his ravings therefore, about Laura,

---

[1] Yellow fever epidemics occurred periodically in Philadelphia in the 1790s. The yellow fevers of 1793 and 1798 were especially severe. As many as 5,000 people died in 1793. The disease, often fatal, was associated with the arrival of refugees from Saint Domingue. All who could—the wealthy—fled the city during epidemics.

[2] Black Philadelphians were thought to be immune to yellow fever and were recruited as nurses and coffin bearers throughout the epidemic. See Appendix C.

excited no attention. Meanwhile all the pangs of suspense preyed upon the bosom of this unhappy girl. The first day of her lover's absence she passed in inquietude; the second in torture, which on the third became so insupportable that she set out on foot to seek him.

On the road she met numbers of people, some in carts, some walking, who seemed to fly in confusion from the town. Near the footpath she observed a young lad endeavoring to raise on a bank an aged woman, perhaps his mother, who had just fallen to the ground; he had scarcely succeeded when she uttered a heart-piercing groan and expired. Not far from them sat a female shrieking in agony over a child that had just died on her knees. The people from the town, their faces pale with terror, kept the opposite side of the road, and hastened on as if the place breathed infection.

Laura shuddered passing on. She had not walked far when she was stopped by a voice from beneath a fence. It was a young woman dressed in black, who begged for God's sake for a drop of water. At her feet sat a child crying bitterly; at her breast hung another, who seemed with languid eyes to supplicate that sustenance the exhausted bosom could no longer supply.

Laura's soul was wrung, as she flew to a neighboring house to seek the water so piteously demanded. A man who stood on the porch bade her begone, saying he would suffer nobody from town near his house. "I am not from town, she said, but there is a poor creature fainting on the road, and I only come to beg of you a little water." He threw her a tin mug and pointing to the well shut the door and disappeared. Laura was shocked by his brutality, but filled the mug and hastened back to the suffering woman, who seized it with eagerness and seemed refreshed by the draught.

Evening was near when Laura reached the town. Far from perceiving the accustomed bustle, scarcely any moving object met her eye. The streets were deserted; the wharves, usually resembling a forest of masts, were naked; three-fourths of the houses shut up. From some of these the dismal howling of dogs, forgotten in the hurry of removal, was heard; from others the groans of the dying, deserted by their faithless attendants. Half-starved cats ran about at a loss for a home, and many were lying dead on the pavement. The air was stagnant. Throughout the whole city a musty atmosphere prevailed like that of a vast building which has remained long unopened. Carts only broke with their rumbling the wide-spread solitude. Some of them, loaded with coffins, were driven with speed, as if their contents could not be quickly enough committed to the earth; whilst others, more slowly moving, presented to the affrighted view the emaciated forms of dying creatures, either motionless extended on the straw, or tearing their hair with frantic gestures and painful shrieks, endeavoring to escape from the vehicle where they were forcibly detained.

Laura terrified hastened on, but turning a corner a new scene of desolation met her eye. A door opened suddenly, and a boisterous landlord, giving directions to some people within exclaimed with anger: "Take him off; I will have none with this fever in my house." At the same moment two men came out bearing a third who appeared on the point of breathing his last. They carried him towards a cart that stood at some distance,—a young woman, with her hair in disorder, and her clothes half torn off, rushed with wild cries from an inner apartment, and seizing the arm of Laura, said in a tone of distraction: "Help, in pity! help me to tear from these wretches my husband;—they bear him to the grave whilst still living!" With a grasp of madness she drew Laura after her, but seeing the men had reached the cart, she loosed her hold, and with the swiftness of lightning flew to join them.

Poor Laura, trembling supported herself with difficulty. A deepened sadness oppressed her soul, and she sunk, exhausted by fatigue and terror, on the marble steps of a house she was passing. But only for a moment did she yield to the weakness that stole on her senses. The recollection of Belfield soon dispelled the lethargy, and roused her to exertion: "Three days have passed since I beheld him," she exclaimed, "and in three days!—Oh God!"

She reached his dwelling. A little negro boy who knew her opened the door; all within was still and gloomy. Without replying to her questions, he led the way to the chamber of his master, and there she beheld the object of her dearest affections, whom so late she had seen glowing with all the ardor of youth, resplendent with all the bloom of beauty, stretched on a couch, pale and exanimate.

His sallow cheek confessed the direful touch of disease. His inflamed eyes rolled with an expression of wildness in their hollow orbits, and rested on Laura without giving a sign of recognition.

Laura gazed appalled on the dreadful spectacle; then overcome with surprise and horror sunk down by his bedside, and found in total insensibility a short suspension of her pain.

When life and consciousness returned she arose, hung over her suffering friend with indescribable anguish, and bedewed his pillow with a torrent of tears.

Determined to leave him no more, she tried with unremitting assiduity every expedient that could procure him relief or comfort, administered herself the remedies prescribed by his physician, and watched with sleepless eye every change in his disorder.

Five days passed on in doubt and agony; but at length Belfield's constitution, the skill of his physician, and the care of Laura prevailed. On the morning of the sixth, awakening from a slumber which had been tranquil, his calmer looks met her tearful eye, and returning reason faintly shone in the glance.

The sudden flow of hope that rushed through Laura's heart, checked by the fear of its being illusory, was almost insupportable. She sunk down by his bed-side; his languid hand pressed her throbbing forehead,—"Is it thee, my poor Laura!" he said, "Has thy love followed me to the bed of sickness, and preserved my life?"

Trembling lest the slightest exertion should prove injurious, Laura laid her fingers on his lips, and with a look of irresistible entreaty, besought him to be tranquil. Belfield smiling obeyed, and fell asleep on her bosom. No feverish starts renewed her apprehensions, no deep drawn groans harrowed up her soul;—sweet and invigorating was his repose, and in the evening he was pronounced out of danger.

CHAPTER XIII

During the languor of convalescence, removed from every pursuit that could divert his attention from Laura, Belfield became more sensible of her goodness. He observed with inward delight, the unbounded extent of her devotion to him, the ardor of that attachment which had rendered her unmindful of danger when attending him in his illness, but above all he admired the purity of her confidence, of her reliance on his truth, unclouded by doubt, untainted by suspicion! His heart paid ample homage to her worth. He saw that in Laura he possessed no common object; he felt that in the face of the world he might be proud to call her his; and he vowed to exert all the powers of his soul to contribute to her happiness;—to consecrate to her a life which he justly regarded as a gift from her hands. Daily were these vows repeated, as he listened to the story of her sufferings during his illness, or heard her endeavour though in vain, to express her joy at his recovery.

When they sometimes threw from their window a glance into the street, or listened to the heavy sound of the hearse as it rattled hastily along, she recollected the shocking occurrences of the evening she had entered the city, and wept for the fate of the wretched beings whose misery she had found herself without means of relieving.

The image of the poor woman by the road-side with her children, continually pursued her. "What has become of the unfortunate little creatures!" she frequently exclaimed. "My heart reproaches me with having left them too soon: yet what could I do, when urged on by apprehension for your safety? And then the frantic woman who followed her husband, with what pain I think of her! why did they not suffer him to die in peace?—why did they barbarously tear him from his home?"

Belfield sought to divert her attention from these melancholy subjects, yet could not cease to wonder when he reflected on the strength of mind, which had supported her through such accumulated horrors. A young creature who had seldom stepped beyond her domestic precincts, thus to rush boldly thro' pestilence and death to perform the sad duties of a nurse to her lover, was a picture indelibly impressed on his mind, and continually before him.

Often, pressing him to her bosom, she said: "If my fate had been like that of so many who now deplore the loss of those they love? if to the grave—but no! all that consoled me was the certainty, in that event, of breathing my last on your lips. Now how different! All is peace,—for you are out of danger."

Again did the glow of transport spread its vivid colours on her cheek, again did her heart beat high and full of gladness when she saw her beloved recover his beauty and his strength; when she heard him bounding towards her with his wonted elasticity. Her gaiety knew no bounds; she played round him with the sprightliness of a happy child, and exerted to please him all her amusing powers.

Led by her creative genius through regions which a warm imagination decorated with endless charms, she once more saw before her nothing but uninterrupted joys. With Belfield by her side, his arm encircling her waist, had she a wish ungratified? Could Laura anticipate misfortune when she was loved by Belfield, was his and was happy?

CHAPTER XIV

The fever, which had so long isolated Philadelphia, began to disappear, and the inhabitants, who had flown from its ravages, returned again to their deserted dwellings.

Belfield unexpectedly received word that his family were coming, and it became necessary at once to find an asylum for Laura.

The people with whom she had lived, in the country, had disposed of their rooms for the winter; she was therefore again to seek an abode among strangers, and it was not easily to be found.

Belfield, concealing from Laura his embarrassment, told her that he intended taking her in the evening to a house in a retired part of the city, where she would be perfectly at her ease, till he could procure lodgings in the country, which they both preferred. At dusk he conducted her to the place he had mentioned. They were shewn into a neatly furnished room, and as in all places, in all possible situations, Laura, if near Belfield, was incapable of fear, she expressed only surprise at the various sounds of tumultuous merriment that reached her ear from the apartments below.

Early in the morning Belfield said he was going to leave her, and desired her on no account to go out of the room, where he said she would be furnished with every thing necessary. When she expressed some reluctance at being left alone in a strange place, he replied that he should set off immediately for the country to seek a retreat to which he would conduct her in the evening. He then repeated his former request, and hurried away.

A silence so profound reigned in the house during the morning, that Laura could scarcely believe it was the same in which she had heard so much boisterous mirth the evening before. Towards noon a servant girl brought in her breakfast. Laura felt no appetite, and passed the day reading a book she had brought with her.

As the shades of evening began to obscure her little apartment, she listened with anxiety to every noise, continually expecting to hear the welcome footsteps of Belfield. As it grew later her uneasiness increased; at last somebody approached her door, but it was not Belfield. A ruddy faced woman of monstrous size entered, and accosted her with gross familiarity.

"You must excuse me for leaving you all day alone, she said, in a coarse masculine voice, and to tell you the truth I forgot you. But it is a pity to sit moping here; come down and dine with my family which happens to be pretty numerous at present, and we shall all try to cheer you."

Laura, shrinking from the vulgarity of this disgusting figure, which she had never seen equalled, excused herself from going down. The woman laughingly insisted; then approaching Laura, raised the hair which shaded her neck and forehead, and, examining her with rudness, said, "well you are really very pretty: ay ay, George knows how to choose.—Come you must go down with me, why are you so shy?"

The disgust of Laura was excited to an intolerable degree, when the impertinent woman continued mysteriously: "Perhaps you are afraid of Eliza? But she does not know who brought you here, or she would have scratched your eyes out before this. No no, every body knows that what they trust me with goes no further. I have the confidence of many people, which I should scorn to betray, and though I have a great friendship for Eliza, I have not given her the slightest hint of your having come here with George Belfield."

"Eliza!" asked the astonished Laura,—"Who is Eliza? What have I to fear from Eliza?"

"Why Eliza is a very pretty girl who has the folly to be in love with Belfield, and has refused many opportunities of bettering her fortune for his sake. Nobody can get a word from her when Belfield is by: though in truth the whim seems lately to be wearing off."

Had thunder fallen at the feet of Laura; had the earth yawned beneath her, less violent would have been her emotions!—A husband who hears that his idolized wife indulges in a licentious passion to the most criminal excess; a father, who learns that his only child, abused and abandoned by some seductive villain, is cast deserted on the world's stage,

"Where those of public fame, insulting hail her, sister!"[1]

cannot feel pangs more agonizing than those that pierced her heart at the story of the fiend-like woman. Her whole frame shook convulsively, and turning away from the odious discourse, she sunk back on the chair from which she had risen.

The landlady was surprised into momentary silence by such an unexpected agitation, but soon recovering, she sought by raillery to end a scene which she thought highly ridiculous.

"Why this is worse than Eliza!" she exclaimed, "are you fool enough to think that Belfield has no mistress but you?"

The tears of Laura ceased to flow. A confused idea of her relation to Belfield, rushed for the first time through her breast. "His mistress!" she thought, "alas! even to that degrading title I have no claim, for here he abandons me to insult and danger!"

The woman, who had not ceased talking, judged, from the silence of Laura, that her remonstrances had produced the desired effect; and repeated the invitation to accompany her below. "Why would you sit moping here?" she said, "why spoil your face with crying?— Such a figure as yours will soon have admirers enough. And then this beautiful hair! why there is fortune lurking in every ringlet."

"For heaven's sake," said Laura wildly, "leave me: only suffer me to remain alone till Belfield returns!" She trembled as she pronounced his name.

"Till Belfield returns!" replied the woman, "why he may not return in a week. He has often promised Eliza to return, and she has not seen him for a month after!—We thought he had some new object in view; and as he has succeeded, you may easily believe that he is in pursuit of another."

The air of raillery with which this remark was uttered, and the too pointed allusion to herself it contained, shook the soul of Laura: to

---

[1]   Adapted from John Armstrong (1709–79), *The Oeconomy of Love. A Poetical Essay* (1736), lines 375–77. *The Oeconomy of Love* is a sex manual for newlyweds and was frequently reprinted throughout the eighteenth century. Armstrong advises against masturbation and premarital sex. He cautions young men not to encourage the affections of women of "abject birth, dishonourable, and mind/Incultivate or vicious." But, if children should result from premarital sex, he urges young men to "Let them be kindly welcom'd to the day" and to "Learn parent virtues." Armstrong was also a physician and he is most widely remembered for his four volume *The Art of Preserving Health* (1744). See Appendix B.

free herself from the impertinence of her tormentor she complained of a violent headache, and begged to be excused from going below, at least till she felt better. The woman softened by this apparent composure, told her to lie down till tea time, and not to be afflicted at occurrences so common as those she had mentioned. Then tapping her on the shoulder, she bade her take comfort, and assured her that nobody should disturb her till evening, when she would come up again herself.

CHAPTER XV

The power of thinking was suspended, and fortunate would it have been for Laura if the power of feeling had been suspended also; she sat motionless and stupefied till roused by the increasing noise from below.

The whole house seemed in confusion; frequent steps passed her apartment. At one time she heard loud bursts of laughter, at another horrid execrations, which were uttered by female voices, and filled her with terror.

"Where am I," she said, "into what den of horror have I been betrayed? oh that I was in the street, for surely I should be safer anywhere else than within these walls!"

She opened the door softly, hoping to steal away unobserved, but perceiving that staircase lighted, and the entry full of people whose looks she dreaded to meet, she shut it again, disappointed and hopeless, and a torrent of tears rushed down her cheeks.

Scarcely was she seated when the tormenting woman again made her appearance,

"Well," she said laughing, "I have returned as I promised, to bring you down; and, fearing you should refuse me, this gentleman has come to join his intreaties to mine; he has not often been unsuccessful."

The gentleman advanced towards Laura whose averted face rested on the back of her chair; he took her hand, which she quickly withdrew; he put his arm round her waist, but she disengaged herself with a sudden start, and her hair falling back discovered a face overspread with deathlike paleness.

Disconcerted by this appearance, and feeling perhaps some emotions of pity, the intruder attempted to speak, but was interrupted by the woman, who, conceiving herself in the way, said, with a significant smile, "well, I must leave you, but you are in good hands, and I dare say will thank me for having brought you so agreeable an acquaintance."

As she turned to put down the light, Laura darted towards the door, flew down the stairs, and in an instant was in the street. She urged her flight with the fleetness of a fawn, and fancied she heard in every sound the steps of a pursuer, nor stopped till obliged by want of breath to check the rapidity of her motion.

Among the variety of sensations that agitated her bosom the satisfaction of feeling herself free predominated. Her disordered mind dwelt on no determined place of refuge, and she continued to hasten forward with no other view than to increase her safety.

After a while she found herself in the fields, surrounded by solitude, fatigued and bewildered. An intuitive desire of security turned her steps towards some lights she saw at a distance, and the thought of the horrors she had just escaped from re-animated her strength. Thus she hurried on, till exhausted by the violence of her exertion, she sunk upon a heap of stones that obstructed her way. There, as recollection struggled with the benumbing power of despondency, and the state-house clock, beginning to strike, announced the advanced hour of the night; its deep-toned sounds awakened suddenly in her breast a new train of feelings, and presented to her mind new images.

CHAPTER XVI

Laura had been raised from her earliest infancy in the neighbourhood of the state-house. Its clock had always been the measure of her pains, the herald of her pleasures; with what anxious impatience had she counted the hours assigned to her lessons or her task, with what delight had she often hailed the return of those which released her from the confinement of school, or called her to a walk with her mother.

With the rapidity of thought, the little events of her early life passed before her; but all her soul dwelt on the period of her mother's illness. At that time particularly had she watched the clock, for it regulated the duties of her attendance at the bedside of her mother, and often with impatience had she marked the slow progress of the lingering night, for she hoped, though vainly, that the coming dawn would bring a favourable change.

Every word, every look of her mother was remembered. She saw her suffering, she heard the interrupted half-broken exclamations of endearment which sink so deep into a feeling heart; felt the full force of her affection in the last effort of her enclosing arms.

The profoundest silence reigned around her while she was thus sunk in reverie, but the darkness began gradually to disappear and objects were rendered discernable by the moon's soft light. Turning her head she recognized the spot where she lay, she saw before her, on the opposite side of the way, the very house in which she had passed the days of her childhood in innocence and peace, she saw the trees beneath whose shade she had sported.

Raising herself on her knees and extending her arms toward the lonely dwelling, she cried, "there, in that house I was fostered by a mother's love; there, beneath that shaded window I caught the last blessing that trembled on the lips of my expiring mother! Sainted being where art thou? hast thou forgotten the promise so solemnly given in that awful moment, that thy spirit should protect from danger thy deserted child?—

"There on that hallowed spot, thy soul soaring beyond the reach of human woe sought an asylum with its God; and here, bowed to the earth, thy wretched daughter knows not where to lay her weary head!"

At this moment, the noise of approaching footsteps reached her ear. Alarmed, she arose and glided along the state-house wall, still weeping, still thinking of her mother; nor stopped till she had reached the church yard where rested her loved remains. The slight enclosure offered no obstacle; she passed it easily, and bent her way amid the silent inhabitants of the dead, toward the well-known grave. The white marble that marked it, reflecting the moon beams, directed her steps, and as she drew near, all the faculties of her soul were raised to frenzy.

Kneeling by the grass-covered hillock, she pressed with her icy lips the sod, wet with the dews of midnight: then falling to the ground, she exclaimed, "I come, dearest mother!—open thy cold bosom—receive thy child!"

CHAPTER XVII

About an hour after the escape of Laura from the abominable house, Belfield returned to seek her. At the door he met Eliza, that Eliza whose name had been productive of so much distress. She seized his arm, hung on him fondly, and appeared to think his visit had been intended for herself.

Acquainted with her violent temper and fearing to excite her curiosity by entering the house, he spoke to her kindly, and made some excuses for the neglect of which she complained.

Eliza, young and beautiful, but born in poverty and unsupported by the advantages of education, had been seduced and abandoned by one of those rapacious prowlers who seek in the destruction of innocence, the only gratification their sated appetites can relish.

Ah why will man, more ruthless than the beast of the forest, employ each wile to destroy that virtue to which his heart yields in involuntary homage! why with fiend-like art seek to sully that purity, the charm of which he is obliged to acknowledge?—Why divest his idol of its brightest ornament, and then regard it with contempt?

Rapid had been the fall of Eliza: yet in the high road of dissipation she preserved a secret wish for that happiness which her misfortunes placed beyond her reach, and under the veil of apparent gaiety, regret and sorrow were the real inmates of her breast.

Among the crowd of admirers her youth and beauty attracted, she had seen Belfield, and, struck by his superior merit, had conceived an affection for him sincere and ardent, which she fondly indulged, being proud of having saved some unadulterated feelings from the general wreck of her hopes and prospects.

Belfield had yielded without resistance to the influence of her charms, and mistaken the fever of the senses for the language of the heart. But tranquil possession soon convinced him of his error, and when she haughtily demanded her due, those attentions which had been continued only from pity, the spell that bound him to the enchantress was in a moment dissolved. Yet when Eliza wept he could not resist her tears; when she supplicated it had not been in his power to refuse her a few hours of that society, which alone, she said, rendered her life supportable.

Thus by indulging, he encouraged a passion, which he hoped

some other object would soon efface, till he became acquainted with Laura. Then for the first time he loved, and Eliza was neglected, and the world itself forgotten.

When the sudden return of his family rendered it necessary to remove Laura from his house, Belfield had recollected a woman who lived in a retired part of the city with whom he had become acquainted during his intercourse with Eliza, and who with great privacy let her apartments for any purpose, provided she was well paid. Not knowing how much the character of her establishment had changed, and that it was now the seat of the greatest disorder, he had conducted Laura thither and left her to seek a better retreat.

On his return he was surprised to meet Eliza; still more so to learn that she had been an inmate of this house for several weeks, and his embarrassment became extreme when she continued to reproach him with having become a stranger to all that concerned her, and pressed him to accompany her into the parlour. He was seeking his mind for some means of escaping from her, when she mentioned that a most romantic adventure had occurred that evening. "Somebody brought here last night a young girl, and very judiciously left her to the care of our landlady, who never thought of her charge till we were all assembled at dinner. She then ran up to apologize for her neglect and to bring her down, but the girl refused to appear, and the old lady returned quite charmed with her new guest.

"Towards evening, when she was again speaking of her, one of our constant visitors, who is always in search of new faces came in, and fired by the description of the stranger, requested to be allowed to see her. I suppose the request was enforced in the usual way, for after a few minutes of whispering, the woman consented, and taking a light went with him up stairs. I was walking in the passage, curious to know how the affair would terminate. Judge of my surprise when, after some minutes her door opened, and the most beautiful figure flew down stairs apparently without touching them, glided by me and was out of sight in an instant."

Belfield had been in torture during this recital, till unable to resist the violence of his emotions—"'Twas Laura," he cried, "it was Laura! eternal curses light on the wretch who dared offend her."

Tearing himself from Eliza, he ran to the room where he had left Laura in the morning; her hat was on the bed; her shawl and gloves lay on the floor, but she was not there. Frantic with rage he sought the infernal landlady, and seizing her by the huge arm, enquired what had become of the young lady.

The affrighted woman attempted to speak; but he heard her not! Urged by some remorse and anxiety he rushed from the house, and ranging through the streets, was at a loss whither to direct his search. He knew Laura had no friend from whom she could ask a shelter. He knew there was no door that would be open to receive her. "She has been driven to despair," he exclaimed, "by insult and outrage; perhaps even now she perishes, and her last words accuse me of having ruined, and then abandoned her to destruction."

Ten thousand deaths lurked in that dreadful thought. Every place that had been dear to Laura he visited. He walked round her house. He hastened through the adjoining squares. He even sought her on the banks of the Schuylkill, on that spot where he had first beheld her, and returned again mechanically towards her once-loved home.

'Twas the sound of his footstep that had fallen on her ear. It was from him that, by an unfortunate fatality, she had flown; from him who would have sacrificed his life to meet her, to see her in safety and obtain her forgiveness.

The dawn of day found Belfield still erring about, engaged in the fruitless pursuit. Hopeless at last he returned to his house, and justice itself might have received the pangs which tore his bosom, as a sufficient atonement for his imprudence.

CHAPTER XVIII

There prevails in our mind, at every period of our lives, some prominent ideas, by which, like so many pillars, the whole fabric of our thoughts and feelings, of our wishes and our prospects, is upheld and supported. Shake them and the whole superstructure totters: remove them and it tumbles into chaotic confusion; leaving us lost in the sensations of nothingness, and weary of an existence which seems no longer to have any end or object.

Such was the state of Laura on the approach of the day. She still lay prostrate on the earth that covered the grave of her mother. Her snowy arms were extended on the damp grass. Her long black hair floated in wild disorder among the clods, and mingled with the dust, when the chilling breezes, which precede the dawn in the month of October, pierced and awoke her from that insensibility, by which beneficent nature sometimes rescues her favorites from the baleful effects of some delirious frenzy.

Belfield unfaithful! Belfield loving another! these were the first obtruding impressions. Benumbed by the cold, she fancied that death was coming to steal her from her woes, and a feeble sentiment, resembling pleasure, hailed the dread messenger of peace.

But he approached her not; a rude grasp seized and raised her from the ground. She opened her eyes and saw an aged man, who, holding a spade in one hand, supported her with the other. Terrified at his appearance, she uttered a shriek and fell in his arms.

He was a grave digger, who had come at this early hour to prepare a last abode for some child of mortality. The white gown of Laura had attracted his notice, and her immoveable posture had led him to think she was dead. As he held her, and looked on her pale face, pity for so young a creature, so unfortunate as she appeared to be, warmed his breast and he determined to carry her to his home.

At the door of the hut he inhabited, his wife met him with an exclamation of wonder. "Be quiet," said the good man, "and help me to restore this poor thing if it is not too late."

As they laid her on the bed she sighed deeply. "Thank god," he cried, "she is not dead;" and having made her drink a cup of coffee, which the old woman had brought: "Come child, he said, let me cover you up warmly, by and by you will be able to tell us how you came in such a sad plight."

These words of kindness fell like balm on the wounded heart of Laura. She pressed the hand of the benevolent stranger and attempted to reply, but was too weak to give utterance to her feelings. A tear of gratitude, more eloquent than words, dropped from her languid eye, while soothed by the friendly care bestowed upon her, she forgot her sorrows and sunk to sleep.

The old man then related to his wife the manner in which he had found her. The delicacy of her appearance, and the fineness of her clothing bespoke her of no common order of beings; the peculiar circumstances attending her excited all their curiosity.

The woman insisted that she was crazy, and that they ought to take her to the hospital. Her husband was of a different opinion, and thought it would be time enough to dispose of her, when they had learned more of her story.

CHAPTER XIX

The setting sun already cast his last faint rays on the horizon, when Laura, awakening from her lengthened sleep, raised herself up on the pillow and fixed her eyes on the old man who was sitting at the bed-side, and whose face she at first endeavored vainly to recollect.

"Well really you have slept finely," said he cheerfully, "come take a little tea that my old woman kept warm for you, and then tell us what we can do to serve you." She took the offered cup, and as she sipped the tea, the old man asked, if she had no friends to whom she wished to send. "Alas," she replied, "I have no friends; I passed last night upon my mother's grave, because the earth contains no spot where I could claim a shelter, where I could seek for pity, or expect repose."

"Poor thing, poor thing," said the old man, "what will you do? We are so poor, and your appearance shows that you have been accustomed to high life; you could not content yourself beneath our lowly shed."

"My good friend," answered Laura, "you are mistaken. I have always been poor; but I cannot think of burthening you with my distress, and even now my heart aches at the thought of my having nothing but thanks to offer for your goodness."

"Nor would we take anything more," he replied, "for the trifling service we have rendered you. But see," he continued, "it grows dark; if you will stay here to night, you are heartily welcome, if not, and you intend going away, go before it is too late, and if you desire it I will go with you."

Laura cast a melancholy glance around the small apartment, and saw too clearly the inconvenience a protracted stay would cause to her kind entertainer. Yet whither to go, she knew not; till by torturing her memory she recollected a person who had nursed her mother during her last illness, and to whom she had often done little acts of kindness. With her she thought herself sure of meeting a friendly reception, and determined at once to go to her house. Rising therefore, to bid her good old friend farewell, she took out her ear-rings and begged him to accept them.—"Take them," she said, "I have nothing else to give you; perhaps they may bring you a few dollars, too small a recompense I acknowledge, but believe me, 'tis all I have."

The old man refused sternly, and Laura was obliged to take them back. But he would not suffer her to encounter the chill blast of the evening, without some additional cloathing to ward off its inclemency. "It blows indeed, he said, a nipping wind, and you are but slightly clothed; here take my wife's old cloak, it is coarse but warm; you will feel no cold with it about you I warrant." Laura, glad to have something that would screen her from observation, wrapped the cloak about her, fastened the hood over her head, and, promising to return it the next day, with many thanks, hurried into the street.

Shrinking from the eye of every one who past, lest she should be known; she hastened with fearful step to the house where she so wished to arrive. Breathless she reached it and with a trembling hesitation knocked at the door. A well known voice told her to come in. She entered a snug little parlour, and throwing off the cloak discovered herself to the astonished woman. "Is it possible," she exclaimed, "that you are here! Why you look as if you have risen from the grave." "And almost from the grave I come," replied Laura faltering, "to beg of you for one night a shelter."

"From the grave indeed!" said the woman with a most repelling air, "no, no, we know very well where you have been. So, instead of marrying the honest husband your father had chosen, you went off with George Belfield; and after all the expense, that was foolishly thrown away on you, turned out no better than you should be. And now Belfield's tired of you and casts you off and you come to me, as if you thought I should have any thing to do with you! no, no, I shall not injure my character by harbouring such creatures."

This torrent of abuse, uttered by a woman who had been raised from want and wretchedness by the kindness of Laura's mother, and owed to her alone her present comfortable situation, shocked and overpowered the unfortunate girl; she leaned against the wall, and burst into tears. "You do well to cry," said the hard-hearted wretch, "but your tears will avail you little. The whole town talks of you and blames you, and the poor young man you were engaged to, was ready to hang himself; but I suppose he thought you were not worth grieving long about, and so he got married to another. For my part, I have heard nobody speak a word in your favour, except Sophia, and every body says she is no better than yourself."

The name of Sophia opened to the wretched Laura a new source of hope. Having been unfortunately married, and abandoned by her husband after he had embittered her days, she lived in profound retirement, with an aged relative. She had been an early acquaintance of the mother of Laura, and the vicinity of their dwellings had rendered them intimate.

Sophia, therefore, had known Laura from her infancy; had cherished her as an interesting child, and admired her as ripening years unfolded her talents and good qualities. During the time of her mother's last illness, Sophia was on a visit to a distant friend; and unfortunately for Laura, did not return until after her fatal flight. But she continued to think well of her; had always expressed much regret and interest on her subject, and had never heard her spoken of by others without entering warmly on her defence.

Laura was no sooner reminded of Sophia, than she determined to go to her. The woman continued talking, without being attended to by Laura, who dried her eyes, took up the cloak, that had fallen on the ground, and turned towards the door. Something like pity, smote the breast of the unfeeling being, as she saw the unresisting victim of misfortune about to depart. Softening a little the harshness of her tone, she said, "But for all, it is a shame to turn you out into the night. You may stay, and can go early in the morning." Laura, remaining silent, passed her with the calm look of indignation, and left the inhospitable roof.

Tranquillized by the hope of meeting at length with kindness, she bent her steps toward the house of Sophia. A light glimmered in the window, and listening beneath it, she heard her soft voice lulling to sleep her infant daughter. Tapping lightly at the door it was immediately opened, and the light falling full on the face of the visitor, discovered to Sophia her altered friend.

With extended arms she flew to receive her, and both for some moments remained speechless. She then led her to the fire, took off the tattered cloak and wrapped her in a warm shawl. She rubbed her icy hands, pressed to her warm bosom her aching head, and by a thousand kind offices sought to convince her that she had found a friend. Never before had Laura felt the power of friendship or the sweetness of its soothing cares. She yielded to her emotions and wept abundantly, whilst her arms clasped the waist of Sophia, who stood bending over her in silence, not less affected than herself by this unexpected meeting.

At length Laura exclaimed, "How kind is this reception, how grateful my heart this goodness; but you know not what you do— you know not what a lost creature your care revives!"

"I know you are my poor Laura," replied Sophia, "the child of that excellent woman whose compassion alleviated my sorrows, whose firm attachment wavered not when I was deserted, and over-whelmed by affliction. To her daughter, my heart, my house, shall always be open. For her suffering child, even though in error, I shall never hesitate, to make every exertion in my power."

Whilst thus speaking words of comfort to the poor girl, Sophia disentangled her hair, bound up her head in a handkerchief, and pressed her to partake of some refreshment which she prepared with her own hand.

When restored to life and warmth by these continued attentions, Laura related to her sympathising friend, all the progress of her inter-course with Belfield, even from its earliest dawn, to the horrid occurrences of the preceding evening, which she asserted terminated it forever.

Laura's despair was renewed by the recital. The delicacy of her feeling shrunk from the idea of her errors being known to the world, and the cruel woman of whom she had sought a shelter left her no longer in doubt on that subject. Sophia wept whilst listening to the distressing tale; but she assured her that she should never again want an asylum. That in herself she would always have an unshaken friend; and that with youth, health, and a conscience free from the reproach of guilt, she ought not yet to despair of happiness.

Tranquilized by these affectionate sentiments, Laura abandoned herself in security to the agreeable sensations excited by Sophia's goodness. She shared her bed, and found on her bosom unhoped for relief from her pains.

CHAPTER XX

Whilst the impressions under which she went to sleep kept possession of Laura's mind, her rest was tranquil. But towards morning
terrifying dreams interrupted her agitated slumbers; and when she
awoke, the sad recollection of the late events nearly plunged her back
into her former despondency.

Constantly led into extremes by an imagination vivid to excess,
she could not recover from the shock occasioned by the sudden
revolution of her prospects. She reviewed her situation, and all was
dark and dismal. Even the avenues of hope seemed to be shut, for
she conceived herself abandoned by her lover. The sink of infamy
to which she had been conducted; the insults to which she had been
exposed; the brutality of the vile woman; the rude approaches of the
stranger; the loss of her reputation, and the ignominious treatment
she had suffered from a creature who, a short time before, used to
receive with full thankfulness the slightest favours from her hand: all
this recurred, and in every thought there was distraction.

Sophia was sitting at a little table where breakfast was prepared.
She endeavoured in vain to induce her friend to partake of it, and
read with affliction, depicted in her countenance, all that was passing in her soul. Their mutual silence was at length broken by bursts
of indignation at the unpardonable levity of Belfield.

"Never," said Laura, "never will I again behold him! He knows
not or values not the heart he has outraged, or he would not have
put me beneath the same roof with Eliza, nor suffered me to breathe
with her the same contaminated air."

Thus they passed the early part of the day in "mournful conference," whilst Belfield, in a state of mind the complicated distress of
which would baffle all description, continued to seek and enquire
for Laura in every place where there was the least possibility of finding her. But all his efforts were fruitless, till at length, by one of those
accidents, which, when they occur, have a tendency to make the
wisest superstitious, he met in the street an elderly woman carrying
a bonnet and shawl which he thought belonged to Laura. Nor was
he wrong: for the bearer, an old friend and confidential servant of
Sophia's, had been sent at Laura's request, to look for them at that
abode of dissipation from whence she had flown in such disorder.

"Where are you going with those things?" Belfield asked in a voice nearly resembling that of a madman. "Home," replied the startled woman, "to the young lady to whom they belong! But what is that to you?" Belfield perceived that he should not have made the question, asked pardon for his mistake, and passed on, but soon turned back, and followed her at a distance, till he saw her enter Sophia's house.

Enquiring in the neighbourhood who lived there, he immediately recollected on hearing the name, that it had been sometimes mentioned by Laura, as that of a lady who had been very dear to her mother. He therefore no longer despaired of finding her, and went directly to the door.

Laura was sitting lost in thought, when roused by a loud knocking, she flew to her friend, and clinging close to her—"Save me, protect me, dearest Sophia!" she exclaimed, "I am sure that must be Belfield!"

Sophia, after assuring her that she had nothing to fear, descended to the parlour where he was waiting.

Having mentioned his name, Belfield stammered an apology for his intrusion, and then with a trembling voice begged her to tell him whether she knew anything of Laura: "Does she live?—Is she with you?" he asked. "Only tell me that she lives, and I shall be happy!"

"She lives, and she is here," replied Sophia, "but—"

"Enough, enough," cried Belfield, "I can hear no more:" and throwing himself at her feet, pressing her hands to his lips, bathing them with his tears—"You have saved me from despair!" he exclaimed, "you have restored me to myself! Laura lives, and she is protected by you! let me dwell on that thought, it is more, infinitely more than I had dared to hope!"

"It is true she lives," replied Sophia, "but to a mind like hers existence must always be a burden when held on the terms she now possesses it;—Laura lives, but she is wretched."

"Oh! talk not thus!" said Belfield, "restore her to me; let me at her feet expiate my fault; let me devote to her a life which shall have no object but to promote her happiness!" With all the ardour of entreaty, he begged to be conducted to her; but Sophia steadily refused:—"Your presence at this moment might prove fatal," she said, "she is too weak to bear it; but if to know that she is soothed by kindness and guarded by friendship can give you comfort, be assured that if she was my sister she could not be dearer to me."

"Then breathe at least one prayer into her bosom for me," said Belfield. "Tomorrow at this hour I will return; let me hope that I shall not plead in vain always."

Sophia was moved. The sincerity of his manner, the paleness of his face, expressive of the torture he had suffered, and the fire which reviving hope had kindled in his eyes, spoke irresistibly in his favour. She continued silent, and Belfield withdrew.

CHAPTER XXI

When Sophia returned to her chamber, Laura was in a state of violent agitation. She interrupted frequently the recital of her friend, and repeated that she would never again behold her destroyer. "Yet whither shall I fly," she said; "how to avoid his persecution? If I stay here he will unceasingly torment you, and alas, I have no choice of abode; beyond your threshold I know of no place of refuge." "Of that we will think hereafter," replied Sophia: "at present consider only your relation to Belfield, and be not too precipitate in your resolutions; at least do not be so unjust as to condemn him unheard. Resentment for the offences of a beloved object cannot long occupy a heart like yours; and regret for your own severity may, perhaps too late, obliterate the recollection of his wrongs." Laura secretly acknowledged the truth of what she heard, but the yearnings of her heart were checked by the jealousy the story of Eliza had created, and her pride recoiled from the idea of sharing with another the object of her affection. She persisted, therefore, in her determination to see him no more; yet, feeling unable to tell him so, she thought that a letter would be the best mode of conveying to him her sentiments.

Sophia placed materials for writing before her, entreated her to restrain the violence of her feelings, and retired to bed, leaving her at liberty to weep and reflect.

The opening dawn found Laura bending over the paper that was to bear her final sentiments to the man she had idolized; to him on whom her brightest hopes had rested, and whom, with every expectation of happiness, she was about for ever to resign. Pale and exhausted by the lengthened effort of the painful task, Sophia perceived her, when she awoke, leaning almost lifeless on the table. Penetrated with sorrow for her sufferings, she entreated her to go to bed; but even the desire of rest had flown with the illusions of love, from Laura's bosom. She closed the letter; she sealed it, and gave it to Sophia, and at the same moment fell fainting in her arms. Long and death-like was her swoon! and as she slowly returned to life, her burning hands and feverish lips betrayed how deeply she had been affected by the painful exertion.

Sophia, alarmed lest such repeated shocks should prove destructive, sought to inspire her with a love of life, by pointing to the many sources of happiness that were still within her reach; but Laura's heart was shut against the illusive hope, and when her powers of reflection arose from the confusion that had overwhelmed them, she saw her forlorn situation in its most horrible point of view. Her confidence in Belfield was destroyed; her passion for him was criminal; its indulgence had proved destructive: life, for her, teemed with misery! In the grave alone, could she expect repose.

Such, and similar thoughts, were passing though her mind as she awaited, in agonizing suspense, the hour of Belfield's return.

At the time appointed he entered the house, and with frantic impatience, enquired for Laura. "She is ill," replied Sophia, "much too ill to support the interview you desire. She passed the night in writing this letter, and exhausted by the effort, is now in bed. She persists in her determination to see you no more!" "And in that determination you support her, cruel woman," said Belfield; "but I will receive no letter; why does Laura write to me? she is mine; why is she concealed from me? if she is ill, who, better than myself, can soothe and restore her?"

"If you intend to destroy her," replied Sophia, "then rush into her presence and kill her by your precipitancy; but if you wish, indeed, that she should pardon, or even hear you, let her recover from the shock she has received, and give time to her softer feelings to resume their influence."

Belfield yielded to the representations of Sophia, and supplicating her to plead for him to Laura, took the letter and hastened home.

"Reduced to the dreadful necessity of conveying to you my sentiments, and sure that I should be unable to support your presence, I must attempt to write. But in what terms shall I write to you? to you, on whom my soul rested firmly; in whom all my hopes of happiness were centered! to you, who saw me sinking to the earth, a sad victim of filial grief, and whose attention gave a new interest to that life to which you recalled me.

"Bitter recollections—departed joys! flow not thus on my tortured heart. Recur not to my thoughts, delightful moments, when his fascinating voice stole like magic on my enchanted ear. Pursue me not, too charming image of the time when he appeared before me, wearing love's sweetest semblance; when my heart hailed him as the messenger of peace. No, let me remember only Eliza! her with whose resentment I was menaced, and the detestable sight of that horrible woman, in whose house I was left; and the grasp of the man from whom I fled— fled, forlorn and desolate, to the grave of my mother, there to expiate the crime of having forgotten her, on the bosom of a stranger!

"There are wounds which time cannot heal; ills which patience cannot teach us to endure. I ask not at your hands the respect of the world, which through you I have lost; you cannot even restore me to my own! My inexperienced heart fancied in you perfection beyond the lot of human nature: the illusion has vanished, but conviction of the sad reality has come too late.

"Oh Belfield, Belfield, seek not to destroy me. Hide rather for ever from my view a being polluted by falsehood; hide from me that form, so late the object of my idolatry, round which, even on the verge of the grave, I twined with agonizing fondness. Through what mazes of delight have I been led to my present state of wretchedness! how was the fatal precipice that awaited me concealed by flowers, and my fall rendered unavoidable! In all the simplicity of unsuspecting faith, in all the purity of affection, I became thine, and I adored in thee the emblem of truth, of goodness, of love! How rudely has the veil that concealed your deformity been torn away? How have you burst on my affrighted soul in all the hideousness of guilt? You led me without remorse, to a den of infamy; you gave me to dishonour, to shame, to public scorn! Ages would not obliterate from my memory that scene, fraught with horror, to which you exposed me—my heart is no longer susceptible of any impressions but those of grief and despair!

"Then spare—in mercy spare me; leave me to that fate which you have so cruelly influenced, nor drive me to distraction by your continued efforts to procure an interview, which my heart will steadily refuse—which my soul abhors. Intervening worlds would not oppose barriers so insuperable as those which now separate us. No longer could my confiding soul repose in peace beneath your protection, which I thought sanctioned by honour, hallowed by the purest fidelity. No longer near you could the slumber of security be mine; no, even in your arms the idea of your Eliza would pursue me; on your bosom my affrighted senses would startle at the apprehension of invading a retreat to which she has a prior, perhaps stronger, claim. Henceforth pain, in whatever form, will assail me in vain, since I have heard that Belfield has a mistress, that he loves another, and I have lived.

"To that other I yield you, perhaps to more than one; to yourself I yield you, whilst degraded, lost—the object of my own abhorrence, of the world's contempt, I hide in some obscure corner the wretched remains of a violated person, and learn to devour in silence the sorrow of a breaking heart."

CHAPTER XXII

No place could have been more calculated to heighten the effect of Laura's letter, than that in which it was opened. It was the same chamber where Belfield had lain prostrate with dire disease, at the period when terror burst asunder the dearest ties of society; when, abandoned by his relations on its first approach, and left to mercenary care—the young, the beautiful Laura, courageous from affection, and regardless of any danger, except that of losing the man she adored, had come, had sought him, had soothed him by her tenderness, and preserved him by her unremitting attention. On the bed before him, her hands had pressed his aching head; across the floor on which he stood, she had supported his faltering steps; near the window which gave him light, she had related to him the occurrences of her dreary walk to town. She was blended with every surrounding object. Her presence, in recollection at least, had given charms even to sickness and pain. And now this lovely, this interesting being, so dignified even in error, from the purity of her heart, and the fullness of the sentiment that guided her conduct, refused any longer to consider him as her friend! Justly offended, because apparently undervalued and neglected, nay, insulted and degraded, in consequence of his imprudence, she intended to tear herself away from him for ever—was it possible to sustain the idea without madness?

When he had finished reading the letter, he remained some moments fixed like a statue; then, starting suddenly, and grasping his hat, he rushed into the street, as if to seek in the open air relief from the anguish that overwhelmed him.

His walk was long, and his extreme agitation for a time prevented him from thinking connectedly. "All this was abominable," he exclaimed at last, "and I can conceive her irritation; yet surely I love her—surely I meant not that she should be thus exposed. She must—she will do justice to my feelings; I have deserved her anger, but she will forgive!"

Calmed by this hope, he at first proposed forcibly to gain admittance to Laura; to throw himself at her feet, and implore her pardon. But then he apprehended that the scene might prove injurious to her health, and he was sensible of the necessity of some explanations to extenuate his guilt, which at such an interview, he would be as unable to give as she to receive. He therefore returned to his lodgings, and wrote the following answer to Laura's letter.

To Laura.

"Banished from your presence—denied all access—shocked by repeated assurances of your determination to see me no more, I am obliged, in justice to myself, and to guard you, perhaps, from painful reflections hereafter, to attempt accounting for my late unfortunate conduct.

"Yet how shall I confine within the cold contents of a letter, the impetuous sentiments that tear my breast?—or how submit to the trammels of language, feelings, prayers, regrets, which should be received into your bosom, in a moment of sympathy; when, seeing me bending at your feet, you would feel, and acknowledge, that I never intended to wrong or to deceive you.

"To deceive you! oh, my dear, my adored Laura, banish from your mind for ever that detestable thought. Let me solemnly repeat the assurance, that I was a stranger to love till you inspired it!—that ever since, absorbed by you alone, no other female for me has had existence!

"And must I mention Eliza?—must that name appear in a page directed to you?—Cruel girl, if you knew what it costs me!—if you knew the indignation that fills my heart at having been thus suspected, and suspected by you; regret would remove your anger, tears and kisses would stifle explanations.

"Learn then that long before I beheld you, in a moment of dissipation, by accident, I met with Eliza; a lovely wreck, at that period, of innocence and beauty. I pitied her; I was kind to her; she mistook these sentiments for attachment. From the time I became acquainted with you, I have not seen her even once, nor had I the least idea that she lived in the house to which I conducted you.

"That house, I confess it with the deepest humiliation, you never should have entered. I ought not to have placed you within the reach of insult, and what would I not give to draw a veil of oblivion over that fatal mistake?—But listen, dearest Laura, listen to the circumstances that led to it; and if I was, notwithstanding, wrong, let me hope at least that I may be forgiven.

"My family were returning unexpectedly. I felt that the moment of presenting you to them had not yet arrived. I dreaded the idea of disturbing your tranquillity, by speaking of my embarrassment, and by explaining it: for the singular seclusion in which you have lived, while it has incredibly preserved your purity of mind, has kept you totally unacquainted with the affairs of the world, and the interests that govern mankind. Absolutely at a loss how to act on so sudden an emergency, and in so singular a situation, I conducted you to a house of doubtful character, but not to a den of infamy, for that such it had become of late, I protest I knew not. I left you to seek a more suitable retreat, and that object alone engaged me, during my absence. I returned a few moments after you had fled, and learned what had happened. The rack itself could have inflicted no agonies like those I suffered. Dread of your fate—self-reproach—despair— all united their pangs to render me wretched.

"Two days elapsed in this state; at last, I discover, by chance, that you are at Sophia's. I learn that you are safe; my frame scarcely resists the sudden transition from distraction to hope. I pant to throw myself at your feet, and am refused admittance.

"Cruel Laura! still more cruel for writing me a letter which for a moment disordered all my faculties, and bereft me even of faith in myself. And can you persist in your resolution? can you read these lines and not feel convinced that however great my error, my heart has been true? Can you believe this heart sincere, and still refuse to see me? You cannot—you will not—you shall not. I will force myself into your presence, and there kneel immoveable, till my looks, more expressive than words, shall have persuaded you, that falsehood can never pollute my lips, not soil my pen, when I am addressing you.

"If still you relent not—Laura, I will whisper in your ear, Laura, consider we are no longer only you and me; a little being exists that will attest our loves, and who may one day ask you 'What has become of my father?'

"I know you will receive me for I feel that I love you. Let me fly then to your arms, let me seal my pardon on your lips!—Celestial creature! Beauteous image of every thing sublime and good! once already you have prolonged my days; oh save me now from worse destruction—restore me to life and to thee!"

The tears that streamed on his paper were proofs of the sincerity of his protestations. The sighs of repentance that burst from his soul, would have softened the strongest resentment; yet still he trembled, lest the impressions Laura had received, should not yield to his prayers.

The letter finished, he threw himself on the bed, but no refreshing slumber approached him. The night seemed eternal, and the morning found him a prey to all the torments of suspense.

CHAPTER XXIII

As soon as it was probable that the door of Sophia was open, Belfield took the letter and went to her house. For a long time she refused to receive it, fearing to offend Laura by too much facility, and thinking that he could not be too severely punished. She represented to him the profound sentiment of grief that had taken possession of Laura's heart, and wished him not to urge his attempts at a reconciliation, till time had softened feelings which had been too violently roused to subside immediately. She hinted at the horror Laura felt at the idea of having been associated with Eliza, and the inhabitants of that abominable house, she said that nothing would induce her to pardon so cruel an outrage.

Belfield listened with impatience, and combated all her objections. "Dear Sophia," he passionately exclaimed, "admit at least that sometimes the very purity of our intentions may prevent us from perceiving the impropriety of our proceedings. Consider that it is dangerous to suffer unfavourable impressions to continue long;—that no one escapes quite unhurt, even from momentary prepossessions against him;—consider that Laura's happiness is at stake. Lose not, I beseech you, time so precious in useless discussion. Extend that goodness which saved your friend, to me;—bear this letter to her hand, and suffer me to remain in the house while she reads it."

Sophia felt the truth of his remarks, and took the letter. She gave it silently to Laura, who averted her eyes from the address, as if she feared to see the well-known characters.

Sophia, regarding her with a look of pity, said earnestly: "I have not taken this letter on slight grounds; and I think you ought to read it before you finally decide."

Laura broke the seal with trembling hand, but for some moments could not distinguish a word. She read it at length, and as her eye glided over the lines, her pale cheek reassumed the faint glow of reviving hope, which heightened gradually to the brightest crimson.

"He remains below," said Sophia—Scarcely had she uttered the word, when Laura let the letter fall, flew down the stairs, and bathed in tears, threw herself into the arms of Belfield.

Both for some minutes continued speechless. Their souls were overflowing, and needed not the tardy conveyance of words, to understand each other.

"Once more I hold thee!" at length said Belfield:—"my Laura! my sweet, my celestial friend! and now let nothing on earth ever separate us again. I knew that in your heart I had an advocate who would be heard in my favour. It pleads for me,—it has brought you to me, and with you happiness and joy. Whatever may occur in the future, dearest Laura, always listen to your heart alone. What it tells you that I ought not, believe me that I cannot do. In this noble trust let our peace be sealed;—for without confidence, without implicit mutual faith, discord will disturb the fairest union, and wither with its poisonous breath the brightest hopes, though fostered by long and tried affection."

Soft as the breath of zephyr whispering among the drooping flowers, fell the words of Belfield on the ear of Laura. Her head reclined on his shoulder; her eye dwelt on his face; her hand played with the ringlets that shaded his brow. To the torments of despair that had lacerated her bosom during the preceding day, the conviction of Belfield's truth succeeded, and the delicious calm of harmony and peace diffused itself through her nerves as she listened to him.

"Forgive me for having doubted you," she said, "nothing again shall disturb my security! Loved by you who can insult,—what can degrade me? Your love is my guard;—to be yours is all my pride. Remember not that once I gave you pain; my life shall be devoted to atone for it."

All further attempts to give an idea of the sensations of Laura and Belfield, to those who have never felt the joy that waits upon a moment of tender reconcileation, would be vain;—and for those who have felt it, enough has been said. Their hearts will supply what language has not power to express.

The strife of the human passions, like that of the elements, may be detailed;—the heavens in uproar, awful as they are to the beholder, may be described. We have words for threatening clouds and lightening and thunder and the roaring storm; but the divine serenity of the ensuing scene,—the azure sky flushed with innumerable shades of mellow yet glowing tints;—the ethereal breath which pervades the vast expanse;—who has the audacity to put his hand to the picture?

CHAPTER XXIV

Laura, revelling in her new-born happiness, forgot that she had been awakened from a dream of similar colouring, to despair and death. She reflected not, that other dreadful moments might slumber in the womb of futurity. She thought only that Belfield was hers, and she was right; for who has ever been wholly exempt from illusion, except at the expense of what perhaps is alone truly desirable?

As she related to him all her sufferings from the moment of their fatal separation; her rapid flight; her fall; the footstep that had frighted her from the wall near which she kneeled;—Belfield was convinced, from the hour and the place, that she had flown from him. He had also passed the church-yard a short time after, but thought not that his hapless friend could have sought a refuge there.

To the poor old man, who had so charitably relieved and sheltered her, he sent, with the cloak, a small present, and promised to go himself to thank him for his friendly conduct. But the generous, the noble-minded Sophia, what words could do justice! Poor and inadequate would have been his efforts to express his exalted idea of her goodness. "Think not," he said, pressing her hand to his lips, "that my silence proceeds from insensibility. Your having saved this lovely girl, was an act of kindness which has sunk deep into my heart, and only the loss of life itself can obliterate the grateful recollection."

Sophia had done nothing but what she had been prompted by her feelings, and she found her reward in the happiness she now witnessed. But, though still young, the mind of Sophia had matured by affliction; and of a temper more sedate, with an imagination less enthusiastic; life presented not to her, the brilliant prospects that again burst on the dazzled vision of Laura.

With soberer views—with hopes infinitely less soaring; she thought it possible, at least, that the bliss of the present hour, so full, so pure, might again be troubled. She saw that a character so susceptible of extacy, must necessarily often tremble on the brink of despair; yet, to dispel by chilling doubts the fairy visions even in their birth, was too cruel; to intrude the cold apprehensions of reason where love and transport had been just restored, was a task too ungrateful. "Be happy," she cried, with more than usual emotion, "be happy while you may, for fleeting are moments so exquisite."

Fearful that the gloom which she felt overclouding her spirits should communicate itself to Laura, she retired to another apartment; and whilst her thoughtless friend intoxicated herself from the cup of rapture, Sophia wept the misfortunes whose approach she dreaded. That Belfield would hallow his intercourse with Laura, by rendering it legal, she believed, and she resolved to press its being done speedily. But his youth, his volatile and impetuous disposition, and his dependent state, filled her with the utmost inquietude.

CHAPTER XXV

When the first tumults of gladness had subsided into tranquil delight; when Laura, Belfield, and Sophia, were assembled round their little fire, and enjoyed the pleasure of social intercourse, the marriage of Laura and Belfield, was often the subject of conversation. Whilst he dwelt on it as an event, the accomplishment of which, was most necessary to secure his peace, he stated also, that the peculiarity of his situation, had been the cause of its having been deferred so long. He represented his brother as a man of haughty and inflexible temper, to whom he owed much, and who would not fail to oppose his marrying so young, nor easily pardon his having formed and engagement so important, without his consent, and without regard to any other considerations except those suggested by his heart. "To shock him at present," he continued, "by any precipitate act, would be in the highest degree imprudent, for I cannot yet dispense with his assistance, which I am sure he would immediately withdraw. A delay of only a few months, will remove all these embarrassments. I shall then have it in my power to decide for myself, to depend on my own exertions; and could they be unsuccessful if Laura's happiness is my aim?"

Perhaps these arguments, though apparently reasonable, might have been easily over-ruled; for if they weighed not against the ruin of Laura, why should they have any weight against the only reparation in his power to make? Perhaps it might have been shewn, that perfect consistency, that the uniform sway of the passions, even in defiance of sense, is less injurious and therefore preferable to a conduct that alternately obeys either. Warmth of feeling, often atones for the pain it causes; But the man who is, by turns, inconsiderate and prudent, will, too frequently, wound, when he ought to spare; and disappoint us, when we reckon on his energy.

Sophia felt all this, but how was it possible to urge it against a man whose intentions appeared so fair; or how còuld she expect to be seconded by Laura, whose confiding soul always on such occasions seized on what was most generous, always preferred what might best convince her lover of her implicit reliance on his truth.

"I am so persuaded that you love me," she said to him, "so sure that you cannot intend what would destroy me, that I rest in tranquillity. Hasten then the period you mention; I shall wait with patience, because I wait without fear, till the moment arrives that will make you—" wholly mine, she would have said, but the word trembled on her lips, and a kiss prevented its recollection.

CHAPTER XXVI

Such being the disposition of Laura, and such the reasons of Belfield, for a short delay of their nuptials, Sophia was obliged to acquiesce; though, from her solicitude for her friend, she would, at any hazard, have preferred an immediate reconciliation between the interests of Laura's heart, and the regard that was due to the established rules of society. She knew that they never can be violated with impunity; that it is necessary to respect them because they exist, and that no one can enjoy perfect happiness, whilst conscious that his conduct is censured by the intelligent and good men of the community in which he lives. She loved Laura too much not to feel the greatest impatience to see her free from reproach; but she was also sensible of the gross inconvenience which would result from disturbing Belfield's career, before his studies were finished. She therefore entered, though reluctantly, into his plan, and shared with the affectionate pair the anticipation of the happy times which they fondly hoped were approaching.

Belfield still retained the apartment he had engaged for Laura, and when mutual confidence and tranquillity had been fully restored, he proposed to conduct her thither. But Sophia would not part with her young friend, and insisted on her continuing to stay with her, till she was married, to which Laura cheerfully consented.

Belfield resumed his studies with renewed and unusual application. All his habits changed. He was no longer seen in the circles of dissipated young men, which he used to frequent; and the companions of his former revels, wondered what circumstance could have wrought so sudden a change. They saw him all day intent upon his books, or engaged with the patients which had been entrusted to his care—but how he spent his evenings, was to them a mystery. They suspected that he was in love, and occasionally rallied him on that account, yet no one could imagine who was the object that thus engrossed his affection.

There is no situation, if we may use the expression, more full of existence than that in which the mind is bent on a laudable purpose; and all its energies are awakened to attain it. This was the case with Belfield, at this period. He was happy, because he was active, and his interests were in unison with his wishes. He approached Laura without regret, for he now considered their marriage as already registered in heaven; and her society appeared to him more delightful than ever, because she had roused his intellectual powers to consistent and virtuous exertions. When in the evening she playfully caressed him, he imagined his gladness arose solely from the superior charms of his love, whilst, in a great measure, it was owing to the satisfaction he felt, when reviewing the day he had passed.

Oh, why does not every woman know, that to be always approved of, to be adored by her lover, she should principally be careful that he may always have cause to approve of himself!—a peaceful bosom is the only congenial climate for the sweetest of all illusions!

Whilst Belfield was engaged in his studies, Laura made preparations for their domestic establishment; and in these the little stranger, to whom Belfield had so forcibly appealed in his letter, was not forgotten.

Thus, several months elapsed, in unison, in tranquillity, in hope. Both were young and beautiful. Both were animated by sentiments of the purest affection. Both aimed at what was right. Both strove to be what, in rendering them most useful to society, would endear them most to each other.—Does human life afford a more pleasing picture?—Who would not regret that their efforts should prove unavailing; or who suspect that, in their past mistakes, lay the cause of their disappointment?

CHAPTER XXVII

The studies of Belfield were now finished. He passed through the ordeal of examination with credit, and received the diploma which qualified him for the exercise of his profession. This event gave great joy to all his friends; but who can paint the sensations of Laura, when flushed with success, glowing with pleasure excited by the applause he had received, he entered her room, and told her, that the long-wished for moment had come; that now he felt independent and free. He informed her also, that his brother, pleased with the steadiness of his late conduct, and flattered by the acquired distinction, had appropriated a handsome sum for his establishment in a neighbouring town, for which he was to set off in a few days. "But before we go," he said, "marriage must sanction our attachment. You must, by accepting my hand and my name, secure to me a treasure, deprived of which, all thoughts of happiness would be folly."

Laura blushed, and concealed her face in his bosom.

Sophia, overcome with gladness, embraced him, and exclaimed: "Dearest Belfield, pardon the uneasiness with which I have sometimes tormented you." He pressed her hand, and then the little group proceeded to arrange the details of the approaching ceremony. The third evening was fixed on, as the time: it was to be privately performed at Sophia's house, and only to be made known after their departure. One friend of Belfield's, in whom he had entire confidence, and Sophia, were to be present; a little supper was to terminate the day.

Sophia charged herself with all the preparatory details, nor did she forget the bridal ornaments of Laura.

All, in the meantime, was festivity and amusement, among the friends of Belfield. His brother gave a dinner to his fellow-students, and his young acquaintances; who, in their turn, had ordered a handsome entertainment at Gray's gardens,[1] to which Belfield was invited for the following day.

He informed Laura of it, when he returned to her in the evening, mentioning at the same time, how willingly he would forgo the honour they intended him; having entirely lost the relish for such parties, and considering as a real sacrifice every hour of separation, since she became more dear, more interesting to him, as the moment drew near which was to unite them for ever.

"But," he continued, "some regard is due to the feelings of my former companions, who seem the more anxious not to be backward

---

[1]   During the 1780s, George and Robert Gray expanded the gardens around the popular tavern at Gray's Ferry on the Schuylkill River. One contemporary visitor described it as "a wilderness of sweets, and the views instantly become romantically enchanting, the scene is every moment changing." The pleasure gardens included fruit tree groves, abundant flowers, exotic plants including aloe and venus fly traps, a "chinese bridge," and a federal temple commemorating ratification of the Constitution.

on this occasion, since they know that I am going to leave the city shortly."

Laura readily acknowledged the justness of this observation, and convinced that Belfield attended his friends more in compliance with what was proper, than to seek amusement, cheerfully submitted to the privation, and felt glad that he should depart with the friendship and regret of those who had known him.

The conversation then turned on their marriage. Nothing could be more amiable than Laura, whenever Belfield mentioned this subject. Her caresses seemed more irresistible, as they were about to become holy; and her heart was so full of the importance of the change which awaited her—a change so long and so anxiously wished for, yet always thought of with a secret fear of disappointment;—she felt so happy and so proud, and at the same time so solicitous, lest in attempting to obtain all, she might lose what she already possessed, that her tears and her smiles were almost constantly blended.

Belfield was never more deeply sensible of his wrongs towards Laura, than now when he was on the point of repairing them; never before had she appeared to him so sweet, so dignified. "I have sinned against thee," he said, "even more than thou art aware of! but let no recollection of my faults embitter the days to come. Henceforth, the whole tenor of my life shall have but one uniform expression—shall only tell, how much I love and adore you!"

CHAPTER XXVIII

The next day, at the hour appointed, Belfield went to the gardens where he was to meet his young friends. When he entered the saloon a numerous company were already assembled, and he felt vexed to see among them the gentleman, who had occasioned the flight of Laura from the house to which he had so imprudently conducted her.

This man, of the name of Melwood, was scarcely acquainted with Belfield, and happened to be of the party more by accident than by express invitation. He had, since the unfortunate occurrence alluded to, mentioned that adventure in several places, and also his intention of leaving no means untried to discover the retreat of Laura, whose name he had ascertained from the mark of a handkerchief which remained behind when she fled. Belfield had heard of this, and as he could never think of the scene itself without remorse, so the man, who had acted a part in it, was naturally odious to him. At table, however, mirth and conviviality presided, and soothed for a time the irritation of Belfield.

After the cloth had been removed the bottle circulated rapidly, and augmented by its vivifying influence the cheerfulness of the guests. But unfortunately, when the usual toasts were exhausted, and each gentleman was called on in his turn to give a lady, Melwood, glad perhaps to seize this opportunity of mortifying a happy rival, named Laura. "And who is Laura?" asked one of the party, after the toast had been drank.

"Laura," replied Melwood, "is a beautiful unknown, of whom our doctor can tell us more. I have myself seen her only once at the house of an accommodating friend, who has, however, promised to procure me another interview."

"Mr. Melwood," said Belfield, with asperity, "the name of that young lady must not be trifled with!"

"Sir," replied the other with a sneer, "I presume that I may mention the name of a girl met at Mrs. W——s, in any manner I please!"

"None but a villain," exclaimed Belfield, "would mention it disrespectfully!"

Melwood started from his chair, as if going to revenge the insult, but recollecting himself, he sat down again and continued silent.

Some more toasts were given, and some more glasses emptied; but the good humour of the company had been interrupted and they soon dispersed.

Belfield hastened to Laura. It was the evening preceding that on which they were to be married. Laura had never passed an afternoon that appeared so tedious, nor ever felt his absence so painful.

At last she heard the sound of his footsteps. It constantly awakened in her bosom the most pleasing sensations, and all his approaches to her were distinguished by some sentiment of increasing happiness; but this time her heart palpitated more than usual. She could scarcely wait till he entered the room; she flew towards him with as much warmth, as much anxiety, as if he had just returned from a long journey.

Belfield's manner was also more than usually impressive; but his tenderness was not blended with that expression of gaiety which had before marked it, and which is so natural when a noble aim has been attained after difficulty and exertion. His face was pale, his eye was restless, and sometimes wild. A sickly energy accompanied every affectionate word he uttered. For moments he would continue pensive and silent, and then redouble his caresses as if his time was short.

"What is the matter?" said Laura, leaning on his shoulder, "You seem uneasy?"—"Nothing," replied Belfield, "only I feel heated with wine and my head aches dreadfully"—"Let me tie this handkerchief round it," she said, "perhaps it will relieve you." She took one from a table; a little cap she had been working and concealed when Belfield came, fell on the carpet—Laura blushed, a tear trickled from Belfield's eye and dropped on the cap as he took it up.

"Tell me what ails you?" she said again after a short pause, "you frighten me; I do not understand you. Your head ached often, but I never saw you thus before! from whence proceeds this sadness? what gives you trouble?—is it me? Alas I know I am but a poor and friendless thing!—perhaps the world will blame you!—Oh rather sacrifice me than be wretched!"

Under the apprehensions which agitated the mind of Belfield, no thought could have escaped the lips of Laura more piercing than that she had uttered. His soul was moved to its inmost recesses. "By all that is holy!" he exclaimed in wild emotion, pressing her hand between both of his, "the world cannot contain a being superior to thee in real excellence! as I believe it, so I would stake my life on that assertion. Sacrifice thee?—No! But that I ever, even for a moment, even through thoughtlessness, could expose thee to insult; that I did not proudly proclaim thee mine the moment thou becamest so; that I did not think every consideration subordinate to that of honoring thee; this wrings my heart! this makes me wretched!"

"But why, dearest Belfield, why all this now?" said Laura, with a faltering voice, am I not thy creature? am I not going always to be so? who will dare insult me when I am thine? or how could I think, when with you, of pangs long passed? Shall we not be happy, dearest Belfield? Oh tell me, shall we not?"

"Undoubtedly we shall!" replied Belfield, with an altered and settled tone, "a being like thee cannot be doomed to suffer!"

There is in the mind, as in the body of a man, a constitutional propensity to resist pain, which often occasions even the most distinguished for intellect and talents to become superstitious, whcn nothing else can afford tranquillity. Thus Belfield seized on the idea that, whatever events might await him, the issue could not be otherwise than favourable, when Laura's happiness was at stake; and it became strengthened by the persuasion, so natural in early life, of the prevalence of a sort of general justice. A sense of what ought to be, too frequently prompts the youthful and sanguine to disregard what is. They hurry on, as if there were a protecting power beyond the reason with which they are gifted.

His countenance gradually brightened, and as he drew his cheerfulness from his conception of Laura's superior claims to the rewards of merit, so she appeared to him more perfect, more deserving of admiration, than ever. His tenderness became sublime, his love was worship.

Laura could not resist the overwhelming torrent of pleasing sensations, called forth by what Belfield said; and though his manner still remained to her mysterious, yet, she was penetrated with the delicious conviction that she filled his soul; that mortal woman could be to man no more. The moment was exquisite, was sacred, and embraced in itself a whole existence. Her thoughts, her tears, were suspended; she asked no further questions, she only felt.

CHAPTER XXIX

When Belfield late at night returned home, his servant informed him that a gentleman had called there twice, and left word that he would come again early in the morning. No doubt remained in Belfield's mind that he had been sent by Melwood, and was probably the bearer of a challenge. He therefore hastily wrote to a confidential friend, whom he requested to come to him at day-break. Having sent it he retired to his room, and reflected how it would be most proper for him to act on this occasion.

To make any kind of apology for the insult with which he had returned an unprovoked offense appeared to him to be totally out of question; particularly as Laura was concerned. He had unfortunately been the cause of her being exposed to ill-natured remarks, and she was going to be united to him by indissoluble ties. He felt therefore the absolute necessity of repressing, by an unequivocal conduct in the first instance, any future attacks on her reputation; and of proving, to his friends and to the world, how far, in his opinion, she was removed beyond all suspicion, and how deserving of every sacrifice, should it be that of life itself. He was moreover sensible that if any accommodation of the affair was at all possible, it must be in consequence of some previous concessions of Melwood, and that of course it might be best effected at the place of meeting. To accept the challenge admitted of no deliberation.

But should he postpone the interview till after his marriage, or press an immediate settlement of the dispute? This question was not so easily decided.—If the event should be fatal to him, what would be the situation of Laura? She would remain behind disgraced, and to his child would be attached the reproach of having sprung from an illegal connexion. On the other hand, might not any procrastination be interpreted as an attempt at evasion? might not the marriage itself, at least by the malignant, be considered as influenced by the hope of getting over the duel? This thought was insupportable. Besides, it would not be in his power to go with a light heart to a ceremony the performance of which ought to be one of the most free, as well as one of the most cheerful, acts of his life. His brow would be clouded;—Laura would perceive it; she would endeavour to ascertain the cause:—The day of joy would become a day of embarrassment. Their matrimonial existence would be ushered in by concealment and deception. And if she knew, he asked himself, what I am now thinking, how would she decide? What is the world to me, she would say, if you are no more? Oh, hasten! if it must be so,—let me have happiness secure, or be wretched at once.

But she cannot be doomed to wretchedness, he continued; mine was the fault, if any there has been committed, and mine is the guilt. To die is nothing, but to live and suffer is dreadful. Eternal justice cannot have marked a being so fair for a destiny so cruel; all must end well. I will meet my fate without delay; and then have peace,— be married and be happy.

Such were the motives that influenced his decision. Seduced by his interests and his wishes he reflected not how fallacious any dependence must be which has no better foundation than our feeble conceptions of just and right; in the eternal, mysterious course of things. He went to bed, and still slept soundly, when a rap at the door awoke him.

CHAPTER XXX

It was Ferguson, his confidential friend, who came in consequence of the note he had received. Belfield told him why he had sent for him, and stated the reasons which, in his opinion, precluded all hesitation with regard to the duel, and made him anxious to bring the affair to an immediate conclusion.

Ferguson, who knew his relation to Laura, and was likewise impressed with the propriety of acting with spirit where she was concerned, approved of them nor did he see why an interview should be deferred, which he felt confident would terminate favourably.

They had scarcely exchanged their ideas on the subject, when the gentleman entered who had been at Belfield's lodgings the night before. As it had been foreseen, he delivered a challenge from Melwood, which was accepted without any discussion; and then the friends of the parties agreed, that they should meet at eleven o'clock that morning, on the other side of the river.

While Ferguson was engaged in procuring pistols, and making some other previous arrangements, Belfield wrote a letter to a General S—, of New York, a man related to his family, in whose house he had passed much of his time, when a boy,—of high standing in society, affluent, singularly liberal, possessed of the most distinguished talents, and whose career would have been brilliant, had the great qualities of his mind suited the country in which he was born—to his protection, he recommended Laura and his child.

To Laura, also, he wrote a note, informing her, that he was obliged to go into the country, but that he should be back by early in the afternoon; he bid her be cheerful, and concluded by saying, "When I return, you will love me more than ever; and in the evening, our happiness will obtain the sanction of the world and of heaven."

He then called on Ferguson, and they proceeded together to the place of appointment.

Melwood and his friend had arrived before them. The former

had said, that he was far from having any ill-will towards Belfield, and would be satisfied to have the affair amicably settled, if Belfield's reputation of being an excellent shot, did not render any forwardness on his part, liable to misconstruction.

Melwood was not a bad man, but having been soured by early disappointments, his manner had become remarkably dry and sarcastic. Attached to nothing, and least to life, he considered a duel on such occasions as perfectly a matter of course, and felt indifferent with regard to the consequences.

Ferguson knew that, with a character of this description, any attempt at explanation would be useless, at least until a shot had been exchanged.

The distance was measured; the parties took their stand; the word was given—they fired. Belfield bounced as if struck by an electric shock, and then fell flat on the ground.

Melwood went to him, and notwithstanding his habitual coldness, seemed deeply to regret the sad occurrence.

On examination, it was found, that the ball had entered the lower cavity of the breast, and probably touched the spinal column.— Belfield remained senseless for a considerable time, though he continued to breathe; but he recovered his recollection after having been taken to a neighboring house.—"Oh, my poor Laura!" were the first words he uttered.

CHAPTER XXXI

The situation of Belfield, who evidently could not live many hours, and the state of the river, the crossing of which was rendered difficult, by enormous masses of drifting ice, forbade his removal to town. Yet it appeared essential to Ferguson, that Laura should be near him, particularly as his declarations, and her conduct, on this occasion, would not be without their effect on the public, whose sympathy, it was, for her sake, of great importance to secure. He therefore wrote a note to Sophia, stating shortly what had happened to Belfield, and requesting her to come immediately with Laura. He also sent for his brother.

Sophia had just finished the simple toilet of Laura. With cheerful alacrity, her tasteful fingers had mingled with the black tresses of her friend, the bandeau of bridal white, and fastened the robe, whose only luxury was its snowy hue. She could not satiate herself with admiring the intended bride; her sweet face alone, would have rendered her charming, but her elegant form, her gracefulness, and her extreme youth, which took from her visible approaches to maternity, all which in that state sometimes offends, made her altogether irresistible.

Laura was at first fearful that she had delayed dressing too long; she now thought she had dressed too soon. She listened to every step; her heart beat at every noise—the hurry of her thoughts was inconceivable.

"What wonderful change is to take place?" she asked herself, "what can happen in a few hours to increase my happiness, and cause all this emotion?"

It was five o'clock; the two friends descended to the parlour, which, always remarkably neat, wore this day an air of uncommon festivity.

Laura, viewing herself in the glass, condemned at one instant the friends of Belfield for thus detaining him, and at the next, blushed for her own impatience, when, hearing a foot in the entry, she cried, "He comes!" Sophia opened the door, and a stranger entering, handed her a note.

Sophia broke the seal, and as she was reading, turned pale, and trembled.—"What is it?" said Laura, snatching the paper from her hand, before Sophia had time to recover.—"Oh, my God!" she exclaimed, when she had seen its contents, and fell senseless to the floor.

Sophia, kneeling by her side, raised her. The stranger handed a glass of water.—When Laura opened her eyes, "Let me go for a carriage," he said, in a voice that shewed how much he was affected, "the boat is waiting,"—and left the room.

He met one, by accident, coming from the theatre, and prevailed on the coachman to render the service desired. When he returned to the room, "Let us go," said Sophia. Laura rose, and jumped into the carriage, as if nothing had happened.—They soon reached the river-side, and went into the boat that waited for them.

The sky was calm and serene. The moon shone bright, as in the night when Laura lay on her mother's grave. The tide, not having yet turned, no rapid current endangered or retarded their progress;

they glided along, in perfect silence, amid the floating cakes, whose margins glittered with the brilliancy of diamonds.

Laura reclined on her friend's bosom, who felt her hand, now burning hot, now cold like the ice which surrounded them. Her breath often became irregular, her eyes seemed deprived of their lustre.—Her silence was not that of tranquillity, but of despondence, which knows no utterance.

Thus they arrived on the Jersey shore. Their conductor led them to a house not far from it. Sophia could scarcely restrain the impatience of Laura, who pressed forward with convulsive energy.

Ferguson, coming down the staircase, met them, "Restrain your feelings," he said to Laura, "I beseech you; appear composed, at least, whatever you may suffer; any violent agitation will prove fatal to Belfield."

Laura made no reply, but disengaging herself from Sophia, stepped lightly up stairs. A door, half-open, leading to a room feebly lighted by a lamp, which burnt on the hearth, seemed to indicate the place she was seeking. She entered softly. An elderly woman sat in a corner; some of Belfield's clothes were scattered about in disorder; he lay on a bed, and over him was spread the listlessness of death.

Covering her face with her hands, she sat down on a chair, by the bedside. After a moment's pause, turning slowly her eyes, as if fearful that even their movement should disturb him, she beheld his distorted countenance, and sinking gently on her knees, bent her head over his hand that lay on the quilt.

A slight noise made at the door, seemed to rouse him. Sophia entered, followed by Ferguson. Belfield turned his head, and pronounced Laura's name.

"Dearest Laura," he said, "thy Belfield is in torture—oh come and relieve him!"

Laura thought he was sensible of her presence, and raising herself looked at him with a heart-rending expression of sorrow, but he knew her not, and a short silence ensued—when suddenly, as if awaking from the sleep of death, he started, recognized her, threw his arm round her, and drew her towards him.

"I knew thou wouldst not leave me," he said, "thou, who art all goodness, wouldst not abandon thy dying friend; but even thy power will be of no avail, they tear me from thee." His nerveless arm loosened its grasp—his languid head fell on the pillow.—But still his eye's intense gaze rested on Laura.

"She is my wife!" he cried, "protect her, for my sake!—Her child is mine, oh shelter it from harm!—

"That I could still hang to thee," he added, after a pause, and again seizing her, "but it cannot be—I go, dearest Laura, all is dark!"—His head fell on his shoulder, and he breathed no more.

CHAPTER XXXII

The sum of the poor girls' misery was filled; her nuptial contract was cancelled by the blood of her lover.

She was borne, bereft of consciousness, to another apartment, and for a long time succeeding fits were only interrupted by momentary exhaustion.

Towards morning she appeared more calm. Sophia sat near her in an arm chair, and slumbered, overpowered by fatigue and pain. Laura, opening her eyes perceived it, and stole with noiseless step to the place where she knew she would find her beloved.

The body of Belfield lay extended on a bier. Laura approached it, and raising the covering from his face, leaned over him; her cheek rested on his clay-cold cheek, her lip pressed to his in frantic anguish.

"It was for this moment that I staid!" she softly whispered, "it was to join thee that I lingered thus long behind!" A thrill of horror seemed to freeze her soul; her knees bent, and she sunk down by his side.

The noise awoke Sophia, who hastened to the spot, and the unfortunate girl was carried back to her bed:—but with returning life she uttered only the ravings of a disordered mind.

★ ★ ★ ★

Ye who revel in the hey-day of youth, and pursue with ardour a phantom which your vivid imagination dignifies with the name of bliss; suspend awhile the arduous pursuit, and reflect for a moment on the wretchedness that will attend its attainment. Does the attraction of beauty, the charm of innocence allure you?—beware of destroying that purity which forms the only solid basis of female happiness. Consider that of fleeting time the passing moments alone are yours, and palliate not in your minds the wrong you do, with the reparation you intend.

★ ★ ★ ★

To trace Laura through the many vicissitudes that awaited her, would be a task too painful. She became a mother,—She found protection from the gentleman whom Belfield had recommended her, and who discerned her worth amid the shades of the deepest affliction.—Her beauty continued unimpaired; her mind acquired new brilliancy: yet thro' every stage of her varying existence, happiness remained a stranger to her bosom; and her life was an exemplification of this truth:—"that perpetual uneasiness, disquietude, and irreversible misery, are the certain consequences of fatal misconduct in a woman; however gifted, or however reclaimed."

THE END.

Appendix A: Biographical Documents

Letter from Leonora Sansay to Aaron Burr (6 May 1803)[1]

[Leonora Sansay's correspondence with Aaron Burr and her appearance in his memoirs and private journals are among the richest of the otherwise sparse sources of biographical information about her life. The letter below of 6 May 1803 confirms that the "Clara" of *Secret History* was at least in part an invention to allow Sansay to write about herself. In this letter, Sansay presents to Burr a consolidated version of the first half of what will become *Secret History*. Evidently, as early as 1803 Sansay had anticipated publishing her letters. Coyly, she writes below, "should the story of Clara, with many incidents which I have omitted, and some observations on all that is passing here, be written in a pretty light style, could it be printed in America in a tolerable pamphlet in french and english, & a few numbers sent here? If it could I should be delighted, & know one who would undertake to write it." The source of the letter below is Charles Burdett, whose introductory comment has been retained. Burdett reprinted this letter in the appendix to his novel, *Margaret Moncrieffe; the First Love of Aaron Burr* (1860).]

In a postscript to Gov. Alston,[2] the night before the duel with Gen. Hamilton, Burr says: "If you can pardon and indulge a folly, I would suggest that Madame —, too well known under the name of 'Leonora,' has claims on my recollection. She is now with her husband at St. Jago, of Cuba."

---

[1]   Source: Charles Burdett, *Margaret Moncrieffe; the First Love of Aaron Burr* (New York: Derby & Jackson, 1860), 428–37. These selections are reprinted in the Appendix to Burdett's novel. The postscript can also be found in a letter from Burr to Joseph Alston, dated 10 July 1804, reprinted in Matthew Davis, ed., *Memoirs of Aaron Burr* (New York: Harper & Brothers, 1838), 324–26.

[2]   Burr's son-in-law. He became Governor of South Carolina in 1812.

[The following letter is from "Leonora" to A. Burr, the orthography of which is strictly adhered to.]

CAPE FRANCOIS, HAYTI, *May 6th*, 1803[1]

I have so much to relate of all that I have seen, heard, and done since my arrival in this country, that I am at a loss where to begin, finding myself in a world where the customs, language, dress & manners were so different from that which I had left. I was at first dazzled & bewildered, but on a nearer view I beheld the passing scene with a cooler eye & I almost despis'd—not the climate, oh no, this charming climate where smiling spring & laughing summer dance their eternal round. I cannot describe the effect it has on me, the nights in particular, love-inspiring nights!— but love was never known in this desolated country, perhaps no one was ever so sensible of this truth as myself—but more of this anon.

Almost a year has passed since I arrived here, during which time I have been coop'd up in the hollow bason in which the town is built, for there is no means of going a mile in any direction beyond it without I chose to make a sortie on the brigands which I have not yet determined on— when I was on the point of leaving the continent, do you recollect having told me, that order would be established here in less than three weeks after my arrival—alas we have beheld months after months passing away & we are still far from that tranquility so much desired—when Toussaint was arrested, it was suppos'd the war was finish'd & it would have been had vigorous measures been immediately pursued, but general le Clerc was without energy—tormented by jealousy for his wife, deceived by his officers, impos'd on by the black chiefs with whom he was alway in conference, he saw himself on the point of being made prisoner by the Negroes, & in the danger which his own imprudence had occasion'd, incapable of forming any project of defence, he only thought of saving himself by evacuating the place—this he was prevented doing by the admiral la touche & the efforts of the garde national which had been organiz'd but a few days before, repelled the Negroes & saved the Cape— the next day he gave a dinner to the officers of the garde national, made them a long speech (they say he was eloquent) and then died of a fever two or three days after. it was the best thing he could do, for if he had continued alive he would have liv'd dishonor'd—

I was presented to his wife a few days before the attack she's small, with

---

[1] The original date of this letter was printed as 1813; however, this is almost certainly an error and has been changed to 1803.

a common, laughing face, that announces neither dignity, nor wit, and I who have always thought that people in superior situations should be superior to common people, was surpris'd to find nothing extraordinary in the sister of Bonaparte—I gave her the Medal of Jefferson[1] which I suppose will figure in the collection of Medals at Paris—I saw her but once for she received nobody living retired at a plantation on the mountain—that is she received no ladies, foul mouth'd fame says she was far from cruel to Gen'l Boyer and all the etat major,—however when her husband died, she cut off her hair (which was very beautiful) to put in his coffin & play'd so well the part of a disconsolate widow, that she made every body laugh—after having had him embalm'd she embark'd with his lov'd remains for france, where she is (as I suppose you know) arriv'd—

general Rochambau, who was then commandant at port au prince, was sent for to take the command here, till a captain general should be nam'd,—he came, and here commences the adventures of Clara—do you recollect her? that Clara you once lov'd—She came to St domingo about the time I did, and at first liv'd tranquilly enough with her husband—but you know she never lov'd him & he was jealous, and sometimes render'd her miserable—but the general arriv'd and the scene was chang'd—

Apropos of Clara, you would not know her, positively not, the climate has had on her an effect quite miraculous, she has acquired a degree of enbonpoint that renders her charming, she has grown fairer and her black hair arrang'd a la greque gives her an air truly interesting her person even in your land of beauty was found passable but here it is regarded as a model of perfection—the general soon after his arrival gave a ball, Clara was invited and went, but in the crowd she attracted general notice without attracting the notice of the general—the week following the admiral la touche gave a ball on board his Vessel, Clara was there & there began her empire like that of Venus rising from the waves—the Ball was superb the whole length of the vessel was levell'd with a false floor and cover'd with a painted awning, ornamented with wreaths of natural flowers, with glasses & with lights beyond number—the seats were enclosed by beautiful palisades & the orchestra was plac'd in a gallery surrounding the main mast—you must observe that the creole women have no taste for dress, they cover themselves from head to foot, & the very few French women that are here, have follow'd the army & know very little of taste or fashion—

---

[1] Sansay or her publishers revised this detail in the novel; in Letter I, Mary gives Pauline Bonaparte a medal of Washington. See note 2, p. 65 (Letter I).

here then was the Theatre on which Clara exhibited for the first time, where she distanc'd all her rivals. Dressed with a licence which can be authoriz'd only by the heat (for she was almost naked) she was led round the room by an officer, where as a belle-femme and a stranger her vanity was fully gratified by the buzzes of admiration, her husband delighted by the splendor of what he deem'd his property follow'd her at a small distance, at length she was seated, but rous'd from her contemplation of surrounding objects by a flourish of music she turn'd her eyes to the door & saw the general who enter'd at that moment, this moment was decisive, he caught her eye, and saw for that night nothing but herself—when the first dance was finish'd, which she did not join (she walk'd again) her husband following as before, the general stopp'd him and ask'd who is that Lady—Madame—replied he—is she not a stranger?—yes an american—she's a charming creature (continued the general) but where's her husband? they say he's very jealous, and bien sot (?)—Monsieur le viola (answer'd the husband) & the general was a little disconcerted—as this conversation finish'd the walse began, he who has not seen Clara walse, knows not half her charms—dance delightful but dance dangerous from a woman fond of walsing, an adroit partner will gain all he wishes—but while she display'd in the mazes of the dance all the voluptuous graces of which her person is susceptible, her eye sought & fix'd that of the general, he alone fill'd her imagination—before the desire of securing that conquest, every other consideration faded, yet 'twas vanity alone that led her to desire it—the general resembles in his person Dr. Brown, rather shorter—and fat you know was always her aversion, but in this country above all things, 'tis dreadful. he has a face agreeable enough, a pretty laughing mouth, but nothing, *nothing* extraordinary, the bitise[1] (sic) he had made with her husband, render'd it difficult to approach her & had a fatal influence on the sequel of their acquaintance. at the dawn of day the ball broke up & the company return'd to their homes,—the general had in his suite an officer who was formerly intimate with the husband—the friendship was renew'd and the officer went to the house to reconnoitre,—it is that Duquesne that was in America during the last war, & as he says an ardent admirer of Miss Sally Shippen (now Mrs. Lee)—this Duquesne informed Clara of what she knew as well as himself, that the general was smitten, but he told her also something which she did not know, among which was that a grand ball was preparing at which he was expected to figure, she was invited, she went, and there large as is her

---

[1] Probably *bêtise*, a foolish act or remark.

portion of vanity, it was amply gratified by seeing the general at her feet, and all the women bursting with envy. The taste of the general influenc'd that of the company, & all the men offer'd their hommage at the same shrine, the eye of the husband saw what pass'd—he saw—& trembled, proud of possessing an object that excited universal admiration, he trembled lest that object should be wrested from him, he knew that the adoring general was a military despot, he knew also that the heart of his wife had never been his, but it was now too late, he had himself placed her on the scene, & it was not in his power to withdraw her.

Suffer me again to repeat that she was guided by vanity alone, & that not one feeling of her heart was interested, there was fifty young men in the room, whose persons, whose manners, could have interested her highly, some of them *had* almost show'd her tenderest favors, but 'twas power, 'twas place she aim'd at, and had she not been thwarted, she would have rul'd St. Domingue; at present she has sunk back to her original nothingness, because she has a husband who would neither shut his eyes and profit by her powers, nor open them and join her to secure & it this husband she owes to you. To return—the acquaintance here formed, was cultivated with indescribable ardor. Breakfasts, (which the french give delightfully), parties, balls, concerts, all succeeded rapidly, & the penchant of the chief was generally known; here admire the inconsistency of the French character, those who before scarcely noticed Clara since her marriage, now sought her with the utmost impressment, & those who pass'd without saluting her, now that she was almost the declar'd mistress of the general, show'd her the politest attention; the train of amusements was interrupted by an insurrection in the southern part of the colony—the general went to port-au-prince where he staid sometime, but at his return it was again commenc'd; a ball was announc'd for the third day after his arrival, where some interesting affairs were to be discuss'd; when lo! on the morning of that third day the brigands attack'd the town in three different directions, at three o'clock in the morning; they had taken the advanc'd posts by surprise, kill'd the officers, their wives, and the soldiers, and advanc'd upon the town; had they been wise enough to have done this without firing (which they might have done) we had been all lost; imagine our position—the cape is open on one side to the sea, the three others are surrounded by high mountains; on the tops of these mountains the negroes were encamp'd and all the country on the other side is in their power; their plan of attack was good, but it was badly executed, for one of the divisions advancing too precipitately spread the alarm; they were repell'd with great slaughter; all the troops that march'd, as well garde national as troops of the line, were order'd to remain on the frontiers; the general did not go out; he sent word to Clara, whose husband had march'd, to tell her not to be afraid, or if she was, to come to his house, & he'd send her on board the admiral's vessel; this she dar'd not do, having receiv'd orders from her husband, not to stir from the house; but towards evening, after repeated messages from him, she determined to go & to learn the fate of her husband, who had been all day, and still was, expos'd to the fire of the enemy. She went, accompanied by her little friend, & after a visit of half an hour, return'd; this was the only time he saw her except in crowded assemblages, and in the presence of another he could say very little; perhaps there was a piano, perhaps a library, but of this I am not certain; perhaps, also, Clara can say with Mrs. Coughlan,★ if he is no better in the fields of Mars than in the groves of Venus,—etc.

the ball was deferr'd till the next day, and the husband was to be kept at his post till it was over; but the next day news arriv'd from a small island near this place, call'd la tortue, that the negroes had pass'd an arm of the sea that divides it from the main land, & kill'd all the Pick, amounting to five thousand, and burn'd all the hospitals & plantations; this was another hindrance to the ball, and the garde national was permitted to descend; you know that the lives of any number of citizens is a very trifling consideration when the commander-in-chief wishes to remove an incommode husband, & on this occasion they were wantonly trifled with; from this moment the structure of Clara's good fortune was abolish'd; her husband had an infernal old servant who told him as soon as he enter'd, that Madame had gone with a servant of the general's to his house, accompanied by Mademoiselle, that the same servant had often brought letters, which Madame had answered (this, by the bye, was true); this, join'd to the fatigue he had been expos'd to unnecessarily, and the jokes that the officers (who all suspected the cause), pass'd on him, render'd him furious; he went to his wife's chamber, told her that all her conduct was known to him, & demanded the letters she had receiv'd; she denied having receiv'd them, and in short denied the whole affair; enraged at being unable to draw anything from her, he lock'd her up, and went to the general's house; he was receiv'd with great cordiality; but without paying any attention to the general's civility, he told him he had not come on a visit of friendship, but to reproach him with having attempted to seduce his

---

★   *Née* Moncrieffe.

wife, and with having seiz'd the occasion of the last attack, to expose to imminent danger him and the company he commanded, in order to be more at liberty to gratify his desires; the general, astonish'd, assur'd him that he was mistaken; but the husband listen'd not, he told him that if he was any other than the general-in-chief he'd have his life; it rests with you to forget that distinction and consider me as your equal, was the reply; this, however, was impossible; after having vented his wrath in a long speech, representing how abominable it was for a person who should be the father of the colony, and the protection of it's inhabitants, to seek to trouble the repose and destroy the peace of family's, he went off; the officers in the antechamber heard the altercation, and the story flew like wildfire through the town; the husband return'd to the house and prepar'd to embark his wife for Philadelphia; passeports were granted as a great favor for Clara and her suite, but the husband was not suffer'd to go; this leads to another observation; when the attachment was first suspected, the husband had arrang'd his affairs to go to Charleston; this did not please Clara; she inform'd the general, and an order was immediately issued that no officer of the garde national could leave his post during four months; & thus you see she had still some influence in public affairs; but the season was so bad at the time the eclat was made, that every body persuaded him not to send her, & the vessel on which she was to have embark'd, perish'd almost in view of the cape.

shortly after another ball was announced; the gen'ral sent Duquesne to the husband of Clara, begging him to accompany him to it, saying it was the only way to stop the storys that were in circulation; but the husband return'd the billet of invitation, requesting that another might never be sent; the ball had been, and such was the effect of Clara's adventure, that in those rooms which on similar occasions were crowded to suffocation, there was that night but fourteen ladies.

to account for this, you must be told that the inhabitants of this Island, that is, the creoles, regard the french army with more horror than the revolted Negroes, & with great reason. They are oppress'd beyond measure, and see daily the wreck of their fortunes torn from them by those who come to restore their property. The citizens are expos'd on every occasion to the fire of the enemy, while the troops of the line rest quietly in their forts. The people of france regard st. domingo as their peru,[1] and each individual that embarks for it becomes fully determined

---

[1] One of the most important Viceroyalties of the Spanish Empire and associated with Pizzaro's quest for New World gold.

to make his fortune at all events, & thus the war has been & will be continued for an indefinite time. They were irritated by these and many other vexations, of which they dar'd not complain; but a grief of a new kind was that of troubling a *menage*, not that fidelity was ever known or thought of here; but it was a novelty to see a husband concern himself about such an affair, & it was at least as great a one to see a simple individual propose a challenge to a general-in-chief. Every body expected to see the rash mortal imprisoned, embarked for france, or perhaps hanged; but as the general suffered it to pass, every one joined the cry, & the people were astonished to find one of their commonest customs made a wonder of. One consideration which, perhaps, had great weight with the general, was his having written very often and very explicitly to Clara. The letters had been destroyed; but the husband said he had them.

The general lost much of his popularity, and went shortly after to fix his government at port-au-prince, & thus ends the adventure of Clara, who, though she was disappointed in her ambitious aims, has been made so much the object of public attention, that she never appears without fixing every regard; for myself, I live retir'd, applying, with unceasing attention, to learn french, & as a proof of my progress, I send you a page written in that language.

Miss Sansay[1] is so near being married that—to-day is Wednesday— and on Saturday the ceremony will be performed. Since our arrival here, her temperament has declared itself, etc., etc. on that subject, one day or other, I intend exciting your regret. should the story of Clara, with many incidents which I have omitted, and some observations on all that is passing here, be written in a pretty light style, could it be printed in America in a tolerable pamphlet in french and english, & a few numbers sent here? If it could I should be delighted, & know one who would undertake to write it. Answer me. I think this long letter deserves an answer. There's certainly matter enough in it to form a romance; but whose life has afforded so many subjects for romance as that of its writer? I hear sometimes indistinct accounts of the United States, but nothing satisfactory. Have you seen many Swiss emigrants? Have you raised an army to hinder the french taking possession of Louisiana? All this I might learn from the papers, but I don't get them. Adieu. Remember, write to me. Apropos—the lady who takes charge of this paquet is driven from this

---

[1] If *Zelica, the Creole* is consulted, the "Miss Sansay" referred to here would be St. Louis' sister. Lapsansky records that Louis Sansay was a widower with a grown daughter when he married Leonora.

country by fear—in the last attack she made a vow to the blessed Virgin to throw herself into the sea if the brigands entered the town, so great was her fear that her person should be exposed to their lascivious desires. This was a rash vow, considering she is only sixty-four years old—there's nothing so diverting as the pretensions of the old women here. One of seventy has vowed to wear neither rouge nor lace, nor trinkets till the revolution is finished; giving for reason that ornaments are useless when the people don't enjoy the blessings of tranquillity, and that, perhaps, she might be deranged in the midst of her toilette by a hostile incursion. Do tell me if I write frenchified english, I dread that, of all things; it has so much the air of affectation, which I always abhorr'd. Couldn't answer the letter addressed to my Mentor—he might find himself indisposed to write, or for some other reason. I should prefer it infinitely.

Adieu, je vous embrasse.[1]

LEONORA.

2. Letter from Leonora Sansay to Aaron Burr (6 November 1808)

From Mrs. —.[2]

Philadelphia, November 6, 1808.

I am again in Philadelphia, my dear friend. But here, as in all places, deprived of your protection, I feel like a corps sans ame.[3] Sometimes the passing pleasures of the hour amuse me; but that support which your unalterable friendship afforded me; on which I leaned in proud defiance of the vicissitudes of fortune, of the caprices of chance, is removed by your absence and the constraint in which I live, obliged to devour my thoughts, my hopes, my feelings, for to whom can I communicate them? is aggravated by the recollection of the hours of delightful liberty in which your goodness once indulged me.

—is kind, almost to a fault. He has been very ill since August, and mends slowly. Yet, notwithstanding, he would have sailed for France if certain events which I suppose he will inform you of had not prevented him.

Everybody here is dull. Nothing heard but complaints of the embargo and the times. Just before I left New-Orleans I received a present of elegant medals from my friend in Mexico.

---

[1] "Goodbye, I embrace you."
[2] Matthew Davis, ed., *The Private Journal of Aaron Burr* (New York: Harper & Brothers, 1856) I:78–79.
[3] A body without a heart.

I wish, if not prevented by more serious business during your stay in London, that you would see Flaxman, the classical engraver, and get him to send me a set of his works, addressed to Bradford and Inskeep.[1] I have one volume of engravings. I believe the only one in this country, from Euripides. The model of this exquisite artist is his beautiful Italian wife. Perhaps, in complying with this request, you may make an agreeable acquaintance.

But, indeed, you are too far off. Approach us. Come only a little nearer. Come where I can meet you, and I will fly to find near you that happiness which none but you can impart; which I have never known except in your presence; which I do not wish to feel till I again behold you.

Y.Z.

3. Letter from Leonora Sansay to Aaron Burr (29 July 1812)

From Mrs. L★★★★★★.[2]

In the month of March, 1809, setting one gloomy day before the fire, turning over the leaves of an English periodical work, in which was an account of the fabric of certain ornamental articles then in vogue, the idea of making artificial flowers suggested itself; and I observed to a gentleman who was in the room, that, if I knew how to die, I could make artificial flowers, the sale of which might greatly contribute to my support; for my literary efforts had been so unproductive of emolument, that I received only one hundred dollars for "*Laura*," though even my self-love, inordinate as it may be, was amply satisfied by the praises bestowed on that little work.

The gentleman replied that, from his knowledge of chymistry and the theory of colours, he could probably assist me. Everything requisite was immediately procured, and I moved to a house in the neighbourhood of Gray's Ferry, where I had lived the preceding autumn. Here the first experiments were made, and they proved so satisfactory that it was thought justifiable to try them on a larger scale.

For this purpose a house was necessary, and the country for several miles round was explored without offering one that suited. At length, after seeking afar in vain, one was found much nearer. In the village of Hamilton, which stands on the hills that rise about a mile west of the Schuylkill, was a neat and elegant house imbosomed in trees; larger,

---

1 Bradford and Inskeep were Sansay's publishers.
2 Davis, ed., *The Private Journal of Aaron Burr*, II:440–46.

indeed, than was absolutely necessary, but, from having been long untenanted, was cheap. It was accordingly engaged. With some articles of furniture that had been saved from various wrecks, and a capital of *twenty dollars*, I began my establishment.

Mr. — lodged at a tavern on the other side of the road, and passed some time with me every day, which was employed in acquiring the knowledge wanting to perfect my little plan.

Chaptal, Fourcroi, Lavoisier, Accum, all the great chymists lent their aid. Every repository of arts and sciences was ransacked. Every treatise on dying consulted. The house was filled with retorts, alembics, chafing-dishes, drugs, and diestuffs.

Owing to the interruption of commerce at that period, artificial flowers were very scarce, and the sale of the first I made, though of very inferior quality, was so encouraging, that I engaged two young girls as assistants. The summer passed on in continued experiments and unremitted industry. The little manufactory had in autumn made rapid progress towards perfection, and acquired some celebrity. But the returns bore so little proportion to the expenditure, that the establishment must have fallen into ruin had not foreign aid contributed to its support.

A gentleman, the only friend of —, the only man who has stood the test of his late misfortunes, after having vainly tried every possible means of procuring him a place in which his talents might have been exerted to advantage, having learned the details of the pursuit in which he was engaged, and thinking it worth continuing, lent him a thousand dollars. This removed the pressure of some old debts, and gave vigour to the manufactory. During the winter its success was so great, that in the spring there were eight young girls and two boys employed. Comforts accumulated, and all in the house was life and activity.

The tables were covered with brilliant imitations of the most beautiful productions of nature; the cheerful voices of the girls mingled with the sound of the hammer on the leaden anvils, and taste and elegance seemed to have taken up their abode in our dwelling.

Three years have now elapsed, and one great object of industry has crowned my efforts, the attainment of perfection. At least, the flowers I make yield not, except in their infinite variety, to those imported from France. But, however agreeable this pursuit, the profits arising from it have been anticipated by its increasing magnitude; and without further assistance obtained from the hand before alluded to, and sums produced by the literary labours of —, it could not have held out. The vice that saps it is want of capital, and it is surprising how it has so long resisted.

For myself, I owe it three years of a novel existence; and a new celebrity which has, in some measure, consigned to oblivion that which marked the earlier part of my career. What I have gained on the score of happiness must be reserved for your private ear....

This flower manufactory gives weight. Its worth is known. Loans have been procured on it. Credits of fifteen hundred dollars at one bank, of six hundred at another, have been had. But, as I before observed, all this is swallowed up before it is obtained. The tools and fixtures cost from fifteen hundred to two thousand dollars, and the hands employed required much training ere they were sufficiently formed to be very useful.

If ever I get into smooth water, I shall laugh at the recollection of my discomfitures. At present they disturb my peace, and almost destroy my faculties.

I am sure, my dear friend, when you see me in the midst of my flock of girls, all rather pretty, from eight to eighteen years of age, you will be proud of me; proud of having discovered the germe of those talents that have borne me through so many vicissitudes. And I should wish no greater happiness, since you have returned, and the hope of seeing you may be indulged, than the continuance of this pursuit, which is more like an amusement than the drudgery of business, and has given me the means of rendering happy so many young creatures, who, in return, repay me with their love.

As for your friend Dr. Bollman,[1] I understand the extent of his wishes to be an employment by which he might gain fifteen hundred, or even a thousand dollars a year. An application was made to him to translate the remainder of Humboldt's Travels in New Spain, but I believe the applicants were too poor to be treated with. He offered to translate and condense that work into one volume, which, stripped of its abstruse parts, would be adapted to popular capacity. But, in these times of war, the people will either fight or groan, and, consequently, have no time for reading.

Reflect on these details for a moment, my dear friend, and think of the happiness I may still enjoy, if near you, in some of those oldfashioned houses in the neighbourhood of New-York. Old Stuyvesant's, where Mrs. Langworthy lived, or some other place. I could supply the city, and Albany, and Poughkeepsie with flowers. Large quantities have been sent from here to those places. You know in France they are an important article of commerce; and even in England I have been told

---

[1] Erich Bollman was a German-born physician and close friend of Aaron Burr's. He, like Sansay, transferred letters written in cipher for Burr to New Orleans in 1806. None of the carriers of Burr's correspondence were indicted for traitorous activity.

that those who manufacture them acquire large fortunes. Think, also, my dear friend, of the pleasure you would derive from the talents, the conversation, the energy of —, and rescue him from the mortification with which poverty and its attendant, neglect, have imbittered his life.

When I consider the miscreants that your goodness has raised, your bounty fed, I think it impossible that the power, which I am sure you would so joyfully exert, should be withheld of raising to distinction one so deserving. Those delightful hours of soul-felt intercourse might then again return, when, unbending from the severe duties of society, I was the soft green or the soul on which you loved to repose; and if, by enjoying, I can impart happiness so exquisite, my heart, my disposition, my feelings, my affections are still the same; glowing with the same warmth, animated with the same ardor.

Had I been the wife of a prince or a king, I should have flown to you as soon as your arrival was announced, bongré malgré[1] the royal permission. But you will readily conceive how much I am the soul of this establishment. So much so am I, that though the city lays before me as if it was painted on a map, I am often several months without going to it, and am very seldom absent an hour. In August I shall give a short vacation, and will fly anywhere to meet you, though even for a moment.

You must expect, my dear friend, to see me somewhat changed. Not the *morale*—that is unalterable; but the *physique* has acquired a great accession of em bon point,[2] which, owing to my height, distributes itself pretty well, so that the proportions are not lost, but the scale considerably enlarged. But this at the first interview you will not perceive, nor anything but a devoted creature irradiated with joy. Oh, I knew this hour would come. During your absence it was strongly impressed on my mind. In my dreams I have beheld you looking benignantly at me; and something whispered to my heart that at length the hour, with feeling fraught, would be given me; that again in your presence I should feel that unmixed delight which from you only I have received—the happiness attending the most pure, most ardent, most exalted friendship.

You receive now the prominent features of my situation. Many are the shades. The trifles which enliven or embellish it will form a corps de reserve[3] for your amusement when we meet. In the mean time I commend myself to your thoughts; but, above all, I wish to fix your attention of the sufferings of

L.

---

[1] Regardless.
[2] Condition of being plump.
[3] A store house.

4. William Wirt's Speech at Aaron Burr's Trial (August 1807)

[During Burr's trial for treason against the United States (held in Richmond,Virginia and presided over by Chief Justice John Marshall), William Wirt was co-prosecutor. He became renowned for his oratory, and this selection from his remarks at the trial were often reprinted in primers throughout the nineteenth century. It is little surprise, then, that the most notorious account of Burr's designs also continued to be the most widely circulated. Harman Blennerhassett (1765–1831) was drawn into Burr's plans and lost considerable land and property.]

Who is Blennerhassett? A native of Ireland, a man of letters, who fled from the storms of his own country to find quiet in ours. His history shows that war is not the natural element of his mind. If it had been, he never would have exchanged Ireland for America. So far is an army from furnishing the society natural and proper to Mr. Blennerhassett's character, that on his arrival in America, he retired even from the population of the Atlantic states, and sought quiet and solitude in the bosom of our western forests. But he carried with him taste and science and wealth; and lo! the desert smiled. Possessing himself of a beautiful island in the Ohio, he rears upon it a palace, and decorates it with every romantic embellishment of fancy. A shrubbery, that Shenstone[1] might have envied, blooms around him. Music that might have charmed Calypso and her nymphs,[2] is his. An extensive library spreads its treasures before him. A philosophical apparatus offers to him all the secrets and mysteries of nature. Peace, tranquility, and innocence shed their mingled delights around him. And to crown the enchantment of the scene, a wife who is said to be lovely even beyond her sex and graced with every accomplishment that can render it irresistible, had blessed him with her love, and made him the father of several children. The evidence would convince you that this is but a faint picture of the real life. In the midst of all this peace, this innocent simplicity and this tranquility, this feast of the mind, this pure banquet of the heart, the destroyer comes; he comes to change this paradise into a hell. Yet the flowers do not wither at his approach. No monitory shuddering through the bosom of their unfortunate possessor warns him of the ruin that is coming upon him. A stranger presents himself. Introduced to their civilities by the high rank which he

---

[1] William Shenstone (1714–63), a popular English poet, who was known for his expensive hobby of landscaping his inherited estate, The Leasowes, in the West Midlands of Britain.

[2] Goddess who tried to seduce Odysseus with the offer of immortality after he was shipwrecked on the island of Ogygia.

had lately held in his country, he soon finds his way to their hearts, by the dignity and elegance of his demeanor, the light and beauty of his conversation, and the seductive and fascinating power of his address. The conquest was not difficult. Innocence is ever simple and credulous. Conscious of no design itself, it suspects none in others. It wears no guard before its breast. Every door and portal and avenue of the heart is thrown open, and all who choose it enter. Such was the state of Eden when the serpent entered its bowers. The prisoner, in a more engaging form, winding himself into the open and unpracticed heart of the unfortunate Blennerhassett, found but little difficulty in changing the native character of that heart and the objects of its affection. By degrees he infuses into it the poison of his own ambition. He breathes into it the fire of his own courage; a daring and desperate thirst for glory; an ardor panting for great enterprises, for all the storm and bustle and hurricane of life. In a short time the whole man is changed; and every object of his former delight is relinquished. No more he enjoys the tranquil scene; it has become flat and insipid to his taste. His books are abandoned. His retort and crucible are thrown aside. His shrubbery blooms and breathes its fragrance upon the air in vain; he likes it not. His ear no longer drinks the rich melody of music; it longs for the trumpet's clangor and the cannon's roar. Even the prattle of his babes, once so sweet, no longer affects him; and the angel smile of his wife, which hitherto touched his bosom with ecstasy so unspeakable, is now unseen and unfelt. Greater objects have taken possession of his soul. His imagination has been dazzled by visions of diadems, of stars and garters and titles of nobility. He has been taught to burn with restless emulation at the names of great heroes and conquerors. His enchanted island is destined soon to relapse into a wilderness; and in a few months we find the beautiful and tender partner of his bosom, whom he lately "permitted not the winds of" summer "to visit too roughly," we find her shivering at midnight, on the winter banks of the Ohio, and mingling her tears with the torrents, that froze as they fell. Yet this unfortunate man, thus deluded from his interest and his happiness, thus seduced from the paths of innocence and peace, thus confounded in the toils that were deliberately spread for him and overwhelmed by the mastering spirit and genius of another—this man, thus ruined and undone and made to play a subordinate part in this grand drama of guilt and treason, this man is to be called the principal offender, while he by whom he was thus plunged in misery is comparatively innocent, a mere accessory! Is this reason? Is it law? Is it humanity? Sir, neither the human heart nor the human understanding will bear a perversion so monstrous and absurd! so shocking to the soul! so revolting to reason! Let Aaron Burr, then, not shrink from the high destination which he has courted, and having already ruined Blennerhassett in fortune, character and happiness forever, let him not attempt to finish the tragedy by thrusting that ill-fated man between himself and punishment.

Upon the whole, sir, reason declares Aaron Burr the principal in this crime, and confirms herein the sentence of the law; and the gentleman, in saying that his offence is of a derivative and accessorial nature, begs the question, and draws his conclusions from what, instead of being conceded, is denied. It is clear from what has been said that Burr did not derive his guilt from the men on the island, but imparted his own guilt to them; that he is not an accessory but a principal; and, therefore, that there is nothing in the objection which demands a record of their conviction before we shall go on with our proof against him.

Aaron Burr

5. Review of *Laura* from *The Port-Folio* (1809)

[Formerly edited by Federalist and staunch anti-Jeffersonian Joseph Dennie, *The Port-Folio* had been purchased by the publishing house of Bradford & Inskeep, the publishers of both *Secret History* and *Laura*, shortly before these reviews were published. Though Dennie remained the lead editor for several more years, the journal distanced itself from its original partisan agenda. Partisan zeal appears to have been replaced by more commercial motives.]

i. *The Port-Folio* (January 1809)

We took up this book, as we generally do modern novels, with the expectation of finding an ordinary love adventure insipidly told, or wrought up with far-fetched words and laboured sentenced into a production still more insupportable; but we must confess that we never have been more agreeably disappointed. It is true, the story has nothing in it marvellous or extraordinary; it neither surprises nor rivets the attention by intricacy of plot. The heroine, a young female, endowed with beauty, uncommon powers of mind, and a glowing imagination, loses her mother, her only friend, at the age of fifteen, and while deploring her loss becomes accidentally acquainted with a gentleman who discerns her worth, falls in love with her, and finds his attachment returned. Pressed by cold relatives to a marriage at which her feelings revolt, she prefers putting herself, to escape from it, under the protection of her lover. From this first false step further imprudencies arise, and misery and destruction, as usual, are the consequences. No tale can be more simple; the occurrences are such as every observer of life too frequently meets with; but they are related with a choice of expression so happy, in a language so elegant and melodious, and at the same time so chaste and unaffected, that we cannot discover the sentence which could be spared, or the word that seemed to be sought for. The thoughts of the author appear to be neatly and harmoniously conceived in the first instance, and such is the genius pervading the whole narrative that we could read it, and actually have read it, again and again, with that exquisite pleasure with which we would attend the execution of a first rate piece of music, though often heard previously, or stand for hours fascinated before the same beautiful picture.

We forbear making extracts, for were we to begin we should not know when to stop; nor do we think it requisite, for we cannot doubt that the book to be read needs only to be known, and that the American public, by showing a due sensibility on the occasion, will encourage a writer of whom it ought to feel proud.

This writer, as we have since perceived by the advertisement, is the same lady who published about a year ago a collection of letters written from St. Domingo. We recognize the style and the talents, which had already obtained our admiration; but the work before us is more finished, and we sincerely hope that the fair author may diligently prosecute a career of mental exertion for which she seems so eminently qualified.

How she acquired or retained the purity of taste to which this narrative is indebted for all its beauties, in an age when writers, from want of superior abilities seem reduced to seek in eccentricity and deviation from nature the means of awakening interest; when most of the fashionable novels disgust by a bombastical assemblage of unmeaning words, appearing themselves astonished how they came together, and are rendered only somewhat less obnoxious by being crammed with the spoils of better times, as a French ragout is with forced balls[1]—we are at a loss to conceive. But we are glad that the fact exists, and while we have availed ourselves of this opportunity of thus expressing the praise due to merit, we feel confident that it will be reechoed by every one who peruses this charming performance.

ii. *The Port*-Folio (March 1809)

Mr. OLDSCHOOL,

Although your first number contained a very spirited, correct, and flattering critique on the novel just published under the title of Laura, I cannot forbear to express the delight afforded me by its perusal. It is a simple tale, told with inimitable pathos; and cannot fail to elicit a tear from all whose hearts beat responsive to the sentiments of humanity.

The author declares it to be founded on fact, and the scenes she describes so closely resemble those which too frequently occur in real life, that her assertion is entitled to the most perfect credit. And this is one of the charms of the work. We are not called upon to yield our sympathy to imaginary distresses, but an attack is made directly upon the heart through the very passes which Nature herself has pointed out as the most exposed to an assailant.

---

[1]   As a French sauce is made richer with "forced-meat balls," small pieces of left-over beef parts, such as liver or heart, congealed with lard.

There is no one situation in which Laura is placed into which we cannot perfectly enter. We feel every pang that rends her bosom, we sympathize in all her joys. Horace lays it down as a maxim—that

"Non Deus intersit, nisi dignus vindice nodus."[1]

Our author follows a better rule, and avoids entangling her story, in such a tissue or circumstances as would require supernatural aid to unravel. Her style is simple, well adapted to narration, and on particular occasions highly energetic. It is pure and polished English, and cannot displease the ear of the most classical scholar. No bombastic epithets, no "sesquipedalia verba"[2] prolong a tedious page. No affectation of conciseness gives rise to obscurity. Had there been less of it the heart could not have indulged sufficiently in the luxury of feeling it excites. Had there been more, the inability of our nature to support, too long, any unusual excitement, would have lessened its effect. We glory in considering it the production of an American. It is as far superior to the crowd of novels daily issuing from the presses of Europe, teeming with the wildest absurdity, in the guise of romance, as the eagle-flights of the immortal Milton[3] to the petty productions of a Bayes[4] skimming like the swallow along the surface of the ground.

The description of the dreadful ravages of the yellow fever is admirably drawn. All the images of horror attendant on such a scene of universal desolation are well conceived and forcibly presented to the mind. If the reader will suffer his imagination to dwell on the description, his sensations will do justice to its force.

The situation of poor Laura after her supposed desertion by Belfield; and at his bed-side in the closing scene, is drawn in the most vivid colours, and must wring the drop of pity from the hardest heart.

The moral of the story is excellent. And throughout are dispersed a variety of pertinent reflections, so artfully disposed as not to detract in the least from the interest of the recital. It affords an impressive lesson to the imprudent female; and speaks home to the heart of the libertine. Those whom fortune has placed above the reach of temptation it may

---

1 "Nor should God intervene, unless his favor be appropriate." The Latin is inaccurately quoted from Horace's *Ars Poetica* (circa 20 BCE), lines 191–92.
2 "One and a half foot long words," i.e., very long words.
3 John Milton (1608–74).
4 Likely the Reverend Thomas Bayes (1702–61), elected to the Royal Society despite a scant record of publication.

teach to commiserate the fate of others. And to those whose situation in life does not exempt them from danger, it will point out the necessity of the most guarded caution, and the inevitable misery consequent upon one single step of an imprudent or vitious nature.

ORIN.

Appendix B: Literary Selections

1. Alexander Pope, "Eloisa to Abelard" (1717)[1]

[Pope's famous poem plays a central role in George Belfield's seduction of Laura. As Gillian Brown explains, Laura succumbs "by putting herself in the place of Eloisa *vis-à-vis* Abelard." Laura becomes a quixotic reader, mistaking the world represented in books for reality, and thus "susceptible to anyone willing to play Mr. B or Abelard to her heroine."[2]]

The ARGUMENT.

Abelard and Eloisa flourish'd in the twelfth Century; they were two of the most distinguish'd persons of their age in learning and beauty, but for nothing more famous than for their unfortunate passion. After a long course of Calamities, they retired each to a several[3] Convent, and consecrated the remainder of their days to religion. It was many years after this separation, that a letter of Abelard's to a Friend, which contain'd the history of his misfortune, fell into the hands of Eloisa. This awakening all her tenderness, occasion'd those celebrated letters (out of which the following is partly extracted) which give so lively a picture of the struggles of grace and nature, virtue and passion.

In these deep solitudes and awful cells,
Where heav'nly-pensive, contemplation dwells,
And ever-musing melancholy reigns;

---

[1] Peter or Pierre Abelad was a French philosopher and theologian who, in 1117, at the age of 38, fell in love with his 17-year-old pupil, Héloise. They became lovers and she gave birth to his child, and the two were secretly married. Héloise's uncle, enraged at Abelard's actions, hired a gang of thugs to attack and castrate him. The two lovers separated, Héloise entering a convent and Abelard a monastery. Both devoted their lives to God and went on to successful careers in the church. Several years later the two exchanged a series of letters in Latin, which were published in 1616. A romanticized French version appeared in 1687, and in 1713 this was translated into English. It was upon the English translation that Pope based his poem.

[2] Brown, Gillian. "The Quixotic Fallacy." *Novel: A Forum on Fiction* 32.2 (1999): 256. "Mr. B" is the seducer from Samuel Richardson's *Pamela* (1740).

[3] Separate.

What means this tumult in a Vestal's[1] veins?
Why rove my thoughts beyond this last retreat?
Why feels my heart its long-forgotten heat?
Yet, yet I love!—From Abelard it came,
And Eloïsa yet must kiss the name.

Dear fatal[2] name! rest ever unreveal'd,
Nor pass these lips in holy silence seal'd:
Hide it, my heart, within that close disguise,
Where mix'd with God's, his lov'd Idea lies:
Oh write it not, my hand—the name appears
Already written—wash it out, my tears!
In vain lost Eloïsa weeps and prays,
Her heart still dictates, and her hand obeys.

Relentless walls! whose darksom round contains
Repentant sighs, and voluntary pains:
Ye rugged rocks! which holy knees have worn;
Ye grots and caverns shagg'd with horrid thorn!
Shrines! where their vigils pale-ey'd virgins keep,
And pitying saints, whose statues learn to weep![3]
Tho' cold like you, unmov'd and silent grown,
I have not yet forgot my self to stone.
Heav'n claims me all in vain, while he has part,
Still rebel nature holds out half my heart;
Nor pray'rs nor fasts its stubborn pulse restrain,
Nor tears, for ages, taught to flow in vain.

Soon as thy letters trembling I unclose,
That well-known name awakens all my woes.
Oh name for ever sad! for ever dear!
Still breath'd in sighs, still usher'd with a tear.
I tremble too where'er my own I find,
Some dire misfortune follows close behind.

---

[1]   In ancient Rome, vestal virgins were those devoted to the service of Vesta, goddess of the
      hearth, and to the maintenance of her sacred fire. "Vestal" later became synonymous with
      "virgin" or "nun."
[2]   Name that has determined Eloisa's destiny, or fate.
[3]   Stone statues placed in damp places collect condensation, which then runs down their
      surfaces.

Line after line my gushing eyes o'erflow,
Led thro' a sad variety of woe:
Now warm in love, now with'ring in thy bloom,
Lost in a convent's solitary gloom!
There stern Religion quench'd th'unwilling flame,
There dy'd the best of passions, Love and Fame.[1]

Yet write, oh write me all, that I may join
Griefs to thy griefs, and echo sighs to thine.
Nor foes nor fortune take this pow'r away;
And is my Abelard less kind than they?
Tears still are mine, and those I need not spare,
Love but demands what else were shed in pray'r;
No happier task these faded eyes pursue;
To read and weep is all they now can do.

Then share thy pain, allow that sad relief;
Ah, more than share it! give me all thy grief.
Heav'n first taught letters for some wretch's aid,
Some banish'd lover, or some captive maid;
They live, they speak, they breathe what love inspires,
Warm from the soul, and faithful to its fires,
The virgin's wish without her fears impart,
Excuse[2] the blush, and pour out all the heart,
Speed the soft intercourse from soul to soul,
And waft a sigh from Indus to the Pole.

Thou know'st how guiltless first I met thy flame,
When Love approach'd me under Friendship's name;
My fancy form'd thee of angelick kind,
Some Emanation of th'all-beauteous Mind.[3]
Those smiling eyes, attemp'ring ev'ry ray,
Shone sweetly lambent with celestial day.
Guiltless I gaz'd; heav'n listen'd while you sung;
And truths divine came mended from that tongue.*

---

*   He was her preceptor in philosophy and divinity.

---

[1]   Good reputation. Abelard's disgrace had ruined his good name and his professional ambitions.
[2]   Remove the need for.
[3]   God.

From lips like those what precept fail'd to move?
Too soon they taught me 'twas no sin to love:
Back thro' the paths of pleasing sense I ran,
Nor wish'd an Angel whom I lov'd a Man.
Dim and remote the joys of saints I see;
Nor envy them that heav'n I lose for thee.

How oft', when prest to marriage, have I said,
Curse on all laws but those which love has made?
Love, free as air, at sight of human ties,
Spreads his light wings, and in a moment flies.
Let wealth, let honour, wait the wedded dame,
August her deed, and sacred be her fame;
Before true passion all those views remove,
Fame, wealth, and honour! what are you to Love?
The jealous God,[1] when we profane his fires,
Those restless passions in revenge inspires,
And bids them make mistaken mortals groan,
Who seek in love for ought but love alone.
Should at my feet the world's great master[2] fall,
Himself, his throne, his world, I'd scorn 'em all:
Not Cæsar's empress wou'd I deign to prove;
No, make me mistress to the man I love;
If there be yet another name, more free,
More fond than mistress, make me that to thee!
Oh happy state! when souls each other draw,
When love is liberty, and nature, law:
All then is full, possessing, and possess'd,
No craving void left aking in the breast:
Ev'n thought meets thought, e'er from the lips it part,
And each warm wish springs mutual from the heart.
This sure is bliss (if bliss on earth there be)
And once the lot of Abelard and me.

Alas how chang'd! what sudden horrors rise?
A naked Lover bound and bleeding lies!
Where, where was Eloïse? her voice, her hand,

---

[1]   Cupid.
[2]   Most likely a reference to Alexander the Great.

Her ponyard, had oppos'd the dire command.
Barbarian stay! that bloody stroke restrain;
The crime was common, common be the pain.[1]
I can no more; by shame, by rage suppress'd,
Let tears, and burning blushes speak the rest.

Canst thou forget that sad, that solemn day,
When victims at yon' altar's foot we lay?
Canst thou forget what tears that moment fell,
When, warm in youth, I bade the world farewell?
As with cold lips I kiss'd the sacred veil,
The shrines all trembled, and the lamps grew pale:
Heav'n scarce believ'd the conquest it survey'd,
And Saints with wonder heard the vows I made.
Yet then, to those dread altars as I drew,
Not on the Cross my eyes were fix'd, but you:
Not grace, or zeal, love only was my call,
And if I lose thy love, I lose my all.
Come! with thy looks, thy words, relieve my woe;
Those still at least are left thee to bestow.
Still on that breast enamour'd let me lie,
Still drink delicious poison from thy eye,
Pant on thy lip, and to thy heart be press'd;
Give all thou canst—and let me dream the rest.
Ah no! instruct me other joys to prize,
With other beauties charm my partial eyes,
Full in my view set all the bright abode,
And make my soul quit Abelard for God.

Ah think at least thy flock deserves thy care,
Plants of thy hand, and children of thy pray'r.
From the false world in early youth they fled,
By thee to mountains, wilds, and deserts led.
You rais'd these hallow'd walls;[2] the desert smil'd,
And Paradise was open'd in the Wild.

---

[1] Punishment.
[2] When Abelard became abbot of St. Gildas-de-Rhuys, he gave Paraclete, the hermitage
     where he had originally established his monastic school, to Héloise. She and her religious
     community had recently been evicted from their property. It was shortly after this that
     the two began their correspondence.

No weeping orphan saw his father's stores
Our shrines irradiate, or emblaze the floors;
No silver saints, by dying misers given,
Here bribe'd the rage of ill-requited heav'n:
But such plain roofs as Piety could raise,
And only vocal with the Maker's praise.
In these lone walls (their day's eternal bound)
These moss-grown domes with spiry turrets crown'd,
Where awful arches make a noon-day night,
And the dim windows shed a solemn light;
Thy eyes diffus'd a reconciling ray,
And gleams of glory brighten'd all the day.
But now no face divine contentment wears,
'Tis all blank sadness, or continual tears.
See how the force of others pray'rs I try,
 (Oh pious fraud of am'rous charity!)
But why should I on others pray'rs depend?
Come thou, my father, brother, husband, friend!
Ah let thy handmaid, sister, daughter move,
And, all those tender names in one, thy love!
The darksome pines that o'er yon' rocks reclin'd
Wave high, and murmur to the hollow wind,
The wand'ring streams that shine between the hills,
The grots that echo to the tinkling rills,
The dying gales that pant upon the trees,
The lakes that quiver to the curling breeze;
No more these scenes my meditation aid,
Or lull to rest the visionary[1] maid.
But o'er the twilight groves, and dusky caves,
Long-sounding isles, and intermingled graves,
Black Melancholy sits, and round her throws
A death-like silence, and a dread repose:
Her gloomy presence saddens all the scene,
Shades ev'ry flow'r, and darkens ev'ry green,
Deepens the murmur of the falling floods,
And breathes a browner horror on the woods.

---

[1] Dreamy.

Yet here for ever, ever must I stay;
Sad proof how well a lover can obey!
Death, only death, can break the lasting chain;
And here ev'n then, shall my cold dust remain,
Here all its frailties, all its flames resign,
And wait, 'till 'tis no sin to mix with thine.

Ah wretch! believ'd the spouse of God in vain,
Confess'd within the slave of love and man.
Assist me heav'n! but whence arose that pray'r?
Sprung it from piety, or from despair?
Ev'n here, where frozen chastity retires,
Love finds an altar for forbidden fires.
I ought to grieve, but cannot what I ought;
I mourn the lover, not lament the fault;
I view my crime, but kindle at the view,
Repent old pleasures, and sollicit new;
Now turn'd to heav'n, I weep my past offence,
Now think of thee, and curse my innocence.
Of all affliction taught a lover yet,
'Tis sure the hardest science,[1] to forget!
How shall I lose the sin, yet keep the sense,[2]
And love th'offender, yet detest th'offence?
How the dear object from the crime remove,
Or how distinguish penitence from love?
Unequal[3] task! a passion to resign,
For hearts so touch'd, so pierc'd, so lost as mine.
E'er such a soul regains its peaceful state,
How often must it love, how often hate!
How often hope, despair, resent, regret,
Conceal, disdain—do all things but forget.
But let heav'n seize it, all at once 'tis fir'd,
Not touch'd, but rapt; not waken'd, but inspir'd!
Oh come! oh teach me nature to subdue,
Renounce my love, my life, my self—and you.
Fill my fond heart with God alone, for he
Alone, can rival, can succeed to thee.

---

[1]   Kind of knowledge.
[2]   Meaning both "sensation" and "faculty of perception."
[3]   Excessive.

How happy is the blameless Vestal's lot?
The world forgetting, by the world forgot:
Eternal sun-shine of the spotless mind!
Each pray'r accepted, and each wish resign'd;
Labour and rest, that equal periods keep;
"Obedient slumbers that can wake and weep;"[1]
Desires compos'd, affections ever even;
Tears that delight, and sighs that waft to heav'n.
Grace shines around her with serenest beams,
And whisp'ring Angels prompt her golden dreams.
For her the Spouse prepares the bridal ring,[2]
For her white virgins Hymenæals sing,
For her th'unfading rose of Eden blooms,
And wings of Seraphs shed divine perfumes,
To sounds of heav'nly harps she dies away,
And melts in visions of eternal day.

Far other dreams my erring soul employ,
Far other raptures, of unholy joy:
When at the close of each sad, sorrowing day,
Fancy restores what vengeance snatch'd away,
Then conscience sleeps, and leaving nature free,
All my loose soul unbounded springs to thee.
O curst, dear horrors of all-conscious night!
How glowing guilt exalts the keen delight!
Provoking Dæmons all restraint remove,
And stir within me ev'ry source of love.
I hear thee, view thee, gaze o'er all thy charms,
And round thy phantom glue my clasping arms.
I wake: —no more I hear, no more I view,
The phantom flies me, as unkind as you.
I call aloud; it hears not what I say;
I stretch my empty arms; it glides away.
To dream once more I close my willing eyes;
Ye soft illusions, dear deceits, arise!
Alas, no more!—methinks we wand'ring go
Thro' dreary wastes, and weep each other's woe,

---

[1] From Richard Crashaw's *Description of a Religious House* (1648).
[2] Certain orders of nuns wear a wedding ring to symbolize their marriage to Christ.

Where round some mould'ring tow'r pale ivy creeps,
And low-brow'd rocks hang nodding o'er the deeps.
Sudden you mount, you beckon from the skies;
Clouds interpose, waves roar, and winds arise.
I shriek, start up, the same sad prospect find,
And wake to all the griefs I left behind.

For thee the fates, severely kind, ordain
A cool suspense from pleasure and from pain;
Thy life a long, dead calm of fix'd repose;
No pulse that riots, and no blood that glows.
Still as the sea, e'er winds were taught to blow,
Or moving spirit bade the waters flow;
Soft as the slumbers of a saint forgiv'n,
And mild as opening gleams of promis'd heav'n.

Come Abelard! for what hast thou to dread?
The torch of Venus burns not for the dead.
Nature stands check'd; Religion disapproves;
Ev'n thou art cold—yet Eloïsa loves.
Ah hopeless, lasting flames! like those that burn
To light the dead, and warm th'unfruitful urn.[1]

What scenes appear, where-e'er I turn my view,
The dear Ideas where I fly, pursue,
Rise in the grove, before the altar rise,
Stain all my soul, and wanton in my eyes.
I waste the Matin lamp[2] in sighs for thee,
Thy image steals between my God and me,
Thy voice I seem in ev'ry hymn to hear,
With ev'ry bead[3] I drop too soft a tear.
When from the censer clouds of fragrance roll,[4]
And swelling organs lift the rising soul,
One thought of thee puts all the pomp to flight,
Priests, tapers, temples, swim before my sight:

---

1   The ancient Romans kept lamps perpetually burning in their tombs.
2   Light used for the dawn service.
3   I.e., rosary bead.
4   Incense was burned and its smoke diffused by the swinging of a container called a censer.

In seas of flame my plunging soul is drown'd,
While Altars blaze, and Angels tremble round.

While prostrate here in humble grief I lie,
Kind, virtuous drops just gath'ring in my eye,
While praying, trembling, in the dust I roll,
And dawning grace is opening on my soul:
Come, if thou dar'st, all charming as thou art!
Oppose thy self to heav'n; dispute my heart;
Come, with one glance of those deluding eyes
Blot out each bright Idea of the skies;
Take back that grace, those sorrows, and those tears;
Take back my fruitless penitence and pray'rs;
Snatch me, just mounting, from the blest abode;
Assist the fiends, and tear me from my God!

No, fly me, fly me! far as Pole from Pole;
Rise Alps between us! and whole oceans roll!
Ah, come not, write not, think not once of me,
Nor share one pang of all I felt for thee.
Thy oaths I quit, thy memory resign;
Forget, renounce me, hate whate'er was mine.
Fair eyes, and tempting looks (which yet I view!)
Long lov'd, ador'd ideas, all adieu!
O grace serene! oh virtue heav'nly fair!
Divine oblivion of low-thoughted care!
Fresh blooming hope, gay daughter of the sky!
And faith, our early immortality![1]
Enter, each mild, each amicable guest;
Receive, and wrap me in eternal rest!

See in her cell sad Eloïsa spread,
Propt on some tomb, a neighbour of the dead!
In each low wind methinks a Spirit calls,
And more than Echoes talk along the walls.
Here, as I watch'd the dying lamps around,
From yonder shrine I heard a hollow sound.
'Come, sister, come! (it said, or seem'd to say)

---

[1] I.e., faith in an afterlife provides the first experience of immortality.

'Thy place is here, sad sister, come away!
'Once like thy self, I trembled, wept, and pray'd,
'Love's victim then, tho' now a sainted maid:
'But all is calm in this eternal sleep;
'Here grief forgets to groan, and love to weep,
'Ev'n Superstition loses ev'ry fear:
'For God, not man, absolves our frailties here.'

I come, I come! prepare your roseate bow'rs,
Celestial palms, and ever-blooming flow'rs.
Thither, where sinners may have rest, I go,
Where flames refin'd in breasts seraphic glow:
Thou, Abelard! the last sad office[1] pay,
And smooth my passage to the realms of day;
See my lips tremble, and my eye-balls roll,
Suck my last breath, and catch the flying soul![2]
Ah no—in sacred vestments may'st thou stand,
The hallow'd taper trembling in thy hand,
Present the Cross before my lifted eye,
Teach me at once, and learn of me to die.
Ah then, thy once lov'd Eloïsa see!
It will be then no crime to gaze on me.
See from my cheek the transient roses fly!
See the last sparkle languish in my eye!
'Till ev'ry motion, pulse, and breath, be o'er;
And ev'n my Abelard belov'd no more.
O Death all-eloquent! you only prove
What dust we doat on, when 'tis man we love.
Then too, when fate shall thy fair frame destroy,
 (That cause of all my guilt, and all my joy)
In trance extatic may thy pangs be drown'd,
Bright clouds descend, and Angels watch thee round,
From opening skies may streaming glories shine,
And Saints embrace thee with a love like mine.

---

[1] Last rites.
[2] It was commonly believed that at the time of death the soul left the body through the
mouth.

May one kind grave unite each hapless name,★
And graft my love immortal on thy fame!
Then, ages hence, when all my woes are o'er,
When this rebellious heart shall beat no more;
If ever chance two wand'ring lovers brings
To Paraclete's white walls and silver springs,
O'er the pale marble shall they join their heads,
And drink the falling tears each other sheds;
Then sadly say, with mutual pity mov'd,
"Oh may we never love as these have lov'd!
From the full quire when loud Hosanna's[1] rise,
And swell the pomp of dreadful sacrifice,[2]
Amid that scene, if some relenting eye
Glance on the stone where our cold relicks lie,
Devotion's self shall steal a thought from heav'n,
One human tear shall drop, and be forgiv'n.
And sure if fate some future bard shall join
In sad similitude of griefs to mine,
Condemn'd whole years in absence to deplore,
And image charms he must behold no more;
Such if there be, who loves so long, so well;
Let him our sad, our tender story tell;[3]
The well-sung woes will sooth my pensive ghost;
He best can paint 'em, who shall feel 'em most.

2. From John Armstrong, *The Oeconomy of Love* (1736)[4]

[Quoted in *Laura*, *The Oeconomy of Love*, a popular and widely reprinted sex manual, advises against premarital sex and masturbation, counsels men to postpone marriage until the age of twenty, and proscribes abortion.]

★ Abelard and Eliosa were interred in the same grave, or in monuments adjoining, in the monastery of the Paraclete. He died in the year 1142, she in 1163.

1 Exclamations of praise.
2 Term for the celebration of the Eucharist (mass), in which Christ's sacrifice is reenacted.
3 Pope is referring to himself. Though these lines are not confessions or autobiographical fact, he probably hints at his feelings for Lady Mary Wortley Montagu, who was in Turkey with her husband at the time. This was well before Pope's fascination with her had turned to enmity.
4 John Armstrong (1709–79), *The Oeconomy of Love* (Philadelphia: William Mentz, 1772).

But if to progeny thy views extend
Paternal, and the name of sire invites,
Wouldst thou behold a thriving race surround
Thy spacious table, shun the soft embrace
Emasculent, till twice ten years and more
Have steel'd thy nerves, and let the holy rite
License the bliss. Nor would I urge, precise,
A total abstinence: this might unman
The genial organs, unemploy'd so long,
And quite extinguish the prolific flame,
Refrigerant. But riot oft, unblam'd,
On kisses, sweet repast! ambrosial joy!
Now press with gentle hand the gentle hand,
And, sighing, now the breasts, that to the touch
Heave amorous. Nor thou, fair maid, refuse
Indulgence, while thy paramour discreet
Aspires no farther. Thus thou may'st expect
Treasure hereafter, when the bridegroom, warm,
Trembling with keen desire, profusely pours
The rich collection of enamour'd years;
Exhaustless, blessing all thy nuptial nights.

        But, O my son, whether the generous care
Of propagation and domestic charge,
Or soft encounter more attract, renounce
The vice of monks recluse, the early bane
Of rising manhood. Banish from thy shades
Th'ungenerous, selfish, solitary joy.
Hold, parricide, thy hand! For thee alone
Did Nature form thee? for thy narrow self
Grant thee the means of pleasure? Dream'st thou so?
That very self mistakes its wiser aim;
Its finer sense ungratified, unpleas'd,
But when from active soul to soul rebounds
The swelling mingling tumult of delight,
Hold yet again! e'er idle callus wrap
In sullen indolence th'astonish'd nerves,
When thou may'st fret and tease thy sense in vain,
And curse too late th'unwisely wanton hours.
Impious! forbear thus the first general hail.

To disappoint, *Increase and multiply*,
To shed thy blossoms thro' the desert air,
And sow thy perish'd offspring in the winds.
Unhallow'd pastime. [...]

Find some soft nymph, whom tender sympathy
Attracts to thee, while all her captives else,
Aw'd by majestic beauty, mourn aloof
Her charms, to thee by nuptial vows, and choice
More sure, devoted. Sacrifice to her
The precious hours, nor grudge, with such a mate,
The summer's day to toy or winter's night.
Now, with your happy arms her waist surround,
Fond-grasping; on her swelling bosom now
Recline your cheek, with eager kisses press
Her balmy lips, and, drinking from her eyes
Resistless love, the tender flame confess,
Ineffable but by the murmuring voice
Of genuine joy; then hug and kiss again,
Strech'd on the flow'ry turf, while joyful glows
Thy manly pride, and, throbbing with desire,
Pants earnest, felt thro' all the obstacles
That interveen: but love, whose fervent course
Mountains nor seas oppose, can soon remove
Barriers so slight. Then when her lovely limbs,
Oft lovely deem'd, far lovelier now beheld,
Thro' all your trembling joints increase the flame,
Forthwith discover to her dazzled sight
The stately novelty, and to her hand
Usher the new acquaintance. She, perhaps
Averse, will coldly chide, and half afraid,
Blushing, half pleas'd, the tumid wonder view
With neck retorted, and oblique regard;
Nor quite her curious eye indulging, nor
Refraining quite. Perhaps when you attempt
The sweet admission, toyful she resists
With shy reluctance; nathless you pursue
The soft attack, and push the gentle war
Fervent, till quite o'erpower'd the melting maid
Faintly opposes. On the brink at last

Arriv'd of giddy rapture, plunge not in
Precipitant, but spare a virgin's pain;
Oh, spare a gentle virgin! spare yourself!
Lest sanguine war Love's tender rites profane
With fierce dilaceration,[1] and dire pangs
Reciprocal. Nor droop because the door
Of bliss seems shut and barricaded strong;
But triumph rather in this faithful pledge
Of innocence, and fair virginity
Inviolate. And hence the subtile wench,
Her maiden honours torn, in evil hour
Unseemly torn, and shrunk her virgin rose,
Studious how best the guilty wound to heal,
Her shame best palliate with fair outward shew,
Inward less strict, with painful hand collects
The sylvan store. The lover *myrtle* yields
Her styptic berries,[2] and the horrid *thorn*
Its prune austere; in vain the *caper* hides
Its wandering roots; the mighty *oak* himself,
Sole tyrant of the shade, that long had 'scap'd
The tanner's rage, spoil'd of his callous rhind,
Stands bleak and bare. These, and a thousand more
Of humbler growth, and far inferior name,
Bistort and *dock*,[3] and that way-faring herb
Plantain, her various forage, boil'd in wine,
Yield their astringent force, a lotion prov'd
Thrice powerful to contract the shameful breach.
Beware of these; for in our dangerous days
Such counterfeits abound: whom next to know
Concerns. And here expect no dye of wound,
No wound is made; the corrugated parts,
With ill-dissembled virtue, (tho' severe,
Not wrinkled into frowns when genuine most),
Relapse apace, and quit their borrow'd tone.
Yet judge with charity the varied work
Of Nature's hand. Perhaps the purple stream,

---

1   The action of rending asunder or tearing (parts of the body, etc.); the condition of being
    torn or rent.
2   Effective for staunching blood.
3   Snakeweed and a coarse, weedy, green herb known to cure nettle stings.

Emollient bath, leaves flexible and lax
The parts it lately wash'd. But hapless he
In nuptial night, on whom a horrid chasm
Yawns dreadful, waste and wild, like that through which
The wand'ring GREEK, and CYTHEREA's son,[1]
Diving, explor'd hell's adamantine gates:
An unessential void; where neither love
Nor pleasure dwells, where warm creation dies,
Starv'd in th'abortive gulf; the dire effects
Of use too frequent, or for love or gold. [...]

          Be secret, Lovers: let no dangerous spy
Catch your soft glances, as oblique they deal
Mutual contagion, darting all the soul
In missive love, nor hear your lab'ring sighs.
But chiefly when the high-wrought rapture calls
Impatient to soft deeds, then, then retire
From ev'ry mortal ken. *The sapient king,*
(Whose loves who could defame?) in the mild gloom
Deep in the centre of his gardens hid,
Held dalliance with his fair Egyptian spouse.
Find then some soft obscure retreat, untrod
By mortals else, where thick embow'ring shades
Condense to darkness, and embrown the day;
There, safe from all profane access, pursue
Love's bashful rites. For oft the curious eye
Of prying childhood, and th'aspect malign,
Waning and wan, of virgin stale in years,
Shed baneful influence on the rites of love.
And thou, my son, when floods of mellowing wine
And social joys have loosen'd all thy breast,
When every secret gushes, this at least,
This one reserve, of love and bounteous charms,
Of trusting beauty, venturing all for thee,
For thy delight, her fortune and her fame;
For her thou nothing. Hold! ingrateful, hold
Thy wanton tongue. Leave to the last of fools,
Of villains! that ungenerous vanity,
Cruel and base, to vaunt of secret joys;

---

[1] Cytherea is another name for Aphrodite. Her son is Aeneas.

Of joys on thee, so vaunting, ill bestow'd.
O dare not thus with mortal sting to wound
The tender helpless sex. Does thy vile breath
So blast my sister's or my daughter's fame, —
By Heaven thou diest! thy treach'rous blood alone
Can wash my honour clean. Prudent mean time,
Ye generous maids, revenge your sex's wrong;
Let not the mean destroyer e'er approach
Your sacred charms. Now muster all your pride,
Contempt and scorn, that, shot from Beauty's eye,
Confounds the mighty impudent, and smites
The front unknown to shame. Trust not his vows,
His labour'd sighs, and well-dissembled tears,
Nor swell the triumph of known perjury.

      Mean while, my son, if angry fate, or love
Grown indiscreet, or loud LUCINA, tell
Th'important secret;[1] is thy mate well form'd,
Virtuous, and equal for thy lawful bed?
Save her, I charge thee, from foul infamy,
And lonely shame; let wedlock's holy tye
Legitimate th'indissoluble flames.
If abject birth, dishonourable, and mind
Incultivate or vicious, to that height
Forbid her hopes to climb, at least secure
From penury her humble state, by thee
Else humbled more, and to necessity,
Stern foe to virtue, fame, and life, betray'd,
A helpless prey. O! let no parent's woe,
No plaints of trusting innocence, nor tears
Of pining beauty, blast thy guilty joys.
Shall she, so late the soft'ner of thy life,
Thy chief delight, whose melting essence oft
Lay with thy melting essence kindly mix'd;
(As far as bodies and embodied souls
Can mingle); she who deem'd thy vows sincere,
Thy passion more than selfish, and thy love
To her devoted, as was hers to thee:
Shall she (O cruel perfidy!) at last,

---

[1] The goddess of childbirth; in otherwords, in the event of pregnancy.

When with her tainted name the winds grow sick,
When envious prudery chides, affecting scorn
Of natural joys, and they of *public fame*
Insulting hail her sister, while each friend
Disgusted flies; shall she not find in thee
Unshaken amity? When to thy arms,
Well-known, with wonted confidence she flies,
To pour her sorrows forth, and sooth her cares,
Shall she then find thy faithless heart from home,
From her enstrang'd? At that disast'rous hour
Wilt thou ungently spurn her from thy love,
To waste in sickly grief her once-priz'd charms,
Forlorn to languish out her life, to lead
Despis'd, unwedded, her dishonour'd days?
Or, if her barren fortune, hard like thee,
Scowls meagre want, (whose iron empire, Pride
Reluctant, and her offspring Modesty
Blushing, at last obey), unskill'd in arts
Of mercenary VENUS,[1] to increase
The rompish band, that, without pleasure lewd,
With deep-felt sorrow gay, thro' TRIVIA's[2] reign
Nightly solicit lovers; oft repuls'd;
Oft, when invited to the barren toil,
Thankless deserted by their slipp'ry loves;
Or to the salt of years, where tedious lust
Uncouth and monstrous creeps thro' freezing loins,
Patient submitted; to the boist'rous will
Of midnight ruffians, to abhorr'd disease,
Hourly expos'd, and DRACO's[3] fiercer rage.
Spare, mighty DRACO! spare a hapless race,
By thy own sex to wretchedness betray'd.
A woman bore thee; by each tender name
Of woman, spare. Hast thou or daughter fair,
Or sister? They, but for a happier birth,
The gift of Fate, and Honour's guardian, Pride
Early inspir'd, had swell'd the common stream;

---

[1] Roman name for Aphrodite.
[2] Goddess of the moon and magic; in Greek, Hecate.
[3] First to codify the laws of Athens, which were infamously harsh. Source of the adjective "draconian."

While she, whom now thy awful name dismays,
Portentous heard from far, with Fortune's smiles
And fair example, might have grac'd thy bed,
A virtuous mate in every charm compleat.

A pious duty next, neglected oft
Demands my song. If from thy secret bed
Of luxury unbidden offspring rise,
Let them be kindly welcom'd to the day.
'Tis Nature bids. To Nature's high behests
Attend, and from the monster-breeding deep,
The ravag'd air, and howling wilderness,
Learn parent virtues. [...]

These precepts wisely keep; by these direct
Thy steps thro' Pleasure's labyrinth. Unhurt
And unoffending thus thy tutor'd feet
May tread the wilds of else-delusive joy.
So shall no sorrows wound, no ruder cares
Disturb thy pleasures, no remorseful tears
Attend thy gay delight; nor sighs make way,
But such as heave the pleasure-burden'd breast,
As utter love, with speechless eloquence
Well understood, and breathe from soul to soul
The soft infection, fondly still receiv'd. [...]

But chiefly thee, fair nymph, behoves to know
That love and joy when in their prime must fear
Decay, the fate of all created things.
Be frugal then: the coyly-yielded kiss
Charms most, and gives the most sincere delight.
Cheapness offends: hence on the harlot's lip
No rapture hangs, however fair she seem,
However form'd for love and amorous play.
Hail, MODESTY! fair female honour, hail!
Beauty's chief ornament, and Beauty's self!
For Beauty must with Virtue ever dwell,
And thou art Virtue! and without thy charm
Beauty is insolent and wit profane. [...]

3. From Germaine de Staël, *Influence of the Passions* (1796)[1]

[In *Secret History*, Mary mentions reading Germaine de Staël's *Influence of the Passions* and admiring it. Madame de Staël, as she was known in the French salon within which she was a central figure, viewed the passions as "the principal obstacle to individual and political happiness," a dictum explored in both of Sansay's novels reprinted here. But Madame de Staël may have offered more than an intellectual inspiration to Sansay. She was the model of the highly educated, witty, world-savvy, influential, and independent woman one can imagine Sansay aspiring to become.]

At what period is it that I have attempted to discourse of the "Happiness of Individuals and of Nations?" Is it amidst the crisis of a wide desolating Revolution, the effects of which no condition has escaped; and when its thunder strikes alike the bosom of the lowly valley and the front of the proudest hills? Is it at a time when, if you but live, you are necessarily hurried on by one universal movement—when the night of the grave fails to secure repose—when the very *dead* are judged anew, and their cold remains, which popular favour had inured, are alternatively admitted into, or expelled from, that temple where factions imagined they bestowed immortality? Yes, it is at this very time, when either the hope or the want of happiness has prompted the human race to rise; it is in an age like the present that one is powerfully led seriously to reflect on the nature of individual and political felicity; on the road that leads to it; on the limits that confine it; on the rocks that rise between and bar us from its enjoyment. But shame, however, be my lot, if during the reign of Terror under which France trembled, if during the course of those two frightful years, my mind had been capable of such a task!—shame be my lot, if it had attempted to conceive the plan, or ponder on the result of this monstrous mixture of all human atrocities. The coming generation will, perhaps, also be induced to investigate the causes that influenced the black proceedings of those two eventful years; but we, the contemporaries and the fellow citizens of the hapless victims sacrificed on those days of blood, could we have *then* retained the power to generalize our ideas, to

---

[1]   Anne Louise Germaine de Staël (1766–1817), *A treatise on the influence of the passions, upon the happiness of individuals and of nations. Illustrated by striking references to … the French Revolution. From the French of the Baroness Stael de Holstein. To which is prefixed a sketch of her life, by the translator* (London: George Cawthorn, 1798), 1–9.

dwell unconcernedly on mere abstract notions, to withdraw from the home of heart, in order to analize its emotions? No, not even now can reason attempt to approach the examination of the unaccountable æra. And, indeed, to appreciate those events, under whatever colours you depict them, argues an attempt to reduce them to the class of existing ideas, of ideas which we are already in possession of words to describe. At the sight of this hideous picture all the emotions of the soul are roused anew: we freeze; we burn; we are anxious for the combat; we are resolved to die: but as for thinking, thought cannot yet repose on any of those recollections; the sensations they impress absorb every other faculty. It is therefore by secluding from my mind every retrospect of that prodigious æra, while I avail myself of the other prominent events of the French Revolution, and of the history of every nation, that I shall endeavour to combine a few impartial observations on the nature of governments; and if these reflections lead me to an admission of the first principles on which is bottomed the French Republican Constitution, I hope that, notwithstanding the violence of party-spirit by which France is torn, and, through the medium of France, the rest of the civilized world—I hope, I say, it may be possible to conceive that an enthusiastic attachment to certain notions does not exclude a sovereign contempt for certain men,* and that a favourable hope of the future may not be irreconcileable with a just execration of the past; and though the wounds which the heart has received must still continue to bleed, yet, after the lapse of some interval, the mind may again raise itself to general contemplations.

In the present consideration of these important questions on which is to depend the political destiny of man, we ought merely to view them in their own nature, and not barely with relation to the calamities which have attended their discussion; we ought at least to examine whether these calamities be essentially connected with the institutions which France is desirous of adopting, or whether the effects of the Revolution be not wholly and absolutely distinct from the consequences of the Constitution; we ought finally to evince sufficient elevation of soul to spurn the apprehension, lest, while we are exploring the foundation of principles, we should be suspected of indifference for crimes. It is with a similar independence of mind that I have essayed, in the first part of

---

* In my opinion, the real partizans of republican liberty are those who most vehemently execrate the crimes that have been perpetrated in its name. Their adversaries may doubtless experience the same horror at those abominations; but as those very crimes supply an argument to their system, they do not overwhelm their minds, as they do those of the friends of freedom, with very possible sensation of grief.

this work, to describe the influence of the passions of man upon his own personal happiness. Neither do I perceive why it should be more difficult to be impartial in the discussion of political, than in the investigation of moral questions: undoubtedly the passions exert as powerful an influence as governments on the condition of human life, and nevertheless, in the calm silence of retirement, our reason is curious to discuss the sentiments we ourselves have experienced; nor, in my opinion, ought it to be a more arduous task to discourse philosophically of the advantages or disadvantages of Republics and Monarchies, than to institute an exact analysis or Ambition, of Love, or of any other passion that may have biassed your conduct, and proved decisive of your fate. In either part of this work, I have been equally studious to be guided solely by my reason, and to steer it clear of all the impressions of the moment. It is for my readers to judge how far I have succeeded.

From the passions, that impulsive force, which domineers over the will of man, arises the principal obstacle to individual and political happiness. Without the interference of the passions, governments would be a machine fully as simple as the different levers whose power is proportioned to the weight they are to raise, and the destiny of man would exactly result from a just equilibrium between his desires and his means of gratifying them. I shall therefore consider morals and politics only in as much as they experience difficulties from the operation of the passions. Characters uninfluenced by the passions naturally place themselves in the situation that best befits them, which is generally the one pointed out to them by chance; or if they introduce any change in it, it is only that which was easily and immediately within their reach. Let us not disturb their happy calm; they want not our assistance: their happiness is as varied in appearance as the different lots which their destiny has drawn; but the basis of that happiness is invariably the same, viz. the certainty of never being either agitated, or overruled by any emotion beyond the compass of their resistance. The live of these *impassable* beings are doubtless as much exposed as those of other men to the operation of material accidents, which may destroy their fortunes, impair their health, &c.

But afflictions of this nature are prevented or removed not by sensible or moral thoughts, but by positive computations. The happiness of *impassioned* characters being, on the contrary, wholly dependant on what passes within them, they alone can derive consolation from the reflections which are awakened in their souls; and as the natural bent of their inclinations exposes them to the most cruel calamities, they stand peculiarly in need of a system whose object it is to avoid pain.

In a word, it is your *impassioned* characters only who, by means of certain traits of resemblance, may, in their aggregate, become the subject of the same general considerations. Persons of the other cast of character live, as it were, one by one, without either analogy or variety, in a monotonous kind of existence, though each of them pursue a different end, and present as many varying shades as there are individuals: it is impossible, however, to discover in them any real characteristic colour. If, in a treatise on individual happiness, I touch only on *impassioned* characters, it is still more natural to analize governments in relation to the play they give to the influence of the passions. An individual may be considered as exempt from passions; but a collective body of men is composed of a certain number of characters of every cast, which yield a result nearly similar: and it ought to be observed, that circumstances the most dependent on chance, may be the subject of a positive calculation, whenever the chances are multiplied. In the Canton of *Berne*,[1] for example, it has been observed that every ten years nearly the same number of divorces took place; and there are several towns in Italy where an exact calculation is made of the number of murders that are regularly committed every year. Thus events, which link with a multitude of various combinations, have their periodical return, and preserve a fixed proportion, when our observations on them are the result of a great number of chances. Hence we may be led to believe that political science may one day acquire the force of geometrical evidence. The science of morals, when applied to a particular individual, may be wholly erroneous with regard to him; but the organization of a constitution is invariably grounded on data that are fixed, as the greater number in every thing affords results that are always similar and always foreseen. That the greatest difficulty which obstructs the march of governments, arises from the passions, is a truth that needs no illustration; and it is pretty evident that all the despotic social combinations would prove equally suitable to those listless and inert dispositions that are satisfied to remain in the situation which chance has allotted them, and that the most purely abstract-democratical theory might be reduced to practice among wise men, whose sole rule of conduct would be the dictates of their reason. You might, therefore, solve whatever is problematical in constitutions, if you could but discover to what degree the passions may be incited or repressed, without endangering public happiness.

---

[1] A region in Switzerland.

But before I proceed further, it may perhaps be expected that I attempt a definition of happiness. Happiness, then, such as we aspire after, is the re-union of all the contraries. For individuals, it is hope without fear, activity without solicitude, celebrity without detraction, love without inconstancy; that glow of imagination that embellishes to the eye of fancy whatever we possess, and dims the recollection of whatever we may have lost; in a word, the very reverse of moral nature, the pure perfection of every condition, of every talent, of every pleasure, unmixed and unadulterated with the ills that usually attend them. The happiness of nations must likewise result from the well-tempered combination of republican liberty with the monarchical quiet; of the rivalry of talents with the inactivity of factions; of the pride of military glory abroad with submissive obedience to the laws at home. Happiness, such as the mind of man endeavours to conceive, is an object beyond the reach of human efforts; and happiness that is attainable, can only be accomplished by a patient study of the surest means that can shield us from the greater ills of life. To the investigation of these means the present treatise is devoted.

And in this attempt, two works may be blended into one—The first considers man in his relations to himself; the other views him in the social relations of all the individuals to each other. Nor are the principal ideas of these two works without some analogy; because a nation exhibits the character of a man, and the force of a government acts upon a nation as an individual is acted on by the force of his own reason. The wish of the philosopher is to give permanency to the transient will of reflection, while the social art tends to perpetuate the actions of wisdom. In a word, what is great is discoverable in what is little; together with the same exactness of proportions. The whole of the universe is reflected in each of its parts, and the more it appears the result of one grand idea, the greater is the admiration it inspires.

There is a wide difference, however, between the system of Individual Happiness and that of the Happiness of Nations: in the former, we may aspire to the most perfect moral independence; that is, to the subjection of all the passions, every man having it in his power to make the experiment on himself; but in the latter, political liberty must be calculated on the positive and indestructible existence of a certain number of *impassioned* dispositions, which constitute a part of the people who are to be governed. The first part of this work shall be solely consecrated to reflections on the individual destiny of man;—the second will embrace the constitutional lot of nations.

4. From [Leonora Sansay?],[1] *Zelica, the Creole* (London: A.K. Newman, 1821)

[*Zelica, the Creole* is approximately three times longer than *Secret History*, the book with which it shares substantial sections copied almost word for word. The publisher identifies the author only as "an American" and lists two other novels written by the same writer also "In the Press," having been "transmitted to the Publisher from America." There are some notable differences between *Secret History* and *Zelica*, including the absence in the latter of the epistolary form, the excision of the post-evacuation travels to Jamaica and Cuba, and the addition of the character Zelica, its eponymous, mixed-race heroine. The *Zelica* author—if not Sansay—also has dialogue copied from *Secret History* spoken by different characters, a transposition that necessarily changes the meaning of these scenes. And unlike in *Secret History*, Clara dies toward the end of the novel. In the excerpt below, Zelica narrates her history to Clara. She presents herself as the victim of her father's political enthusiasm.]

"Whence arises this despair?" asked Clara. "Tell me all your sorrows: if I cannot serve you, you are, at least, sure of my sympathy,—of all the consolation I can offer.—Alas! How little is that all."

"I will tell you," replied Zelica, "the story of my sorrows, that you may be convinced that they are without hope of relief:—

"My mother, an amiable and beautiful woman, was descended from the African race, and was, consequently, marked with the stigma that attended those people. My father, captivated by her beauty, and won by her merit, had resolution enough to combat the prevailing prejudices of his country, and married her. This union, that formed his happiness, has devoted me to indefinable misery. He entered, ardently, into the interest of the people of colour; sought to ameliorate their condition, and to induce the inhabitants of the island to consider them as human beings.

"At five years of age I was sent to France, to be educated; but chiefly, as my father declared, to keep me from imbibing the prejudices of my country against my maternal ancestors. In France, all traces of my early impressions were effaced. No expense was spared in the cultivation of my talents, and I was happy in all the happiness of youth, enjoying the

---

[1]   Vol. 3, 124–30.

fullness of existence, having no wish ungratified. At sixteen I was taken from the convent in which I had passed the happy hours of my early years, and conducted to the chateau of a relation of my father, who lives in Champagne. In that gay and delightful country I became acquainted with the original of the portrait that I wear on my heart, —first felt the pressure of the hand that traced those letters over which you have seen me weep with the ardour of passion and the bitterness of regret. From my mother I inherited the fervour of the children of the sun.—I loved, as only those born in burning climes can love.—I was separated from the object of that passion. Pardon me for not entering into details. The horrible change that followed these bright, but fleeting moments, has thrown a gloom over my soul, and renders me incapable of tracing scenes of happiness. I was recalled to my country by my father, and I obeyed the summons with joy, relying on his affection,—assured that he would be delighted with the perfection I had attained in the arts he wished me to cultivate, particularly music,—and that he would give me, with a princely fortune, to my lover. I thought only of the orange-groves of my native land, as I had heard them described in France,—the unfading verdure, the endless spring, that reigned there,—and anticipated a life of transport, passed with my father and my husband. But how different was the fate that awaited me! On my arrival, my father, I learned, was no more; and the country, ravaged by a cruel war, was in a state of frightful anarchy. The revolution that had desolated France, extended its fright-ful ravages to the colonies, and St. Domingo was the theatre of all its horrors. My father has espoused with enthusiasm the cause of the blacks, and opposed all measures taken to reduce them again to slavery. This, as it was with him a matter of opinion, I had no right to condemn; nor should I have presumed openly to blame what I did not entirely approve; but my father, with a despotism more cruel than that he had so ener-getically opposed, had decided my fate. My blood still curdles with horror when I think of the moment when this fate was announced to me. The ardour of my father in the cause he had embraced, degenerated to madness; and, to cement the union that had been formed between him and the black chiefs, he promised to bestow on one of them his vast estates, and the hand of his daughter.

"When I arrived at the Cape, Christophe, the husband my father had chosen for his unfortunate Zelica, came to me. I had not yet learned the conditions on which I was to retain the affluence I had been accus-tomed to; or, if I refused to comply with them, to be reduced to the most abject poverty. My long residence in France had entirely effaced from my mind all idea of the people of colour; nor can I, even now, accustom myself to them. Conceive, then, the horror with which I recoiled from the presence of Christophe. When he imparted to me the will of my father, I rejected the conditions there offered me with the most violent indications of horror. 'Death,' I exclaimed; 'death would be a thousand times preferable.'"

Appendix C: Contextual Documents

1. From Baron de Wimpffen,[1] *A Voyage to Saint Domingo, in the Years 1788, 1789, and 1790* (London: T. Caddell, Jr. and W. Davies, 1797)

[...] I have determined, Sir, to give you a description of *one of my days*; it will be the simplest method of giving you, once for all, a summary idea of the manner of living at St. Domingo, in what is called a town. [...]

The cracking of whips, the smothered cries, and the indistinct groans of the negroes, who never see the day break but to curse it; who are never recalled to a feeling of their existence but by sufferings—this, Sir, is what takes place of the crowing of the early cock; and by the strains of this infernal harmony, was I awakened out of my first sleep at St. Domingo. I started, screamed, and fancied that I had waked in the gulph of Tartarus, between Prometheus and Ixion[2]—And I was among Christians! Among the worshippers of God——who died to mitigate the sorrows of the afflicted!—Custom has already weakened the effect of the impression; it will never obliterate it altogether.

A walk of an hour served to dissipate the chagrin of this gloomy awakening. I came back in time to see a troop of male and female negroes lying against the wall, or squatting upon their heels, and waiting amidst a universal yawn, for the master's giving the signal of going to work, by loud cracks of the *Arceau*,* on their back and shoulders—for, you will hardly conceive, and indeed it cost six months observation to convince me of the truth of it, there are negroes who must absolutely be beaten before they can be put in motion. The arceau is the true key of this species of watch—If I had chosen to take the word of the masters for it, I should have looked no farther for the cause of this singular disposition of the slaves, than to their natural sloth and inactivity: but on considering the matter a little more narrowly, I fancied I could see

---

* A kind of short-handled whip, so called in the colonies.

1 Alexandre-Stanislas de Wimpffen (1748?-1819?). Pierre Pluchon identifies him with a well-known family from Wurtemberg, in southern Germany. More is known of his distant cousins, François-Louis and Georges-Félix, who were officers general for both the French Monarch and later served the French Republic and Napoleon. It is possible that Alexandre-Stanislaus served with Rochambeau during the American War of Independence and afterwards in the West Indies.

2 In Hell, between Prometheus, whose crime was giving humanity fire, and Ixion, who was the first in Greek mythology to slay his own kin.

that these dispositions were marvelously seconded by the inactivity and sloth of their masters, who, for the greater part, too ignorant and too unindulgent to comprehend that the vices of education can only be subdued by time and patience, find the plan of beating more practicable than that of instructing! The natural consequence of which is, that the negro, once accustomed to this mode of treatment, can only be wrought on by rigour and severity. I have persisted, month after month, in lavishing on those who attended me, nothing but patience, gentleness, and good offices of every kind—all were in vain: the bent was taken, and nothing was left me, after all my endeavours, but the alternative of waiting on myself, or of having recourse to the *arceau*. [...]

A lady, whom I have seen, a young lady, and one of the handsomest in the island, gave a grand dinner. Furious at seeing a dish of pastry brought to the table overdone, she ordered her negro cook to be seized, and *thrown into the oven, yet glowing with heat*—And this horrible Magæra,[1] whose name I suppress out of respect to her family; this infernal fiend, whom public execration ought to drive with every mark of abhorrence from society; this worthy rival of the *too famous Chaperon*,★ is followed, and admired—for she is rich and beautiful!

2. From Absalom Jones and Richard Allen, *A Narrative of the Proceedings of the Black People During the Late Awful Calamity in Philadelphia in the Year 1793* (Philadelphia: Woodward, 1794) 3–9

[Absalom Jones (1746–1818) and Richard Allen (1760–1831) were leaders of the free black community of Philadelphia. Both were former slaves who had purchased their freedom. Together they established the first independent black church in America. In this pamphlet, Jones and Allen contest in print the censorious account of the behavior of the free black community during the Yellow Fever epidemic of 1793 published by Mathew Carey. Carey accused the black community of taking advantage of the distressed white inhabitants of the city, overcharging them for care and assistance burying the dead or pilfering their homes. In Chapter 12 of *Laura*, Laura finds a sick Belfield, abandoned by his friends, attended to by a black

---

★   A planter of Saint Domingo, who, in the same circumstances, seeing the heat shrivel and draw open the lips of the unhappy negro, exclaimed in fury, "The rascal laughs."

---

1   With Alecto and Tisiphone, one of the three Furies.

nurse. The following account gives voice to the unnamed "negro" in the novel. It also illustrates the extent of the crisis caused by the Yellow Fever epidemic. It was widely believed that the Yellow Fever came to Philadelphia with the French-speaking refugees from the revolution in Saint Domingue and from the slaves who accompanied them. It was also a common opinion that black people were not susceptible to the fever, a misnomer that, in the complete version of the pamphlet, Jones and Allen refute.]

[...] In consequence of a partial representation of the conduct of the people who were employed to nurse the sick, in the late calamitous state of the city of Philadelphia, we are solicited, by a number of those who feel themselves injured thereby, and by the advice of several respectable citizens, to step forward and declare facts as they really were; seeing that from our situation, on account of the charge we took upon us, we had it more fully and generally in our power, to know and observe the conduct and behavior of those that were so employed.

Early in September, a solicitation appeared in the public papers, to the people of colour to come forward and assist the distressed, perishing, and neglected sick; with a kind of assurance, that people of our colour were not liable to take the infection. Upon which we and a few others met and consulted how to act on so truly alarming and melancholy occasion. After some conversation, we found a freedom to go forth, confiding in him who can preserve in the midst of a burning fiery furnace, sensible that it was our duty to do all the good we could to our suffering fellow mortals. We set out to see where we could be useful. The first we visited was a man in Emsley's alley, who was dying, and his wife lay dead at the time in the house, there were none to assist but two poor helpless children. We administered what relief we could, and applied to the overseers of the poor to have the woman buried. We visited upwards of twenty families that day—they were scenes of woe indeed! The Lord was pleased to strengthen us, and remove all fear from us, and disposed our hearts to be as useful as possible.

In order the better to regulate our conduct, we called on the mayor next day, to consult with him how to proceed, so as to be most useful. The first object he recommended was a strict attention to the sick, and the procuring of nurses. This was attended to by Absalom Jones and William Gray; and, in order that the distressed might know where to apply, the mayor advertised the public that upon application to them they would be supplied. Soon after, the mortality increasing, the difficulty of getting a corpse taken away, was such, that few were willing to do it, when offered great rewards. The black people were looked to. We then offered our services in the public papers, by advertising that we would remove the dead and procure nurses. Our services were the production of real sensibility;—we sought not fee nor reward, until the increase of the disorder rendered our labour so arduous that we were not adequate to the service we had assumed. The mortality increasing rapidly, obliged us to call in the assistance of five* hired men, in the awful discharge of interring the dead. They, with great reluctance, were prevailed upon to join us. It was very uncommon, at this time, to find any one that would go near, much more, handle, a sick or dead person.

Mr. Carey, in page 106 of his third edition, has observed, that, "for the honor of human nature, it ought to be recorded, that some of the convicts in the gaol, a part of the term of whose confinement had been remitted as a reward for their peaceable, orderly behavior, voluntarily offered themselves as nurses to attend the sick at Bush-hill; and have, in that capacity, conducted themselves with great fidelity &c." Here it ought to be remarked, (although Mr. Carey hath not done it) that two thirds of the persons, who rendered those essential services, were people of colour, who, on the application of the elders of the African church, (who met to consider what they could do for the help of the sick) were liberated, on condition of their doing the duty of nurses at the hospital at Bush-hill; which they as voluntarily accepted to do, as they did faithfully discharge, this severe and disagreeable duty.—May the Lord reward them, both temporally and spiritually.

When the sickness became general, and several of the physicians died, and most of the survivors were exhausted by sickness or fatigue; that good man, Doctor Rush,[1] called us more immediately to attend upon the sick, knowing we could both bleed; he told us we could increase our utility, by attending to his instructions, and accordingly directed us where to procure medicine duly prepared, with proper directions how to administer them, and at what stages of the disorder to bleed; and when we found ourselves incapable of judging what was proper to be done, to apply to him, and he would, if able, attend them himself, or send Edward Fisher, his pupil, which he often did; and Mr. Fisher manifested his humanity, by an affectionate attention for their relief.—This has been no small satisfaction to us; for, we think, that

---

* Two of whom were Richard Allen's brothers.

[1] Benjamin Rush.

when a physician was not attainable, we have been the instruments, in the hand of God, for saving the lives of some hundreds of our suffering fellow mortals.

We feel ourselves sensibly aggrieved by the censorious epithets of many, who did not render the least assistance in the time of necessity, yet are liberal of their censure of us, for the prices paid for our services, when no one knew how to make a proposal to any one they wanted to assist them. At first we made no charge, but left it to those we served in removing their dead, to give what they thought fit—we set no price, until the reward was fixed by those we had served. After paying the people we had to assist us, our compensation is much less than many will believe.

We do assure the public, that all the money we have received, for burying, and for coffins which we ourselves purchased and procured, has not defrayed the expence of wages which we had to pay to those whom we employed to assist us. The following statement is accurately made:

CASH RECEIVED.

The whole amount of Cash we received
for burying the dead, and for burying
beds, is, £.233 10

CASH PAID.

For coffins, for which we have
received nothing £.33 00
For the hire of five men, 3 of
them 70 days each, and the
other two, 63 days each,
at 22s6 per day, 378 00

411 00

Debts due us, for which we expect
but little, £.110 00
From this statement, for the truth of which we
solemnly vouch, it is evident, and we sensibly feel
the operation of the fact, that we are out of pocket £.177 98

Besides the costs of hearses, the maintenance of our families for 70 days, (being the period of our labours) and the support of the five hired men, during the respective times of their being employed; which expences, together with sundry gifts we occasionally made to poor families, might reasonably and properly be introduced, to shew our actual situation with regard to profit—but it is enough to exhibit to the public, from the above specified items, of *Cash paid and Cash received*, without taking into view the other expences, that, by the employment we were engaged in, we have lost £.177 9 8. But, if the other expences, which we have actually paid, are added to that sum, how much then may we not say we have suffered! We leave the public to judge.

It may possibly appear strange to some who know how constantly we were employed, that we should have received no more Cash than £.233 10 4. But we repeat our assurance, that this is the fact, and we add another, which will serve the better to explain it: We have buried *several hundreds* of poor persons and strangers, for which service we have never received; nor never asked any compensation.

We feel ourselves hurt most by a partial, censorious paragraph, in Mr. Carey's second edition, of his account of the sickness, &c. in Philadelphia; pages 76 and 77, where he asperses the blacks alone, for having taken the advantage of the distressed situation of the people. That some extravagant prices were paid, we admit; but how came they to be demanded? the reason is plain. It was with difficulty persons could be had to supply the wants of the sick, as nurses;—applications became more and more numerous, the consequence was, when we procured them at six dollars per week, and called upon them to go where they were wanted, we found they were gone elsewhere; here was a disappointment; upon enquiring the cause, we found, they had been allured away by others who offered greater wages, until they got from two to four dollars per day. We had no restraint upon the people. It was natural for people in low circumstances to accept a voluntary, bounteous reward; especially under the loathsomeness of many of the sick, when nature shuddered at the thoughts of the infection, and the talk assigned was aggravated by lunacy, and being left much alone with them. Had Mr. Carey been solicited to such an undertaking, for hire, *Query*, "what would *he* have demanded?" but Mr. Carey, although chosen a member of that band of worthies who have so eminently distinguished themselves by their labours, for the relief of the sick and helpless—yet, quickly after his election, left them to struggle with their arduous and hazardous task, by leaving the city. 'Tis true Mr. Carey was no hireling, and had a right to flee, and upon his return, to plead the cause of those who fled; yet, we think, he was wrong in giving so partial and injurious an account of the black nurses; if they have taken advantage of the public distress? Is it any more than he hath done of its desire for information. We believe he has made more money by the sale of his "scraps" than a dozen of the greatest extortioners among the black nurses. The great prices paid did not escape the observation of that worthy and vigilant magistrate, Mathew Clarkson, mayor of the city, and president of the committee—he sent for us, and requested we would use our influence, to lessen the wages of the nurses, but on informing him the cause, i.e. that of the people overbidding one another, it was concluded unnecessary to attempt any thing on that head; therefore it was left to the people concerned. That there were some few black people guilty of plundering the distressed, we acknowledge; but in that they only are pointed out, and made mention of, we esteem partial and injurious; we know as many whites who were guilty of it; but this is looked over, while the blacks are held up to censure.—Is it a greater crime for a black to pilfer, than for a white to privateer?

We wish not to offend, but when an unprovoked attempt is made, to make us blacker than we are, it becomes less necessary to be over cautious on that account. [...]

3. [Anonymous], "Renewed War in St. Domingo" *Balance and Columbian Repository* 1.25 (1802): 198

[What follows is an example of how news from Saint Domingue appeared in the US press as the Haitian Revolution unfolded. Note that the breathless account of fighting in the Caribbean precedes coverage of a domestic slave insurrection.]

[...] By the snow George, Bell, from Cape Francois, in ten days, we are informed, that Toussaint had revolted, in consequence of which, three divisions of Leclerc's troops had been engaged with the blacks, and very roughly handled; no quarters given.

[Aurora.]

————

In corroboration of the above, (says the Philadelphia Gazette) we have obtained the subjoined extracts of letters, received in this city, from the most respectable authority:

CAPE FRANCOIS, MAY 28.

"We have just received information that a French fleet lately arrived at Guadaloupe, met with the same fate as the fleet that arrived here, likewise the inhabitants; the town was entirely consumed by the fire as well as the country. On the landing of the troops, 800 of the French were killed. Pelage, as well as all the rest had surrendered; but one commandant, his name and station I am unacquainted with, on the 25th, surprised a French post and killed every man.

"In a few days after Toussaint had surrendered, he asked permission to go to one of his plantations, which was granted by the Gen. in Chief. We have just received information by General Christophe, that Toussaint had decamped with a strong body of troops, in opposition to the French.

"In the small time of his being here, he discovered the force of the French, which, out of 30,000 soldiers brought into the island, there only remain about 18 or 20,000, and there are dying every day ten or twelve in this one place. There are in the hospital at the Mole, 2000 sick men. I feel convinced, if there should not arrive from France, some reinforcements in a very little time, we shall find ourselves in a great deal of trouble, and not unlikely that Toussaint will still be Governor of St. Domingo, which is the fear of every citizen."

MAY 29.

"TOUSSAINT HAS AGAIN TAKEN UP ARMS, BUT I IMAGINE WILL NOT BE ABLE TO DO MUCH, AS HE IS ONLY JOINED BY DESSALINES, AND A CONSIDERABLE FORCE IS EVERY DAY EXPECTED HERE FROM FRANCE. WE HAVE RECEIVED INFORMATION THAT GUADALOUPE IS IN A STATE OF REVOLT, AND THE CONSEQUENCES MAY BE EXPECTED TO BE WORSE THAN HERE, IF POSSIBLE."

LAST MAIL.

—

INSURRECTION IN NORTH-CAROLINA.

In the Norfolk Herald of the 10th inst.[1] are the following articles. *"We are authorised to state, that an insurrection of a very serious nature has broken out amongst the Negroes in Perquimens and Hartford Counties, N. Carolina. The particulars, we are constrained to observe, must be withheld for the present, from motives of precaution. It may not, however, be improper to remark, that too much vigilance cannot be used in our own neighborhood.*

---

[1] Is short-hand for "this month."

"We are informed, that five negroes were executed at Halifax court-house, on the 15th ult.[1] for sedition."

4. Charles Brockden Brown, "On the Consequences of Abolishing the Slave Trade to the West Indian Colonies," *The Literary Magazine, and American Register* 4.26 (Nov 1805): 375–81 (1805)

[Charles Brockden Brown (1771–1810) was among the United States' first professional novelists. He is best known for his four gothic works, *Wieland*, *Edgar Huntly*, *Ormond*, and *Arthur Mervyn*, written in a brief period from 1798–1800. But Brown wrote much more than fiction. His book *Alcuin, A Dialogue* (1798) takes up the issue of women's rights. As a member of *The Friendly Club*, a literary society that included among other New York intellectuals the doctor Elihu Hubbard Smith, playwright and theater-manager William Dunlap, and the minister Timothy Dwight, later president of Yale College, Brown immersed himself in Enlightenment philosophy from the works of Rousseau up through the writings of British radical William Godwin. In 1803, Brown turned to the task of editing *The Literary Magazine* and later the *American Register*, periodicals that reviewed British and American books, commented on matters of socio-cultural import, and recorded, in the form of annals, the signal historical events of the day. Brown did much of the writing for these ventures himself. Brown also wrote two anonymous pamphlets concerning the disposition of the Louisiana Territory in 1803. With reference to the war in Saint Domingue, he warned the Jefferson administration that the French would turn from their defeat in the West Indies to re-colonize their western holdings in North America. Brown urged Jefferson to rally the western inhabitants to the national banner, anticipating the Louisiana Purchase.]

The probable fate of the negro race in the American colonies, is an interesting subject at all times, in a merely speculative view. It comprehends various questions of high importance in the philosophy of man; it touches on the destines of a large portion of the species, on the event to be expected from the grandest and most cruel experiment that ever was tried upon human nature; the sudden and violent transportation of

---

[1]   Of the preceding month.

immense multitudes of savages to distant regions and new climates, and their forcible and instantaneous exposure to a state of comparative civilization. The fate of a large empire, with all its wealth and power, depends on this experiment. The colonial establishments of Europe in the new world, form a mass of dominion scarcely inferior in magnitude to the proudest dynasties of ancient or modern times; and though their ruin would not necessarily involve that of the mother countries, it would completely subvert all the established relations between the different members of the European commonwealth, besides absolutely diminishing their prosperity.

What form will the colonial society assume during the continuance of the slave trade? In all human probability, one of two events will speedily happen; either the fate of St. Domingo will suddenly become the fate of all the negro settlements, or the West Indian system will remain a little longer on its present footing. The impending blow may possibly be warded off for a season: negroes will continue to be driven, tortured, and wasted, in proportion as new recruits can always be obtained from Africa. A scanty portion of the dregs of Europe will still reside in the islands, and compose the whole of that colonial body on whom the preservation of the system depends. Each attempt of the enemy in St. Domingo, or each effort of the slaves themselves to imitate the example of that settlement, will shake to its base the whole western wing of the European community, till, in the course of a few years, the frail tenure will give way, on which are held those fine possessions; and all the monuments of Europe, in the insular part of the new world, will vanish before the tempest which a short-sighted and wicked policy has for ages been raising.

With emancipated Africans there can be no faith, no treaties, no fixed connexions of neutrality, not even the honourable and settled relations of modern warfare. The suppression of such a monster in policy is a duty incumbent on every civilized state connected with the West Indian system. The efforts of France and Spain may possibly be successful in St. Domingo, but what will be the effects of a contrary event on the colonies that remain tranquil? The negroes in St. Domingo are already acquiring something like a navy; they have proposed to Great Britain conditions of alliance, which no civilized government can listen to. These two facts speak loudly of the dangers necessarily inherent in such a neighbourhood. What has England to expect? or what can she do to brighten her prospects? Till the slave trade is at once boldly and totally abolished (for in the present circumstances delay is not prudence; it is rashness, in fact, though it may result, like many other kinds of temerity, from real cowardice); till the root of all the evil is hardily struck at, and the main, universal cause of all danger destroyed, an hour's quiet cannot be expected in the slave colonies, nor any sensible alleviation of the manifold evils which crowd the picture of West Indian society. Whether all the mischiefs of negro liberty come at once, or only undermine the system gradually, and then cover it with ruin in the end, the alternative is almost equal. The abolition of the slave trade alone can rectify those abuses, and counteract those frightful dangers. But what are the steps by which the abolition is likely to lead to so desirable a consequence?

Every one is aware of the dangers of the slave trade in its natural effects upon the *security* of the West Indian establishments. Nothing can tend more obviously to prevent proprietors from residing on their plantations, than the constant, and, at present, just fear of insurrection. When a native of Europe is about to leave a home, in which the value of perfect security is only overlooked because it knows no interruption, he is forced to reflect on the blessings he has hitherto enjoyed, and to consider that they are not the gift of every government. In his choice of a new place of residence, the change on climate enters perhaps far less into his comparative views, than the change from a state of safety and protection to one of perpetual alarm; of real dangers, which no length of time can disarm of their terrors; and sufferings, which no seasoning can palliate. Even in the regular communities of the old world, the difference of the rights enjoyed under various governments, has no small influence on emigrants in fixing on new abodes. And what are all the fears of banishment to Siberia, or of French conscription, compared with the risks to which every white inhabitant of Jamaica is exposed, so long as Dessalines is emperor of Hayti, and has a troop of allies in the slaves of every British plantation? In proportion as the British plantations are peopled by homebred negroes, who their masters are forced to treat well by the impossibility of filling their places; the danger of the planter is diminished, and the just obstacles to choosing the colonies for a place of residence is removed.

The tendency of men is always to follow their stock. When it is vested in foreign trade, they *may* remain at home; but they generally reside where they see it oftenest. When vested in the carrying trade, it generally draws them to one of the spots between which it circulates. When vested in foreign agriculture, it seldom fails to draw them after it. In these employments, no doubt, impolitic restrictions may prevent the capitalist from following his stock; climate is seldom any obstacle: the general tendency is strong, and as soon as artificial impediments are removed, this tendency is manifest. And this would cause the great colonial proprietors to reside on their plantations, were not two principal causes now to prevent them; the dangerous nature of their colonial residence, and the superior attractions of European society. The latter is of much less consequence than the former, because it operates chiefly on the more wealthy and less valuable, as well as less numerous class of inhabitants, and because it must daily lessen as the improvement of the colonies advances. We have proofs, in all the accounts of St. Domingo during the last year of its greatness, that the whites were rapidly increasing, in numbers, elegance, and even splendour, merely from the strength of those inducements which connect men with their property; and such inducements operate with accelerated force; for every family that removes to the island, is a new tie to those which remain. Nothing but the dangers of insurrection could permanently counteract this propensity, and the measure which removes or lessens that danger, will remove or lessen the non-residence, hitherto so hurtful, both to the interests of the proprietors themselves, and to the general character of colonial society.

The excellent management of the negroes in the colonies where no supply can be procured, and where the great proportion of the whites reside, is sufficient proof of these propositions. Various circumstances have placed the settlements of Spain and Portugal nearly in the predicament. Scarcely any of the blacks, in these colonies, are of African birth; the trade being extremely insignificant, and the natural increase of the blacks very rapid. The whites, too, reside upon their properties, and in the large towns scattered over South America, in a proportion elsewhere unknown. The privileges of slaves have gradually been extended, first by custom, and then by law, till the period has actually arrived, when a Spanish or Portuguese slave hardly conceives himself less comfortable, or even less important, than the lower order of free inhabitants. The good treatment of those negroes is partly owing to the residence of their masters, who are guided by their own eyes and interests, not their overseer's, and in its turn tends to encourage that custom of residing; and to the difficulty of procuring recruits from Africa, the necessity of which is lessened by the consequences of this treatment. The condition of the slaves in those states of North America, where importation has long been discontinued, is another striking proof of the truth of this representation.

That the bad qualities ascribed to the negroes, often with great justice, belong rather to their habits than to their nature, and are derived either from the low state of civilization in which the whole race at present is placed, or from the manifold hardships of their situation in the colonies, is not only consistent with analogy, but is deducible from facts. The travellers who have visited interior Africa, where the influence of the slave-trade is much less felt than on the west coast, assure us, that the natural dispositions of the negro race are mild, gentle, and amiable in a high degree: that, far from wanting ingenuity, they have made no contemptible progress in the arts; and have even united into political societies of great extent and complicated structure, notwithstanding the obstacles arising from their remote situation, and their want of water-carriage: that their disposition to voluntary and continued exertions of body and mind, their ˙ capacity of industry, the great promoter of all human improvement, is not inferior to the same principle in other tribes, in similar situations: in fine, that they have the same propensity to improve both their condition, their faculties, and their virtues, conspicuous in the human character over all the rest of the world. Let us compare the general circumstances of any European nation; the character, both for talents and virtues of its inhabitants, at two distant periods. How remarkable is the contast between them! Little more than a century ago, Russia was covered with hordes of barbarians; cheating, drinking, brutal lust, and ferocious rage, were as well known, and as little blamed, among the nobles of the czar's court, as the more polished and mitigated forms of the same vices are at this day in Petersburgh; literature never appeared among its inhabitants; and you might travel several days journey, without meeting a man, even among the higher classes, qualified for one moment's rational conversation. [...]: Though the various circumstances of *external* improvement will not totally conceal, even at this day, and among the first classes, the "vestigia ruris,"[1] yet no one can deny that the stuff of which Russians are made has been greatly and fundamentally improved; that their capacities and virtues rapidly unfolding, as their habits have been changed, and their communication with the rest of mankind extended. A century ago, it would have been just as miraculous to read a tolerable Russian poem, or find a society of Boyars where a rational person could spend his time with satisfaction, as it would be at this day, to find the same prodigies at Houssa or Tombuctoo:[2] and those who argue about races, and despise the effect of circumstances, would have had the same right to decide upon the fate of all the Russias, from an inspection of the Calmuc skull,[3] as they now

---

[1] Vestiges of a rural past.
[2] African cities in present-day Nigeria and Mali.
[3] From the region of Northern Asia ruled by the Mongols in the thirteenth and fourteenth centuries.

have to condemn all Africa to everlasting barbarism, from the craniums, colour, and wool of its inhabitants. If we allow that there will always be a sensible difference between the negro and the European, yet why should we suppose that this disparity will be greater than between the Sclavonian and Gothic nations? No one denies that all the families of mankind are capable of great improvement. And though, after all, some tribes should remain inferior to others, it would be ridiculous on that account to deny the possibility of greatly civilizing even the most untoward tribe, or the importance of the least considerable advances which it may be capable of making. That the progress of any race of men, or of the whole species, in the various branches of virtue and power, must be infinite, was never maintained by sound reasoners. But that this progress is indefinite; that no limit can be assigned to its extent or acceleration, is beyond all reasonable controversy.

The superiority of a negro in the interior of Africa to one on the Slave Coast is notorious. The enemies of the slave-trade reasonably impute the degeneracy of the maritime tribes to that baneful commerce. Its friends have, on the other hand, deduced from thence an argument against the negro character, which, say they, is not improved by intercourse with civilized nations. But the *fact* is admitted. Mr. Park observed it in the north, and Mr. Barrow in the tribes south of the line, who increase in civilization as you leave the Slave Coast. Compare the accounts given by these travellers, of the skill, the industry, the excellent moral qualities of the Africans in Houssa and Tombuctoo, &c., with the pictures that have been drawn of the same race, living in all the barbarity which the supply of slave ships requires; you will be convinced that the negro is as much improved by a change of circumstances as the white. The state of slavery is in no case favourable to improvement; yet, compare the Creole negro with the imported slave, and you will find that even the most debasing form of servitude, though it necessarily eradicates most of the moral qualities of the African, has not prevented him from profiting intellectually by the intercourse of more civilized men. The war of St. Domingo reads us a memorable lesson; negroes organizing immense armies; laying plans of campaigns and sieges, which, if not scientific, have at least been successful against the finest European troops; arranging forms of government, and even proceeding some length in executing the most difficult of human enterprizes; entering into commercial relations with foreigners, and conceiving the idea of alliances; acquiring something like a maritime force, and, at any rate, navigating vessels in the tropical seas, with as much skill and foresight as that complicated operation requires.

This spectacle ought to teach us the effects of circumstances upon the human faculties, and prescribe bounds to that arrogance, which would confine to one race, the characteristics of the species. We have torn those men from their country, on the vain pretence, that their nature is radically inferior to our own. We have treated them so as to stunt the natural growth of their virtues and their reason. Our efforts have partly succeeded; for the West Indian, like all other slaves, has copied some of the tyrant's vices. But their ingenuity has advanced apace, under all disadvantages; and the negroes are already so much improved, that, while we madly continue to despise them, and to justify the crimes which have transplanted them, it has really become doubtful how long they will suffer us to exist in the islands.

We may be told, that brute force and adaptation to the climate, are the only faculties which the negroes of the West Indies possess. But something more than this must concur to form and maintain armies, and to distribute civil powers in a state. And the negroes, who in Africa cannot count ten, and bequeath the same portion of arithmetic to their children, must somewhat improve before they can use the mariner's compass; rig square-sailed vessels; and cultivate whole districts of cotton and coffee for their own profit in the Antilles.

The improvement visible in the negroes brought over to Europe as domestics, and their superiority to their countrymen in Africa or the West Indies, is a new evidence of these truths. There is surely a wider difference between one of those blacks and a native of the Slave Coast, than between a London chairman and the Irish shepherd who lived a few centuries ago. The fidelity, courage, and other good qualities, remarkable in freed negroes, distinguish them as much from the slaves, of whose cowardice and treachery such pictures have been drawn, as the feats of valour recorded in the annals of the Welsh, place them above those wretched Britons who resisted their invaders only with groans.

There is nothing in the physical or moral constitution of the negro, which renders him an exception to the general character of the species, and prevents him from improving in all estimable qualities, when placed in favourable circumstances. Nay, under all possible disadvantages, we see the progress he is capable of making, whether insulated by the deserts of Africa, or surrounded by the slave factories of Europeans, or groaning under the cruelties of the West Indian system. This progress will be accelerated in proportion as those impediments are removed; while Africa is civilized by legitimate commerce with the more polished nations of the world, the negroes already in the West Indies will rapidly improve, as soon as the abolition shall begin to ameliorate their treatment.

It will not be long before milder treatment will increase the productive powers of negro labour. The first two or three seasons may possibly be less prosperous, in consequence of the change. Indeed, changes of every kind have a tendency at the beginning to produce disorder in all political systems; for, it is true, though lamentable, that the correction of the greatest evils in society generally increases, for a time, the bad effects of the original error. But the connexion is so constant between freedom and industry, that we may reasonably expect these evils to be of short duration. The history of all Europe demonstrates the effects which the mild treatment of the labouring orders naturally produces on the value of their industry.

The proprietors of Hungary, almost immediately after the reform of Maria Theresa,[1] began to feel the salutary consequences of the limitations of the corvées[2] due from their peasants. When, instead of full power over the whole of the serf's labour, the lord could only take two days in each week, he found those two worth much more than all the seven had been before; though at the same time, he lost the right of retaining the peasant on his ground against his will. If such mitigations are favourable to the master, still more advantageous must they be to the slave. And can any improvement be made in the condition of the lower orders, more effectually, than by augmenting their wealth, and their importance to the upper classes? It is not unlikely that the number of holidays will next be increased, or the hours of work in the day diminished; that the negro will, by degrees, be left more and more to his own care, and will begin to feel himself more dependent on the produce of his industry. The less interference from the laws, the better for the master, and still more for the slave. The mutual interest of the parties will be the best law, and, indeed, the only one capable of being accurately executed. When something like industry has taken root, it may be time to introduce, in the same silent, gradual, and voluntary manner, the grand improvement of task-work. This has already been attempted, with the happiest effects, in several of the colonies; in Brazil; on some parts of the Spanish main; in the Bahamas, and elsewhere. It has been introduced also into Surinam; though, from peculiar circum-

---

[1]   Maria Theresa (1717–80) was the reform-minded Habsburg Queen of Hungary and Bohemia from 1740–80.
[2]   Unpaid labor, performed in lieu of taxes.

stances, it has not there produced such salutary changes as in other settlements. Indeed, while the bad effects of the old system flourish in full vigour, preventing the general improvement of the slaves in their habits of voluntary exertion, it is only in certain kinds of work that tasks can be distributed. The new mode of treatment would render *universal* task-work, not only an easy, but a necessary improvement. And when these changes shall have been effected slowly, and with the consent of all proprietors, not taken by vote, but freely given by each individual; will not the lower orders in the islands be exactly in the state of the *ascripti glebæ*[1] under the milder feudal governments of the old world? It is but one step to make them *coloni partiarii*,[2] or serf tenants paying a proportion of their crops to the lord. Such they are already in some parts of Spanish and Portuguese America, where the richest ores and pearls are obtained, by means of this very contract between the master and his slave. Nor does it much signify in what form the last change of all shall then be effected by the total emancipation of the negro. He will, by this natural gradation, have become civilized to a certain degree, and fully capable of enjoying the station of a free man, for which all are fitted by nature. In the course of time, we may hope to see the same relaxation of prejudice against him among the whites, which has made the European baron cease to look down upon his serf as an inferior animal. The mixture even of the races, is a thing by no means impossible, and will remove the only pretext that can remain for supposing the West Indian society, as new-modelled by the abolition, to be in the smallest degree different from the society in Europe, after the successors of the Romans ceased to procure slaves in commerce.

5. Engravings (by J. Barlow), from Marcus Rainsford's *Historical Account of the Black Empire of Hayti* (1805)

[Marcus Rainsford served as a captain in the Third West-India Regiment of Britain. He arrived in Saint Domingue in 1799 after being shipwrecked during a hurricane while en route from Jamaica to Martinique. Rainsford circulated liberally among the reigning elite under Toussaint until his arrest for espionage—he pretended to be an American, but had no passport to prove his citizenship. Ultimately his death sentence was commuted. After his return to

---

[1]   Unenrolled tenant farmers.
[2]   Enrolled serf tenants.

England, he published two books about Haiti, the first a personal memoir and the second the *Historical Account of the Black Empire of Hayti* from which the following engravings are taken. Rainsford was the first Englishman to offer his views of the Haitian Revolution. He regarded himself as an advocate of Haitian freedom, writing in his introduction, "It is on ancient record, that negroes were capable of repelling their enemies, with vigour, in their own country; and a writer of modern date has assured us of the talents and virtues of these people; but it remained for the close of the eighteenth century to realize the scene, form a state of abject degeneracy:—to exhibit, a horde of negroes emancipating themselves from the vilest slavery, and at once filling the relations of society, enacting laws, and commanding armies, in the colonies of Europe" (xi).]

"The mode of training Blood Hounds in St. Domingo
and of exercising them by Chaseurs."

"Blood Hounds attacking a Black Family in the Woods."

"Toussaint Louverture."

"Revenge taken by the Black Army for the Cruelties
practised on them by the French."

"The Mode of exterminating the Black Army as practised by the French."

6. From Condy Raguet, "Account of the Massacre in St. Domingo, in May, 1806" *American Register or, General Repository of History, Politics and Science* (1 January 1807): 137–44[1]

[...] [Dessalines] instantly decreed the destruction of all the remaining whites. His orders reach Christophe,[2] who retires to fort Ferrier, and singles out twelve or fifteen whites who must be preserved. Some of these he has with him, and some remain in town, but under the immediate eye of the commandant of the place, who is directed to see that no injury is done them. Except very few, all other whites are in the country, where, as I have above stated, they were sent a short time before. These arrangements are carried on so secretly, that not a word is known of the intentions of the government, until Tuesday morning, the 13th of May, when we learn with horror and concern that all the unfortunate whites, except those marked for preservation, were assassinated during the preceding night. As it was done out of the city, our ears were not assailed with the shrieks of the dying victims, nor were our gutters, as in the preceding massacre, floating with streams of blood. The only trace of murder to be seen in the streets was one spot of about half a gallon of blood; one unfortunate family however were butchered in the town, and as it will give some idea of the modes of murder pursued by the Haytians, I will give the particulars. It was publicly communicated through the town on the following day, by the nurse of the family, a negro woman, who openly pointed out the individuals employed on the expedition.

Mr. Selle was a baker, and a man of respectability; Dessalines and Christophe had long expressed a great friendship for him, and, after having saved him from the general massacre of 1804, appointed him baker of the army. His wife was a handsome, genteel woman of about thirty-five, and they had three small children, the youngest of which was at the breast.

Richard, commandant of the place, with a guard of soldiers, went to the house about midnight, and, knocking at the door, called Mr. Selle to come down and let him in. He said he had just received orders from the emperor, to send out of the city all the house servants, and that he wanted theirs. Madame Selle, upon hearing this, called out, "I hope, commandant, you don't intend taking my nurse, I have a young infant, and rather than you should take its nurse you might take me." Richard insisted upon entering,

---

1   Though published without attribution and without the author's consent, Raguet claimed authorship of "Account of the Massacre" in a letter to the editor of the *American Register*, published in January 1808.

2   See note 1, p. 62.

and Mr. Selle was obliged to open the door. He entered, and, at a certain signal, four black grenadiers rushed in, and throwing a rope with a noose round Mr. Selle's neck, and one round his wife's, hauled upon the ends till they were both strangled. They then mashed the baby in their hands, and strangled the other two children who were asleep in bed. The chests were then broken open, and the money taken off by the commandant.

After this barbarity, the wicked assassins, instead of burying the bodies of this unfortunate family, to hide their guilt from the eyes of the world, dragged them to a ditch on the very edge of the town, about two hundred yards from their house, where they lay uncovered and exposed, till the dogs and the vermin had devoured them. Several of the Americans went to see the horrid spectacle, and an indigene of veracity one day assured me, that he saw a dog running through the streets with one of madame Selle's hands in his mouth.

The massacre in the country was not executed as the former had been, by the troops solely. Christophe said that the soldiers had already waded deep enough in blood, and on that account allotted a great part of the labour to the cultivators of the plantations, who on the occasion made use of their great knives, and butchered the men, women, and children, in perfect *sang froid*.[1]

7. From [Condy Raguet], "Memoirs of Hayti—For the Port Folio. In a Series of Letters" (1809–12)

[Condy Raguet published serially the following account in *The Port-Folio* over the course of three years from May 1809 to January 1812. *The Port-Folio* had been one of the most important—and partisan—periodicals of the early republican United States. Edited originally by Joseph Dennie, *The Port-Folio* launched vicious attacks on Thomas Jefferson and the Republican party after Jefferson's election and the political defeat of Federalism in 1800. Purchased after Dennie's death by Bradford and Inskeep, *The Port-Folio* shifted emphasis away from polemics and discourses on religious controversy to the more genteel collection of materials comprising "portraits of great men," "Remarkable Trials, Law Reports, and Pleadings of a peculiarly entertaining, interesting, and eloquent character," "Epistolary Correspondence of men of literary eminence," and "Papers on topics of Moral and Physical Science, Rural Economy, Useful Projects, Miscellaneous Essays, Romantic Adventures,

---

[1]   Cold blood.

Tours and Travels, Foreign and Domestic Literature, Criticism and Poetry, Levity, Merriment, Wit and Humour." With something for everyone—the editors promised to "please the ladies" by attending occasionally to "the Toilet of Fashion"—Bradford and Inskeep aimed most not to offend: "The squabbles in the State, and polemical brawls in the Church will be habitually shunned by all the prudence of a pacific policy," they wrote. It certainly bears mentioning that Bradford and Inskeep also published both of Sansay's novels, reprinted here. And also worth noting that they published the only known reviews (both favorable) of *Laura*, an innovation in cross-marketing.]

Introduction

Hispaniola, the most beautiful and fertile of the West India Islands, has for many years been the seat of one of the most sanguinary rebellions recorded in the pages of history. The ruder ages of antiquity have scarcely produced such direful events as this unfortunate country has exhibited.

The writer of the following letters, in the early part of the year 1804, in the course of some mercantile pursuits, visited Hispaniola. This being his first voyage, afforded him pleasing objects of speculation. The novelty of the scene to which he was introduced, in a country emerging from a state of slavery to the rank of an independent nation, produced those strong impressions which the sensibility of youth is so naturally formed.

He there first conceived the idea of recording, as correctly as his opportunities for information would enable him, the transactions most worthy of notice which occurred about this period: but the unsettled state of the government rendered it dangerous for a stranger to commit to writing any relation that would represent things in their true light. The only mode of accomplishing his views, which could be pursued in safety, was the making of memoranda of dates, with a mere hint of occurrences connected therewith, but for the most part, he was compelled to rely for a short time upon his memory.

On returning to the United States, a detention at the Lazaretto afforded the first period of leisure which presented itself, for placing on paper the fruits of his observations, and shortly after his return to Philadelphia, he published in the American Daily Advertiser, "A Short Account of the Present State of Affairs in St. Domingo." To this account was prefixed, as introductory to the then state of the country, a brief notice of the events that occurred at the commencement of the Revolution, which, from misinformation, was, in several particulars, incorrect; and the narrative itself being written in haste, and perhaps under the influence of some prejudice against the Haytians, was destitute of order, and contained, perhaps, many trivial details.

In the latter end of 1805, the writer again visited that country, where he remained upwards of seven months. From frequent opportunities of intercourse, and even intimacy, with many officers and people of distinction, (some of whom were men of talents and education) he was enabled to add much to his former stock of information, and after his return, he wrote for publication, "A circumstantial Account of the Massacre in St. Domingo, in May, 1806," which appeared in several of the city papers.[1]

The intention of writing a connected and circumstantial history of the Haytians subsequent to their independence, after which the writer's acquaintance with that people commenced, has been long entertained, and has indeed been with him, a favourite and frequent subject of reflection. He has consequently availed himself of every opportunity, that presented, of gathering information relative to this object, from respectable gentlemen, with whom he has corresponded or conversed, and upon whose veracity he could rely.

The epistolary form may perhaps require some explanation. The writer conceives there are many circumstances which do not strictly appertain to the department of history, and yet, as they tend much to show the manners and customs of a people, and their treatment of strangers, are well worthy of relation. In fact, a great part of his work will probably consist of such matter, and as he makes no claim to the rank of a *historian*, he is very willing to be considered merely an annotator. The epistolary style seemed best suited to his abilities, and to avoid the imputation of egotism, to which he might be exposed, if he wrote in any other form, he concluded that his narrative in a series of letters addressed to a friend, would be the most unassuming mode, in which he could speak as often of himself as occasion would require.

The history of Hispaniola from its first discovery by Columbus, in 1492, to the commencement of the revolution, in 1789, and during several years of that dreadful era, has been fully and circumstantially related by Mr. Bryan Edwards, in his History of the West Indies: Rainsford also in his Empire of Hayti, published at London in 1805, has treated the subject at large, and has continued his narrative to the commencement of that year.

The writer means to confine himself *chiefly* to that portion of the history of Hayti, which succeeds in independence, but if the reader

---

[1] The article is reprinted above in this volume under the title "Account of the Massacre in St. Domingo, in May 1806."

wishes to acquaint himself with the early part of the revolution, he may receive ample information by referring to the works already mentioned. He will there see recorded the particulars of an event which has justly excited general attention.

R.

Letter III

The Cape, Island of Hayti, February 1, 1804.

Unlike the generality of travellers, who endeavour to entertain their correspondents with circumstantial details of their adventures from the moment they embark upon their voyage, I have in my two first letters entered at once into the substance of my narration. This was done for the purpose of giving you full information of the state of affairs in this country at the period of my arrival, which being accomplished, I shall begin to speak of myself.

On the 23rd of January, we received a pilot off the harbour of the Cape, and in about one hour anchored before the town. We were immediately visited by a mulatto officer of the port, dressed in a kind of uniform and a military *chapeau*, who directed the captain and myself to accompany him on shore, with the papers of the vessel, invoices, letters, and newspapers. On our landing, an American gentleman came up to speak to us, but was prevented by the officer, who hurried us through the streets, and would permit no person to converse with us. In a short time we arrived at the office of *Sangos*, captain of the port, where our vessel was reported. Thence we proceeded with the same rapidity up one street and down another, until we reached the *bureau* of *Richard*, commandant of the place. Here again a report similar to the former was registered, and we were called upon for our newspapers and letters. Fortunately of the latter we had none, for it is a fact well known here, that no letter deposited in that office ever reaches its address. Thence we were hurried to the house of citizen A. the interpreter. It there appeared that I had forgotten one of my papers, for which I was instantly sent on board, with directions to return without delay. The sailors being employed in mooring the vessel, I was not able to procure a conveyance to shore as soon as could have been wished, and when I landed again on the wharf, was not a little astonished to find the mulatto officer *diabling* and swearing at me in a violent manner with his stick raised in a threatening attitude. Having never been accustomed in my own country to *argumentum bacculinum*,[1] especially with one of his

---

[1] "The argument of the cudgel," i.e., an appeal to force.

complexion, I was mortified in the highest degree, but refrained from any retaliation, as I knew the consequence would be an arrest by a guard of black *gens d'armes*, who were there, listening to the abuse of the officer. He then reconducted me to the interpreter's, who treated me with much civility, and expressed his sorrow at the necessity which obliged him to be so particular, observing "the man with whom we have to deal is not to be trifled with," alluding to Christophe. We were then conducted with the interpreter to the house of the general, where we waited up stairs in an antichamber, until his excellency was at leisure. He at length appeared, as if disturbed from sleep, in a dishabille with a Madras handkerchief round his head, and having, with all the dignity and importance of a great man addressing his inferiors, asked us several questions, such as whence we came, what passage, the latest news from France, &c. we were dismissed, and permitted to go where we pleased.

As we passed through the town, my attention was busily engaged in contemplating the surrounding scene. Being a little after midday, when the powerful rays of the sun were scorching the very streets, scarcely a human being was to be seen. The dreary desolated walls which surrounded huge heaps of ashes and rubbish, too plainly pointed out the ravages of a destructive element, and produced in the mind of the observer, a train of melancholy reflections.

Cape François was once a city of much magnificence and splendor, and perhaps the richest of all the West Indies. Two conflagrations have now reduced it to a desolate situation, but the vestiges of its former grandeur, are still in many places to be traced. The walls of the houses are all standing, and the number of those which have been since rendered habitable by repairs, is comparatively small. The buildings are all of stone, roughcast, and either of a white or yellow colour. They are but two stories high, having a hollow square in the centre exposed to the sky, in which is usually the kitchen and a well. From this area the staircases ascend, and around it on a level with the second story is a gallery into which the chamber and parlour doors open. The stairs and floors, with few exceptions, are all of stone, tile, or brick; the ground floors are occupied for stores, shops, and stables, and the upper stories for the accommodation of families. The houses are generally ornamented with iron balconies, which have withstood the fires, and the window casements, as no glass is used, are hung with Venetian or close shutters. The streets are narrow, but well laid out into small squares, neatly paved, and perfectly clean, and there are three of four hollow squares, in the centre of which are fountains adorned with the heads of animals, constantly spouting pure and delightful water, which is conveyed to them in subterraneous aqueducts from a neighbouring mountain. This is the water used for drinking and culinary purposes, as that contained in the wells is brackish and unwholesome.

The space of ground occupied by the city is about three quarters of a mile in length, by half a mile in breadth, and contains no vacant lots or gardens. It is situated on the west side of the harbour, near to the bottom of the bay, and is open to the sea on the north east. The entrance into the harbour is apparently several miles wide, but a large reef of coral rocks extends nearly across it, leaving but a small passage for vessels, breaks the impetuosity of the waves, and renders the west side of the bay, on the outermost point of which *Picolet*, a very strong and powerful fort, is situated, and sufficiently protects the entrance. The town is encompassed on the north and west by lofty mountains, the acclivity of which commences in the very town. On the south, a plain of flat country as level as a bowling green, extends for fifteen miles, and on the east is situated the harbour, on the bank of which is an extensive battery and parade. At the north east of the town is the suburbs called *carenage*, from its being the place appropriated for the repairing and careening of vessels. There are but *three* warves: one, at which all the mercantile business is transacted; another, for the accommodation of the country people who attend the market; and the third, called the government wharf, is little used: all these wharves are guarded day and night by soldiers, who suffer no one to pass them without examination. The lamps suspended at the corners of the streets are lighted every night at the expense of the occupiers of the nearest houses, and small parties of guards patrole the city, to preserve tranquillity and arrest suspicious persons.

The chapel, the only place of worship in the city, is a very commodious building, situated on the south side of a large hollow square, called *Place d'armes*. Its external appearance is magnificent: the floor is a brick pavement without pews, and entirely open to the sky, as there has been no roof on the building since the last conflagration of the town. In one corner however of the church is erected a small shed, which serves to shelter the altar and the priests from the weather. The matin service, at which I have more than once attended as a visitor, is performed very early every morning. The church is crowded with devotees, kneeling, and to every appearance perfectly sincere in their religious exercises. They were mostly females, but of every shade of colour, from white to black, promiscuously intermingled. Of men there were few, and these chiefly black, and all very old or mendicants. On one occasion, I observed *fifteen*, who were blind, standing by the door, counting their beads and asking alms. There are three priests who officiate, two whites and one black. A large fine-toned bell announces the hours of service.

The market-place is a hollow square, known by the name of *Place Clugny*, of about 400 feet in length, and of the same breadth. On Sunday, which is the market day, this whole area is covered with merchandize of almost every species, foreign and domestic, spread out upon benches and stalls, and even upon the ground, in such abundance as scarcely to leave room for passengers. Here you will see, meats, fish, poultry, turtle, eggs, fruit, vegetables, coffee, sugar, wood, grass, charcoal, bread, dry goods, and in fact almost every article which agriculture, commerce, and manufactures can collect together. In addition to this, the stores and shops, of which all the houses surrounding this area consist, are opened, and the most lively scene of small trade is carried on. Many thousands of people attend this market, abounding in all the delicate and luxurious productions, which any of the Antiles[1] are capable of furnishing. The peasants bring in the produce of the plantations from the distance of twenty or thirty miles, on mules, horses, and asses, and in return carry away articles of dress, ornament, and convenience. To speak on reasonable grounds of calculation, there must be, some market days, as much as twenty to thirty thousand dollars of specie[2] in circulation.

The number of the inhabitants of the Cape may be estimated at 10,000. Of the population of the whole Island, from the dreadful state of carnage and massacre which has for fifteen years existed here, it is impossible to make any correct computation.* Of the inhabitants of

---

* The term Island, as heretofore, is to be understood as relating only to the part formerly French. In the year 1789, prior to the revolution, the population of this division was estimated at 40,000 whites, 24,000 free people of colour, and 500,000 black slaves. Since then the population has been daily decreasing. The cruel conduct of the French, in burning, drowning, suffocating, hunting with blood hounds, and otherwise destroying thousands of these ill-fated people, added to the fortune of the war and a very extensive emigration, has in all probability reduced it to 300,000. In this opinion I am in a degree supported by a declaration, made in an official proclamation of Dessalines, in which he states his military force to be 60,000. About *one-sixth* of the population of a country is usually considered as capable of bearing arms, but as in Hayti, boys are put into the ranks at the age of fourteen, we may fairly conclude that *one-fifth* are soldiers. Dessalines no doubt swelled his roll to the fullest extent, and from these circumstances we may safely infer that the present population does not exceed the above stated.

---

[1] Spelled "Antilles," these are the islands of the West Indies (except for the Bahamas), separating the Caribbean Sea from the Atlantic Ocean; they are divided into the Greater Antilles to the north and the Lesser Antilles to the east.

[2] Coined money.

the Cape, about 3000, as stated in a former letter, are whites, and the number of that colour in the whole Island, is about 10,000. The people of colour in the northern parts of the Island bear a small proportion to the blacks, but in the western and southern departments they are a very considerable part of the community. The island may perhaps contain 50,000, including those who were formerly free. The inhabitants are then composed of three distinct classes, viz. whites, blacks, and people of colour, which last I shall generally term mulattoes. The whites consist of about an equal portion Europeans and Creoles. Of the blacks a great number are Africans, the rest Creoles, and the mulattoes are all Creoles.

The African blacks, though sanguinary and cruel, appear to be a tractable and obedient people, easily managed by proper treatment, but excessively ignorant and slothful. From their employment under the former government in the cultivation of estates in the country, and their consequent seclusion, they are quite barbarous and uncultivated, and are in the intellects little removed from the brute creation. This class composes, with those of the Creole blacks who were formerly also plantation negroes, and who do not much differ from them, the great body of the army, and the present cultivators of the land. The Creole blacks, who have not been bred in the fields, are of a different character. From their former habits of associating with the white masters on the estates and in the towns as domestic barbers, cooks, valets, &c. they have acquired a degree of politeness and urbanity of manners scarcely conceivable. Many of them are even well informed intelligent men. Some indeed have had good educations; and I understand there are a few in the island (free formerly) who have been educated in France. The Creole blacks, from their superior knowledge, address, and talents, were, during the revolution, among the conductors and leaders of it, and are, with some exceptions, those of the blacks who occupy the most important stations under the government, particularly in the civil departments. In the army, courage and military skill have been consulted more than learning, and in several instances, Africans and plantation negroes have held important commands.

The negroes generally appear to be brave, but this is no doubt partly the effect of severe discipline. Christophe, in one instance, where some of his men showed a disposition to give way in battle, had their heads instantaneously struck off, as an example to the rest. They are remarkably polite and civil to each other. If a quarrel take place, which however is not frequent, they never strike, and if words and epithets will not settle their dispute, they quietly retire to a private place, and determine it with their swords. A glove is thrown by one as a gauntlet, and as soon as the challenge is accepted by the other's taking it up, the duel commences. This system of single combat extends itself even to the lowest classes, and you will scarcely find a boy ten years old, who has not some knowledge of the use of the sword. Though most of the negroes have proved themselves to be remorseless inhuman villains, some few are possessed of morality, virtue, and benevolence. The ignorant negroes speak a language which is called Creole, but is a mixture of that language with the African. Those of the better class speak the Creole with some French, generally however very corrupt French.

The mulattoes are composed of people of colour of the various shades between black and white, of which five are defined.[1] Many of these people are the sons of the former wealthy white planters, and have been educated at colleges in France. Classical scholars and men of talents and learning are therefore not unfrequently to be found, and it has generally been the knowledge and abilities of these men that have conducted the revolution. Most of them have some information, and many of them were formerly rich proprietors. A great portion of the important stations, as well military as civil, are supplied by them, principally perhaps, because a sufficient number of blacks of capacity and understanding are not to be found for those offices that require scholarship. The mulattoes possess all the ferocity and sanguinary disposition of the blacks, combined with a superior grade of intellect. They are said to have been the most savage actors on the stage of the revolution, and notwithstanding their affinity to the whites, who were their fathers, they have carried their revenge and cruelty far beyond what was ever practised by the blacks. They are also stated to have been formerly the most severe masters to their slaves, and it appears that the blacks remember it to this day, with the determination of retaliating at some future time. A very perceptible jealousy already begins to manifest itself, and as the government is professedly *black*, the man who approaches nearest to that colour, feels himself the most independent and safe. The mulattoes who were the instigators of the rebellion in the first instance, when they made common cause with the revolted negroes, little expected to be left in the back ground, when the independence of the island should have been

---

[1] Moreau de Saint-Méry's system accounted for 128 shades of color spanning white to black grouped into 11 larger categories. The names of these categories vary from the familiar Black, White, and Mulatto to the obscure Sacatra, Griffe, Marabou, Metif, and Meamelouc. See *Secret History*, Letter X for Sansay's description of racial castes on Saint Domingue. See also note 1, p. 308.

obtained. Their pride, which is excessive, has been greatly mortified, and many of them now regret the destruction of the *ancienne regio*.[1] But death would be the immediate consequence of such a sentiment, if publicly expressed. As a stranger I have several intimacies with men of colour holding public stations, and have more than once heard dissatisfaction expressed by them, in strong language. On one occasion a well educated mulatto officer observer to me in speaking of Dessalines, that "in point of cruelty and wickedness he was far before Nero."

R.

From Letter IV

The Cape, Island of Hayti, Feb. 1804.

[...] Since my last we have been alarmed to a serious degree, by a strange and uncommon transaction. On Sunday, the fifth instant, the town was filled with soldiers, who had orders to kill all the *dogs*. Some were stationed at the corners of the streets, with drawn swords, while others entered the houses and drove the dogs out, who no sooner appearing in the streets, were crushed with stones, bayonetted, or cut to pieces with sabres. This barbarous and inhuman conduct excited universal terror and consternation among the whites, who considered it as a signal to notify them of their approaching fate. Few ventured into the streets, and those who did, appeared pale and gloomy, and bearing every mark of distress and fear. In the evening the streets were full of dead dogs, and most of the poor animals that had not been destroyed, appeared with the loss of some of their limbs. This piece of cruelty, it was afterwards said, was done by the direction of Christophe, in consequence of a dog having made an attempt to bite his horse as he was riding. But this is hardly to be credited. I am satisfied in my own mind, that it was done with a view of affrighting the whites, by displaying the vengeance to which they were themselves soon to be devoted in the destruction of the animal which had been so wickedly employed in torturing and tearing to pieces so many of the blacks.[2]

The foreigners now in this place consist of very few others than Americans, who, you know, are to be found in every part of the world. Some are resident merchants, but the chief part of them are sojourners. The treatment we receive from the Haytians may be considered as *civil*; as for *respect*, we see very little of that, and I am sorry to find that they have no higher opinion of the American character, than other

---

[1] The former ruler, the French monarch.
[2] See images from Rainsford in Appendix C, pp. 288–89.

people, who form their judgment of us from mercantile intercourse. We are considered as a nation of traders, whose sole pursuit is money, and who, for the attainment of their favourite object, would sacrifice probity, virtue and honour. Dessalines has been heard to say, that "If a bag of coffee was to be placed on the brink of Hell, an American would be the first man to go for it."

★★★

Some days since, a mutiny was detected at the arsenal by the commanding officer. There was a company of artillerists, about eighty in number, who had a long time tamely submitted to their hard treatment, and who refused to do so any longer. They remonstrated with their officers—"Have we not," said they "fought for liberty, and been victorious, and are we still to be slaves?" Their question was answered significantly. They were cast into a dungeon, for the purpose of learning the sweets even of that liberty of which they complained.

It would be natural to suppose that Toussaint L'Ouverture, the former commander in chief of the blacks, who effected so much for their advantage in the revolution, and who so powerfully assisted them in the cause of liberty, would be remembered with gratitude and love. This is not the case; his name is seldom mentioned, but in terms of reproach. Christophe said to a friend of mine in conversation, that Toussaint was a *fool*.[1] The fact is, that every man appears to be jealous of another's fame, and endeavours to detract from his reputation, thinking thereby to add to his own. For my part, I am fully persuaded that the spirit of freedom which originally actuated the *negro slaves* of St. Domingo, to throw off the yoke of bondage, is now completely and effectually extinct, among the *grandees of Hayti*. It has given place to a spirit of insolence, of oppression, and self-importance. Every one is seeking for power, and the happiness of the inferior classes of the people never occupies a moment of their attention. They are like the rest of mankind, as soon as they have gained their ends by the agency of *the people*, they forget past favours, and behold with contempt the insignificant, credulous fools who raised them into power.

---

[1] Toussaint Louverture became an icon for abolitionist and antislave-trade activists. They compared him favorably to Napoleon Bonaparte as a great leader, lionizing his dignity, his rise from servitude to self-possession, and his restraint in victory. The hagiography of Toussaint also allowed for the presentation of a stark contrast between him and his successors. Thus, some could celebrate Toussaint and simultaneously lament the barbarism of the Haitians.

The *grandees* of Hayti, I mean those who are admitted in the *first circle*, and who participate in the *style* of high life, are, the officers of the army as low down as a *commandant* or major, (a captain being seldom, a subaltern never admitted into company, unless he be an aid-de-camp) the officers of the civil departments, the priests, judges, lawyers, physicians, and a few citizens of different denominations. The great body of the people of the second class are, however, noticed, and are often invited to the tables of the *great*.

Some of these gentry are nabobs of the first order, and live in a most sumptuous and extravagant manner. They have spacious houses splendidly furnished, servants and equipages, and a guard of soldiers at their doors, to prevent informal visits, and to convey a high and mighty idea of their importance. Their tables are furnished with delicate and expensive meats, fruits, and pastry, served up in the most elegant manner, and accompanied with the choicest liquors, while they themselves appear in all the grandeur of nobility.

★★★

Not long since I had the honour of being invited to a party given by this lady, and as a particular description, I knew, would be amusing to you, I took the pains to observe every thing with attention. [...]

★★★

There were *two hundred and fifty* guests at the table, besides many who could not procure seats. The company consisted of the general of division Christophe, who occupied the centre, with Lady Dessalines, our hostess, on his right hand, and Madame Christophe on his left, six or eight black and mulatto generals, as many colonels and others of high rank, with all the officers of any distinction, civil and military, then in the Cape, the captain and officers of a British man of war, about thirty American merchants and captains, a great number of the white French inhabitants of the most respectable class, male and female, a few black and coloured *professional gentlemen*, and citizens, and a great crowd of mulatto and black damsels. The table was surrounded by about a *hundred* domestics and waiters, and a guard of soldiers to keep off the rabble, who had rushed in like a torrent to see this beautiful exhibition, and a grand band of music performed fine pieces during the whole of the repast. Except the meschianza given, during the American war, in the neighbourhood of Philadelphia, I doubt in any *fete* ever given in the United States equalled this in luxury, variety, or splendor.[1]

***

At the conclusion of the feast several toasts were given by Christophe, and drank with loud expressions of applause; among these were, "The Governor General of Hayti," (who was absent) "His Britannic Majesty," and "The President of the United States." The greatest harmony prevailed, and upon the occasion, the time-serving Frenchmen, who were present, had a glorious opportunity of displaying their gallant attention to the distinguished *fair ones*. After this the company retired into various parts of the house and garden, to keep out of the way, until the tables should be removed, and preparations made for the ball; when this was arranged, the music struck up, and the whole room was in motion. As I declined dancing, I amused myself by lounging about the room as a silent spectator. Their chief dances were cotillions; most of them danced well, and some of them elegantly; but the checkered appearance of the floor, was to me a novel, and, I must confess, an unpleasant sight. In one place would be seen, a handsome gentlemanly Frenchman *dancing to* an ugly, vulgar-looking negro wench, and in another, a delicate young lady, fair as a lily, and the picture of virtue and innocence, *going right and left* with a savage looking negro, bearing the very front of an assassin. I pitied the poor wretches who were obliged to submit to such degradation for the purpose of preserving their lives; and when I reflected, that, perhaps, at a future day, they might be butchered by these same partners, the very blood chilled in my veins.

From Letter XI

[...] This destruction of the whites must be viewed by every friend of humanity, as one of the most deliberate and wicked acts of barbarity that has ever polluted the pages of history. Nine thousand men, women and children, most of who were entirely innocent of any agency in the cruelties committed against the blacks, after being enticed to remain in the island under a solemn pledge of the protection of the government, were in the most wanton, barbarous and cruel manner inhumanly destroyed.

---

[1]   The meschianza was a highly theatrical pageant celebrated 18 May 1778 by British troops under the command of General William Howe.

I can conceive of no excuse which can be set down as an extenuation of their crime. Their uncultivated and rude state may be adduced perhaps by some as an argument in mitigation, but not with reason; their leaders have proved themselves capable of distinguishing between right and wrong, and this particular enormity has been the effect of studied and deliberate premeditation. It is true that the injuries and flagitious cruelties inflicted upon them by the French during the revolution, were highly calculated to produce a severe retaliation, and had their vengeance been exercised upon those who came within their grasp immediately after the departure of the French troops, or afterwards upon those only who had been instrumental in their sufferings, some allowances might have been made for the passion of human nature. But suppose we could for a moment admit, with the Haytians, that deliberate vengeance upon the whole white population for the crime of the wicked part, was justifiable in the present instance, we must surely be convinced that the whole merit or virtue of the act is tarnished by a base passion for pillage. Instead of beholding an act of retribution "which the justice of God has urged," as expressed by Dessalines in one of his proclamations, we see a band of robbers and ruffians rioting in plunder. [...]

From Letter XVII

[...] A description of the persons and characters of the women, constitutes a very important branch of the duty of the traveller, who undertakes to write an account of any particular nation; and I should consider myself as falling very far short in my respect for the ladies, were I to pass unnoticed the gay and sprightly damsels who make so conspicuous a figure in the *beau-monde* of Hayti, or who display their charms with such fascinating lustre at the imperial court of *Jacques the First*. I anticipate the smile which will be excited, as you picture to yourself a *sable* belle decorated in all the splendor and taste of fashion, tripping down the mazy dance, and rivalling even the very Graces, in a display of her accomplished movements and graceful attitudes. But pardon the interruption, I mean not to embellish my narrative with such fancy coloured descriptions, as your imagination may invent, but to delineate the Haytian ladies in their true *colours*, that you may yourself form a judgment of their merits. You, as well as others must know, that the inhabitants of the United States have been accustomed to see people of colour in no other capacity than that of slaves, servants, or labourers, without education and consequently incapacitated for any stations in life but those of the most humble nature. This being the case, they have very naturally imbibed certain prejudices, which have become so habitual as to be with difficulty removed. They are accustomed to consider all those who are possessed of even a single drop of African blood in their veins, as belonging to the class of negroes, and the only idea they are disposed to form of people of colour, is founded upon what they have been in the constant habit of witnessing. Thus it is extremely difficult for an American to believe, that there can be in this island, mulatto men who have been brought up by their white fathers, with all the care and attention, which parents usually bestow upon their legitimate offspring, who have been educated at colleges in France, and who are accomplished classical scholars. Yet the fact is so, and perhaps when this information is premised, it may not appear so extraordinary, that among the Haytian women also, many should be found who are adapted for different sphere of life, from those of our own country.

During the existence of the ancient system of colonial government, which was terminated by the French revolution, when peace and tranquillity held their united empire within the bosom of this then happy island, Hispaniola possessed in a profuse degree, all that wealth and luxury, which the fertility of its soil was calculated to produce, and the inclinations of its inhabitants predisposed to enjoy. Hospitality then extended her downy wings over the splendid mansion of every opulent planter, and with joyful welcome invited the sun-oppressed and weary traveller, to partake of the festive board of her generous patron. But unfortunately it not unfrequently happened, that tokens of domestic kindness, and of zeal for the accommodation of the guest, were not confined to the social pleasures of the table, or the unbounded varieties with which it was loaded. A looseness of morals had by degrees been introduced, which corrupting the virtue of a chaste hospitality, transformed her sacred rights into the lewd practices of a brothel. The master too was not ashamed to indulge in a similar illicit and disgraceful commerce with his *own* female slaves, and hence was produced a race of people, whose approximation in colour to the white, advanced with every new generation, until in the year 1789, a population equal to *four fifths* of that of the whites, was extended over the island. As the colonies became gradually more and more accustomed to the sight of persons of a mixed blood; it was in the same proportion deemed less discreditable in a white father to rear and educate his coloured child. But a deep-rooted prejudice against people of colour as regarded their claims to any degree of rank, so completely governed the European as well as the Creole white, that a woman of the latter complexion would never associate with one of the former, neither was a coloured man permitted to hold any office under the government or practise any liberal profession, although many of them were men of education, and proprietors of great estates. Had not this bitter prejudice been carried to such an unlimited extent, it is highly probable, that the unhappy revolution which has caused so much banishment and bloodshed, would never have terminated as it has, for the mulattoes would have had no cause for revolt, and without their talents and counsel it could never have been successfully conducted. But to return from my digression.

The women of Hayti, like those of all other communities, are composed of various classes, according to their stations in life. I shall consider them under the three general heads, to which I think they may with propriety be reduced. The highest class, of *first circle*, comprizes the ladies, and daughters of the chief officers military and civil, the maids of honour attendant upon the empress, and her daughters the *princesses*, and a few women of *degree*, who are perhaps related to, or very intimate with, some of the families of distinction. Of this rank, there are some of all colours, from the lightest shade, to the purest black. In the second or middling class, may be included the wives and daughters of merchants, subaltern military officers, mechanics, and the great body of shopkeepers, mantuamakers, and milliners. The division of labour is here so justly apportioned, that all the easy light work, such as that of retailing dry goods, belongs exclusively to the women. By this means they are enabled to support themselves respectably, and to be highly useful to their country, for in consequence of their industry, more men are left to devote their services to the various military and agricultural employments, for which they are required. Of this class, there are likewise some of all colours. The lowest class, composed of servants, plantation wenches, washers of clothes, &c. are nearly all black. You will seldom see one of a lighter shade than the *mulatresse*, and of that colour but very few.[1]

---

[1] The child of one white and one black parent. According to Moreau de St. Méry's classificatory system designed for colonial Saint Domingue, a mulatto or mulatresse had at least 56 and no more than 70 shades white. To make Moreau's abstruse system somewhat less confusing, consider that according the system, a mulatto child might have two parents of color so long as the shades of color of each parent were roughly equal to the category of the mulatto, in other words 64 shades white and 64 shades black. Given the link between class status and color that Raguet describes above, it is possible to imagine the utility of such a complicated taxonomy of skin color and blood. It is worth noting that even by 1896, when the US Supreme Court established at the federal level the doctrine of segregation known as "separate but equal," the legal description of what constituted whiteness or blackness varied from state to state.

That particular portion of them which is the most likely to attract the attention of strangers, is composed of those who belong to the three lightest shades of colour called *quinterone, quarterone,* and *mistive.* The great body of these women are handsome, and many of them beautiful. The short curly wool of the negro is lost in their fine long flowing tresses of hair, and there is scarcely any thing in their appearance which indicates the least consanguinity to the black. The colour of many so far from appearing to be produced by the mixed nature of their blood, resembles entirely the effect of the sun and climate, and there are not a few of a much lighter complexion than some American *brunettes.* Their persons, particularly those of the *young* women, are generally slender, and well proportioned, their features delicate, and their deportment lofty. Their mental acquirements are generally limited, though many of them have excellent educations. But in some accomplishments they are by no means deficient. They sing with elegance and melody, play on the guitar with judgment, and dance with gracefulness. Of these fashionable amusements they are extravagantly fond, but of others again they are entirely negligent. I have never seen, for instance, a Haytian lady seated at a gambling table, with a pack of cards in her hand, exhibiting a countenance expressive of such interest as if her whole happiness was involved in the issue of the game. Their leisure time is employed in pursuits of industry, and as they excel in all the nice branches of needlework and embroidering, they are enabled to procure a maintenance. Their language, which is the refined Creole, (for even this simple tongue has its various dialects and styles) is extremely fascinating, and with the soft and melodious accents with which it is artfully uttered, is well adapted to the science of making love, and is often successfully displayed.

The Haytian lady is excessively fond of dress, and in her *costume* exhibits a great deal of taste and neatness. Jewels, trinkets and rings of considerable value and splendour form a considerable part of her wealth, but the article which is more highly esteemed of all the rest of her wardrobe together, is a fine *Madrass handkerchief* for her head.[1] So great is the predilection for this article, that if a Haytian lady was in want of one, and at the same time of an *under-garment,* and had only money enough to purchase one, she would buy the former. A single Madrass handkerchief, of a singular and beautiful pattern, has been known to sell for *sixty-four* dollars, to such extent has vanity and extravagance been carried.

---

[1]   See note 1, p. 65.

The Haytian ladies are haughty, proud and disdainful, artful, high-spirited, of jealous dispositions, and very apt to tear caps, scratch, and pull hair, if any dispute arises between them upon affairs of love. Pugilistic encounters are therefore not uncommon. In their social inter-course however with each other and with strangers, they are polite, ceremonious, and complimentary. They pay great attention to their health by the frequent use of the bath, and are always clean in their dress. Their teeth are of the purest white, to preserve which they continually rub them with a kind of soap-stick, and the constant use of the most fragrant perfumes, completely subjugates all native odours.

Marriages are not frequent. I recollect of hearing of but one, the cere-mony of which was performed in church, and it created a sensation of envy and jealousy throughout the whole town. The bride was a young *mulatresse* of character and respectable connexions; the women consid-ered it as a public declaration made by *mademoiselle*, that she was resolved not to conform to the established custom, as setting a higher value upon her reputation, and that of consequence, she considered her claim to chastity as superior to theirs. But although the connubial ceremony is usually omitted, states of concubinage, preceded by regular courtships, are adopted in their stead, which oftentimes continue during the life of one of the parties. In this state fidelity is as much revered as though enjoined by the solemn contract of a priest or magistrate, and it is under this system of domestic establishment that many of the officers and their ladies live. The emperor is married, and has several daughters, as is also the general in chief, who has a family of young children growing up. It is worthy of remark, that it is extremely rare, that a woman of colour resides with a man of a darker shade than herself. The husbands are generally of a lighter cast than their wives, though instances are not wanting of women nearly white, being married to, or what is equiva-lent to it, residing with men perfectly black. This, however, I presume only occurs in instances where *great men* have been concerned, and where the female has sacrificed her feelings to her ambition.

The women all assume the appearance of chastity. Those who are of a respectable class, and above the temptations to which poverty might expose them, really are so, and the number of those is exceedingly small, who are so degraded as to be classed with the common women of our country.[1] They are very much attached to the whites, inasmuch, that did the subject rest with them, they would most heartily unite in the restora-

---

[1] Prostitutes.

tion of the colony to its former proprietors. This observation will hold good of nearly all the women, even those who are black, excepting indeed the ladies of officers and men in distinguished stations, whose ranks would be affected by such an event. From their having been spectators of so much revolutionary horror and carnage, the Haytian women have acquired a degree of courage and heroism which is by no means common to the female sex. But yet this masculine temper of mind is in no way indicated by any harshness of manners, for the same softness which should every-where characterize the female, is fully preserved in their deportment.

Although I have drawn lines of distinction by which the women are classed into different grades, yet I should observe, that the intercourse between those of the two highest is upon so familiar a footing, that they appear to be upon an equality. Their stations in life, alone mark the difference, and I have not observed that the ladies of great men, often assume much consequence upon the superiority of their ranks, in their conduct to inferiors.

Having thus given you as particular account of the *fair sex* of Hayti, as my present acquaintance with them, enables me to do, I shall leave you for a while that you may endeavour to reconcile my account with the ideas you had formed of them, when under the influence of prejudice.

From Letter XIX

[...] The appearances exhibited to the view of a traveller, when survey-ing the face of the country, are of a melancholy character, and cannot fail to excite in his mind the most gloomy sensations. He beholds, all around him, the remains of the princely mansions of the ancient proprietors of the soil, fast crumbling to dust. He sees the tottering pillars on which still hang massy gates of iron, almost eaten up by rust; walls, pyramids, marble statues, and many other vestiges of magnificence and splendour falling to decay. Instead of these proud structures, the devastation of which has been accompanied by such horrible transactions, a mean solitary cabin is presented to the sight. Instead of the comforts and luxuries which here once so highly abounded, a miserable horde of ignorant negroes, scarcely enjoy the necessities of life. These uncheering appearances are eminently conspicuous on the *Plaine du Cap*, which extends many miles to the southward and eastward from the Cape, and which was formerly so abun-dant in luxurious gardens, fertile plantations, and splendid edifices.

But the gloominess attendant upon such scenes of destruction, is in some measure alleviated by the civility, which one meets with from the peasantry in travelling. There is a strong contrast between the insolence of soldiers, who are stationed in the large towns and the politeness of the simple cultivators. Not an individual passes without taking off his hat with the friendly salutation of *"salut monsieur"* or *"bon jour capitaine,"* which latter appellation is the one indiscriminately given by the lower class of people, as well in town as country, to all white men who, they perceive, are not Frenchmen. Thus a negro speaking to a merchant, captain, supercargo or sailor, never forgets to entitle him *capitaine*, that appellation with him being synonymous with *stranger*, and at the same time the most dignified and respectful title for a private citizen, which his vocabulary affords. The females are equally polite, and never fail in passing to drop a low curtsey, and with a modest smile to greet you with *"bo jou moucher."* [1]

The peasantry of Hayti exhibit a sad spectacle of the effects of a mistaken policy. They are miserably poor, and live in wretched hovels. The clothing of the men consists of a shirt, and sometimes a pair of pantaloons, made of coarse German linen, and their food of cassada bread, yams, and roasted plantains, seasoned perhaps with a salted herring, which answers the purpose of being *pointed at*. The women, particularly those of the younger sort, are like the ladies of the city, extravagantly fond of ornaments, and elegant rings are frequently to be seen pendent at the ears of a damsel, who has scarcely any other dress to appear in, but a *chemise*. [...]

8. Agostino Brunias, Scenes of the West Indies, ca. 1780

[Agostino Brunias (1728–96) was an Italian painter who recorded scenes of West Indian life from his first visit to Barbados in 1765 until his death on Dominica in 1796, where he had lived and raised a family since 1775. Brunias' paintings record a romantic view of colonial culture, featuring whites and people of color together at marketplaces, folk dances, and in town. He never recorded slaves at labor in the fields or images of plantation violence. The paintings are valued for their meticulous representation of architecture and clothing on the islands.] [2]

---

[1]   A creolization of *bon jour monsieur*.
[2]   Lennox Honychurch's essay on Brunias contains more images and an excellent overview of the artist's career. See http://www.lennoxhonychurch.com/brunias.cfm.

Market Day, Roseau, Dominica
Agostino Brunias, 1728–96
c. 1780
Oil on canvas
Yale Center for British Art, Paul Mellon Collection

A West Indian Flower Girl and Two other Free Women of Color
Agostino Brunias, 1728–96
c. 1780
Oil on canvas
Yale Center for British Art, Paul Mellon Collection

Works Cited and Recommended Reading

Aptheker, Herbert. *American Negro Slave Revolts.* New York: Columbia UP, 1968.

Bénot, Yves. *La Révolution Française et la fin des colonies, 1789 –1794: Postface inédite.* Vol. 164. Paris: La Découverte, 2004.

Berlin, Ira. *Many Thousands Gone: The First Two Centuries of Slavery in North America.* Cambridge, MA: Harvard UP, 1998.

Blackburn, Robin. *The Making of New World Slavery: From the Baroque to the Modern, 1492–1800.* New York: Verso, 1997.

Bogues, Anthony. *The Haitian Revolution and the Making of Freedom in Modernity.* Paper presented at the Philadelphia Political Theory Workshop, University of Pennsylvania, 2005.

Bolster, W. Jeffrey. *Black Jacks: African American Seamen in the Age of Sail.* Cambridge, MA: Harvard UP, 1998.

Branson, Susan. *These Fiery Frenchified Dames: Women and Political Culture in Early National Philadelphia.* Philadelphia: U of Pennsylvania P, 2001.

Brown, Charles Brockden. *An Address to the Government of the United States, on the Cession of Louisiana to the French: And on the Late Breach of Treaty by the Spaniards; Including the Translation of a Memorial, on the War of St. Domingo, and Cession of the Mississippi to France, Drawn Up by a French Counsellor of State.* Philadelphia: John Conrad & Co, 1803.

———. "On the Consequences of Abolishing the Slave Trade to the West Indian Colonies." *Literary Magazine, and American Register* 4 (1805): 375–81.

Brown, Gillian. "The Quixotic Fallacy." *Novel: A Forum on Fiction* 32.2 (1999): 250–73.

Brown, Gordon S. *Toussaint's Clause: The Founding Fathers and the Haitian Revolution.* Jackson: UP of Mississippi, 2005.

Buck-Morss, Susan. "Hegel and Haiti." *Critical Inquiry* 26. Summer (2000): 821–65.

Burr, Aaron. *The Papers of Aaron Burr.* Mary-Jo Kine, et al., eds. Ann Arbor: University Microfilms International, 1978–81. 27 reels and guide, 1 supplemental reel.

Burr, Aaron, and Matthew L. Davis. *Memoirs of Aaron Burr with Miscellaneous Selections from His Correspondence.* 2 vols. New York: Harper & Brothers, 1836.

Danticat, Edwidge. "Ghosts of the 1915 US Invasion Still Haunt Haiti's People." Opinion. *Miami Herald Online.* 25 July 2005. <http://www.miami.com/mld/miamiherald/news/opinion/12214452.htm>.

Dash, J. Michael. *Haiti and the United States: National Stereotypes and the Literary Imagination.* New York: St. Martin's Press, 1997.

Davidson, Cathy N. *Revolution and the Word: The Rise of the Novel in America.* Expanded Edition. New York: Oxford UP, 2004.

Dayan, Joan. *Haiti, History, and the Gods.* Berkeley: U of California P, 1995.

Drexler, Michael. "Brigands and Nuns: The Vernacular Sociology of Collectivity After the Haitian Revolution." *Messy Beginnings: Postcoloniality and Early American Studies.* Ed. Malini Schueller and Edward Watts. New Brunswick, NJ: Rutgers UP, 2003. 175–202.

Du Bois, W.E.B. *The Suppression of the African Slave-Trade to the United States of America, 1638–1870.* Millwood, New York: Kraus-Thomson, 1973.

Dubois, Laurent. *Avengers of the New World: The Story of the Haitian Revolution.* Cambridge, MA: Belknap Press of Harvard UP, 2004.

———. *A Colony of Citizens: Revolution & Slave Emancipation in the French Caribbean, 1787–1804.* Chapel Hill, NC: U of North Carolina P, 2004.

———. *Slave Revolution in the Caribbean, 1789–1804: A Brief History with Documents.* New York: Palgrave Macmillan, 2006.

Ferguson, Moira. *Subject to Others: British Women Writers and Colonial Slavery, 1670–1834.* New York: Routledge, 1992.

Fick, Carolyn. "The French Revolution in Saint Domingue: A Triumph or a Failure?" *A Turbulent Time: The French Revolution and the Greater Caribbean.* Ed. David Barry Gaspar and David Patrick Geggus. Bloomington and Indianapolis: Indiana UP, 1997. 51–77.

———. *The Making of Haiti: The Saint Domingue Revolution from Below.* Knoxville: U of Tennessee P, 1990.

Finkelman, Paul. "Jefferson and Slavery: 'Treason Against the Hopes of the World.'" *Jeffersonian Legacies.* Ed. Peter S. Onuf. Charlottesville: UP of Virginia, 1993. 181–221.

Fischer, Sibylle. *Modernity Disavowed: Haiti and the Cultures of Slavery in the Age of Revolution.* Durham: Duke UP, 2004.

Fleming, Thomas. *Duel: Alexander Hamilton, Aaron Burr and the Future of America.* New York: Basic Books, 1999.

Gaspar, David Barry, and Darlene Clark Hine. *More than Chattel: Black Women and Slavery in the Americas.* Bloomington, IN: Indiana UP, 1996.

Gaspar, David Barry, and David Patrick Geggus. *A Turbulent Time: The French Revolution and the Greater Caribbean.* Bloomington, IN: Indiana UP, 1997.

Geggus, David Patrick. *Haitian Revolutionary Studies.* Bloomington, IN: Indiana UP, 2002.

———, ed. *The Impact of the Haitian Revolution in the Atlantic World.* Columbia, SC: U of South Carolina P, 2001.

Genovese, Eugene D. *From Rebellion to Revolution: Afro-American Slave Revolts in the Making of the Modern World.* Baton Rouge: Louisiana State UP, 1979.

Gilmore, Leigh. *Autobiographics: A Feminist Theory of Women's Self-Representation.* Ithaca: Cornell UP, 1994.

Goudie, Sean. *Creole America: The West Indies and the Formation of Literature and Culture in the New Republic.* Philadelphia: U of Pennsylvania Press, 2006.

Harris, Sharon M., ed. *Women's Early American Historical Narratives.* New York: Penguin, 2003.

Hunt, Alfred N. *Haiti's Influence on Antebellum America: Slumbering Volcano in the Caribbean.* Baton Rouge: Louisiana State UP, 1988.

James, C.L.R. *The Black Jacobins.* New York: Random House, 1962.

Jameson, J. Franklin. *The American Revolution Considered as a Social Movement.* Boston: Beacon Press, 1926.

Jefferson, Thomas. *Notes on the State of Virginia.* Ed. William Peden. Chapel Hill: U of North Carolina P, 1982.

Kadish, Doris Y. "The Black Terror: Women's Responses to Slave Revolts in Haiti." *The French Review* 68.4 (1995): 668–80.

———, ed. *Slavery in the Caribbean Francophone World: Distant Voice, Forgotten Acts, Forged Identities.* Athens, GA: U of Georgia P, 2000.

Kaplan, Amy. "Manifest Domesticity." *American Literature* 70.3 (1998): 581–606.

King, Stewart R. *Blue Coat Or Powdered Wig: Free People of Color in Pre-Revolutionary Saint Domingue.* Athens: U of Georgia P, 2001.

Kolchin, Peter. *American Slavery, 1619–1877.* New York: Hill and Wang, 1993.

Kukla, Jon. *A Wilderness so Immense : The Louisiana Purchase and the Destiny of America.* New York: A.A. Knopf, 2003.

Langley, Lester. *The Americas in the Age of Revolution, 1750–1850.* New Haven: Yale UP, 1996.

Lapsansky, Philip. "Afro-Americana: Rediscovering Leonora Sansay." *The Annual Report of the Library Company of Philadelphia for the Year 1992.* Philadelphia: The Library Company, 1993.

Latrobe, Benjamin Henry, et al. *The Correspondence and Miscellaneous Papers of Benjamin Henry Latrobe.* New Haven: Published for the Maryland Historical Society by Yale UP, 1984.

Levine, Robert. "Race and Nation in Brown's Louisiana Writings of 1803." *Revising Charles Brockden Brown: Culture, Politics and Sexuality in the Early Republic.* Eds. Philip Barnard, Mark Kamrath, and Stephen Shapiro. Knoxville: U of Tennessee P, 2004. 332–53.

Lewis, Linden. "Culture, Labor, and Caribbean Freedom." *The Cultural Contradictions of Caribbean Freedom.* Eds. Linden Lewis, Hilbourne Watson, Reneé Gosson, Glyne Griffith, and Elizabeth Crespo, unpublished manuscript.

Martin, J.P., "Rights of Black Men," *The American Museum, or, Universal Magazine.* 12.5 (Nov 1792): 299–300.

Martin, Wendy, ed. *Colonial American Travel Narratives.* New York: Penguin, 1994.

Matthewson, Tim. "Jefferson and Haiti." *The Journal of Southern History.* 61.2 (1995): 209–48.

Moreau de Saint-Méry, M.L.E. *Description topographique, physique, civile, politique et historique de la partie française de l'Ile Saint-Domingue avec des observations générales sur sa population, sur le caractère et les moeurs de ses divers habitants, sur son climat, sa culture, ses productions, son administration, etc. Renfermant les détails les plus propres à faire connaître l'état de cette colonie à l'époque du 18 octobre 1789.* Paris: Guérin, 1875.

Newman, Richard, Patrick Rael, and Phillip Lapsansky. *Pamphlets of Protest: An Anthology of Early African-American Protest Literature, 1790–1860.* New York: Routledge, 2001.

Nussbaum, Felicity. *The Global Eighteenth Century.* Baltimore, MD: Johns Hopkins UP, 2003.

Popkin, Jeremy D. "Facing Racial Revolution: Captivity Narratives and Identity in the Saint-Domingue Insurrection." *Eighteenth-Century Studies* 36.4 (2003): 511–33.

Rainsford, Marcus. *An Historical Account of the Black Empire of Hayti: Comprehending a View of the Principal Transactions in the Revolution of Saint Domingo; with its Ancient and Modern State.* London: J. Cundee, 1805.

Scott, Julius S. *The Common Wind: Currents of Afro-American Communication in the Era of the Haitian Revolution.* Unpublished dissertation: Duke University, 1986.

Sheller, Mimi. *Democracy After Slavery: Black Publics and Peasant Radicalism in Haiti and Jamaica.* Gainesville: UP of Florida, 2000.

Smith-Rosenberg, Caroll. "Black Gothic: The Shadowy Origins of the American Bourgeoisie." *Possible Pasts: Becoming Colonial in Early America.* Ed. Robert Blair St. George. Ithaca and London: Cornell UP, 2000. 243–69.

Socolow, Susan M. "Economic Roles of the Free Women of Color of Cap Français." *More than Chattel: Black Women and Slavery in the Americas.* Eds. David Barry Gaspar and Darlene Clark Hine. Bloomington, IN: Indiana UP, 1996. 279–97.

Stabile, Susan M. *Memory's Daughters: The Material Culture of Remembrance in Eighteenth-Century America*. Ithaca: Cornell UP, 2004.

Thornton, John. *Africa and Africans in the Making of the Atlantic World, 1400–1680*. Cambridge [England]; New York: Cambridge UP, 1992.

——. "African Soldiers in the Haitian Revolution." *The Journal of Caribbean History* 25.1 & 2 (1991): 58–80.

Tobin, Beth Fowkes. *Picturing Imperial Power: Colonial Subjects in Eighteenth-Century British Painting*. Durham, NC: Duke UP, 1999.

Trouillot, Michel-Rolph. *Silencing the Past: Power and the Production of History*. Boston: Beacon Press, 1995.

Vietto, Angela. "Leonora Sansay." *American Women Prose Writers to 1820*. Eds. Carla Mulford, Angela Vietto, and Amy Winans. *Dictionary of Literary Biography*, V. 200. Detroit: Gale Research, 1999. 330–36.

White, Ed. "The Ourang-Outang Situation." *College Literature* 30.3 (2003): 88–108.

Wimpffen, Alexandre-Stanislas de. *Haití au XVIIIᵉ siècle: Richesse et esclavage dans une colonie française*. Ed. Pierre Pluchon. Paris: Édition Karthala, 1993.

Wood, Gordon S. *The Radicalism of the American Revolution*. New York: Vintage, 1991.

Yellin, Jean Fagan and John C. Van Horne. *The Abolitionist Sisterhood: Women's Political Culture in Antebellum America*. Ithaca: Cornell UP, 1994.

Zuckerman, Michael. *Almost Chosen People: Oblique Biographies in the American Grain*. Berkeley: U of California P, 1993.